The Patio

The Patio

Monika Pistovčák

authorHOUSE®

AuthorHouse™
1663 Liberty Drive
Bloomington, IN 47403
www.authorhouse.com
Phone: 1-800-839-8640

Published by AuthorHouse   02/29/2012

ISBN: 978-1-4678-8969-8 (sc)
ISBN: 978-1-4678-8970-4 (e)

The author utilised information related to the subject of "DMD" and to the subject of "ILLEGAL LOGGING" from www.wikipedia.com

1

I looked desperately at the puncture in my tyre, hoping it was only a disagreeable dream. I was leaving the most beautiful district of our country; it brimmed with majestic hills and the white snow-capped summits of a mountain range. In spite of the fact that it was the middle of summer, the snowflakes were not yet willing to give up their reign and sublimate into water foam. Sunbeams slid downhill. The old guardians had been keeping an eye on the colourful gardens hidden in the valleys for ages, on and on. The scenery was unquestionably breath-taking but there were many kilometres directly in front of me. Despite all the beauty surrounding me, I was not able to enjoy and absorb it with every inch of my body as I once had in the many times I had crossed this part of my country.

"Excellent." Talking to myself and walking towards the boot of my car, I tried to keep a cool head: I was sure I´d be able to change the punctured tyre. I opened the boot and leaned over the items scattered across the whole space and began picking them up one by one. A fringe of different things rose next to the ditch near the roadside. Each of them was hidden by the tall grass and weeds growing everywhere, making the edge of the road rather peculiar. I lifted up the floor of the boot. Looking all around for a spare wheel and a lifting jack, I wanted to change the tyre as quickly as possible so I could leave this place and continue my journey.

"No! No! No! This cannot be happening!" A desperate laugh left my mouth; the words flowed past a lump in my throat.

"Great!" A corroded latch was sitting on an equally rust-stained screw. "I need a screwdriver to loosen it." I quickly checked the rest of the space. On the left, there was something stuck: it looked like it could be a screwdriver. I took it. Immense relief circulated through my mind. It did not take long for me to understand that the situation was more difficult than I had thought: the screwdriver´s head was the wrong sort of point, so I wouldn´t be able to undo the latch.

"No checking before the trip, no comfortable trip." Smiling at how stupid I had been, I began looking around me. There were no houses, no shops and no human beings. Just me, my car and the road. Shielding my eyes from the sun´s extremely sharp beams, I looked about the vicinity again. My gaze stopped at an old, faded petrol station in the distance. Estimating the number of metres, perhaps kilometres, I began piling all my things from the grass onto the car´s back seats. I decided to make a beeline for that station. A member of staff might have been there or somebody might have strolled there coincidentally. I did not know why, but as the distance between me and the petrol station grew shorter, my inner stress got bigger. Approaching that place, I could see two petrol pumps and a building with an exceedingly old facade. The colour of the walls used to be red, maybe wine-coloured. The roof was coated with many islands of moss and bryophyte. It was hard to say if the green colour was the paint or the colour of the new habitants from the plant kingdom. The windows had not been washed for an awfully long time. The stress inside me decreased and I was convinced nobody else was at the scene.

"O.K. First, I must go check if I am the girl still and then I´ll make some phone calls to find help." Looking for a good place to answer the call of nature, I did not notice a man standing behind me. I made one step more and bumped into him.

"Goodness gracious!" My heart was jumping up and down. I was not able to get calm.

"I am truly sorry. I didn´t mean to bump into you," he said. Apologising and holding my palms to my chest, I tried to console myself.

"Can I help you?" the man asked me in a very polite way, his lips twirling into a warm smile. Many wrinkles built little paths around his eyes, which joined together into lots of shallow fans. What gave him a look younger than his age (he was, in fact, in his fifties) was that he was slender and one head taller than me. I could not hesitate. Time was racing forward to night and I was supposed to reach the capital by 10 pm at the very latest.

"My tyre is punctured, the latch is rusty and broken, and I´m looking for help." I shot the whole sentence at him in just a few seconds. Contemplating, he returned inside the building. A short while later, he brought out a gear looking like a sizeable crowbar or a solid steel stick.

"That car?" His gaze focused on my car in the distance. Barely did I nod. He headed towards my car and I followed him: not a word was uttered. There walked two people who were utter strangers to each other. I was a little bit afraid. Arriving at the car, it only took a moment for me to unlock it. He peeked into the boot: a miraculous chemical reaction of three common factors (water, iron and time) covered the latch and the screw too. He withdrew from the boot, winking at me from underneath the shield on his cap.

"I have to damage it more than it already is." It was more an assumption than a question about my spare tyre latch´s future.

"All right. No problem." I let a shy smile settle on my cheeks and sat down on the grass beside the road. The man whistled while metal components creaked intermittently.

Bang! My insides jumped. I had not expected such a loud shot.

"Here you are, my girl." His grin was the grin of winners. Pulling out the tyre, beads of sweat trickled down his temples.

"Oh. I´m grateful." Getting up from the ground, I approached him, trying to help.

"I'll fix it. Thank you," I said. He raised his eyebrows in unspoken surprise. I took the spare wheel and put it down on the ground, rolled it next to the punctured one and laid it flat. Firstly, I loosened the wheel screws; after a while, they were removed. Using my screw jack, I raised the car until it hung almost half a metre above the road. In the end, the wheel was replaced and fixed. The car was lowered onto the tarmac. My hands were dirty and my forehead was covered in sweat. All that remained was to tighten the screws as much as possible. I felt the light touch of a hand on my shoulder.

"Could I do it?" the man asked. I shrank back without a word. Screw by screw was clawed by the wrench and tightened with adequate power in the correct way. He handed me the wrench.

"What do I owe to you?" I enquired.

"Nothing."

"Yes, I owe you something. Tell me, what would you like?"

"Your smile." His answer amused me. I smiled. The stranger's response was not the only reason that the situation was full of ridiculous and confusing feelings.

"Nice to meet you, young lady." He gave me a quick wink and lightly tapped my back; the mischievous grin of a little boy skipped across his lips. Without waiting for my "thank you" or "goodbye", he went back to the petrol station and left me gasping.

"Nice to meet you, too." Talking to myself, I settled on the grass and weeds and found the cigarette box in the rear pocket of my jeans. After taking the first drag, cupping my hands to prevent the flame from dying, I raised my head.

"Oh." A fox stood in front of me, maybe only one year old and three or four feet in length. His gaze met mine. A very strange shiver went through my body; butterflies began floating in my stomach.

"Have I already met you? Yes, I have." A whisper came out of the air.

"You are Daniel's cemetery guardian, aren't you?" I dropped words into the silence again.

After a while, I got up and put my cigarette out against the tarmac. I headed back to the driver's car door. I hesitated for a second, then I suddenly felt the need to turn back. I did not know the reason. I just turned and faced the fox, watching it.

"Tell him hello, will you? Do you know a way?"

The sunny day was aiming to finish its journey. The pictures of many towns, villages, mountain ranges and fields were exchanged for images of the capital. Tall street lights along the motorway invited me and my body relaxed with the familiar atmosphere.

2

"Nina! Can you come here?" The voice of my mum arrived at the door of my kingdom. It was pleasant to listen to it, again. I smiled. I knew what would happen.

"Coming, Mum!" My answer leaked out through the closed door of my room.

The next moment, I announced to my mum that I had applied for a scholarship at a Faculty of Forestry a few months ago: a secret I had kept from her. An unusually long silence helped to rein in her disagreement, hiding in that kitchen of ours for a while. She had barely taken in this information when I attempted to go straight to the heart of the issue.

"Mum, it is a very prestigious competition of tenders and I tried to enter it." A giant ball had enlarged in my throat in a short time. My throat got hot and I felt as though I had become a person accused of committing a delinquent act.

"Where is it?" She pretended to prepare the ingredients for dinner later to keep herself cool-headed.

"At the University of British Columbia."

"What is the state like? What is the city like?" She did not return, she did not begin our discussion, she did not even change her attitude at the kitchen sideboard. She calmly threw all the ingredients into the sink to be washed.

"The state is Canada, the city is Vancouver." I began trying to think of ways that could free me from this ridiculous investigation. None came.

"Why?"

"'Why' what mum? I don´t understand your question."

"You understand me pretty well." An irritation snaked in her tone.

"I won the competition? Perhaps, it is the right answer." I attempted to resolve the unspoken questions I strived to do it my best. Mum had a slightly different viewpoint on it.

"Mum, I love the subject of my study: I love the terrain work, I love to have an opportunity to learn and . . ."

"Stop it! Why Canada? Do you know how far away it is?"

"Do I?" There was only one tiny movement and a kettle holder landed on my face. Mum was facing me and giggling. Getting up from the chair, I approached Mum and pressed a light kiss to her cheek.

"I love you, Mum." My exceptionally quiet answer mixed with the whispering of water flowing from the tap.

"I love you too."

I must have fallen asleep. An impressive variety of colours flooded the surfaces of clouds as the sun sent its beams through the sky. The little round window revealed as much of the outside as I was able to soak in. Every time I travelled by plane, I enjoyed every each inch of the journey. An object of envy to birds, I was only afraid of landing. But until it was time to land, I was calm. The exact time and world latitude were written in the bottom-right corner of the TV screen in front of me. It was only half an hour until the landing of my plane.

I was like Dorothy in "The Wonderful Wizard of Oz". Sun rays were everywhere around me. The vast expanses of glass allowed a large amount of natural light to proceed into the airport lounge. Wooden sculptures, made by natives, greeted me and invited me to learn as much as possible about their land. They were dressed in blue and green, like they needed to demonstrate the colours of the land, sky and the ocean that had washed the shores of Sea Island for ages. People dragged baggage behind them, trolleys creaked on solid marble tiles, escalator belts sang their strange songs and an unidentified buzz surrounded each and every object in the building. I gazed around to find the right direction. The meeting point was, according to the orders in the email, at the Pacific Coach Lines counter in the International Receiving Lounge, Arrivals level. On gigantic information panels above me, a lot of miniature orange lights formed capital letters. Going slowly, row by row, I stopped reading at the line "THE INTERNATIONAL RECEIVING LOUNGE". I followed several arrows directly to it. A thrill boiled in my veins. The new goal of my life could arise in a few minutes.

Bang! Holding fast and rubbing my arm, I tried to meet the eye level of the tall man who I had bumped into. I waved one hand in the air to say "sorry". The second hand landed beside the handle of my luggage. Rushed by embarrassment, I strived to resolve the awful situation and leave the place as soon as possible.

"Rudi, or Nina Rudić." In spite of my warm smile, I hesitated in my head due to my struggle to act as expected. I looked like a loony—it was obvious. Reaching out my arm to him for a little while, I recognised there was no place for friendly gestures. So the hand was shoved back into the pocket of my jeans.

"Phew." I breathed again, grasped the handle of my suitcase in a second and went tearing along without any hindsight.

"Good, I´ve found it." A couple of feet separated me and the counter of Pacific Coach Lines. The nice green-blue coloured slogan "Pacific Coach—travel easy" decorated the billboard. Searching in all directions and trying to find a face similar to the professor´s, I compared each face that I saw to his, which I had seen in our email correspondence. Two hours later, having read everything that interested me, I made a sudden decision. I left the lounge.

Taxis and coaches lined the pavement. People were swallowed by them and their bags disappeared into the boots of the vehicles. Nobody was there. No sign with large letters in bold, my name printed or hand-written. No one was waving and calling my name. I decided to sit down on the curb, my chin bolstered up by my palms, which rested on the brim of my luggage. I strived to pull out the printed email from my small coloured rucksack.

The opened A4 paper gave me the information I needed, which I had memorised many times. I could not comprehend why nobody had met me at the meeting point. My eyes skipped all the formalities and were caught by a sentence that was full of valuable points: "*. . . and, at the end of this letter, I attach some important meeting point information. No matter whether your plane arrives on time or if your flight is delayed or cancelled, I will be permanently verifying (with the airport information desk via the Internet) the arrival conditions of your flight to be able to pick you up. After collecting your baggage, look for the International Receiving Lounge. It is situated on the same floor as Arrivals. Look for the Pacific Coach Lines stand. I will wait there for you.*"

I jumped over the few sentences below and continued reading.
"*. . . I attach my latest photo so you´ll be able to recognise me.*"

3

"Why? How is it possible that you don´t know it for sure? Switch me on to my assistant immediately!" There was a small interval of waiting. The calmness of the night was spreading everywhere. Only a soft sound of drizzling tinged the night.

"Да, я тебя слушаю." (Yes, I´m listening.) The strong, reserved voice cut the air.

"Я сказал после завтра. Это значит, мой самолёт будет причаливать после завтра, в пять часов Ванкоуверского часа."
(I said the day after tomorrow. I meant my plane is going to land the day after tomorrow, at 5 am Vancouver time.)

Tranquillity sneaked out with the beginning of his penetrative walking. Pit-a-pat, pit-a-pat, pit-a-pat, the old melody from primeval times was coming from Albert´s Docks near the River Mersey out onto the streets of the ancient city centre of Liverpool.

A rental car was speeding along the shores connecting Vancouver International Airport with the north-west peninsula, where West Point Grey lay adjacent to University Hill. The University of British Columbia was the target of his trip. Strictly speaking, a tremendously valuable interview with Professor Andrew Dragonsky, the Associate Dean for Research and Graduate Study at the Faculty of Forestry, had caused his arrival in British Columbia. The colourful Indian summer was spreading everywhere during this late September afternoon. Shades from warm yellow through to orange and dark red painted over the leaves of all the broad-leaved trees, which shone like little suns among the many dark green twigs of the conifers. SW Marine Drive cut across many streets and in the end dived into the forest area of Endowment Lands Ecological Reserve. Following the GPS, the steering wheel of the rental car was turned by the driver left to join 16th Avenue. The next phase of his course was East Mall and, finally, the University of British Columbia.

"It´s very late. You should go to bed. You have to get up at 7.30 am." She stopped in front of the TV screen.

"Mum, please. Just ten minutes." He leaned from right to left. He would have liked to stay watching the crime serial.

"I´ve already said." She approached her son and simultaneously rubbed his shoulder and kissed his forehead tenderly. She switched the TV off and snapped the light off. Leaving her son in the dark space, she slowly retired to her room.

Bit by bit the wheels in their circular movements were nearing the slab floor again and again. His wheelchair left the living room with its nocturnal atmosphere. Wheeling himself along the wide corridor, he shortened the distance to his children´s room.

He stopped his wheelchair at the opened window. He rested there for a small while, as was his daily habit. He loved looking over all the roofs of the historical city and watching the regiment of little twinkling spots on the wings of the Liver Bird. Its silhouette was majestic and royal. Peace and silence abounded. Nobody asked him anything.

"Is everything O.K.? Do you need anything? Can I help you?"

If you are on your own, it does not automatically mean you must be unhappy. His parents were the unhappy persons, not him. Of course, they attempted to conceal their misery in the best manner they knew. He could see it—it was obvious.

The reason was his wheelchair and his illness. Sitting in silence, he did not want to make even the most miniature of movements. His irises absorbed all the beauty of the old maritime mercantile city. His heart began sailing through the early stories hidden under every one of those roofs. Drizzling raindrops were tapping on their surfaces, rolling downwards along iron eaves and down the pipes to the pavement. Streams of drops combined into rivulets. Some streams found canal nozzles and disappeared under the ground´s surface. The remaining streams kept on in their journeys along an uncountable number of buildings. Some of them rested in puddles without any movement. He might have loved this mizzle theatre just on account of its similarity to his dystrophy. Some of his muscles acted like brave puppets in hellishly precise ways, cooperating with his brain cells. Then, there were muscles without any teamwork ethic. Those muscles only adored relaxing and sleeping like the drops in their puddles. They waited for dawn, when a shoe or a tyre would cross the puddle and they could move for a while again.

The engine of the rental car stopped working. He got off. Facing the university building, looking at the alumni gathered directly in front of its wood and concrete construction, he checked his watch. Half an hour remained until his appointment with Professor Dragonsky.

"Can I disturb you?" Trying to get the attention of the man behind the desk, he knocked on the glass of the university´s information counter.

"Yes sir, can I help you?" The man, who was in his mid-sixties, ripped his gaze from his newspaper and gave his full attention to the newcomer.

"Yes, I would like to know where I can find the office of Professor Dragonsky?"

"Sir, can I see your passport or ID card, please?" Stretching his arm to the mouth of the counter, he looked at the newcomer.

"I´ve already arranged my meeting with the professor. He must have written a note in the computer system somewhere, or on a piece of paper." His reaction was a little cross.

"Sir, I´m sorry. Unless I enter your ID data into the university system I can´t let you enter the building." The politeness in his voice was petering out. The friendly face was exchanged with a poker face.

"O.K. Here you are." Each molecule of air between the two of them was like a big purse full of anger.

A couple of keyboard taps soon settled the matter. The little misunderstanding was solved. The man behind the information desk explained step by step the way to get to the professor´s office.

"I´m not sure he will be there," he reported, but the man with the Russian accent disappeared into the distance, swerving around the nearest corner and up the stairs.

"Never mind, he´ll realise that for himself," he said, continuing to read the unfinished paragraph on the left page of his newspaper.

"You have puffy eyes, Gregory." Checking him from head to toe, she was wondering, what is the basis of his attraction to her. He was not even eighteen.

"Non-event, madam." A mischievous smile jiggled up and down from his lips to his cheeks and from his cheeks to his lips.

"Your project explanation was excellent. It might be a little bit grown up in comparison with your age, but I enjoyed it." The coquetry mixed the meaning of her words.

"Can I return to my place?" He nodded towards his desk. He tarried until she noticed the sentences in her notebook. No answer, no allowing movement, he decided to leave the field of the examination.

"Oh, Gregory. I almost forgot. This is for you from the headmaster." A white sheet hung from her fingertips to deliver the letter to its recipient.

A reverse movement of wheels brought him back to the teacher´s desk. Hesitation covered the face of the teenage boy. The confirmation and acceptance of his distance learning would be the perfect gesture for him. If the answer was negative, he was not certain what his first reaction would be. Would he be disappointed, depressed or mad? His trembling hand held the important paper.

> *". . . Considering all relevant and necessary responsibilities . . . I can confirm the distance learning of the student Gregory Wronskij under the following conditions . . . signed Donald Derbhall, headmaster of . . ."*

Overwhelming heat flooded through the grid of veins in his body. He did not know what to think. Should he have screamed or should he have celebrated in silence? Should he not have done either?

"Thank you, madam." Folding the paper, he returned to his school desk.

A long ringing sound swam along a vast corridor. Its song, tangled with many sunbeams, created a light air, which spread all around and swayed from wall to wall. It brushed the gloomy atmosphere away and hopped like a child in autumn´s defoliated leaves.

He successfully withdrew his mobile phone from his jacket pocket, finally. Reading the display name, he slowly raised it to his ear. He listened to a voice coming from a distance, his mood elevated, his face growing warmer and his lips curling up into a smile.

"Это очинь хорошие известие."
(It is really good news.)

Suddenly, his attention was captivated by the letters printed on the name plate next door. He continued his conversation. He knocked at the door and waited for an answer.

"Я люблю тебя тоже."
(I love you, too.)

He finished his call and again knocked at the door. No answer came. It was only 10 minutes until their appointment. His eyes swept the room, looking for somewhere he could sit down.

4

I stood up from the kerb, where I had made the decision to get in a taxi and go to the university on my own. I had never been in a taxi on my own. A whit of anxiety, a bit of joy and a touch of doubt were suddenly twirling inside me. I stopped shilly-shalling and crossed the road between me and the taxi rank. My mind began pulling from its rear brain boxes all the previously considered possibilities, one by one, not missing any of them. The rollers of my luggage started rolling. My steps crossed the path to the taxi rank.

I could not believe the fact I was in a pretty comfortable taxi alone, without any company. Doubting my determination, my mind wandered.

"Would you prefer a nicer or a quicker journey?" The driver´s glance rested on my reflection in the rear mirror.

"Sorry, I wasn´t listening. What did you say?"

"I asked you whether you prefer a nicer or a quicker journey." The repetition was voiced.

"The nicer one?"

The ignition began with a muffled sound and the engine of the car began its four-stroke song.

There was extensive bustle everywhere. Glancing from the shoreline to the dark water and back, in the next instant my eyes slid a few metres away. There was a rope tied to the edge of a dock. Elsewhere, a man stood tarrying for another order. Everything was locked up in the big circle of daily life. The busy life of docks was not peculiar to me—I had known it before. I used to visit the docks of my home town during the early hours of dawn. I used to sit down on the grass banks of the Danube. I adored inhaling the breeze of morning dock life. I loved watching the worming cargo harbour lining one of the several arms of the Danube. I liked looking at Habsburg´s old town, which towered in the distance for miles.

Here, there was nothing. Pacific endlessness filled the horizon. Oh, no, I was wrong. There were many logs floating on the ocean surface like subtle toy boats.

Beep-beep-beep. I tried repeatedly to dial the phone number of the professor´s office. The answer was the same every time. Beep-beep-beep. I may have written down the wrong phone number, I thought.

"Excellent."

The shoreline was gone behind thick strip fields of coniferous trees, which were intermittently tangled with leafy woods. Yellow spots were exchanged with orange points. In the end, they gave up to the red. A brilliant patchwork stretched across the scene. The taxi left all this beauty behind it and headed on to the uncountable number of unfamiliar and unseen streets of University Hill.

"Ma mademoiselle. Vous à la." the driver said. I leaned over his shoulder.

"Combien ça coûte?" His forefinger pointed at the digital display showing the cost of the journey.

"Merci beaucoup, monsieur." I gave a quick innocent wink to the sitting driver. I hoped my attempt to create a friendly air would be successful—It could be useful to have a friend in this big world. I slid a Canadian banknote into his palm.

"Thank you." The taxi driver got out of the car, opened the boot and unloaded my luggage onto the pavement, next to a little iron mailbox.

"Thank you. Have a nice day," I said. Turning to the university building, I wanted to be inside as soon as possible. Exhaustion began reigning over my whole person and my desire urged me inside with each coming watch tick.

"Excuse me." I disturbed a small group of alumni standing in front of the university.

"Yes?" If I had not been so tired, I would have certainly appreciated the handsome look and polite manner of the boy who had addressed me.

"I´m looking for something like an information desk?" I threw the incomplete question at him. My behaviour became like a teenager´s. In spite of the fact that I had acted like a fool, I was unable to drag my gaze away from his piercing blue ponds.

"Inside, to the left, and look straight ahead. It´s written on a big glass counter." In my adolescent-like confusion, I did not notice his friendly manners. Bowing to my height, he showed me the direction.

"I see it, thank you. Nice to meet you." The words dropped from my lips into the air in a style that felt strange to me.

´Nice to meet you.´ Am I an idiot? Why did I smirk at him that way? At the speed of light, I disappeared inside the university walls, as invisible as water evaporation in a chemical laboratory. The smell of wood was everywhere inside the pompous large entrance foyer. It was spreading to the sides; the wall decorations were made of wooden components. Clumps of students were cheerily chatting there. A large bulletin board displayed the activities for the week, perhaps for the term. Other alumni were flowing out, passing by me, into the warm bright autumn afternoon.

"Afternoon, sir." Knocking lightly on the glass, I attempted in a polite manner to get his attention.

"Yes, madam?" His answer was sunk somewhere in the last paragraph, in his unfinished journal. He drew a tiny loop with his pencil, without looking at me.

"How can I help you?"

"Oh. Rudi. Nina Rudić. It´s my name." A sparkle emerged in his eyes and a terrifically warm smile twisted his lips. Two dimples took their places in his cheeks.

"I´ve heard your name before . . . Where is it? Where did I see it?" He raked through the paper piles surrounding the counter desk on the opposite side of the glass. "Found it. Are you looking for the professor of The Faculty of Forestry? I´ve pencilled it, right here." He offered me an envelope.

"Thank you, sir." I took the envelope and pulled out a pamphlet. Opening the pages hesitantly, I tried to grasp two cartoon cards as they slid down towards the floor. They landed on my feet. I bent down and picked them both up. Reading the pamphlet patiently and scrutinising every word, I gasped.

"Phew." I returned to the concierge counter. I could have felt, as the ground under my feet started moving. My stability trailed away.

"Could you be so polite to explain to me the way to my accommodation? The professor wrote it here." My finger tip glided to an address attached to the bottom-left corner of the first card.

"OK," he replied. I looked at the map spread on a slender ledge at the edge of the counter´s glass. "You need to go in this direction," he continued, tracing the route on the map.

My walk only took a quarter of an hour. I was so tired that I did not actually notice the weight of my luggage. Dragging it behind me, I walked absent-mindedly and let my senses absorb the magnificent beauty of the Indian summer. Sunbeams smoothed my cheeks, a chill evening breeze played with my hair and tiny spider webs got caught in my hair accessories. A young girl in her early twenties ran past me, jogging. The rattle of a scooter reached my ears. The chirping of two birds exchanging their daily experiences cheered my mood.

I completed all the forms required by the staff of the university. I loved the professor, he had fulfilled all papers. I knew about all the obstructions I was obligated to pass before I obtained my campus room. My acute need sounded: "I desire to know the number of my room!"

"I've found it!" After a quick search on the notice-board, there it was. The 4th floor. I looked around: any staircase could have been the right solution to reaching the fourth floor.

A satisfying click of the door lock.

"Finally! A shower, water and cleanness." Soon, the whisper of water filled every inch of the misty space. My whole body was calm. A disturbing banging sound interrupted the air of satisfaction.

"Oh no!" I snarled. Sneaking myself out of the shower and trying to throw anything on me, I tried to detect the direction of the noise. Somebody very impatient must have been waiting behind the door because the bagging continued.

"Are you crazy?" My voice was full of vexation. Opening the door using all my strength, I pulled it strongly.

"Hello!" Only a choked voice came out. "Hi." He repeated his greeting.

"Phew." All the words remained latched somewhere between my neck and lips. ´Am I a teenager?´ This question re-sounded in my brain.

"Mathew, Mathew Sander." The outstretching of his arm and his introduction were simultaneous.

"Rudi." I gave an extremely short answer, desperately struggling to regain my composure and retract my immature rudeness. I did not usually act like an adolescent fool. ´Consolidate, Rudi!´ I ordered myself.

"Rudi, I asked you . . ."

"Yes? Sorry, I wasn´t listening to you."

"I would like to invite you to a new term welcome party. Almost all my classmates are coming. It´d be a good opportunity to meet new friendly faces. Will you join us?"

Finally, I´d done it! I tore my eyes off his dark blue ponds. I was cheerful and proud of myself at the same time.

"An immensely attractive offer. But no." The reply caused a selfish grin to form on his lips.

"The reason is?" Lifting his eyebrow, he awaited my response.

"None." A feeble smile appeared on my lips.

Sitting on the edge of the bed, I faced the window. The tree tops created a truly amazing and fascinating picture in one scene. Confusion floated in my brain. What to do? I fumbled for the envelope that I had left on my wooden bedside table a night ago. The card folded in it by the professor had a couple of hand-scrawled sentences, both apologetic and explanatory.

"I would be very grateful if you would help me. A few weeks ago, I launched an interesting programme developing forest areas. This is similar to the bachelor research you did in your country. All permissions were confirmed and granted by a local organisation and the Ministry of Nature too. Your support is needed due to the need for smart hands and educated brains. I attach a printed sheet with the important instruction so you can collect your ticket at the airport counter. Thank you for your patience, I appreciate it."

My pupils crossed each row twice to consider other possibilities, like the opportunity to remain in UBC´s labs and help important research or to join the rest of the alumni at my study level and attend lectures or seminars. Neither compared to what was scribbled. My head had been relaxing for a while, now I had to deal with this new strange situation. What to do? I opened the zip of my suitcase at a snail´s speed, bit by bit. Pulling out my 60-litre-big backpack, I began stuffing it with clothes and things that would be required for a two-week-long expedition. I suddenly smiled.

"It´s so crazy!"

It was the second time I had been at Vancouver International Airport in the span of one and a half days. Diurnal haste and clutter surrounded me. Memorising the facts folded in my posterior brain cells, I quietly walked around and looked for a digital boarding panel, which would provide the details of my departure.

The 5th row from the top of the boarding panel showed my departure gate: Gate 5. It was quite easy to remember. I fused with the airport´s haste: time ticked too slowly. I would´ve loved to have been at my destination already. First, I had to collect my ticket from the Multiple Airlines counter. It was now a familiar place, with the stands of many airline companies offering their services to anyone, and I supposed to anywhere.

"Hi, I´m Nina Rudić. A ticket should have been left for me." Hesitation came across in my voice and the clerk woman´s face became wrapped in consideration. I looked at the advertising displays. Two-coloured slogans covered the plywood walls of the Multiple Airlines stand. Photos reflected stewards´ smiles, expressing overly happy feelings. These artificial smiles produced doubts in your brain and the luxurious air was step by step diminished. I caught a movement in the corner of my eye: a second clerk approached the counter.

"Hi. Are you having a nice day? Can I ask you for your patience? It will take only few minutes. Might I ask for your passport please?" These learnt phrases were given to me in an extremely neat and devilishly polite manner.

"Here you are." She took my claret-coloured passport and opened it. After scrutinising the data and comparing it with the computer database, she slid a ticket into the passport and handed it back to me.

"Have a nice day."

"You, too."

My sight wandered from one direction panel to the next: I followed them and advanced to Gate 5. Many shops smirked at me and attempted to entice me in. A rainbow-coloured store with items made by natives got my attention. Only one step in and I was trapped. A wooden fragrance hovered above stands made of many shelves. Logs framed the shelves and plywood got their filling. Items were piled on them, telling their long fairy tales. I listened to their tales and enjoyed myself. Twisting round and round, I noticed a boy sitting in a wheelchair looking at a small figure of a fox, examining its pointed ears all the way down to its paws for quite a while.

"Hi," I said. The intensity of my gaze disturbed him from observing the subject between his fingers.

"Hi." His answer was accompanied by a weak smile.

"Why the fox?" I asked, my head cocked. I could see something whirling in his mind, then he shot at me a funny grimace.

"A similarity, perhaps? Can you see it?"

"Sorry? No connection."

"To you."

"Me? Why?" I frowned. I didn´t know what he meant.

"Turn back! You´ll see the response." A narrow piece of mirror hung on the wall behind me, just showing my reflection. The ring of a phone cut the little thread of coquetry between us two.

"Да папа, я слушаю тебя. Нет, я только пошёл в магазин. Это всё.
(Yes Dad, I´m listening to you. No, I just went into a shop. That´s all.)

Chatting with his dad, he wheeled his chair to the exit. On the exit line, which could have been an imaginary threshold, he stopped, winked and saluted at me, and was gone.

I took the ginger statuette from the shelf and approached the cash desk. Bright green figures announced the exact price.

"Thank you. Have a nice day." The fox was mine. Heading off, I was attracted by the charm of that Russian speaking boy. I was amused. Thoughts swam in my head.

My laptop was ready again. Its battery supplied it with energy so I could connect to my email inbox and finally send an email to my mum. I could imagine her checking her inbox every hour, as fear or powerlessness crept into her mind.

> *"Hi Mum. Your child arrived at the university yesterday afternoon. My palm gripped the door handle of my campus room about an half and a hour later."*

I strived not to lie and to write the truth as much as possible. I disguised the sentences so that the spy concealed in my mum would not get a hint of any suspicion. I pressed the SEND button.

"Phew. I hate lying." Skipping to the next email, I opened it. A message in three short rows shone at the screen:

> *"Hi Rudi, don´t be silly. I thought we solved our misunderstanding. Why didn´t you come to the pub yesterday? Write back. Daniel."*

´As arrogant as usual. Can I be annoyed with him? ´ I thought.

The next two were from the Professor of Soil Sciences who had taught me at the University of Comenius back home. The last email was sent from my sister´s email address. Both had almost the same topic.

"Hi, Sun. How is it going? Can you send me a couple of nice words? I look forward to it." My mood rose and an absent-minded smile nestled on my cheeks. After a while, I shut the laptop and put everything back in its place. The voice of an airport staff member flew from loudspeakers through the halls of each gate to passengers. A shadowy image hovered above the surfaces of the runways, lightly touching the bitumen, grass field and airport-buildings.

"Flight number 65871 E25 from Vancouver International Airport to Belize City, Belize—Philip S.W. Goldson International Airport with Multiple Airlines, stopping in Seattle and Atlanta . . ." The voice died amid my thoughts. My flight, which would last nearly twelve hours, would start in a couple of minutes.

I walked slowly down the stairs onto the runway at P. S. W. Goldson International Airport in the coastal town of Belize City, the former capital of British Honduras. The hot tar under my feet adhered to my trainers´ soles. The air near its surface shimmered. The quicksilver must have jumped to the high position on every thermometer in the area. In comparison to the airport buildings I had seen before, this one was like a little box of matches standing next to a refrigerator. Big fan blades in the entrance hall rotated round an axis. It was the most satisfying sound I could have heard at that moment. "TAXI" was written on boards, which were resting on the roofs of scratched yellow taxis.

"Excuse me, are you Nina Rudić, señorita? I´m in charge of delivering you to the professor´s laboratory as safely as possible." My back was tapped by somebody´s hand. It was not a taxi driver, or a member of staff from the University College of Belize.

"Have you arrived here by the flight from Vancouver?" he asked. The sentence sneaked out through his squeezed teeth. It seemed he did not expect to see me. I squinted to improve my sight in order to see more clearly, making sure that my eyes did not lie me.

"Of course!" I replied. A grin dominated his lips.

"Fine, cowboy, fly off, and I´ll cope whit it myself." I gave him the same kind of rude smirk.

"A little brave schoolgirl in a strange world?" He looked me over. He reversed to face me. A knock at the roof of a taxi cut our conversation. The driver´s window was opened.

"Yes, señorita?"

"To the University of Belize, please." My palm gripped the door handle, vigorously tweaking it. My only intention was to slide in and to be taken to the professor.

"Wait!" He hit the door.

Standing wordlessly, I faced him.

"The brave schoolgirl is leaving." An ironic smile, I sneaked in and a door banged.

"Sir, can you take me to the university please?"

The taxi entered Belmopan, the capital city and the home of the university. The university was a neat-looking construction in white with the central part coloured with red bricks; it was covered with many tall rectangular windows. A spacious parking area was spotted with islands of bushes.

"Your destination, señorita" I looked at the numbers on the display and pressed Belizean dollars into his palm.

"Nice to meet you, sir."

Noisy steps echoed behind me. The sound became sharper and quicker as the length between me and the runner got shorter.

"Hey." A snappy grip stopped my walk.

"You? Again?" I freed my arm from his clutch and continued in my former direction. "Why—do—you—do—it?" I spelled the words out one by one. "I suppose you are a very clever boy and a gentleman all in one, who is in charge of delivering me to the professor as safely as possible." I paused to letting him understand the basics of the matter.

"Oh, I´ve got it. That is the right reason why you let me fly on my own?" I left him, my whistling bouncing from wall to wall. He was stunned, remaining in his place.

"Call at the airport, please. Check the possible delay of their flight. Thank you very much. I´ll be back immediately." The speaking man faced his colleague in front of him and backed into the corridor behind him. He was approaching me. I was almost directly behind him. One step more and . . .

"Sir." I addressed him hurriedly to avoid jostling each other. With an unexpected hug, I was latched in the grip of his arms.

"Finally! Finally! You are both here. I´m Andrew Dragonsky, your new supervisor." He offered me his hand.

"Rudi. Sorry, Nina Rudić." I blushed into the silence.

"I hope, Rudi, the most polite young gentleman you´ve ever met was chosen to accompany you." He gave me a boyish wink and continued squeezing my hand.

"I´m obliged to you. He personally arrived at the college to invite me. Then I became a member of a very unbelievable welcome party one night ago. He mentally supported me during the whole flight and I was very grateful for his company. I´m scared of flying." The last declaration was conspiratorially whispered.

"You are welcome." His satisfaction was interrupted by his sudden sense of urgency. "Come in." Opening the laboratory doors as widely as possible, he led us into the magical world of the forestry laboratory. There was a kingdom of measuring devices, instruments, digital scales, glass pots, pipettes, chemical substances, stainless instruments, dossiers placed on many shelves and a lot of other noteworthy things necessary for the science of forestry.

5

Everywhere sounded like a huge beehive. Sellers of various stalls shouted at each other. Different animal noises pierced the sellers´ shouting every now and then. The engines of miniature vehicles purred along the streets, passing by crates, containers, canvas bags and by stalls, of course. The smell was a terrible composition of fish, fruits, vegetables, flesh, spices and the seafood, which streamed among the stalls, people and animals. I strolled from one stand with tropical fruits to another with smoked fish, returned a ´hello´ to someone and smiled to another, savouring the items offered and relaxing. The market was a fascinating world with vivid, beautiful people speaking in many dialects. I did not why, but a strange feeling like a strong pang hit me. Starting to sway, I attempted to discern the reason. There, directly next to a faded post office, was a small boy. He was about the age of five. An animal similar to a dog faced him, barking at him and exhibiting its fangs unrelentingly.

"Sorry. Sorry. I´m terribly sorry." I apologised to everyone that I accidentally bumped into as I struggled among the crowd, trying to get to the boy. I successfully grasped the boy and placed him between two parts of a banister lining a staircase.

"Stay here! Can you understand me?" The answer in his big wide-opened eyes showed me he agreed.

My gaze stopped at the white fangs displayed at me in warning. I was stunned and frozen. My touch with reality was lost and I began sinking deeper and deeper into my own memories. A flashback came to me . . .

"The first one at the Stefanik Chalet takes turns!" I understood—it was not necessary to dash.

"No problem, guys. The last will make dinner for everyone." I shot to them over my shoulder, giggling and listening to their jokes as I ran over.

"Hey, Rudi, does a fire blaze in your bottom?"

"Honey, look at it." One wink and my arm pointed to the sky. "The dark. There. A big storm is coming soon. Start the ignition of your propellers! Hurry!"

Instead of replying, a broad snigger flew at me. I did not return it. My speed walking uphill only took a short while, while the sky was cut by dazzling lightning. Heavy drops fell on the rock path: the streams of water speeding downhill made the ascent more and more difficult. Unable to see anything through that heavy, thumping rain, we sped up. The hammering sounds of thunder spread in many directions and lighting slapped anywhere and anything. Bad timing—there was only one solution in front of us.

"Go ahead and nip towards the Chalet!" I said. I repeatedly ordered myself not to stop. "Hell! Why are you sitting here?" I could not believe it. "Have you gone crazy?" Danica was sitting on the ground as though she had not seen the heavy storm coming.

"Perfect!" I shouted. She gave a sort of low sob. "Are you mad? Danica, stand up immediately!" My voice died among the thunder, which gave way to an enormous amount of lighting a couple of seconds later.

"Stand up!" Shouting at her, I pulled her up.

"Leave me! I am exhausted!"

"No, you are the mother at the first place. Do you remember? You have the child, at home! You can´t afford to be exhausted! Stand up!" Fierce dragging followed. She curled into a ball and began crying.

"What are you doing here? Have you not noticed that coming storm?" The guys asked as they arrived.

"She wants to stay right here!"

"Right here? Is she mad?" Ron smirked and continued with his group, saying something terribly funny to Daniel.

"Leave her here, we´ll find her on Sunday and take her home." Ron´s sarcastic response irritated my ears.

"Can you stop? Help me! Are you an idiot? We can´t leave her here!"

Daniel separated from the rest of their group. "Where is her backpack?"

"She´s leaning against it! Give it here!" I dragged it away. She lost her balance, looking at me angrily. I handed him the rather wet pack.

"Thanks," I said.

"Not at all. Give me yours, too." Aiding me with my backpack, he was outraged.

"No, I´m fine thank you. I might need it. But thank you."

"Again her! Nobody ever has a problem, but she always produces one!"

"Leave it, please! Go! I´ll cope with it!" The next few rumbles of thunder came from nearby, with lighting following afterwards. The path was so bright I was able to see every small stone. He left us wordlessly, joined his fellows and accompanied them uphill.

"Stand up!" No response. She kept on crying with her head between her knees. I pulled her hard. She jumped up and began screaming hysterically at me.

Slap! I smacked her, my palm landing on her cheek. She had not expected it. I gripped one of her arms. The second was clutched by my hand. My back slid under her body. Happiness flooded me because she did not struggle against me. The first step of her transfer was behind me. The storm grew stronger as time passed. I desperately desired to see just the tiniest beam of the watch light on the chalet roof.

´Yes! Yes! Yes!´ My mind screamed. A small beam from the watch light periodically crossed my face. One step, two steps, ten steps.

"Hell!" I barked. There was a couple of shining fox eyes. It looked at me. I was like a rock, hard and hypnotised. We glared at each other. I jumped when the next thunder rattled through the sky. At first, an almost inaudible growl could be heard from the fox´s jaws. In a few heartbeats, it got more threatening. When the reddish creature showed me its fangs in their full beauty, I flinched back for a second. Danica´s body weighed me down. I stumbled, moving backwards awkwardly. A truly flesh-creeping snarl approached my ears. My skin was covered with goose bumps. The fox´s snarl changed to sharp barking and the beast ran towards us. In a desperate attempt to escape, I was just able to get my legs in order.

"RUN!" I shouted. Not turning back, I backed away faster and faster. One leg stumbled into a hole and I felt my ankle twinge with pain. The fox barked and barked. The metres were left behind its reddish tail.

Bang! An ear-deafening and blinding streak of lighting cut into a monstrous spruce. The tree´s top landed on the ground, then it jumped back in the air and repeated this a few more times. Behind a veil of skipping spruce branches, I could see the fox´s silhouette. It seemed as though the reddish animal was checking conditions. Then the creature turned and left. A silent thanks pressed a giant lump inside my throat as I carried Danica into the chalet.

"Rudi!" The slightly drunk professor came over to us. I was determined not to tell him anything. All the guys suddenly became like bumblebees striving to attract the queen bee´s affection. I smirked and left for my room to take off my wet clothes.

"This is your key." A man, who I presumed was the owner, handed me a labelled key. I nodded thankfully and shuffled to my room.

"You are the winner. You won the one-bed room," he announced as he was descended downstairs, smiling.

"Daniel, it´s nice to see you," I hoarsely remarked. An exhausted climb up the stairs followed. I disappeared behind the room door.

"Hey, Rudi. Can you open the door?" No rustle, movement, creak or word followed, only a long silence.

"All right. I´ll leave your bag next to the door." A thud sounded from the hallway, sneaked into the room over the threshold. Opening the door, I leaned over and pulled my bag in. I noticed someone sitting on the edge of the staircase.

"Daniel?" Leaving the bag where it was, I neared him and settled down next to him.

"Thanks for helping Danica," I said.

"You should have let her stay there." His monotonic voice stung me.

I swallowed hard. "Why? Are you crazy?" I could not believe what I had heard.

"She is the biggest egoist I´ve ever met! It was her decision to stay there. The weather in the mountains usually varies in a minute. Did she lose her brain during the climbing? You weren´t obligated to share her destiny. You´d have died."

"She would have as well." I percolated words through jammed teeth.

"She has a son and she is the mother. Is it the reason why you´ve helped her? I can´t understand you. Translate your wrath! You are pissed off! Why?" he asked. My temper rose. I stood up and walked out. Dragging my bag in the room, I fought against my desire to scream at him. I would have loved to do so. But I did not do it.

"It was worth helping her!" I snapped over my shoulder. My insides were shivering—I´d hit the roof. I pushed my backpack into the room with a final shove. Holding the door aside, I went to slam it.

Thud! Daniel´s palm stopped it. He approached me, gripped my arm, pushed me back and shut the door. The room got smaller than it actually was. He cupped my face. His thumbs tenderly strolled along my jaw, then up to the lower lip, resting there for a while, then to both sides of my cheeks. His vileness passed and a warmth settled in his pupils. He brushed the edge of my lips with his. Continuously, they walked over my neck. He emerged, glancing into my eyes as if he had found something unusual.

"Why?" he faced me and smirked. His face blurred as he neared me. I was dizzy, unable to move or speak. Great emotive pressure was everywhere, circulating around my body. My stomach cracked from the pressure, caused by the fluttering of many tiny butterfly wings. We became one mind, one pleasure, one feeling, one yearning and one desire of two bodies. I shivered under waves of his shaking. I gasped after the kisses he covered my body with. Goose bumps flooded me from head to toe. Things were scattered on the ground: furniture, my backpack, clothes . . .

"No, I don´t believe!" he whispered. The pleasure died. He moaned and sat up on the edge of the bed.

"Are you a virgin?"

"Why? Is it important?"

"How old are you?"

"Nineteen." Sitting in the bed corner, I hugged my knees.

"You are nineteen in the sixth term?"

"I started school when I was five . . . and had passed exams of two years during one year, at university."

"Why?"

"I wanted to evade a teacher, we didn´t get along." I replied. Leaning over a rug, he picked his clothes up. He finished dressing.

"Rudi, I can´t." He pressed his lips to my forehead. It was a long caress, like he wanted to apologise that way. He dragged himself from me.

"You really are like an angel." With his steps, the sentence petered out, and he left the room.

"Señorita! Señorita!" A Creole man tugged at me patiently. I jerked. He was about one head taller than me, perhaps more, looking straight at me and smiling. The boy was settled on his arm.

"Señorita! Charlie would love to give you something."

"Do you waaaant?" He prolonged his question to create a secret around his gift.

"Sure." His grin melted my dumbness. His giggling was so infectious that it provoked me to smile at him.

"Close your eyes and flatten your palm!" The wee hand tickled my palm. "You caaan?" A coral branch of around one square centimetre lay there.

"Nice. Thanks." The tips of my fingers touched the coral.

"Dad, tell her!"

"Señorita! I would like to ask you . . . can you dive?" There was both hesitation and shame in his voice. I did not comprehend why, but I answered as politely as I could.

"With a snorkel, if that's good enough?" A contrite feeling twirled through me.

"It´s enough, señorita!"

"Hurry, dad!" Charlie said.

"I would be glad if you would accept our invitation." Expecting my reaction, he was worming around like a little boy.

"I would be delighted, but I don´t know if . . ." I took a deep breath. There was a tranquil gap.

"Don´t be afraid! I´m sorry, I´ve not introduced myself yet. Sander, Trevor Sander, the head biologist at Chiquibul National Park." He offered me his hand.

"I´m Rudi. Nice to meet you."

"Dad!" Charlie nudged him.

"This Saturday morning? Would that be possible?" the man asked.

"I don´t know. I´m a student at the local university. I´ll ask the professor if I need to stay in the lab or go research the forest areas and . . ." I did not finish my thoughts.

"There. Write it there." Charlie´s forearm was right under my chin.

"What?" I cocked my head.

"Your phone number."

"I haven´t got one. I´ve not bought a SIM card yet. It´s only my second day in Belize."

"Write the name of your Professor," he suggested. I undid my small backpack and removed a fountain pen from its inner pocket.

"Professor Dragonsky, University of Belize." Pretty towering letters appeared on the tiny forearm. He suddenly leaned forwards to me. He wrapped his arm around my neck and brushed a wee kiss against my cheek.

"I´ll call you baby." He winked at me. I giggled.

"Have a nice day, Rudi." He turned and they both left. Putting the pen back in my pack, I was attracted by something strange on the ground. I squatted to take a look. Examining the object next to the tip of my shoe, I picked it up: it was a spider.

6

"Morning, professor. It´s a nice day, isn´t it?" A large amount of packed equipment was stored in a row close to one of the desks in the laboratory.

"Are you leaving?" I asked.

"No, we are heading into the Maya Mountains," he corrected me, continuing to pack while responding to my questions at the same time. He paused his activities every now and then as if he were revising the necessary steps that he wasn´t supposed to forget.

"The Maya Mountains are quite a large area." There was a break between the previous statement and his last. He re-counted all the items again, scrutinising his list row by row. One of the many packed items remained hanging across my shoulder, my second hand was occupied with a backpack: the overstocked sack gave the impression that it would burst any second.

"Is it connected with my work in Belize and me helping you? Remembering the information in your letter, is this the reason I´m staying here?" He ceased his haste.

"Yes. We need to go to the Macaw River area. It´s the natural boundary of Chiquibul National Park. We need to take as many samples as we are able to carry."

"What kinds of samples?"

"Samples of soil types—they are the most important for us. Then we need to extract samples of plant species to detect the biomass productions of particular species growing in the area. Unfortunately, I don´t have time to go into all the details. Anyway, you surely already know all this—it was the object of your bachelor project." There was no pause, no glance: only rapid packing.

The progress of our dark green Land Rover Discovery was more like childish capering than a fluent drive. We had left the comfortable southern highway a couple of minutes ago. We had used it to reach our destination quicker: in spite of the fact that it was more than one and a half times the length of the other route, the highway was completely without holes. We now joined a road covered with a great number of ditches and crevices. I´d never experienced anything like it.

Belize had impressed me from my first step after descending the airplane stairs. However, this place was incredible and amazingly breath-taking. My whole body absorbed the beauty presented to us from tree canopies. In the hide of the Rover, I became invisible, but I could observe almost everything. Colourful birds, smart monkeys, tree leaves wrapped with sunbeams, flowers looking like a brooch pinned on the breast of an exquisite princess and the sound—no words were enough to form a description similar to it. Spending hours in the car, as the road got narrower and the vegetation got richer, I got a little bit tired, my excitement grew weaker and I failed in my battle against sleep.

"Hey, Rudi, we´ve arrived." The quiet words vibrated around my eardrums as I woke up. As my eyes adjusted, I tried to remember where I was. I had fallen into a truly deep sleep because the two long flights one after another had shut my body down.

"Hi. I´ll be ready in a few seconds." I hastily grabbed all my items from beside me and jumped down from the Discovery. Opening its boot, I recognised it was empty.

"Who took all the things out?"

"Me."

"I thought you didn´t like me."

"Don´t make false illusions! Honey! Professor Dragonsky asked me for." His sarcastic response woke me completely. A bitter and self-glorious grin from ear to ear appeared on his face.

"Are you much papal than the Pope? Am I right?" I gazed at him and then followed a course heading to small clay houses with cane roofs, a subtle village on the edge of the Mayan jungle.

My notebook was continuously filled with details of science area No. 1:

> *"The canopy layer has a cover of foliage 99%; the understory layer less than 25%; the amount of sunlight shining on the understory is only 5%; the forest floor has a cover of foliage less than 5%; the amount of sunlight shining on the forest floor is about 2%."*

Figures were listed under the rows of *"Vegetation diversity . . . number of species in the science area . . . ratio of a particular species to all species in the area . . ."*

The rows combined into pages and the pages created a scientific resume. Despite constantly arguing with each other (me and Mathew), every one of us was in fact working hard. I pitied the professor because he was forced to become an involuntary neutralising factor, usually calming down the tempers between us two. We were obligated to handle 65 little areas in 11 biologically different areas. We continued by taking soil samples from those 11 areas. A lot of work was crammed in less than three weeks. Exhausted, we would approach our small accommodation in the evenings and not be sure whether we would be able to continue in the coming morning.

"I´m going to give you one day off," Professor Dragonsky said, interrupting the feeble tinkling of aluminium cutlery. The looks of the other two members at the table made the same face, checking that they had correctly heard the professor´s announcement. "I´ve assumed for today that we will only work this morning. We can hit the road between 2 and 3 pm."

The trek to the nearest civilised city took at least three and a half hours—it always took that long no matter which direction you headed in, whether to the north to San Ignacio or to the south to Mayan villages or Punta Gorda. The majority of each road usually lead through tough and rugged jungle terrain, where one common kilometre took four times as long as you would have expected.

"Are you going to return to Belmopan?"

"No, we have been invited to Caye Island."

"Whose invitation did you accept? Who is the host?"

"You know him, and I´m sure, you like him even. It´s a boy. I could not refuse."

"Is that our plane? No! Way!" Dismay sounded in my voice.

"It is just a bad joke, isn´t it?" The twelve-seat plane was waiting for take-off. The aircraft crew consisted of two members: the captain and a second pilot. The plane was like something from an "Indiana Jones" film or the aircraft from spaghetti western films with Bud Spencer in the lead role.

"Could Her Majesty The Princess Rudi get on the board?" The ignorantly sarcastic tone tickled my soul.

"I´d be glad, my dearest servant. You can test the plane´s safety on your own." This retort rather nastily slapped his superior-grinned face.

"She is a nice hot-blooded kitten, isn´t she?" A friendly co-passenger said as he jogged next to him.

Soon, the tiny line of the local runway disappeared as we reached higher altitudes. Jungle vegetation fields merged into one large green flat sheet, blurred here and there with the transparent veils of padded clouds floating under the plane. There were some pretty visible clearings with Mayan pyramids, which seemed from this height like little indefinable peaks in the middle of a forest. The green patchwork ended and small mangrove islands appeared, tangling in many directions. They comprised an impressive rich lace that decorated the coast of the mainland; this unabridged beauty met turquoise ocean water. My breath stopped: I was not sure whether it was due to the faint turbulence that had caused the plane to seesaw or whether it was the picture created by the hands of Mother Nature. The image captivated me for a pretty long time. A friendly nudge disturbed me.

"Look there." The professor pointed at a dark blue ring amid the turquoise of the Caribbean. I supposed it had been built over many centuries by microscopic animals named corals. Many small fields of green vegetation grew on the loop's surface, providing a basic platform for new life.

"It's the Great Blue Hole, isn't it?" I asked.

"Yes. I like it." The professor's face shone. "We are close to Ambergris Caye—that's our destination." A shy smile returned to him.

The flight was smooth but the thought of the upcoming landing dragged all my uncomfortable feelings up from my insides. A lot of butterflies began fluttering in my stomach; I got nervous and scared. I would have loved to disguise I had ever been afraid of landing. I had no idea how.

"Her Majesty has lost her colour." His sarcasm and my cynical sneer became our tools for conversation at that moment. He understood and I did not need to stay in rude reflection. As the aircraft descended, the blurry shore shapes of the mainland became sharper and more noticeable. After a while, I could recognise the runway heading to the Caribbean on one side and to San Pedro Airport on the other. The quiet thud of the airplane wheels against ground trailed away, my heartbeat slowed down, my breath stabilised and my common sense finally returned. Everyone around me applauded. I joined them warily. I had seen this for the first time after the landing of my plane in Vancouver. People in Europe did not express their satisfaction this way. All twelve passengers emptied the plane in a bustle. Approaching the building of the relatively small airport, they scattered and became fused with natives, newcomers, taxi drivers and perhaps with staff too.

"Rudi! Rudi! Rudi!" The intensity of the voice calling my name was increasing. Looking around, I attempted to locate the source. There was a five-year-old boy, skipping and waving at our three-man group.

"Charlie!" I squatted in front of him and pressed a kiss on his cheek.

"I am graced with your presence, señorita." His wink caused me to smile.

"I'm glad to meet you again, Mr Trevor, it's nice to see you." Shaking hands, we felt like old friends.

"What is all this? Can you explain what's going on?" Mathew's annoyance surrounded each one of us. When it had died down, his nuisance followed it in the fragment of a second.

"Are you crazy, Mathew? Is something wrong?" Charlie stopped him in the middle of his unspoken sentence. "She is my friend! Stop shouting at her!" His little face reddened.

"I think it's time to apologise, Mathew." Mr Trevor entered the debate. Mathew's reaction swept the opposite way to what Mr Trevor had expected: Mathew waved at a taxi and disappeared in it.

"I'm really sorry. Everything will be O.K., believe me. I hope so, anyway."

"Hi! Andrew!" Trevor´s hug was lasting and very tight. Their friendship must have been deeply cemented in their hearts, but I did not have any idea of their friendship.

"Dad, can we go?" Charlie urged him, not willing to wait a minute longer.

"Dinnerrr!" a female voice screamed at anybody who was awake in the rooms on the first floor. Doors slowly began opening one by one and the owners left their rooms as though they were earthworms leaving the land because of rain. An ocean whisper tangled with its scent floated through the wooden patio into every corner of the kitchen, which was furnished in an old marine style. It tickled all the senses.

"Evening." The professor dragged his chair away from the table and sat down.

"And Rudi?" Charlie asked impatiently, squirming.

"I´m sure she´s been following me."

"It seems, our Princess isn´t here." The response whipped into the space.

"She isn´t as attracted by him as he wanted. It seems." Charlie threw his notice in the air and giggled, clapping his hands together.

"Señorita apologises—she went outside. She wanted some fresh air," a cook in her late fifties said, resolving the subject.

"Our rude Rudi." Mathew whipped words into place, again. He felt the desire to grumble for a little while under his breath, but instead he made space to allow the cook to serve him.

It was only around 6 pm but it was already twilight. Houses, coconut palm trees, wooden jetties, stilts supporting booths with cane pavilion roofs used by local fishermen, the sand´s surface . . . everything was wrapped in its warm shades. On the equator, a fellow could be sure that sunrise and sunset would occur at six. Ocean waves played with little marine boats tied by ropes to ferrous loops on the jetties. And there in the distance, they were playing in the same way with cabin cruisers anchored near the villa houses surrounded by many blooming bushes. Sand grains overflowed through the tiny gaps between my toes. My eyes were attracted to the sleeping pelicans´ bodies seesawing on the water´s surface and my eardrums trembled with the soft sounds of rolling waves, which faded among the sand grains on the shoreline.

"Evening." Somebody´s voice cut through the silence.

"Hi. It´s a nice sunset, isn´t it?" I said, tucking my hair behind my ears and turning to the direction of the voice.

"Might I accompany you? I´ve had a long evening."

"Why not," I replied. The boy did not stand up. I supposed he could have been a teenager because of the sound of his voice. The dark of the shadow created by the patio´s ceiling was darker than the sand in front of it. His chair moved backwards, suddenly turning and sliding along the long, spacious wooden slats towards me. I understood.

"Could you tell me, young sir, where the main promenade is?"

"Right here, under my wheels, mademoiselle."

"O.K. Can I sit down next to you, if you don´t mind?"

"You are welcome to."

Hours of chatting had eaten the night away bit by bit. We shared pleasure, tinkling laughter and an enjoyment of each moment shared by us two as we hovered above the beach.

"Do you smoke?" He offered me a cigarette from a paper box wrapped in cellophane.

"From time to time." I took it, bowing my head to his cupped hands, protecting the small flame of the cigarette lighter.

"Are you from Liverpool? The Beatles, Yellow Submarine, Hey Judie . . ." he asked.

"Why? I was only whistling their melodies. I like them," I replied.

"I´m Gregory, by the way."

"Cool." I stretched my arm out to him to introduce myself. Before I could say anything more, I was stopped.

"You are that girl from the airport shop, aren´t you?"

"I´m impressed." My brain worked hard. All my memories were dragged from their deepest cells to the surface. "Yes! Yes, you are the boy from Vancouver airport!"

"Yes."

"Why did you leave so suddenly?"

"Dad called me."

"Are you here together?" I asked. He replied with a wordless nod. "On holiday?" I continued.

"No. My dad has a business in Belize."

"And you?"

"I´m going to enjoy my life."

"A fine aim." An uncomfortable silence settled between us two. Looking at the black surface of the ocean, we were not able to find a thread to continue the conversation.

"It´s getting late. Tomorrow will be a busy day too. Have nice dreams," I said.

"You too," he replied. I faced him once again and waved. Walking away, I had to go back: he called something to me but I couldn´t hear him. Then the words clinked sharper.

"DMD."

"I didn´t want to ask about it. I am not interested in."

"I know. You will do. Everybody has asked." I did not know what those three initials meant. Strange uneasy feelings whirled inside me: they bit me and filled me with inexplicable panic. I was afraid of being frank, as strong as my heartbeat was.

"If you want, I´ll stay?" I offered.

"No. You said it´s too late. I can look forward to next evening."

"I´d be glad."

"Let me help you with your wheelchair."

"No. I must do it on my own."

"O.K. See you tomorrow."

A table lamp shone next to my laptop during the early morning hours. My forefinger scrolled the circular part in the middle of the mouse. I was waiting for the results for the term I had put in Wikipedia´s search bar: *"DMD."* Wikipedia´s page listed several possibilities related to *"DMD"*. They explained everything, from Disability Mentoring Day, through Dendermonde, which was a city in Belgium, to the Digital Micromirror Device. I scrolled through the rows again and again. A row placed under a row named Disease Modifying Drug caught my attention. One double mouse click was done and my suspicions came true.

"No!" A singular word slid out under my breath. My pupils widened; a hefty lump was growing in my throat.

"Why? It´s not fair!" The definition was vibrating in my ears. I attempted to reread the article again and again. I desperately wanted to find something among the rows of text.

"Duchenne muscular dystrophy, DMD for short, is a recessive X-linked form of muscular dystrophy, which results in muscle degeneration, difficulty walking, breathing, and death. The incidence is 1 in 3,000. Females and males are affected, though females are rarely affected and are more often carriers. The disorder is caused by a mutation in the dystrophin gene, located in humans on the X chromosome (Xp21). The dystrophin gene codes for the protein dystrophin, an important structural component within muscle tissue. Dystrophin provides structural stability to the dystroglycan complex (DGC), located on the cell membrane."

I wrote down all the medical terms on a piece of paper. Putting them in the search windows of Google and Wikipedia, I tried to collect information that could have brought a sliver of hope or light. I clicked from one site to another.

"Symptoms usually appear in male children before age 5 and may be visible in early infancy. Progressive proximal muscle weakness of the legs and pelvis associated with a loss of muscle mass is observed first. Eventually this weakness spreads to the arms, neck, and other areas. Early signs may include pseudohypertrophy."

The pseudohypertrophy. The letters were put into the search bar one by one, creating a word, creating sense.

"Pseudohypertrophy can be specified as the enlargement of calf and deltoid muscles, low endurance, and difficulties in standing unaided or the inability to ascend staircases. As the condition progresses, muscle tissue experiences wasting and is eventually replaced by fat and fibrotic tissue (fibrosis)."

I clicked back to the previous page to continue reading the definition of DMD.

"By age 10, braces may be required to aid in walking but most patients are dependent on a wheelchair by age 12. Later symptoms may include abnormal bone development that lead to skeletal deformities, including curvature of the spine. Due to progressive deterioration of muscle, loss of movement occurs, eventually leading to paralysis. Intellectual impairment may or may not be present but if present, does not progressively worsened as the child ages. The average life expectancy for patients afflicted with DMD varies from late teens to early to mid-20s. There have been reports of a few DMD patients surviving to the age of 40, but this is extremely rare."

"Rudi. Rudi. Can I come in?" Charlie´s voice followed a zippy knocking at the door. After I answered him, he slowly opened the door and slid inside.

"Wake up, Rudi! We are going snorkelling at the atoll reef. It´s really worth diving there! I bet you´ve never seen beauty as you can see it there! It´s the second biggest reef in the world!" He excitedly spoke the words at a loving speed. Without a break, he continued explaining, continuously shaking my arm.

"Rudi!" A muffled scream constantly bounced in my head from ear wall to another.

"Ow!" I jerked away, rubbing my earlobe. "Charlie, have you lost your mind?" A broad and happy smile was his reaction.

"If you don´t have ears, you could look like a hamburger." I returned him a drowsy smirk.

"Whyyy?" He asked.

"The top part of your head could easily be opened and filled with meat and vegetables." He giggled.

"Wait, I´ll need just a second!" I disappeared behind the bathroom door.

"You really aren´t a common girl," he said. I cocked my head incomprehensibly. I could not find the thread between our previous conversation and his last sentence.

"It didn´t take as long as for another common girl," he added to his explanation. The words ´ANOTHER COMMON´ were strongly emphasised. It amused me. I offered him my hand. A small one slid in. Vivid chatting, giggling and teasing down the staircase became more and more tangled with the fragrance of just-made coffee and pastries, rolls or cookies, which came out from the kitchen door.

"Morning, Señorita Isabell," Charlie said to his favourite member of their family, to his cook and nanny, all in one. She bowed to Charlie. He kissed her on her soft cheek.

"Morning!" she replied. A second butterfly-light kiss was placed on her other cheek and we left her there in her own surprise and contentment.

"Belle, my girl, just Belle." She told herself so quietly that nobody could hear.

"Morning!" As I settled at the table, I could strongly sense Mathew´s bad mood.

"Her Majesty the Princess is late." A sharp addition arrived. "Again, of course."

"Again?" I asked. I could not believe what I had heard. "What´s wrong, Mathew? Come on, be polite and explain it." My voice was calm, not trembling, but aimed directly at the target.

"What´s wrong? Are you so naive or so stupid? What´s wrong? You come here! You sneak into my family and you ask ´what´s wrong´?"

"I don´t understand. The professor invited me." In spite of the flips jumping in my stomach, my exterior remained serene.

"The professor was invited by my father," Mathew went on, angrily whipping his reply into the air.

"That´s enough, Mathew!" Trevor interrupted him in a resolute way.

"I asked her to visit us a few days ago, at the market in Belmopan. Might you be so polite and accept that fact? Rudi is my guest!" Each word brought such a high degree of authority that goose bumps rose on everybody´s skin.

"She saved me!" Charlie yelled to Mathew with childish enthusiasm and determination. The density around us was no problem for Charlie in that instance. Mathew lifted his eyebrows.

"A dog snarled at me and wanted to bite me. She grabbed me and put me on a staircase," Charlie declared, bug-eyed.

"I didn´t save you really. The dog could have been growling at this. I found it on the ground after your leaving." I pulled out the tiny piece of leather lace hidden behind my top. I opened it and passed it to Trevor.

"A strange creature," he said as he examined the approximately two-centimetre big animal gripped between his fingers.

"Its home is usually Australia and one species occurs in Chile or the western part of South America. Somebody could have brought it into our state like a kind of pet, perhaps. The distance between Chile and Belize is too great for it to have spread via natural species migration." He let sunbeams fall on it. They allowed him both to see better and to ensure he was in the right.

"The mouse spider," he alleged. "Its bite is uncomfortable, especially to young children. You feel great pain at the site of the bite. Nausea and abdominal pain follow. There can be breathing difficulties and a general weakness or muscle numbness. You sweat and cough heavily." His forefinger paced along the red spider´s body, checking each nook.

"I was right! She saved me!" Charlie made a ´winner´ gesture.

"Nice work. You have smart fingers. It is too small. I like it. Did you do it on your own, a very nice decoration?" I silently nodded, did not want to make the situation worse than it was.

"I should go. Excuse me, please. I need to borrow snorkelling equipment," I said.

"You don´t. You just need to bring yourself in your swimsuit," Trevor replied. His palm covered mine and postponed my leaving for a short while. Giving me a smiling gaze, he lightly and encouragingly rubbed the back of my hand.

"Mathew isn´t all bad," he said.

"He is just a little bit jealous." He faced me for a moment like he would have loved to say "yes" but the effort was too much. He loved him in the same way as Charlie. Mathew was his son too.

7

The wooden jetties glowed with heat absorbed from the sunbeams falling straight down on them. A cabin cruiser waited, anchored near the wooden booth at the end of the jetty, which sheltered it from the sun´s hot beams and gave it a small shadow. A square of canvas was fixed above the cruiser. I supposed it was necessary for an all-day ocean trip. We could have transferred to roasted chicken. We needed a shelter, a protection against sunbeams. A flock of pelicans circled and floated above the fishing boats tied to the wharf close to us. Watching the fishermen throw fish remains into the water, they dived in head first.

"Are you Sander´s friend?" The query finished my observation of the pelicans´ spectacle. A brown-skinned boy was climbing up iron bars hammered into the wooden pier, one of many attached to the jetty.

"Yes. Is that good or bad?"

"Mathew told me that . . ." he started. I did not allow him to finish the sentence.

"Is what Mathew says important here?" Facing him, I could read the confusion reflected in his face. He reddened.

"My name´s Rudi. By the way, Mathew calls me Rude Rudi. You can choose which you prefer." An unpleasant grin settled in the corner of my mouth.

"Sorry. I don´t think badly of you." He awkwardly wormed about. Offering me his hand, he hesitated. He might have assumed he had insulted me. "I´m Tristan, the captain of your atoll trip." With a mischievous wink, he attempted to fix the ill position that had arisen accidentally and unconsciously.

"Is Isolde the name of your cruiser?" I asked, shoving my hands into the side pockets of my jean shorts. I cocked my head to one side, waiting for his reaction.

"What?" His uncomprehending expression unveiled he had not understood. "Oh, I see. One day, I might explain that story to you. I just want to say: don´t believe first impressions."

I stretched my arm out to him. "O.K. I am Rudi." I was wriggling now. He let me boil in my own juice for an instant.

"Friends?" He gripped my hand for an instant.

"I would like that."

"Here comes the rest of our crew." Shielding his eyes with his palm horizontal to the ground, he pointed to the start of the jetty.

"The fun´s gone—Mathew has arrived," I snapped under my breath.

A sea of turquoise spread under the cruiser´s floor window, which allowed us to study the underwater world on the ocean bed. Exciting, nothing more and nothing less, was the right word, which expressed the state of my mind, my soul and my whole body. The master of a philharmonic orchestra had brought all the instruments in harmony to make the most incredible ocean symphony. The life under the water was brilliant: fish painted in rainbow colours, ray fish of different sizes, coral islands, starfishes and one shark. I pressed my body tighter against the cruiser. In my head, one thought was whirling, not showing my respect. Looking around, I would have loved to have a tiny spot of somebody´s support.

"The shark! Rudi, did you notice it?"

"Yes I did, Charlie." My tone did not sound as excited as Charlie´s.

"Hey Rudi, we´ve achieve our destination. The atoll gate!" Charlie said as he tugged my arm to turn me in the right direction. In the middle of the vast water was a similar cruiser to ours, anchored and waiting for newcomers. Nearing the left side of our boat, the men on board exchanged a few words to cheer one other. Something that looked like tickets was given to Trevor. Without any order, he gazed at Tristan. The anchor was cast over the cruiser's edge and, after hitting its usual place under the water on the ocean bed, it bit into an unknown point. The cruiser became an anthill of activity. Everybody knew what to do: clothes were taken off, flippers and diving goggles were put on and snorkels were made ready for use.

"There´s your equipment, Rudi." The professor nudged me, encouraging me to put it on. My hesitation at seeing the shark was relieved by renewed enthusiasm.

"Thanks." Each one of the crew members disappeared into the water, waiting for me. Sitting on the boat´s side, I suddenly somersaulted into the water.

There was such a marvellous amount of colours that a rainbow in comparison with this underwater world was only a sequence of grey shades. Turning our heads in all directions, we enjoyed the views offered by the ocean. Charlie followed me, showing me the most prominent species according to him. Becoming a member of a fish shoal, I swam calmly in order to not make any movements that could have startled them. Charlie touched his breast in a brief gesture, pointing to his heart. I did not get it. Pointing upwards, I emerged on the surface.

"I meant they like you," he said, repeating the last gesture. We re-dived to carry on our ocean adventure. The world of the second biggest coral reef opened its kingdom for us again, and we piled picture after picture into our memory cells.

"It was a great trip."

"Yes, it was. Enjoy the rest of your day, Trevor and Professor. Bye Mathew, bye Charlie!" Tristan said goodbye to each trip member.

"Have a nice day, Tristan." Giving him back the borrowed equipment, I stumbled against the edge of the cruiser and landed on the jetty. No situation could have been stupider than this. A giggle pushed through my lips. Tristan joined me, dragging me up from the jetty.

"Thanks. Bye, Tristan." I hurried to reduce the gap between myself and the others.

"Gregory, Gregory," I screamed. The squeaking of a door sounded from behind the house. I rushed behind it to check who or what could have caused the noise. "Are you mad, Gregory?" My temper calmed now I was winding him up.

"Why didn´t ask you someone?" I asked.

"Nobody was home." His sharp answer hit me. Finally, I was successful in settling him in his chair. "Are you going to be fed up with me?"

"I´m not fed up," he replied.

"Do you know how to swim?

"What?" His face reflected as much comprehension as the size of a pin head.

"Are you able to swim? Have you understood my question?"

"It is a very uncommon question. If we assume I´m a 'wheelchair boy', your query is strange, at least." He emphasised the word 'wheelchair', ensuring I would understand him in a suitable and correct way.

"Are your arms strong enough that you are able to swim just by using them? Is my query clear enough?"

"Stop your mockery! I am a wheelchair boy."

"I´ve already heard, Gregory! Would you be so polite and answer me?"

"I´ve never tried to swim in that way."

"O.K. We´ll check tomorrow."

"Have you heard me say yes?"

"I´ve not asked for your agreement." My snapping retort hit his eardrums. Wheeling him to the rear patio, I began whistling.

"Have a nice day and see you in the morning," I said. I blew a kiss as I was leaving.

"Why?" he asked. Facing him, I raised my eyebrows and cocked my head.

"Life is too short to waste sitting around on your backside. No patio isn´t worth it."

8

Many sweet orange beams from the sunrise covered each cane roof, chair, table and object in the Admiral Nelson Bar area. Some guests of the Victoria House Hotel usually had their breakfasts in this part of the resort just to see the incredible morning sunrises. There was another guest type as well, who decided on this particular place just for the views. The Belizean people used them to persuade anybody who crossed their path: they were views no one could have seen anywhere else. According to them, the Great Barrier Reef was the most magnificent around world. No explanation had the power to change their minds.

At this early hour, there were only two men and a highly recommended bartender at the scene. The urgent meeting had been arranged by them so they would not be disturbed or overheard by anybody else. The delicate business, according to their appointment, would take place on the beach of this romantic luxury hotel, mainly used by rich people or romantic couples. The sugary air did not accord with their business issues.

"The business related to Chiquibul National Park has a singularly strange attitude. The local people are suspicious, and that Prussian Mennonite community in Spanish Lookout is convinced that you aren´t interested in their crude oil but in something more powerful and different at the same time."

"Don´t be silly! One community? They arrived from Europe two centuries ago. We are living in the 21st century, my dear fellow."

"But swietenia macrophylla is not a weed in the middle of a wheat field. You can pass one tree, but such a big amount will be noticed by anybody crossing that area."

"Please don´t panic, Andrew. Don´t panic, stay calm! You´ll finish your botanical and soil research and then I´ll give you the right numbers to put in your final documentation. And the Belizean government will be able to see them." The ash tip of his cigar lightened his face in a red colour as he dragged a long breath into his lungs. A very satisfied, sarcastic and selfish smirk accompanied his cool-headedness. Exhaling cigar smoke, he wrote some letters on a piece of napkin placed on a decorative rail on their table. His pen found its place in the pocket of his shirt again. He shifted the napkin piece towards Andrew.

"That'll be the amount that will be in your account if our business is successful. The bottom number is the sum that your faculty will obtain for services realised following my job demands."

After an instance of hesitation, he grinned, screwed up the scribbled napkin and shoved it in his back pocket.

"You persuaded me quickly. The deal has been done."

"Something to drink, sirs?"

"No, thank you. Just the bill."

"Of course, sirs."

A quite new taxi stopped in front of the building.

"Could you wait for few minutes?"

"No problem, sir." In a half-turned sitting position, the taxi driver offered him a favour: "I can vanish for quarter of an hour or more, if necessary."

"Great." Question-less, the passenger passed him a rolled note from the rear seat. The driver's door was opened, the door was slammed and the coast was clear.

People walked in both directions along the pavement between the cab and the building next to it. They passed by, hung around or crossed Princess Margaret Drive; they chatted to each other, giggled or were alone with their thoughts. From the back seat, he could see the main entrance decorated with a metal label. The engraved letters announced the importance of the edifice's owners:

"The Russian Federation Honorary Consulate"

A little chink in the taxi's window permitted him to listen to every voice or movement coming from the busy street. A well-known figure emerged from the gate's mouth, pacing towards the cab.

"Здраствуй Филип, друг мой."
(Hi Fillip, my dear fellow!) A man slid into the cab, offering his hand to the sitting man.

"Здраствуй. Для меня нет время. Иди прямо торговать.
(Hi, I don't have any time. Go ahead with our business!)

"Здес номери членов сообщество и час когда надо телефонироать, когда они находятся вне Меннонитов." (Here are the numbers of the community members and the precise times when they are free, unless the Mennonite community gets suspicious.)

A sheet of paper dropped into the passenger´s jacket pocket; he nodded and tucked it deeper so it would not have any chance of getting lost.

"Спасибо." (Thanks.)

No other words were spoken. The taxi´s guest disappeared into the street rush. Fillip´s hand patted his jacket´s side. Thoughts whirled in his brain, processing a new strategy for how he could secure the cooperation of old-fashioned people, frozen somewhere in the 19th century, with the new options of the 21st century. Nothing would easily rise in front of him. The crude oil business stood on one hand like a camouflage and, on the other hand, he was offering an extremely difficult trade, but much more profitable than any oil business. This kind of business had died during the 20th century due to loss of attractiveness. This business was related to swietenia macrophylla: ordinary mortals called it mahogany.

"Интриги. Как я это люблю."
(Machinations are the loveliest matter.) Satisfaction hovered above him.

Bang! The driver slammed his door shut behind him. No query was raised, just a key clicking in the metal ignition and the taxi woke up into a long, delicate, gentle purr.

"To B.C. Municipal Airport?"

"Yes, home."

The tiny runway line got wider as the Maya Island Air plane lowered its altitude. The same applause, cheering and clapping from happy passengers that he had heard many times dragged him away from his thoughts. He had never comprehended the exact reason for this habit. Little six to twelve-seat planes were as popular for public transportation there as buses were in the UK or in any other developed city around the world. They were not used to clapping or cheering at every bus stop.

A sour mood trapped him. He was fed up with all these people being happy every moment of every day, in spite of mostly being poor. Did they not have any life aims? When did they lose their need to become successful? What was their life purpose? Disgusted by their lifestyles, he pierced his way through the small groups scattered near the runway exit.

"Next time, I´ll fly by private plane. Quality deserves quality," he muttered, unable to shake his prior crummy mood. The distance to the long taxi line was shortened by his accelerated pace.

"Gregory! Young Sir! Your breakfast!" A buxom landlady in her early forties with a large wooden tray in her hands followed him from one room to another.

"The patio, Bernicia," he replied, just loud enough to be audible.

"Did you watch the dawn again, young sir?" Wave splashes and the whistling wind were the only things that answered her for a pretty long time.

"Can you hear it, Bernicia?" He did not twist to face her. He remained in the same numbness. You could have heard a pin drop.

"Gregory, you need to eat something. I can only imagine how early you got up. I can hear your intestines. They are doing flips, at least." Her voice was full of taunts. Laying the tray down on a table, she scanned him narrowly. She would have liked to continue her speech, but . . .

"Hush, Bernicia. Please listen!" The past numbness trailed off. She could not let him stay trapped inside himself. She was not going to let him succumb to his thoughts, his lethargy. "Gregory, you need a friend. A good friend who would be able to bring light into your days." The mosquito net door frame was slammed.

9

I was whistling "Yellow Submarine" as water splashes filled the bathroom. It was only 5.15 am, but my eyelids had refused to remain closed at five, so I had got up. I tiptoed along the staircase, trying not to make any squeaking sounds and disappeared behind the bottom door leading to a slatted veranda. The familiar ocean fragrance hovered everywhere, wrapping around me and titillating all my senses. I descended the last two wooden stairs, holding a beautiful hand-made, carved wooden banister, the moonlight covering it with a light grey-blue hue.

Fine sand grains flew over my toes and soles, tickling me in a comfortable way. The movement of my feet brushed them off and they fused with their brothers, joining them repeatedly as I walked along the silent, sandy beach. I must have been crazy: when my sight wandered over to the ocean's surface, I could see pelicans sleeping with their heads folded under their wings, seesawing on the waves and enjoying their dreams. The night was losing its sovereignty, descending from its throne bit by bit and letting the coming day ascend and develop an entirely new day. I had never seen a more beautiful and spectacular dawn at home.

"Tristan. Tristan. Can you hear me?" Knocking, pacing from one window to another and whispering his name, I attempted to discern whether there was movement inside.

"Yes?" The question was accompanied by a slight squeak. I jumped.

"Hi."

"Do you know what time is, Rudi?"

"Around, 5.45?"

"A little early, isn´t it?"

"I need your help, please."

"Whom did you get my address from?"

"I only need your help Tristan, please. Don´t keep moaning, please," I said calmly. Tristan looked at me for a while as though he was counting.

"What kind of help?"

"A swimming lecture."

"You are a very good swimmer. I don´t understand." Some confusion reflected in his face. "Even if I wanted to help you, I wouldn´t be able to—my job begins at 6.30."

"O.K. Can you lend me a life jacket?" My previous enthusiasm slowly trailed off. "Can you?" I repeated my query.

"No problem, sure." His silhouette melted into the house´s shadow for a short while. "Here you are. Can you tell me your secret?"

"Later, maybe. I haven´t got time right now."

"Rudi, wait."

"Thanks for helping," I said. Letting my backpack rapidly slither along my arm, I stuffed the orange phosphorous life jacket inside.

"Not at all, Rudi."

"See you later, Tristan. I´m obliged to you." Leaving him there, I headed in a direction known just in my mind. A fairly long time later, I heard him say something. Turning to face him, I just saw his blurred silhouette standing in the house´s shadow.

"Who told you my address?" he asked. A satisfied smirk settled on my lips.

"I´ll tell you another time."

"Morning." I was surprised—he was sitting there, wordless, with a breakfast tray on the table in front of him looking like it was pinned to him.

"Will you join me?" he said. His gesture flew above the table top, inviting me to share his breakfast.

"If you have got a full coffee pot, I could think about it."

"With milk?"

"Sure, Gregory," I said.

"A croissant?"

"With nuts and cream?"

"Sure, Rudi." He returned my own ribbing.

"What kind of dawn is it for you?"

"For me?"

"Where you come from."

"O.K. I understand now. I used to watch twilights. I´ve never seen a dawn." He kept looking in the distance as though he desired to find the ocean´s end.

"Oh. It´s different for me. As a child, I used to go on the top of a hill near my granddad´s flat to observe the dawn. During summer, when the first sunbeams ran across the little mountain range and down their slopes, we would sit in the fields full of flowers and green grass below. Under the shelter of a tree, we would look for the first sunbeams piercing the morning fog floating between Morava River and the sky. In winter, we used to go there to count snowflakes falling down to the ground. And every spring Sunday we would stand there and taste the fragrance of newly woken nature. There were four of us grandchildren: three girls and one boy. We used to go there to make our own dawn reproductions on paper. We used to draw it—we totally enjoyed it. All our childish feelings were put onto white pieces of paper. Then we used to ask granddad for his decision. He just used to say: ´no winner. We are all winners.´ Then we would laugh for a long while, feeling satisfied, happy and loved. It was thrilling. I love remembering my childhood."

I bit a croissant and took a sip of coffee as he continued.

"I couldn´t watch the twilight until later; not until I became a teenager. My parents were old-fashioned and stern. My mum used to have an iron hand in a velvet glove. I´m sure you know what I mean. ´Be in bed at 7.30, latest.´" He smirked at this memory. "I like observing the sun´s movements, I really like it"

"It´s a colourful performance." My thoughts were lost in the distance.

"I like all the colours reflecting from one roof to another: red beams bouncing off window glass, dazing me in so many ways. But, I prefer the twilight without the sun." He checked my reaction, my interest and stopped his speech: he melted into rows of a never ending twilight-story.

"I love when subtle drizzling drops knock on different surfaces, producing the same sound but in many variations, then quietly roll downwards to join bigger raindrops, finding tiny paths that lead them down to the ground. Then they find a crack, which will deliver them to the powerful river, to Mercy. None of those drops knows whether it´ll achieve its aim or not: they just try. Their destinies are different, but the rolling adventure is so thrilling."

"What is your life´s aim?" Looking directly into his eyes, I waited for an answer.

"To have the opportunity to be thankful for each new morning."

"On the patio?" I cocked my head in surprise. I was conscious of being sarcastic and a little bit rude, but politeness was not the right way to kick his ass into gear and drag him away from his lethargy. "How old are you, Gregory. I estimate close to ninety or more? Too young to be old, am I right?" My smiling eyes stopped teasing him.

"I brought something for you," I continued. Snapping back the lace end of my backpack, I fought to free its belts caught under my chair leg. Finally, it was opened. An unidentified orange padded thing landed on his tights. Scrutinising the subject, our chat died. A nervous silent pause remained.

"A life jacket?" I could have sworn he was counting in order get calm. "Do you mean I´ll go swimming?" he asked. He raised his head, piercing the early morning air. His stable glance examined my resistance, stinging me in the core of my heart.

"I hope so." I did not let him derail me. I followed the previous context of our last conversation, not giving him any time to stop me.

"I would like to show you something really breath-taking. You must see it: it´s worth having a couple of swimming lectures to be able to go snorkelling there." My rapture hovered in every inch of that place.

"No!" His resolution whipped me. There was no possibility of negotiation or offering a second option. He smacked his wheelchair against the table as he swivelled towards the kitchen door. My arm shot out and my palm gripped his, blocking the wheels from going on in haste.

"Don´t leave, please. I´m your friend." Now I was piercing him to the core; I was not going to evade the situation or back off and let him withdraw into himself. "You just miss your tuxedo. Nice swimming trousers." I sent him a ribbing wink, handing him the orange phosphorous life jacket.

"Have you invented a way of approaching the water?" he teased, maybe waiting for me to give my plans up. I raised my eyebrow and stood up. Gregory stopped his wheels next to me.

´What are we waiting for?´ I thought. Removing myself from the edge of the stairs behind the wheelchair, I bowed down to his ear.

"Vous à la, monsieur." A nearby path had been created while he was getting changed, made from a set of wooden slats. I wheeled him pretty comfortably across the wooden parts of the course; a subtle shaking occurred on the slat junctions. The last slats were immersed under the water's surface.

"Is your wheelchair stainless?" I asked. He did not reply.

Wordless, he looked at the ocean: even tiny waves were thwarted and remained perfectly flat. He pushed down the ball growing in his throat. I let him win his own fight. I was tarrying. Quietness floated around us, wrapping his decision in many untouchable layers.

"I've not swum for years." Finally, he broke the awkward silence.

"It's O.K. I expected it. Don't worry." A faint smile sneaked onto my lips. "Be happy." Laughter shackled our ear-splitting whistles as the familiar melody reached our eardrums. Gregory kept laughing as I started counting . . .

"One, two, three, and ruuuun!" I pulled the wheelchair in front of me slowly at first, but after a while it absorbed the power of my arm and dashed forwards to the water. The water friction finished the movement in an exceedingly short fraction of a second: the wheels stopped twisting and we were shot into the water by the power of friction. Splash! We both landed in the liquid. Sincere laughter cracked the dense air and poured into the surroundings without any warning. I knew the life jacket was as reliable as Tristan's sincerity, innocence and dignity, which were attributes so rarely seen. There was no question of me wearing it in case I forgot how to swim. I alternated swimming with jumping in the dark water (the sunrise had not reached a high enough level yet to change the liquid into its true turquoise hue) in an attempt to reach Gregory.

"Your first feeling . . . ?" Face to face, we laughed and laughed.

"You are crazy, Rudi. I can't believe it. You did it!" he exclaimed. A water splash produced by his palm dispersed on my face, flowing down my cheeks in many miniature drops. With one hand in a protective position, my second hand replied to him in the same manner. A water fight started.

"Stop! Stop! I give up!"

"Promise! Say it! Say 'I promise.'"

"I promise." Splashing noises, laughter and repeated loud requests for promises swallowed his answer. The guarantee trailed off in a matter of seconds.

"Are you standing on your feet?" I asked. My surprise, which in brief jerks had disturbed the fight, must have been evident in my voice.

"The salt water. It's aiding me." Gregory's voice was hoarse.

"You can stand up. That's great!"

"Can we continue swimming?" Embarrassment hovered above his words.

"Sure. Let's go!"

"Leave me! Stop! Don't help me! I'll cope on my own," he said. No words of defiance fell out of my mouth. Standing aside, I became a bystander. Unless he decided so, my words would not change his actions. His whole person sank into the water. Every muscle, every inch of sinew and every thought joined him in his effort. Neither of us became the sole winner: both of us became one. Happiness, satisfaction and euphoria satiated all our senses.

"Are you exhausted?"

"Yes, exhausted and thrilled."

"At 2.30?"

"At 2.30? What?" I did not understand his question.

"Our trip meeting. You told you want to show me something breathtaking."

"Next weekend, I promise." I made a grimace to reduce his disappointment. He was used to listening to similar answers many times.

"The professor is going to leave for the jungle about lunch time, I suppose. One journey usually takes about a half a day. It´s far better to travel during the day light."

"Is the park important?"

"We´ll see. The research isn't over yet."

"Is it important to you?"

"Yes. And it´s my graduation project as well. We´ll see soon. Later, Gregory."

Bernicia´s buxom shapes trapped his mind for quite a long moment. Healthy-looking curved lines did not let him pass by without noticing such precisely created parts of the woman´s body. Joy shone from every particle of Bernicia´s personality. Her vivacity was unconsciously displayed to the whole space. She was the kind of person who usually exuded an ambiance wherever she decided to settle. Old gentlemen used to say "She is slightly broad in the beam." In spite of "twiggy ladies" being fashionable, his starved gaze had missed buxom girls.

"Hm." A raspy cough distracted Bernicia from her kitchen cleaning. It was more similar to "Hospital Sterilisation" than to a common house cleaning. It allowed no bacterium, no microbes, no germs: nothing that could have caused a tiny sneeze.

"Oh, sir, I didn´t hear you coming." Her palms, with each finger wearing a ring with rainbow stones, were pressed to her chest as she strived to get calm.

"Gregory is . . ." he started. She cut him short.

"I have the greatest news, sir. I´m terribly happy. A girl visited him. They spent all morning together." The secret radiated from her gestures.

"Really?"

"Yes. Yes, sir." Showing her cute bottom, she continued with her unfinished work, a jolly melody pouring from her throat.

"Too many drops of white rum in your coffee this morning, Bernicia?" he ribbed her.

"You are welcome to my morning coffee. You´d appreciate it, sir." Her waist brushed from side to side in time with the swing of her own crooning.

"And he´s now . . ."

"In his room." Again, she did not let him end his sentence.

"Very lovely dress, Bernicia."

"My coffee invitation still stands, sir!" Swinging and crooning, she kept on with her job.

"Bernicia, I am not hungry yet. I´ll call you if things change." The click of a light switch forced him to turn his head.

"Oh, papa. I have not heard you come in." He read words over Gregory´s shoulder. Big letters on his laptop screen fused into the title "CHIQUIBUL NATIONAL PARK".

10

The dense jungle foliage at the canopy levels did not allow sunlight to reach the ground, so the plant inhabitants of the jungle floor were scattered in various circle areas where strong, bright beams touched the ground. I was struggling across tangled plants, stumbling through roots and fallen branches and trying to free my backpack. It kept getting trapped in the grid of plant species, which got continuously richer and thicker. My skills and knowledge told me to stick at it because the compact and almost impenetrable vegetation meant only one thing: the jungle's edge must be nearby. During the last day, the terrain work and the environment had forced me to learn how to use machete. My first practice brought a lot of fun to the members of the small family consisting of the professor, me, Mathew and two young local boys. Advancing the speculative edge, I got more exhausted and my temper rose.

"Hell! They should have taught me how to use a chainsaw!" My arms, shoulders and wrists hurt me and an uncountable number of scratches were causing my skin to burn.

"Pull out the GPS! Pull it out!" The orders I gave myself sounded like a cheerleading song. After a firm press on the start button, the GPS awoke and began loading its software. Finally, it was ready to cooperate.

"I´m not far—it´s about 25 minutes straight ahead to the research areas." I judged it to be 2, maybe 3, kilometres.

I rummaged carelessly through the backpack, looking for antiseptic liquid. I had thrown it in the inner pocket the night before, knowing we would be staying away from our temporary home (the little cane-roofed and baked clay houses) for more than five nights. Leaning my back against a gigantic tree, I rested, letting the liquid´s drops fall on my bleeding scratches. Tiny cuts absorbed them and distributed each one of them to my veins, which delivered the droplets to every last inch of burning skin. I fingered in the backpack to find the bottle full of water. The liquid slid down my throat, gently touching its dry walls in two abiding swallows. In an unsynchronised rapid movement of hands, all the items found their former places. I rose to continue on in the direction that I had decided on, irregularly cutting with the machete to open new corridors in front of me.

"Shit!" A sudden falling branch startled me. Twisting my head round, I looked up and down the canopy and back to the floor. I tried to catch glimpse of the cause of the flying limb. My eyes skipped from twig to twig, scrutinising them in all directions. I walked backwards, my legs proceeding along the path. My next step did not meet with the ground.

Bang! I was suddenly rolling down a slope, my fingers striving to snag any root, twig or branch poking out from the soil bank.

"Ow!" The massive slide finished in the indisputable thud of my hip on the solid ground. My hands checked all my painful body parts to make sure it was not as terrible as it seemed. Mud lines had accidentally sketched interesting pictures on my trousers. One of the several twigs that I had met during my flying and rolling exhibition had torn the linen fabric and allowed my knee to peek out. No injuries; just a few new scratches accompanying their older brothers, which sent subtle flames to close my skin´s crevices.

"Shit!" I pulled the GPS from the muddy remains of a puddle, pressing my forefinger on the start button and praying that it would work. I felt an intense need to pay attention to something that was shivering in my view. My eyes fastened on the quick movement: thousands of colourful fluttering and shivering flecks flew in all directions near the surface of a pond. Other swarms of animated spots floated close to the edge of a cave´s mouth among an uncountable number of hanging orchids, whose stems tangled into glorious blooming falls. The next group of small flying rainbow-flakes shook their tiny wings just a few feet in front of me, within reach. A butterfly paradise. If I had been an entomologist, I could have observed them for many years. And I´m sure I would not have been able to discover every one of the species flickering around. My ability to breathe had been lost somewhere in the first moment when my gaze had stopped and had been trapped by this unspeakable beauty.

"Rudi." I gave no reaction.

"Rudi!" A boyish yell hit me. I jumped. Bum-bum, bum-bum. My heart sounded like a grandiose church bell.

"Rudi, is everything all right?"

"You just startled me. What is this place? Have you ever seen something similar?" I was stunned and thrilled and needed to pour out and express all my feelings.

"We´d better go, it´s very late. In less than quarter of an hour, it´ll be twilight. The forest gets dangerous then." His offered hand helped me get up.

"Wait, wait, please. I want to snap a couple of pictures." Firmly rummaging through my backpack, I quickly looked for my camera. The loosened lens cover swayed as a clicking sound cut through the air several times. Putting the camera away, I hurried to obey Joseph.

"You´ve not answered me yet. What is this paradise?"

"Paradise," he replied with a grin and the whistle of an unfamiliar song.

"Hey cowboy, you´re behaving like Matt!"

"You´ve hurt me, señorita."

"So . . ."

"It´s the Chiquibul Cave System."

"Do you know it?"

"Of course, my lady. Let´s go, Rudi, it´s late!" I could subconsciously feel the indefinite persistent pain of my muscles sending burning sensations to all my senses. But the vision of the dark jungle forest drove me to go back to our temporary camp.

"Wait, my machete!" I disappeared. Rapidly running back along the corridor I had gone through an hour ago, the reason was obvious: nobody was safe in this forest without a weapon. There it was, right on the slope´s edge. My hand must have loosened its grip at the moment when I had unexpectedly started falling. I bowed down to pick it up.

"Rudi . . ."

"Have you got something better in your bag?" I asked. Out of breath, I let the words slip out one at a time until I had caught my breath.

"Let´s go!" No conversation, no jollying or teasing; we hurried onwards. The dark arrived at the forest floor earlier than we had expected. The night wildlife initiated in several dubious steps, but with the waxing hours the wild voices got louder and the noises became more distinct.

"Are you afraid?" he whispered in my direction.

"No, thrilled. I´ve never experienced anything like it."

"Hush!" Joseph dragged me down. He pointed at two silhouettes just five feet away from us.

"Listen! Can you hear that?" Squatting among dense foliage, which gave us cover, we listened to the voices approaching us.

"Когда я сказал это правильно, это правильно! Да, ты понимал очень правильно! Да красное дерево! Это самая важна торговля для меня и я не позволяю чтобы она не била осуществленна!" (When I said it is right, then it is right! Yes, you understood correctly! Yes, the red tree! It is the greatest business in my life. The deal is too important not to be finished!) The man yelled to another next to him. Our observing position could not have attracted anybody´s attention, due to the dark and the private zeal mixing with the furiousness of the screaming man.

"Do you understand them?" Joseph asked.

"He is a stranger."

"I´ve comprehended nothing. What is the language?"

"Russian."

"How do you know it?" The surprise affected Joseph´s voice, making it a little bit louder unconsciously.

"Hush! I come from the former eastern communist part of Europe, which included European countries with a political regime similar to Vietnam or North Korea." His frozen expression betrayed that he did not understand a word of my explanation.

The shouting died down, the two men receded and then the black of the forest vegetation swallowed them. We rested in the shelter of the shadows for a couple of minutes until we knew we could emerge safely.

"I´ve thought, people living in North Korea or Vietnam are too poor. I´ve not known they can afford to study at a university."

"The political system of former European communist countries was similar to the political system of North Korea. It´s the only similarity to North Korea. But these countries were developed, have pretty good social, educational and trade level. They are similar to other European countries, today. There was the only difference. People were allowed to visit just the communist countries. The capitalist world was closed to them. Perhaps, there was the second difference. People used to earn less money than their western neighbours. Don´t you watch TV? How old are you?"

"Seventeen."

"Let´s go." I stopped our strange conversation. It was time to go.

"Has Joseph come back yet?"

"No, professor."

A round circle of smoke rose up, carrying the scent of cooking food and burning wood into the air. The light produced by the fire ran across all their faces, illuminating with soft hues the cupola-shaped tents stood in a semi-circle and the figures shuffling around them.

"Evening. We´ve brought some chunks of wood."

"Jesus! Finally!" The professor gripped us both in a strong hug of relief.

"Her Majesty has dignified us with her return." Matt´s sarcastic teasing, as a rule, passed by me. I left wordlessly. My desire to wear dry, clean clothes was bigger than my desire to react to Mathew´s rudeness. A lamp gave enough light in my little round tent that I could see every crawling insect, inside and outside the space, in explicit detail. Warmth, dry clothes and the night silence cheered my mood and I was ready to challenge Matt´s sharp comments. My guts produced a strange noise and the smell of the now-finished meal dragged me out.

"Did she hurt you? You behave like an idiot."

"It´s not your problem."

"Yes, it is. We are occupying one place."

"She´s rude, impolite and selfish."

"It´s your description."

"Joseph, can I offer you a bowl of stew?"

"Yes, thank you professor." Joseph was hungry, so the spar between him and Matt did not warrant him refusing a nice-smelling dish. The professor´s hand reached me as I returned to the middle of the tents. His encouraging look told me all that I needed to know in that instant. Sharing our private silent smiles, I approached Joseph and settled on the same log. Sparkles jumped high above the flames, piercing the air with their miniature orange bodies and building a secure atmosphere around the different people joined into one hilarious family.

A subtle spoon rattling sounded from time to time, cutting through the nature noises twisting around one other and creating a beautifully amazing jumbled song.

"Good morning. A cup of morning coffee, professor? It seems a nice day is in front of us," I said.

"Hi Rudi. Have you been in the forest?"

"For a morning shower. You know it."

"Women matters." An amused smile tickled his lips.

"Women matters?" I slightly wrinkled my forehead. I was giggling, enjoying this awkward moment. An unexplainably close friendship had been growing between us. Our conversations were many times wordless: many times we needed to just use gestures or facial expressions. Many times touches and gazes solved or eased ambiguous tasks.

"Here you are, your coffee with cane sugar and milk."

"I´m sorry, I wasn´t listening . . ." A coffee aroma was hovering under my chin. A plump kaolin mug was cupped by my hands.

"Thank you, professor. You are polite to me." His raised eyebrows expressed his surprise.

"I like any woman´s accompany. The world would not work without both women and men. Balance and stability are two words that create one very important rule." A toucan´s squawk finished his speech.

"It was the comma behind the sentence." A short glance, we quickly shared our amusement. He settled next to me and the giggling trailed off, leaving a more than comfortable silence.

"Such an irresistible fragrance, isn´t it?" A fuzzy haired head peeked out from one of the four canvas copulas. His glued eyes did not let him see things in the surroundings in their distinct shapes, so his estimation was not as exact as he had expected: one tent peg crossed Joseph´s step and immediately caused a disaster. Joseph hectically balanced between walking and stumbling.

"Such a nice performance, Joseph."

"Thanks, professor. Can I help myself?"

"Yes, do you have a mug?"

"No, I haven´t. You know, my father wanted to pack me—I let him do it for me. Thank God for that plastic bottle, which hit his sight and he fortunately put in my bag. So, I have water, at least."

"We´ll share. Do you like sweet coffee, cowboy?" I nudged him with my shoulder. I chuckled: his story entertained us. His palms cupped the half-full mug of coffee given to him. Patting the log, I gestured for him to sit down and accompany me.

"Do you like it?"

"Oh, too sweet, Rudi. I´ll cope though."

"Hey cowboy, you are too brave!" I ribbed him.

"Maybe sweeter than Rudi." His arrogance whipped through the air.

"Morning everybody," Mathew said.

"Nice to see you again, Mathew."

"Don´t you offer me a cup of sharing coffee, Rudi?"

"Such a clever boy! No, I don´t." I snapped the response over my shoulder as I headed to my tent to prepare all the necessary items for the day´s terrain work.

"O.K. boys, we are obligated to complete all our research at two pm. The last three areas are an estimated two kilometres from the Las Cuevas Forest Research Station in the middle of the Chiquibul Forest Reserve. Trevor Sander, Matt´s father, will be waiting there for us to give us a lift to Belmopan." Ignorance was the right way of successfully managing Mathew´s behaviour. He effortlessly casted him out from the centre of attention that Matt loved.

"My decisions for these areas have been due to logging. Every area picked is different. The first contains the remains of salvage logging in the 1950s. The second field represents logging from the 1980s. And the last area shows a sustainable way of timber logging that started being used after the 1980s. That was the explanation of today´s work in short. Details will be given to you at the place. So, let´s go pack our bags and load them into the Discovery! After quarter of an hour, we are going to leave."

A big wide clearing invited the Discovery, which was covered in a dried mud shell. All the arrangements were in place. According with the professor´s agreement with Trevor, next to a long building a terrain jeep occupied a grass area, hidden in the trees´ shadows. The clearing was surrounded by a typical local jungle forest space and had four other much smaller wooden buildings intended for use as accommodation, as well as research areas for scientists coming from all over the world and many prestigious universities. I was exhausted after finally finishing my terrain work. But, I was stunned and impressed by this unique scientific accommodation/work/resting area. Only the dark grey sky had the power to destroy my pleasure. The nearing storm pushed the darkness in front of; it did not forecast anything decent. We could not leave the camp before traversing through the Las Cuevas Forest Research Station, abandoning our footprints behind us in an uncountable number of diverse, vivid streams, which flowed in all directions. Broken and up-ended objects were scattered throughout the area. Each one of us had to accept the fact that our departure to Belmopan was delayed until the storm was over.

"I feel like a drug tycoon."

"Do you know a tycoon who is interested in clean plates and hot dinner?

"It smells good. Can I join you guys?" I disturbed boys´ joking.

"Your fragrance is incredible, Rudi."

"I reveal you my secret. Take a shower. I´m sure you´ll smell very good, too. Try it, it works." I sent him a wink.

"We´ll be late. Hurry up Rudi!" Joseph urged me.

"Hey Joseph! I´m hungry! Don´t take my plate away!"

"We are supposed to be in the conference hall in five minutes. The professor is waiting."

"In the conference hall?" I lifted my eyebrows. An amused expression of my face reflected my attitude to his demand.

"I´m not joking, Rudi. Let´s grab Julian, too."

"All right, Joseph."

I caught them almost at the staircase´s edge. The banister was wrapped in a thin, wet foil of rain created by many little raindrop ribbons rotating around it again and again. The intense rain whipped buildings, cut the air into many large strips and covered the ground with a number of puddles. No one had any chance of getting into one of the other buildings without getting sopping wet.

"Can you hold this?" Julian offered me the second brim of a canvas sheet. I assumed he must have been naive: I was not convinced that this kind of protection would be enough, but I took it anyway.

"Hands up! And run!" The canvas protected just the body parts hidden under it; the unshielded parts got drenched in a few seconds. We ran across the grass field, skipping among increasing puddles.

"Yes, we are the winners!" Joseph shouted when he hit the first dry paving stone under the overhanging wooden roof. Julian let the canvas sheet slide down, brushing away drops from its surface. Looking at each other, we started giggling. The giggling transformed into laughter.

"Ladies and gentlemen, it is the elite of the scientific world!" Three wet creatures processed along a short corridor into the so-called conference hall.

"Evening, professor." The greeting disturbed two persons in the middle of a conversation. Considering what they were saying, which they said so loud that it was easily audible, we recognised that they were talking about tomorrow.

"Oh, we haven´t heard you coming."

"Trevor, let me introduce you to my team. This is Julian and Joseph. And you already know Rudi and Mathew." He looked behind us.

"Good evening, Dad, professor." A familiar voice hovered in the space. Nobody returned the greeting. There was no reason to.

We sat and listened for nearly three hours. Every step made during the terrain work in the three different research areas was discussed in detail so no aspect would be missed out. Mr Sander´s experience and education formed a strong basis for the laboratory work.

"You are supposed to look through the samples, facts and comments in the notebooks to find solutions and invent actual projects that local specialists can apply in local forest re-cultivation and the long-term sustainability of it." Trevor reminded us of the purpose of our work.

"That´s all. I know we could continue for hours, but you would be unable to listen to any more. You´ve had a pretty long, exhausting day, I think," the professor added.

The rustling of papers gave a full stop to the discussion. All graphs, maps and plans were taken down and the dim screen light was turned off. I unconsciously perceived how they left the space one after another. An A5 piece of white paper attracted my gaze. Big bold black capitals published in three short rows presented the engaging offer of a small library hidden behind a slatted wooden wall:

"UP-TO-DATE PUBLICATIONS
EMAIL FACILITIES
COPY AND FAX FACILITIES"

The thrill inside me and my desire to read all the emails in my inbox were growing; moments later, my finger pressed the computer's start button and the device woke up into life. My fingers bounced from one keyboard button to another with rapid speed, the letters fusing into a URL address. With the correct user name and password, my inbox was opened.

"The first step: emails from Mum." I could only imagine what would be written in them. I surprised myself in spite of the fact that I looked forward to reading them.

"Hi my Sun,

I'm impressed, those snaps are wonderful. The country, the people, the cities, the countryside—everything looks so bright, so beautiful . . .

Autumn has undoubtedly pushed summer away. The temperature has decreased below 14°C. And, in the mornings and evenings, it falls below 4 or 5°C. I'm a little bit envious. Summer has gone . . .

I almost forgot—your granny sends you many kisses. Laura helped me attach a couple of home-made pictures.

I love you,
Mum. ;o)"

As I had expected, I was so amused, happy and thankful that for a short while, I was back at home. I felt as if I could smell the aromas of Mum's kitchen: the scent of the cakes or cookies made by her every other day. My eyes fell on the subject of Laura's email: *"HELP!"*

"Hi Nina,

You are just a common rat, a snake and a Judas. Take your butt, put your foot on any plane, fly across whatever ocean and come home! Now I've expressed all my emotions, I can be a bit nicer to you . . .

I think it's not really news to you that, as I write, our mum is coming slowly, but surely, to senility. For example: one warm sunny day, she ran around the flat helplessly looking for her keys. I couldn't just watch her, so I checked the front door from the corridor side. Guess what! Yes, the keys were there. What a big surprise! And one night, I was snaking along the hallway so quietly that you could have heard a pin drop and . . . what do you think happened? She was waiting for me there and she said her favourite question 'do you know what's time?' and I thought I would blow my top! My heart banged rapidly for the next two days . . .

Laura, your ex-sister. ;o)
Honey, enjoy yourself!
I love you and I miss you. ;o)."

I was laughing: many funny pictures, with my mum playing the leading role, were flashing through my mind.

"Rudi, are you crazy! What did you do? Why Belize? Shit! It's on the equator! . . .

Rudi, I would like to explain my stupid behaviour from that night, I've wanted to say from the last morning . . .

I want to do it personally, not via email . . .

Rudi, there is nobody else with your ironic style of humour. I'm bored.

Hey, don't be a jerk and let me know your arrival date.

Daniel."

He had fulfilled my expectations: he remained faithful to his character. He was as polite as usual. There were many emails packed in unopened rows. I quickly skipped through their subjects to be sure I read the most important ones. I was too tired to keep reading. I decided to abandon this cheering but energy draining activity for the next evening.

"Tomorrow! Stand up, Rudi!" Ordering myself, I switched the computer off and rose. Stretching my hand to snap off the light switch, I was stopped by a title of a book written in fairly massive dark green capitals: *"THE RED TREE—SWIETENIA MACROPHYLLA—AND OTHER SUBSPECIES".* The Russian man in the forest had shouted at the other man something like . . . I returned in my mind to one night earlier, striving to remember every word spoken by that furious Russian. Yes, he had said "Да красное дерево"(the red tree). I pulled out the book from the library, walked back to my chair, sat down and began thumbing through the pages. I paused at a chapter named *"IMPORTANCE AND BENEFITS OF LOGGING".* I found the chapter's end. It contained more than forty pages, which were covered with text, pictures of devastating logging activities, diagrams, data tables and graphs, pointing to a repressive attitude towards the environment: the word *"SUSTAINABILITY"* seemed to be an unknown phenomenon. I read line by line to not skip any significant facts.

". . . in the country, illegal activities were caused by citizens of the neighbouring country . . . within Belize's borders . . . in one year alone, specialists from Chiquibul National Park declared that over 1,000 acres were illegally cleared for cultivation . . ."

My eyes slid to the sentences in the paragraph above.

". . . timber extraction increased threefold . . . the uncontrolled cutting and exporting of the economically valuable red trees generated more than usual . . ."

I found a pencil and some paper and wrote down the author and the title of the book. I shoved it in my trouser pocket. The book found its former place in the library. A snap switched the light off.

Darkness and jungle voices entered the scene. They replaced the whipping rain and the thudding of rolling things during the storm. It had been scary and shocking at the same time. My course was clear: straight to my accommodation, it was early morning and I had just one wish—to sleep without any dreams disturbing my rest. I was advancing to the cottage construction when I spotted two gleaming points strangely piercing the dark. I kept on in the same direction, pretending as though I had seen nothing. Not turning to the left or to the right, just going straight on. Two small lights followed me. I could feel breath near my calf.

"O.K." I suddenly changed my mind and decided to face the creature.

"What do you want from me?" I asked. The question was addressed more to me than to it to encourage myself. There stood a nice, friendly looking animal more similar to a fox than a dog. It looked grey, but I was not convinced whether it was really grey; in the dark, all things have a grey shade.

Crack! The sound startled me. I pushed myself against a wall. The shadow gave me the advantage of invisibility; I comfortably waited for an opportunity to leave my sanctuary.

"I´m not sure if you correctly understood the agreement."

"I can assure you . . ."

"No! You can´t assure me nothing! Change the agreement for real! Then I´ll be satisfied." The voice sounded as if it was making a threat. A strange stunned feeling circulated through my veins. I unconsciously slipped to the ground, not paying attention to the creature observing me the whole time. It seemed to cock its head as if showing its satisfaction and disappeared into the blurry black distance.

"I´ve gone mad. Foxes like me," I whispered sarcastically. I rose with the help of my arms. The cold reminded me that it was time to go to bed.

"Who was that man? Do you know him?" A voice came from nowhere.

"Jesus! Shit! Jesus!" I thoroughly gasped. My breaths were latched right behind the gates leading to my lungs and were not able to fill them with soothing air.

"Are you an idiot?! You almost gave me a heart attack."

"Sorry, I´m really sorry." He hugged me, swaying from side to side. It took a while, but I finally caught my balance.

"I´m Rudi, fella." Giggling, I ribbed him. He joined in.

"Better?" I nodded. He awkwardly undid arms.

"Who was it?"

"No idea. But the voice was familiar to me."

"Who was the second man?"

"I didn´t see anything—I stayed hidden in the shadows."

"I was right to come back from my father´s office, I just heard that threat."

"Perfect."

"You are shaking. Go to bed!" A door creaked then banged against the wall behind it and we stepped into the small hallway.

11

The boot of the Discovery was utterly unloaded and all the bags, equipment and samples were stored in the university´s biological laboratory. The remaining passengers shared the journey back to their homes. Julian lived on the same side of Belmopan as Joseph. It was not far from the university campus, but the professor gave them the lucrative offer of conveying them home. Both were inhabitants of the Salvapan region and the way to the municipal airport crossed that Mayan side somewhat. I saw the blurry boot door with its obscure licence number rectangle. The mountain backpack resting on my back reminded me of earth´s gravity, pushing it down onto my knees. The vision of my dormitory room got stronger than anything else. The fresh scent of my washed body occupied my mind and commanded my walk.

A beautiful sunset dragged me outside. Looking for a free bench in the campus park, I tried to steal as much privacy as the place offered. A giant acacia in the middle of a green lawn stood near a dark brown bench. Its yellow blooms brushed my palms. I settled there, my back leaning against the tree trunk. I placed my laptop on my thighs; it sprung into life on my command. My fingers began typing and scrolling, criss-crossing through the pseudo-mouse rectangle.

"Hello, I´ve come back from Belmopan. I am in front of my room on the campus." I waited. His Skype name showed that Gregory was online, but "online" must not have meant he was at his computer.

"Hi Rudi. It´s nice to chat with you again. Thanks for your last email."

"I´m sorry we lost one day, but if you want, we can make our trip tomorrow or the day after."

"Why didn´t you take the same flight as Mathew Sander?"

"Do you know him?"

"No, I don´t know him personally. His father is an important person on Ambergris Caye; he is the Director of Chiquibul National Park. I guess you met him."

"Yes, such a nice, open guy. :o)"

"And handsome?"

"I didn´t notice. Such a polite nature. Hey fella, what is going on?"

"I asked the professor a favour. He bought me a ticket at the airport. My ticket is waiting for me at the local airport. I think my flight will land at 11.30 am. We can arrange our trip."

"Tomorrow?

"Yes. Enjoy the rest of your day. I´m looking forward to seeing you."

"Good morning, madam. Can I ask you something? Is it possible to rent a bike for more than two days?"

"Yes, of course." A plump chocolate-skinned lady in her late forties smiled at me in a friendly way.

"Can I pay for three days now and then I´ll pay the rest?"

"Yes, just give me your address here and your passport number or ID number." I dictated the address of Sander´s home to her. She stopped writing.

"Trevor Sander is your host?"

"Yes."

"Oh girl, you are too young. You know he has been a widower for a pretty long time? And he is a handsome man too. I know it´s hard to resist his attraction. Oh my little girl, you are too young." Her muffled voice contained a little-known secret: she leaned across her office desk to me as she spoke.

"Madam, Mr Trevor is my host. I´m Mathew´s classmate. Professor Dragonsky was invited too." It was hard fighting with my own amusement and confusion. Only my attempt not to insult her in any way permitted me to keep a poker face for a prolonged time. Her curiosity resolved, I let a mischievous smile settle on my lips. My eyebrows rose higher than normal and the corner of my lip shifted up.

"Madam, I´m grateful for your concern, but I´d better leave not be too late. It would be pretty impolite not to arrive on time."

"Of course. You are Matt´s classmate. It´s such a horrible faux pas." Her face would have reddened but the chocolate hue hindered it.

"Don´t worry. It´s been nice to meet you, madam." I took my rental bill and my passport. Heading to the airport rental stand, I giggled at her reaction.

Any news spread across San Pedro quicker than a newcomer would expect. Many aluminium sticks hanging from massive shells announced my arrival in the small scuba diving shop, giving a lovely muted sound.

"Good afternoon," I said. A shaggy haired young man peeked his head out into the shop in answer to my greeting. A broad grin appeared around his mouth.

"Hi girl, my services are here just for you." The same facial expression continued. There was a strange kind of coquetry apparent.

"I would like to buy two sets of snorkelling equipment and one life jacket. Is that possible?"

"Sweetheart. It´s strange. It can´t work. The life jacket and snorkelling equipment? It´s such a funny demand."

"Yes, it can, sweetheart."

"O.K. You are the customer. You are the guest. What colour would you like?"

"Many luminescent colours if your shop possesses something like that." He placed on the shop counter a variety of snorkelling sets. The counter soon became host to a towering pile containing diving goggles, snorkels, flippers, water cameras and everything that a fantastic scuba shop could have offered. Finally, the right sizes and hues were chosen. The deal was done.

"Have a nice day, sweetheart." His last flirtation fused with the door´s creak and street noises.

Every inch of the bright streets absorbed sunbeams, which gave everybody the delightful feelings of happiness and satisfaction. Everyone scattered along the streets smiled at me and their palms waved to greet me. There were children on the playgrounds chatting, laughing and ribbing one another. Life was calm and vivid, surrounded by many rainbow-coloured shops, houses, pubs and little restaurants. Small vehicles similar to golf trolleys (maybe they were real golf trolleys) passed my bike. I turned in all directions, amazed by the air radiating from all sides. I simply enjoyed it. The scent of something baked tickled my nose. A modest stall standing at the market entrance, consisting of just a couple of stands, crossed my path. A longer sniff followed my previous one. The fragrance attracted me and trapped all my senses.

"Afternoon, señoras." I comprehended they were members of the Mayan community living in Ambergris Caye. The food was similar to European pancakes but looked slightly different, mainly in colour.

"What does it taste like?" My question caused them to chuckle.

"Do you like spicy food?"

"Hm. If I could taste a bit of it I would have the opportunity to decide," I hesitated. According to the Internet, Caribbean cuisine contained a myriad range of spicy dishes.

"Here you are, my girl. Try it." Her tone was so gracious, I could not refuse. My fingers clenched the offered piece, nearing it to my mouth. The pancake smelled wonderful, so I pushed my teeth uncertainly into the piece.

"Delicious. I ask you for one, señora." Their fingertips handily formed a paper rectangle into a decent pocket shape, which the pancake was put into.

"Gracias, señoras. Have a nice day." Wheeling the rental bike beside me, I enjoyed the sense-shaking taste of the pancake. It disappeared bite by bite into my tummy. Near to me, on the fence of part of a playground, a five-year-old girl was eating some chocolate titbits.

'I forgot—presents!' I thought.

"Hi. Can you tell me where I can find a grocery shop?" I asked. Her chubby arm pointed out the right direction and a chirping song came from her lips, singing the exact explanation in detail.

Señora Isabell´s dance with her broomstick was visible from afar. She was nearly sixty but her temperament did not show it. Neither her accumulating years nor any illness had the power to change it. A Spanish song hovered around the whole patio and tangled with the sounds of stomping steps.

"Nice noon, Belle, isn´t it?" She jumped a little bit.

"Rudi." She hugged me very tightly.

"Belle, Belle, please," I protested.

"Oh, honey." She released her clutch: I could freely breathe again. Both her palms covered my cheeks and faint flashes shimmered in the middle of her black pupils.

"You are as fresh as a daisy, Señora Belle."

"Hey honey, you aren´t a man, you aren´t obligated to flatter me."

"I´m not."

"Let´s go inside. Have you already had a lunch? You´ve had none. I guessed as much. Don´t you have a mirror in your room?" she asked. I smirked.

The open door invited me with the scent of just-made fruit cake. A thin chocolate sauce was left on a biscuit surface to harden and dry into a flat glaze shape. I felt as if I was home in the kitchen with my mum. A boyish voice dragged me out from my thoughts.

"Belle, Belle, it smells marvellously!" An avalanche flew into the room. The objective was clear: the wonderful-smelling cake.

"It´s too hot, you´ll scorch fingers." Belle pulled his arm away from the blazing baking sheet.

"You don´t like me, Belle." He turned, offended, and headed back. Then he noticed me standing there. "Rudi!" He skipped and the little monkey clutched me around my neck with both his arms. Two legs wrapped around my waist and his mouse-like teeth dazzled me.

"Will you share a trip with me?"

Several cabin cruisers had their massive ropes tied to the wooden piers. They enabled divers to comfortably get off their boats onto a local jetty. The muscles on the man´s back ran up and down, reflecting the movement of his body. Many sweat beads rolled down and covered his tanned skin. Goggles followed snorkels, flippers and breathing equipment onto the white jetty battens.

"Tristan. Tristan."

"Hi Charlie. Have you come alone?" Charlie left a moment for Tristan to decipher his unspoken riddle.

"Hi Tristan." He shielded his face with his palms to protect them against the beams stinging his eyes.

Three figures, enveloped in the red shades of the sunset, sat calmly and wordlessly sniffing the ocean fragrance, letting the warm breeze caress them. When the fire red sun set, with just a little half circle visible, they rose, shuffling along the jetty.

"It looks as though he has observed us for a while."

"Who?"

"There, on the path behind the sand bank." Tristan jerked his chin to indicate a person on the edge of the sand.

"I know him."

Our running feet brushed the sand grains aside, leaving a shallow ditch behind them. Small fingers tickled my palm, striving to hold hands. As we shortened the distance, the figures became sharper. The gripped fists toyed with the wheels to force the wheelchair forwards, backwards, to the left and to the right. This sequence repeated in many variations, as if the wheelchair was dancing.

"It´s a nice afternoon, isn´t it?" he asked. A slight irritation of his query drummed on my senses.

"I hope so. Is something wrong?" The question might have been asked at a bad moment. His wheels turned and we could only see the wheelchair´s back. I ran closer to him, caught the chair handles and pulled him back.

"Let me go, Rudi!" He shouted, one word at a time.

"No!" I childishly snapped at him as I imitated his behaviour.

"Rudi, I´ve thought it through seriously."

"No! I´ve thought it through seriously too." I continued in the manner of an offended child.

"Rudi, I asked you to let me go!"

"No!" I said with a chuckle, which changed to a friendly laugh that teased and finally melted him. He faced me. Subtle knocks titillated my back.

"Oh, I´m sorry Charlie." My arm pushed him forward, next to me. I squatted to be at the same level as Charlie.

"Charlie, this is my good friend Gregory."

"Oh, it must be fun to wheel around all day," he proclaimed with childish excitement. At first, Gregory´s frozen face did not persuade me that he had properly understood what Charlie meant. But then he broke into giggles and an extensive smirk occupied his cheeks.

"Young sir! Young sir!" A startled scream, coming to us from afar, penetrated the atmosphere.

"I´m supposed to go. See you tomorrow," Gregory said.

"O.K. At 10 am?" I replied.

"Here?"

"Here. Bring just . . ."

"I know. Bernicia is frightened. So, see you tomorrow. Rudi."

Leaning his back against the side of Tristan´s cruiser, he rested. His removal from the wheelchair was not as easy as it had seemed at first glance. Tristan locked his wheelchair into a pale wooden booth, which served as a store for different kinds of equipment, a sanctuary against a sudden storm, a resting place after returning from diving and Tristan´s office, all in one. I finished fastening the belt around Gregory´s hand. A white rope connected it to a light red buoy. The life jacket made his sitting more comfortable because its padded structure was filled the air.

"Is everybody on board?"

"Fella! Wait, please." A member of the cabin cruiser´s crew pointed to the side of the coming demand.

"Didn´t you say you don´t need to see the reef twice a month?" Mr Trevor threw into the space, not connecting eyes with his son.

"Bro, you are like a girl." Charlie teased him, chuckling under his breath, thinking nobody could have caught it.

"Shut up, Charlie!"

"Andrew, Gregory?" Trevor´s sight scrutinised their faces as though he was afraid of finding a bit of disapproval.

"It´s O.K." They answered together.

I searched for a couple of scared hints in Gregory´s expression but he sat calmly, his eyes glued to the glass bottom of the cruiser. His whole person sucked in the beauty spreading under the boat on the ocean bed. Fish in many varieties of colours, sizes and body shapes played their roles in the underwater theatre. It took hours before the cruiser was stopped, the engine silenced and the anchor thrown down to fasten the cruiser to the sea bed. The crew members put on their flippers and goggles with snorkels attached and somersaulted into the ocean. They disappeared under the turquoise surface, then popped up one by one like noodles in boiling water.

"I´ll help you to the edge of the boat, you aren´t supposed to do anything like that. Just sit, turn to face the water and jump," I instructed him. An awkward silence emerged instead of any response.

"Gregory, are you listening to me?" I asked. I fully understood his cursory glance. "Give me your hand, don´t worry. I´ll count to three then we´ll jump," I whispered, giving him an encouraging smile as my palm gripped his. "One, two, three. Jump!"

The liquid substance surrounded us and air bubbles headed to the water´s surface. I could not easily pulling him upwards with one hand. I pointed the forefinger of my second hand to attract his sight to my legs. They were moving in a synchronised rhythm, forwards and backwards. A slight stirring in his flippers and his life jacket helped me a little bit to reach the surface easier.

"Yeees! Rudi! Yes!" He gasped, not able to breathe regularly at first, but his joy was contagious.

"She´s my friend." Charlie´s hug throttled me. I gently freed myself from his hug, faced him and gave him a quick wink.

The reef was in a magnanimous nature that day. It opened its arms and allowed us to discover as many secrets as we were able to. Gregory´s soul was undoubtedly lost among the corals, fish, tinted shades and forms. Everything created an uncountable number of pictures, which changed in an instant or remained unchanged for a longer while. Charlie and Tristan persisted in accompanying us, sharing our amazement, our thrill and our presence. The other crew members were lost somewhere among the adjacent breath-taking part of the ocean kingdom. Time fused into one excellent minute.

Stomping our feet on the jetty, drops fell from snorkels and flippers. The chatter was never-ending and laughter could be heard now and then. The sun´s red wore us down with its tone and the moored boats jingled with their iron bars as they peeked out from their jetties.

"Rudi, can you accompany me home?" No words, only a nod.

The houses sank into darkness as the sunbeams gradually lost their power and a black hue squeezed among the warm shades. The shimmering light of a porch lantern illuminated a pretty crucial part of the patio. Somebody occupied a rocking chair. He may have been smoking a cigar because a strange scent tickled my nose and a bright orange tip pierced the darkness from time to time.

"Evening, Mr Trevor."

"Evening, Rudi. It was very nice day. You can leave your bike in the corner of the patio." Wordlessly, I put it in the darkness. The bike rested on the veranda´s banister.

"I´m thankful to you all, I appreciate your help," I said.

"Gregory is a good boy. I´m glad I was a small part of your plan," He noticed. I suddenly felt confused. "Mr Trevor." There occurred an uncomfortable gap. I was squirming.

"Yes?"

"Just . . . hm . . . nothing." I would have liked to share the same space as him, if that strange piece of information had not been eating away at my brain. Each time that I met him, it emerged. "Have a nice night, Mr Trevor." He nodded to reply to my greeting. I went to the kitchen door and opened it. He stopped me.

"Rudi, are you annoyed by something?" he asked. I returned to him, leaning against the patio banister. I had no idea how to start. There was an uneasy gap of silence. "Did you see something?" He tried to help me start my explanation.

"I don´t know, I´m not sure, but . . ."

"I´ll ask you, O.K?" There was a breach of the quietness, again.

"Did it happen during your stay in the forest research station?"

A set of approving nods came after his query. I sniffed the air.

"I was returning from the conference hall at the Las Cuevas Forest Research Station." An enormous chunk was growing in my throat and I did not know how to push it down. I supposed the story could seem a little bit unbelievable. I was thankful that Matt had been witness to the threats too.

"A stranger was standing on the staircase and threatening someone who shared the same accommodation as me.

"What sort of threats?"

"The stranger said he was not sure if the second person correctly understood the agreement. The second man tried to reassure the stranger, but the stranger cut him short. Then he added that the unknown man can do nothing to change their agreement in reality," I said. Trevor remained wordless. His rocking chair swayed in slow movements and the porch lantern light shimmered from time to time, as though it was attempting to help to solve the mystery.

"Who did you share the accommodation with?"

"Joseph, Julian and the professor. I trust all of them."

"Me too. Was it the building opposite the conference hall?" My quiet nod expressed unspoken approval.

"There were two members of staff as well," I continued.

"Did they come from Russia?"

"From Russia? That's odd, to say the least. Why Russia?" He wondered. A terrific surprise settled in his look. "I think . . ." I knew it was an extremely absurd situation to describe without raising any suspicion. I did not want him to think I was embellishing the facts. "Me and Joseph had already met him, in the jungle. I'm almost sure the voice of the threatening man was the same as the voice of that shouting man."

"Whom was he shouting at?"

"The second Russian-speaking man. It was pretty dark, so we weren't able to recognise their faces or anything else."

Listening to my testimony, his forehead became filled with different wrinkles. The rocking chair produced a muffled noise and the wooden slats creaked under its weight. I felt strangely like I was a fool.

"I'd better go, Mr Trevor." He stayed buried in his thoughts and didn't notice as I left. Even though the loud click of the mosquito-protected kitchen door caused a piercing sound in the night's quietness, it did not allude him to my presence.

"The red tree." My unfinished testimony forced me to return.

"What? I didn't hear you." He jerked suddenly.

"I said the red tree. They, the Russian-speaking men, mentioned it. I think it's the mahogany. The logging. The illegal logging. I read about it. There were many indirect connections." He listened to me patiently, scrutinising every word. I decided to go. I had said enough already to look like a real fool. "Have a nice night, Trevor." The door clicked and the mad night's talk melted behind it.

"Good evening, Señora Bernicia." Her fingers handily tweaked wilted blossom petals from the plants growing in pots edging the window sill.

"A very nice evening, Mister Fillip." She kept on without letting up her activity, dancing and crooning together. "Mister?" She allowed him to near the villa entrance. He stopped, turned and peeked out from the shadow of the house into the light coming from the window.

"Señora?" He waited for her reply. His eyes drank in her coquettish movement, her body language and her marvellously and highly attractive appearance. "Have you forgotten my invitation? Have you avoided me on purpose?" A smug smirk slid across lips. He became wrapped deeper and deeper in her femininity, consciously and willingly. Knocking on the door of her private house part, his flutter in his stomach rose up.

"It´s nice to see you, mister." The opened door offered him free entrance to a world full of warmth, scent and comfort. She approached a white and blue sideboard to pour water into the kettle and let it boil. In no more than a snatch of a second, he sniffed her perfume. Pace by pace he strolled towards her, not leaving even the smallest part of her skin without goose bumps. His lips brushed every naked sliver of her body, screaming and asking to make love. His fingers found the edge of her dress, rolling it slowly upwards. Stalking her feminine curves, the tips of his fingers finally achieved their goal. An excitedly wet and hot place invited him, calling him to slip inside. Her bottom continuously pressed against his erected member, stubbornly trying to free its grip. Her small fingers skilfully, slightly and effortlessly opened his zip and a blissful warmth was radiated along his member by her palm. Suddenly using extremely high strength, he pushed her onto the sideboard. With the spreading fingers of both her palms pressed against the wall, her salacious bottom peeked upwards and revealed the secret of her shell. She was ready to approve him sliding comfortably in her. Absolute thrill flew around their veins; the two shivering bodies caused delicious goose bumps for both of them and the small room was filled with never-ending bliss. Again and again, he immersed himself and rammed her thrilled insides, his dipping causing her such tremendous pleasure that she groaned and screamed. The open window brought in the song of ocean waves and the fresh air of the tropical night in irregular intervals.

The wheels rotated from their goodbye point and kept going in the villa´s direction. The beach stopped the ocean tide, not allowing it to cross an imaginary frontier. Pelicans slept satisfied on the water´s surface and a clip-clopping coming from a distance reminded him of the old pit-a-pat melody of his home town. A weird noise broke his reverie.

"Señora Bernicia is watching a spicy movie." Gregory was playing whit this thought. A smirk spread along his lips and the sounds unconsciously led him to her private window: curiosity could have been the cause. He wheeled nearer. After all, he was a teenager full of testosterone. Girls and women were a big secret to him still, but a spicy movie could have been the right end to an amazing day.

"A lush pictures, I like it." His wheelchair was stopped. The hot scene went on, the intensity grew, their climax was imminent. The hot scene in the kitchen, Señora´s TV was switched off. The man hugged señora, turned her and, with one simple push, he settled her on the board.

"Shit! I hate him!" Gregory´s recognition took him breath.

The man stopped as though somebody had thrown a cup of boiled water at his face. He immediately slid out, hastily fastened the jeans and ran out from Bernicia´s kitchen. Nobody was there.

12

The Indian summer was nearing its end. Leaves gradually started to fall to the floor, warm shades of red turned brown and tree branches and twigs lost their clothes, through the free space among them ever green needle-limbs of softwoods were visible. Spider webs flew away to somewhere afar, so the sunbeams could not get trapped by their fibres any more this year. At the turn of the two seasons, the majority of the local trees looked more like coat hangers than majestic rulers with fabulous multi-coloured leaf crowns. Now, they resembled jackstraws more than the highest level of forest vegetation. This transparent adaptation of the forest enabled one to see a far greater distance than during the spring or summer. After almost one month spent in the jungle, this part of the world, so similar to the place I came from, seemed more familiar and warmer than at any time before. The shades of brown and grey implied that winter was behind the door. The sky got dark grey in a couple of minutes. Raindrops changed to heavy rain drumming on the floor. I could see my Vancouver residence in front of me. I ran; my speed increased with the rain´s growing intensity.

Standing in the lobby of the student residence, raindrops rolled down my cheeks, dripping from my jacket onto the floor. Students passed me in pairs, groups or on their own. The numbers written on the elevator buttons lit up every time somebody got in or out of the lift. The fourth floor, finally. Feelings of satisfaction and comfort and a homely air surrounded me, in spite of fact that I had only spent one night there.

"Matt, where is Rudi?

"Oh. Hi, Gregory." The wheelchair boy disturbed him from his morning musings. He jumped up from the rocking chair on the veranda to talk to him. He sat down on the first step of the small staircase connecting the patio to a wide tile path sank in the sand next to the house. He stretched his arm out to greet him.

"She left. I suppose she is already in Vancouver. Her lectures start tomorrow."

"Why didn´t she mention it?"

"The professor told her it yesterday, in evening. I think she had no idea. Her departure was changed by Professor Dragonsky."

"You are classmates, aren´t you?"

"Yes."

"Why didn´t you fly with the same plane?"

"She didn´t say bye, apparently." A sarcastic tone crept between them.

"Are you jealous of Rudi?" A slight teasing was hidden in his words.

"I´ve not understood your question."

"Forget it. Is Mr Trevor at home?"

"No, he already left for his office in the Chiquibul reservation."

"What a pity I´ve brought him something."

The wheels gripped by his palms took him back in his former direction. He crossed the local hard-stomped sand main road, which was wide enough to be used by pedestrians, cyclists, small trolleys or supply vehicles.

A light knocking on the door interrupted an oddly omnipresent afternoon silence, as a rattle coming from the opened kitchen frame was more natural for the place and familiar to him.

"Gregory? I´m coming in." No response, no hint of any movement. A handle was pushed down. The door was opened to reveal Gregory´s temporary kingdom and he swam into the room. Nobody occupied the room, just a working laptop and the sound of muffled clicks every now and again. A black colour was spread across the screen. One tap on a sensible rectangle and the computer woke up; the screen changed to an online document. Every row was filled in. His eyes scrolled in haste, swallowing information after information. The payment confirmation by bank card had been done at 4.08 am and the flight time was right in the middle of the screen.

"Shit! The flight departed at 4.55 pm." From Philip S.W. Goldson International Airport in Belize City, the first stopover airport was Quebec City Jean Lesage International Airport, followed by an international airport in the Netherlands; his final destination was Liverpool John Lennon Airport.

"Shit! He saw us." Fed up with himself, he switched Gregory´s laptop off. It was the last Christmas present from him to Gregory, the latest version made by HP. He had asked for it. Gregory had been so happy when all the wrapping paper was removed onto the floor. Now Gregory didn´t want it any more.

On the second floor, classroom 12, I stood in the Forestry Department. Scrutinising my school schedule, I had assured myself that I had not exchanged one little field for another. The students trickled into the classroom in small groups. Some arrived in a hurry, some entered vividly chatting and others settled wordlessly on the chairs. I became an observer, invisible and unheard. My eyes skipped from one group to the next, trying to remember as many faces as my memory was willing to absorb and input their images into my brain cells.

"A nice day, people." The voice approached me from the front of the classroom, stopping me from scrutinising my classmates and bringing me back to reality. "Kids, today I am going to continue with the topic from the last lecture. So, my colleagues, can I ask you for its name?" The assistant lecturer pointed his question at a boy in the third line.

"The accumulations of heavy metals in soils."

"Yes, you are right!" The lecturer brought a white projection board down by pressing a green button peeking up from a small plastic box squeezed in his fist. The bright light coming from the projector changed beams to letters, figures or photos, presenting forest examples pertaining to the topic. Pens wrote notes carrying the most pertinent information about the topic and keyboards typed translated orders given by someone´s fingers into words and consequently into sentences. A tiny red laser circle stopped on each paragraph, which was then accurately explained. There were questions asked, there were engaging discussions and someone made a joke to make the air more comfortable. Finally, we finished. The lecturer closed all the devices and we closed our notebooks and laptops.

"Oh, I almost forgot, you need to bring and introduce your projects in the next lesson. The themes were mentioned during the last lecture. It´ll be classified as your first exam." He gathered his files into a pile and folded them under the arm.

"Excuse me." I grabbed his attention. I struggled along the lines of seats, descending down the stairs to the bottom.

"Yes, can I help in any way?"

"I´m sorry, but I unfortunately missed three lessons. I would like to ask you for the titles of the themes." He looked at me as if I were an alien.

"I´m afraid that I can´t accept such a long absence during my lectures. Has any staff member said you were allowed to miss three lectures of each subject?" His sense of importance towered above him so visibly. The situation went from ridiculous to silly. My muscles did not obey me; in spite of trying hard, a naughty smile settled in the corners of my lips.

"No, I arrived yesterday."

"But university study should stick out above all your other ambitions. You had enough time to arrange to get here on time."

"I did. If I were a billionaire I would have taken a flight with a private company," I snapped. No hesitation arrested me and no doubts were present in my mind. I had worked hard for three weeks. I got angry. "Flights from Belize to Vancouver aren´t as popular as around the U.S. or Canada. Thank you for your help. I´ll attempt to ask my classmates. Have a nice day. See you next lesson." I must have exerted my entire brain power to calm my temper down. I strolled upstairs, not knowing if I had become a hero or a loser. He had given me no chance to defend myself or to explain the facts.

"It´ll sort itself out," I encouraged myself under my breath.

The taxi left Liverpool John Lennon Airport. It swallowed one Liverpudlian street after another, driving through the spreading grid of roads and following road signs announcing directions. The taxi driver ensured he had perfectly understood the orders and continued to Lancashire. Hours later, a gentle drizzle had altered the roads from their common autumn look. The cars in front us pressed their tyres against the tarmac, pushing tiny layers of water to both sides and leaving two paths behind them along the whole road. Windscreen wipers constantly paced from left to right, carrying a familiar noise.

The taxi arrived at its destination. "Church Street, Lancaster, Lancashire. The house number is right too, isn´t it?" asked the driver.

"Yes, thanks."

"It´s raining, stay inside. I´ll help you with your wheelchair."

"Thanks, you´re very kind, sir."

A brown canvas backpack, covered with a navy print and various pin emblems, rested on his thighs. His fists gripped the wheel frames to send his wheels forward along the tile pavement that connected the street to a red-brick house hidden at the end of a small private park behind tall white cedar trees. Ringing the bell caused an insignificant movement from inside the house. A person appeared at the window, peeking out to investigate the visitor. As well as the visitor, she saw the pavement, trees and the drizzling raindrops rolling down the glass. It did not take more than a minute for a lock click to quietly pierce the air and the handle to be twisted towards one of the walls.

"Gregory!" She bent down. A long squeezing hug supplied him with the eminent warmth of home. "Your mother knows you´re here?" she asked. He faced her for a pretty long time, wordlessly. "She doesn´t, does she?" Just a dumb nod vouched his recognition.

A sweet scent coloured the air, calling them to taste the cakes, perhaps cookies, resting on granny´s kitchen windowsill. They waited until they had cooled down.

"Come in, Rudi." The professor came out of his office.

"You wanted to meet me?"

"Yes. I´ve arranged for you to practice in one of our forestry laboratories."

I approached his desk and picked up a sheet of paper. Scrutinising all the fields, I stopped at the small schedule rectangle.

"I´m afraid you must shift this time." Putting the schedule back on the desk, my finger pointed at the badly arranged schedule rectangle. "It´s clashing with another subject."

"Which?" His eyebrows lifted up, expecting my response.

"Forest soils."

"Oh, Rudi, it´ll be O.K."

"Really? I´m not so sure."

"I´ll manage it. The assistant lecturer, Flywick, is my student. It´ll be O.K., really."

"We had, I would call it, an argument, maybe a disagreement. Putting it simply, I was rude and he was arrogant. That´s all." I waited for his reply. None came. There was silence: he was oddly looking at his desk with his head between his shoulders.

I eventually got his answer: "Rudi, it´s necessary to finish our Belizean work to be able to get on with the next piece of research." I observed his reaction wordlessly. He continued in a very relaxed manner. "I´ll find a new time and space for your lab practice. I´ll tell you as soon as I´ve sorted it."

"Fine. Thanks, professor. Can I leave?" Biting my lower lip, I faced him. No reaction: I assumed it was time to go.

Watches sent needles to the numbers nine and twelve. My guts grumbled. A canteen would have been the best way to satisfy them. This was only the second time I had been to a lecture, so some parts of the school´s facilities were not as familiar to me as those at my alma mater at home. Re-entry into the professor´s office did not seem like a good idea. From his facial expression, I recognised that Flywick was his least favourite. Students passed me, crossing the hall space in many directions. I stopped one of them.

"Hi, are you going for lunch?" I asked.

"Yes." I was lucky: my first choice was successful.

"Would you like some company?"

"Why not? I´m Patricia."

"Rudi. It´s nice to meet you."

We were vividly chatting for a while. I fell in love with her polite and warm manner. She was half-Indian. Her granny originated from the Mi´kmaq tribe. Patricia´s Indian features had not changed, even after years of tribal evolution and the genetic influence of immigrants coming into Canada centuries ago. We fitted well with each other. Her refined manners and exaggerated interest in my country caused us to lose track of time.

"Oh, gosh! I must fly!" I exclaimed. I fished inside my backpack for a pen, wrote down my email address and the name of my residence in haste and disappeared among a crowd of hungry students moving around the canteen.

Due to the Belizean laboratory work, the last week in October ran at such a terrible speed that I did not notice and found myself in the middle of November. The Canadian autumn finished a little bit earlier that year. The ground behind the residence´s windows wore a delicate white dress, the trees had snow caps and the branches were decorated with tiny chains of snowflakes. Sucking in all this winter beauty, I was disturbed by voices snaking in from the corridor outside my room. I was obligated to put all the analysis of the last lab session into a schedule, diagrams and graphs. I wanted to finally finish that Belizean job. Sitting at the laptop again, my eyes were attracted by repeating blinks on the PC´s toolbar. I clicked on the blue ´S´. I could not believe my eyes.

"Hi, my honey. What do you think? Am I smart?

"You or Laura? :)" A teasing response was sent with a small smile added.

"Me."

"O.K., Mum, you are the cleverest mother I know."

"What´s new, honey?"

Our conversation took three hours because Laura returned home and joined us. Our never-ending joking and teasing was stopped when a glance at the PC´s clock revealed the exact time. I disconnected immediately so I would not be interrupted by anybody. I burrowed into the results of my lab work, striving to create a perfect project.

I jerked as the alarm clock effected an invisible spasm inside me. The flashing figures *"7.35"* were featured on the alarm´s screen.

"Hell!" I saved my work, compressed it into one file, clicked on the connection banner on the laptop screen and waited for a connection. The second click opened my email box; my fingers typed letters that fused into the professor´s email address, and a couple of additional clicks attached the documents to be urgently sent to his inbox.

"Call your mum. I´m sure your dad has already told her what you did."

"Don´t be naïve, granny. I think he would be asked for an explanation," he replied. His granny turned to him, dullness apparent in her face. She raised one eyebrow, causing some wrinkles on her forehead to increase.

"What happened, Gregory?" She pushed through her coming anger.

"He cheated on her, my mum." She felt his mighty wrath. He did not have the mental power to press it down and any sham expression could not have disguised it. He did not act in that way. He was not going to camouflage his dad´s behaviour.

"Are you sure?"

"Yes."

"Yes and . . . ?"

"I saw him stick his hellish stinking member in her vagina!" He got red. His furiousness grew. A hard thud landed on the table next to him. A small teacup jumped up a little and cold tea spit a couple of drops on the table´s surface. Granny twisted her back to a wall behind a kitchen cupboard. She desperately needed a bit of privacy.

"A lot of men do it," she said. She was calmer than Gregory wanted her to be. He was one uncommonly sensible teenager full of fury and emotions. It was enough to create a dense atmosphere.

"My son isn´t any exception. I´ve never expected he will act in a different manner. Your granddad behaved in the same way."

"But, Mum thinks he is her prince."

"No, your mum knows about it."

"I don´t believe you!"

"Gregory, your mum is one extremely clever woman: she is conscious of all the possibilities in front of her. Dad´s infidelity plus his money means we have money to buy your drugs and pay for your hospitalisation. Yes, she could say NO. But I´ve already said: she is very clever and the most loving mum I´ve ever met." Granny spoke for a long time, emphasising every detail to give him space and time to absorb them and see the situation for what it was. A long-lasting stillness hovered around the kitchen, tangling with the cookies´ scent. Granny´s words stirred within him. He was lost in the chaos of human values.

"You´ve always taught me to be honest, sincere and a real man. Is there something that´s change your mind?"

"Life. Just life."

"What?"

"Your mum had two possibilities. The first was to have a happy child and help him live as long as possible or she could have been proud, asked for a divorce and caused many health problems to her child."

He wheeled his chair near to the window. Raindrops streamed in many sheaves down the glass, blurring everything behind their water veil.

"Did granddad leave you for another woman?"

"Honestly?" She asked herself more than Gregory. "Yes, she was from Russia too. They went back there together."

"I will read the names of the people who have not yet presented their projects and they will come up to the projector to make their presentations." The rustling of paper started the lesson as the lecturer crossed names off his list. One student's work fused into another project and the same topic was discussed from different angles. Several questions interrupted every presentation. I was not convinced whether Flywick, our assistant lecturer, used this method to allow the class to get more information about the presented subjects or whether he desired to attract the students' attention to his own person.

"Rudić, Nina." I slipped the first transparent foil sheet onto the projector's glass panel.

"THE NATURAL HIGH COPPER CONCENTRATION IN FOREST SOILS"

Big bold capital letters appeared on the white board.

"THE AREA:
Europe

THE RESEARCH AREA:
5 research fields 10 × 10 m (100 m²)

SPECIFICATION OF THE RESEARCH AREA:

1. *forest ecosystem with 100% coverage at the canopy level*
2. *forest ecosystem with 50% coverage at the canopy level*
3. *glade ecosystem without any canopy level*
4. *research fields with human implementation of selected trees*
5. *research fields with human implementation of selected trees and application of alkali and acidic substances*

THE CONCENTRATION OF COPPER IN THE RESEARCH AREA:

1. *natural concentration*
2. *concentration immediately after human implementation*
3. *concentration 1 year after human implementation"*

I felt a lump whirling from the lower part of my throat to the upper. My voice was shaking. I attempted to stop the shivering in my stomach.

Click! The classroom door slightly creaked open. All heads followed that sound to check who the interrupter and saviour was.

"Excuse me, I need Rudi. Can I take her with me?"

I did not wait for the lecturer to reply. I grabbed all my prepared documents, thanked my classmates for their attention and evaporated from the place.

"Thanks, professor. I appreciate it. You saved me." He began smirking.

"I have worse work for you than a project presentation."

"Anything." I winked at him. We headed to the B-block of the university building.

13

"Hi Gregory, nice to see you." He sent classmates back a smile and advanced to the office of their head teacher. One metre more and he would have been hurt by the sudden swinging open of the door.

"Shouldn´t you be on the equator?"

"Good morning, Mr Derbhall. I´ve come to see you. I would like to re-arrange my external tuition." Great hesitation entirely buried his courage. There was a big amount of the unanswered question.

"Do you need to postpone your exams?"

"Oh, oh, no."

"Gregory, be quick. I´m in a hurry—my first lesson begins in five minutes."

"Is it possible to do my exams earlier?"

"Of course, but are you sure? Have you timed it precisely?"

"Definitely."

"What month would you like?"

"November."

"November. I´ll see what I can do."

"Here is your group, Rudi."

"My group?" I looked at him, not knowing what kind of work the professor had put aside just for me.

"Your alumni group."

"What?" There must have been another explanation. A group of five students was observing something extremely small, clenched with the arms of stainless steel tweezers. A worm was the object of study. It was scrutinised in detail. A young man immersed in scientific observation seemed stunned: "What is it?"

"Vermin." I still didn´t understand the exact reason, why I was there.

"Tree diseases—I studied it in the summer term."

"These people are specialists. They already work with insects for four years. It´s to your benefit to know it. I need you to learn everything."

"My benefit?" I still didn´t understand.

"You need a multi-level experience."

"Am I here to learn everything about vermin?"

"Yes, certainly." I was pushed forwards into the biology lab. The powerful amplified clapping of his hands got their attention. An introduction followed his theatrical behaviour. Professor Dragonsky explained me all his purposes of my work in the biology lab to avoid wasting any more of their time.

"So, we can return to your unfinished presentation." I gasped, not able to believe what I had heard. The lab door clicked shut and adhered to a magnet above it. The professor´s poker face stubbornly persisted in the same position. A childish chuckling penetrated the density radiating from me.

"Have you swallowed the bait?"

"Completely." I joined in with his laughter.

The sound of crunching snow was everywhere. People hurried along the pavement on their way home from work; others swept snow piles from car roofs. Pedestrians waited for green lights, cars beeped in an afternoon traffic jam and, among all this chaos, snowflakes quietly fell in unnoticed harmony. Closing the distance to my well-known residence, a concentration of alumni was growing in one square metre.

"Rudi, Rudi! Just a moment."

"Hi Patricia."

She breathed intermittently. "I followed you from the bus stop." I cocked my head, shifted one brow.

"When did you get off? I did not notice you on the bus."

"I didn´t get off. It seems we occupy the same residence."

"What bus number do you use?"

"37."

"37? I don´t know that bus line," I smiled.

She stopped, flicking snow from her shoulder onto the ground. Evidently, she did not understand my reply.

"It´s my shoe size, I´m used to walking. I´ve not been on a bus in Vancouver," she laughed.

"Nice skis." Patricia tried to lift her skies from the ground back on the shoulder, but they slid down again and again.

"Do you know ski?"

"Usually, I cope go downhill. Is it enough?"

"You can join us. We are going to ski into Whistler Blackcomb Mountains. It´ll be fun. We´ll go back on Sunday perhaps on Monday."

"I´ve got tree lectures in my schedule on Monday afternoon. I´m grateful for your offer, but maybe next time."

"Just two days, it´ll be a great weekend. Rudi, join us!" I held open the residence´s door and she slid inside. I followed her. The warmth, the bustle around the foyer and the aroma of the canteen were inviting.

"I don´t have skis?"

"It´s no problem."

"Patricia, I´m not sure, if it´s such a great idea."

"O.K. See you at 6.30 in the morning. We´ll pick you some skis up from Whistler´s rental place."

"So, see you morning." I resigned.

"Aren´t you going to use the lift?" A slight wonder sounded in Patricia´s voice.

"No, thanks." We went our separate ways.

The room´s windows were decorated with many floral ornaments created by the frost. The lights of the street lamps outside shimmered in the darkness of night. Their twinkling changed the shadows of the park benches in many different ways. Pedestrians gradually disappeared from the snowy paths with the waxing hours and the night became the queen of these hours. Closing the blinds, I continued drying my washed hair. With the push of a finger, my laptop began waking up. I went back into the bathroom. I left my wet towel on one round rib of the radiator to dry. The moisture of my bath had spread around the space, causing the steam to condense into many little water drops that rolled down the surfaces of the room, or covered them with a tiny foggy layer. Back in my bedroom, a comfortable chair was pulled back by the conscious movement of my leg. Sitting down on the padded seat, the mouse pointer made irregular circles across the laptop screen and, after several clicks, my email inbox showed me all its secrets. My eyes skipped from one row to another. "My clever mum, no email—she´s recognised the comfort of Skype." I told myself to carry on.

"My fella, Daniel. What´s his news?" I was prepared for his extraordinary writing style. I must confess, I looked forward to it.

> *"Rudi, don´t you take things seriously? It´s the middle of December! Have you gone mad? I´m already in my sweet home. Do you hate me? By the way, the guys are missing you, all jokes were spent. We need a new inspiration. Are you in touch with our professor? Write to him! Be polite!*
>
> *Daniel."*

I passed by rows with advertisement offers, striving to find a line with the professor´s address: there wasn´t one.

"Write to him! Be polite!" The words urged me to write him. Daniel was a truly strange card, but I liked him. He had not written it unreasonably.

> *"Good evening, professor. I hope to come home in the middle of December. I would love to meet you, perhaps for a Christmas drink somewhere among the Christmas market stalls.*
>
> *I miss you.*
> *Sincerely, Rudi."*

I pressed send and read the next non-spam email, which was from Laura:

> *"Hi sister. You aren´t allowed to change your arrival date. Our old gang is going to meet up and YOU are a member too, darling.*
>
> *Bye, I´m looking forward to seeing you.*
> *Laura."*

My mailbox was not as full as usual, so it had taken me just an hour to finish going through it. I reloaded the page again to be sure I hadn´t anybody´s mail. Nobody awaited my answer. The mouse cursor was about to click on the small cross to shut down my emails when the Skype banner twinkled to grab my attention.

"Gregory." After a curious click, he asked me for a video call. It was not possible—my web camera did not work.

"Hi Gregory, my camera doesn´t work. I´m sorry. ;o)"

"That´s a pity, it would be nice to see you."

"You have some news?"

"Yes, he had an affair!"

"Who´s he?"

"My dad." I was stunned. I knew Gregory adored both his parents.

"Somebody told you?"

"I saw it," he replied. I could not believe what he had written.

"When?"

"The night after the reef trip."

"I accompanied you near to your villa. Only Bernicia´s window was lit up."

"Yes! Hurray! Have you got it yet?"

"Your dad and Bernicia?"

"Yes!"

"Did they see you too?"

"Just my dad."

"Wow."

"Wow?"

"Has he apologised to you?"

"No, I´ve not seen him yet."

"?"

"I went to my granny´s in Lancashire, near Liverpool."

"Have you told her?"

"Yes."

"Her reaction?"

"Strange."

"Strange?"

"She told me something like men usually behave in this manner, it's a casual thing and that my mum is a very loving mother because she decided to tolerate it. Because we need money for my disease's sake."

"Oh."

"Oh?"

"Your granny is clever too."

"Rudi!"

"You need money. Money gives you more time."

"What do you mean?

"He earns that money."

"Mum takes care of us!"

"Do you hate him?"

"Yes!"

"Forgive him."

"Rudi!"

"Have you told your mum? How did you explain that you are at your granny's?"

"I used to do it all the time. She knows I love her."

"Are you going to tell her?" I asked.

"It'll surely hurt her."

"That's right. She loves you though, doesn't she?"

"I don't understand," he replied.

"He loves you as well, doesn't he?"

"Yes, they both do."

"They both love you, from the bottom of their hearts. Am I wrong?"

"Of course."

"Forgive him."

"?"

"Just try, nothing more."

No answer arrived, although I waited quite a while. Checking his connection, the banner hue announced that he was offline.

"Это надо зделать дорогая Анна."
(It is very important for me you will do it, my dear Anna.)

A flat sheet of paper was slid onto the coffee table that she sat at. According to his behaviour, it seemed its content was of great importance to him. She picked it up and read slowly and carefully.

"Если у вас большой интерес зделать эту торговлю дла международного права нам надо зарегистрироваться у FSC." (If you have enormous interest in doing everything according to international law, it is necessary to register with the FSC.)

"Перше всего нам надо стать членом FSC."
(The first step is to become a member of the FSC.)

"Зделайте как это необходимное, вы зделайте дорогая Анна. Вы юрист."
(It is inescapable that you should do it, dear Anna. You are a lawyer.)

They exchanged a couple of informalities with each other. It took less than a few minutes. She rose, offered him her hand and, in an impressive leaving walk, she disappeared behind an office door. Her manner caused him to be amazed every time they cooperated with each other, but she was unattainable. Her attitude clearly proclaimed that any deal was just a deal. No feelings, no relationship: just hard work to achieve the client's goals. He wished that she was not so terribly sexually attractive. A fairly loud wall clock gong pulled him back to the present.

"Я должен позвонить моему другу, ли вещи двинусь для хорошего курса."
(I need to call my friend about whether things have developed the right way.)

Checking the particular local time did not give him any positive information about progressing his business. It was too early to call. There was the night in his target destination.

"Yes, I´m ready." The quiet opening of a door responded to her knocking. I had already risen almost half an hour earlier. I did not let Patricia wait for more than a few seconds. My small mountain backpack had already been packed: a flask full of hot tea and some baguettes were put in the front part, and clean clothes were put in too. I was sure, I would need them.

"Hi, can we leave?"

"Yes."

"Do you want to go skiing in baggy trousers?"

"No. I´ll buy a ski trousers. There are some skiing-equipment-shops in Whistler, aren´t they?"

"Just a moment." A corner prevented me from recognising where she had vanished to. I slid down along the wall next to my door to settle on the doormat, which partially covered the floor in a rectangle shape. Nobody strolled there: students usually sleep through such early morning hours. Some had come back to their dormitory rooms only a few hours ago, some worked on their unfinished projects and others slept, indulging deep dreams.

"Try it on, please." My room was unlocked again. Trying on the clothes had to be done in a very short time.

"Yes, that´ll do. It´s O.K." Patricia´s comment full of satisfaction sounded like an official confirmation.

"Yes madam, I agree," I said. She threw my baggy trousers at me, laughing. We left the room.

We barely caught the 6.55 bus from the university bus stop. We could not miss it: our Pacific Coach departure was at 7.30 and the next would be one hour later. The thrill inside us grew with every passing bus stop.

"Run, Rudi. The coach is just waiting at its stop," Patricia said. We jumped on the pavement and rushed, passing other coach lines.

"Two student tickets to Whistler Blackcomb Ski Resort, please." Patricia, out of breath, shot her entire sentence at the bus driver.

"O.K., but your skis must go in the baggage space."

"No problem, sir."

The Pacific Coach met its schedule. The door closed and downtown Vancouver vanished behind the rear glass shield. It was more than a month since I had returned from Belize to start attending UBC. But every time when my eyes hit a new section of Vancouver, I was stunned and amazed; I was never disappointed. The unspeakable harmony of the ultra-modern city with the surrounding nature took the wind from my sails. I was able to just look at it and enjoy it, to sniff the atmosphere into my body. The coach had already traversed the whole second half of West Georgia Street; on the left, Lost Lagoon had magically transformed into a snow-white sheet offering children skating or hockey games.

One more curve and West Georgia Street fluently fused into Stanley Park Causeway. Coniferous trees edged the road in somewhat irregular queues, creating an army of young cadets. Stanley Park got sparser. The peninsula showed us all its coastal beauty. The bus neared the massive Lion Gate Bridge. Joining the bridge, the vehicle transported us across the dark sea water, allowing its passengers to be comfortable in their seats and look over the bridge, where cabin cruisers created many foamy lines like a black drawing with white ornaments. Leaving Marine Drive and Capilano Road in a rear panorama, the coach made a loop and joined the Trans-Canada Highway. It did not take long and we copied the lines and curves of the Sea to Sky Highway. First, the highway snaked along the coast, then it lead through small towns and finally it emerged into a large wood area, surrounded by a number of hills towering towards the sky: the beginning of a mountain range. A road panel read *"WHISTLER BLACKCOMB MOUNTAINS"*, delivering the cheering information to the passengers.

"Where do we go?" I asked.

"Seventh heaven," she replied. I looked at her in amusement, but she was the boss.

"Patricia! Hey, honey! Wait!" We turned; a guy was coming towards us from a shop with an oversized claret billboard reading *"WHISTLER BLACKCOMB RENTALS"*. After a long hug full of kisses, their eyes took in the presence of each other.

"Jacob, this is Rudi, my friend. Rudi . . ."

"This is your boyfriend. Jacob, it´s nice to meet you." I finished her sentence, offered my hand to Jacob and smiled.

"Has Patricia told you your skiing aim?"

"Yes. Seventh heaven." Directly looking at him, I announced it as convincingly as if I were an old inhabitant of Whistler.

"Has she shown you the trail map?"

"No," I grinned. "I can´t keep up. I´m lost."

"Seventh heaven sounds pretty nice. That´s enough to know. Or isn´t it?" Patricia laughed.

"O.K. girls, come into my kingdom." We headed into the rental shop. He held the door open and we slid in. The vast space was full of skiing and snowboarding equipment, things to rent or buy, trail maps, postcards expressing the mountains´ beauty, bags, shoes and mountain clothes.

"Wow. Might I look at those?" I asked.

"Of course." He took down a pair of skis and passed them to me. "Here you are."

"Thanks. Could you fit them on me?"

"Are you sure? They are normally used for . . ."

"For free-riding, I know."

"Honey, you told me you had slid down some smaller hills." Patricia said, lifting her forehead up.

"Looking at that map, I think they might be the best . . ." I pointed to the trail map of the resort. The seventh heaven trails were scattered across the surface of the Horstman Glacier. I did not suspect that any snow machine would have been able to climb to that altitude and flatten the glacier terrain.

"Do you really want this pair of skis?" They asked me. The hesitance rang in their voices.

At first a cabin, later a four-seat lift and then a double-seat lift transported us to Horstman Hut. In one way, the hut was remarkably similar to those in the European Alps, but in other ways there was a presence of Canadian simplicity.

"Hi Jacob, the keys are behind the cash desk."

"Thanks, Mathew."

I jumped. I must have smiled to myself as I checked the boy named Mathew. I laughed under my breath. ´Am I missing his arrogance?´ I asked in my mind as I followed the turtledoves in love in front of me.

"Is this Rudi´s room?" Patricia´s question distracted me from my thoughts. They stood outside a room with its door ajar.

"Is fifteen minutes enough, Rudi?" Jacob asked.

"For you maybe! Are you so terribly quick?" I replied.

"A good breakfast (at 10.30) and a new snow blanket are waiting for us." He showed me what our priorities were. Patricia made a face at me.

"O.K., darling, I´ll be there." Waving, I closed the door, trying not to hear their private conversation.

"I´ll wait for you every few metres., O.K?" Jacob described his plan for the imminent descent.

"Which direction shall we go?" Patricia´s hesitation tickled my senses.

"Hey fellows! It´s a sunny day! Let´s just go!" I shouted. The deep snow powder hid both my skis and my calves disappeared in an uncountable number of new white snowflakes as my skis ran downhill in many curves, drawing bends in the snow´s surface. There was speed, pleasure and crazy screams.

"Woo! This is great!"

The wet blanket created by the drizzle that had fallen for a whole week caused the pavements to glisten and reflect the lights of the lamps shining along them. Lancaster´s local pubs woke up to nightlife and people looking for any fun flew inside them, leaving their problems at the door. Rain streams washed everything crossing the roads into the sewers.

"One more!" he shouted at the top of his voice, trying to attract the barman´s attention. The band was producing quite loud big beat music. The songs filled the whole pub, not leaving anything in silence.

"No!" The bartender´s negative answer surprised him.

"I can´t . . ." he tried to finish his sentence. ". . . hear you!" The sentence´s end died in the shouting of people having fun. The bartender had no problem reading lips though, given that he functioned daily among a screaming, laughing and shouting crowd.

"No! I said NO!" He repeatedly spelled out his reply.

"I´m your customer." His tongue refused to obey him. He tried to repeat the sentence. This time he successfully said his statement in one piece.

"You´re totally drunk," the bartender replied.

With a dismissive wave of his hand, he left, struggling through the dancing and stomping mass until he reach an entrance.

´When did this hill grow here?´ he asked himself. He looked around, searching for somebody who would be willing to help.

"Fella, could you . . ." Without any hesitation, a guy approached him and they were outside in a moment.

"Thanks, my fella." His helper descended back into the pub, smirking the whole time.

"Am I drunk? That´s bullshit! Hic-hic." He waved his hand dismissively as though he did not know which direction was the right one and his second hand moved him ahead. A terribly loud and unremitting beep from a bus horn suddenly startled him. An extremely long dazzling light with many flashes was the last thing he could remember.

"Honey, honey." A slightly shaking palm moved in front of his eyes, trying to distract him from his dreams. His eyes zoomed in and out as he attempted to focus on the person above him. He wanted to recognise the voice of the person stroking him gently. A strong conviction vibrated around his brain: he had heard that voice and experienced that touch before . . .

"Honey, honey, everything will be alright."

There were more tangled voices coming towards him. There was the thud of a door slamming and then quietness surrounded him. Finally, he could see things in their true shapes, forms and colours. He looked about, scrutinising each inch of the room. He knew it. He had been in similar spaces so many times before. But why was he there now? Was his illness getting worse? His eyes were arrested by a female figure resting in a slightly yellow armchair.

"Granny." The tranquil word pressed through lips. "Granny, why am I here?" The woman jumped.

"Oh, honey." She came over to the bed, took his hand from the blanket and squeezed it gently and carefully.

"What happened? I can remember an enormous white light." A hoarse tone wrapped around his sentences.

"A bus knocked you down."

"Where?"

"Two streets away from our house. Near McDeclain´s pub."

"McDeclain´s pub?"

"You were totally drunk," she replied. Some flashes of memory flitted through his brain. There was the bartender who had refused to pour him a drink and the argument with Rudi via Skype. He reddened. A long silent interval allowed him to organise his thoughts and emotions.

"Granny, I´m so sorry. I was angry with life." She squeezed his hand again and tapped the back of it but did not say anything.

"Could you do me a favour?" he asked.

"Yes."

"Can you give me a pen and some paper please?" His grandmother rooted in an old sack that looked vaguely like a woman´s handbag.

"The basic core of every handbag is a total disorder." She did a winning gesture, holding up a yellow plastic pen.

"Can you help me sit up?"

He attempted to write something on the paper, but without something to lean against it was not possible. The writing using his hand in its splint looked comical; he had transformed into a child learning their first letters.

"That's the address of my email box and that's her email-address." The pen pointed to two rows, more scribbled than readable.

"You know how to send mails, don't you?" Granny raised her eyebrows. An expression of her mimic-muscles replied everything. "O.K., O.K. I'm joking." They giggled.

"Please, tell her I'm sorry. Could you do it for me?" he asked.

"A terribly mad evening?" With her head in a cocked position, her mouth spelled the words out loudly.

"Something like that," he replied. She placed her hand on his shoulder and bent down to kiss him.

"Some smaller hills?" Patricia stopped next to me, laughing and asking together.

"Girl you are a bad dream," Jacob said as he breathed deeply, trying to catch the air swirling around his lungs.

"Is it possible to get there?" My gloved finger pointed to a turquoise surface on the left part of a hill.

"That's the glacier." Patricia's response was enough to satisfy my curiosity. The sun was constant in the sky; the smallest cloud did not accompany it. A perfectly clear and lively panorama was placed in the Blackcomb's skiing-menu. Snow powder flew everywhere, twisting, rotating or hovering above and around every skier as they glided elegantly through deep white fluff built of thousands of snowflakes.

14

An answering machine finished its regular announcement: any caller was supposed to call again later. There was nobody in the university lab. Shining figures on a wall clock reported the time: 7.32. Along the corridors, the first morning rush began, lecturers arrived at their offices, university cleaning staff put their equipment into storage and some students trickled inside the classrooms.

"Professor! Professor!" Running, he tried to catch him before he vanished into his office.

"Yes? Oh, morning, Matt." Face to face, they both waited for the next question.

"You have not answered my questions yet about the results I sent by email."

"Really? I thought I did."

"I´ve checked it many times. I can´t continue. I need your approval to be able to progress with my work."

"Of course, I understand. I´ll send you my acceptance with all the potential corrections today."

"But I´ll lose a day."

"Rudi´s part is already finished, you could use her results. I have considered all aspects of it for a rather long while. It is necessary to comprehend each part of our equatorial research."

"What´s that mean for me?"

"Your co-operation with Rudi." Sarcasm crept into his voice as if were trying to discern whether Matt´s attitude towards Rudi had changed.

"Have I got another option?"

"Wait until I send you my acceptance," the professor mischievously smirked.

Ring-ring-ring. A vigorous ringing touched their eardrums.

"Your phone, professor."

"O.K., O.K., O.K., I´m coming." The office´s door was pulled energetically. Tracing the ringing phone sound, he suddenly stopped and ran out of his workroom.

"Matt!"

"Yes, professor?" He was almost at the corner of the corridor.

"Let me know when you´ve decided." Mathew laughed under his breath. The professor´s absent-mindedness was nothing new to him.

A sunbeam tickled my eyelids. A weird feeling suddenly flooded my body. My subconscious screamed at me: wake up immediately! I jumped. My mobile phone alarm had let me sweetly dream too long. Gathering my things into my backpack, I knocked on the wall joining my room with Patricia and Jacob´s. No rustle, no hints of any movement: just noises coming from the hallway that lead to every room.

"Patricia, hey Patricia, we overslept! Pat, open the door!" Perhaps nobody was inside their room. I gave up. Entering my room, I thought about all the possibilities to solve the situation. I put my jacket on. In a tearing hurry, I wrote a short message to the two of them with a borrowed pen, which I had found on the small table in my room, in case of their miraculous appearance. I had reached the fourth staircase step when a door behind me creaked. Peeking his head round the door and scanning the hallway, my eyes met a man standing in the middle of the space, wrapped in a towel.

"Are you leaving?" he asked.

"Are you deaf? I knocked so loudly the dead would have opened the lids on his coffins."

"Rudi are you leaving?"

"Do something! It´s late! 7.30! We overslept!" Turning back, I made a great effort to urge them to understand that we should have left the hut already. With a bit of luck, we could catch the Pacific Coach. "Keys. Please." I shot my hand out to grab them. "Don´t look at me like an owl, give me your keys, I´ll take your skis outside. Comprende amigo?"

A Styrofoam cup was embraced by my hands as I tried to get warmer. I was sipping the last drops of tea when Patricia and Jacob pushed open the wooden wing of the hut´s exit door. With six snaps, we fastened our skis on. There were no skiers, no resort staff, no snow machine adjusting the hills to make them flatter and more enjoyable for skiers and no movement anywhere. Three colourful points slid downhill, abandoning the three white snakes created by their various curves behind them. The first passage of hill vanished and the next slopes waited patiently for us to let them perish in a similar way as the first had. The horizon spreading in front of us was built of a white blanket covered with a new small amount of snow powder as far as the human eye could see. No questions, no answers, no breaks. The kilometres uphill faded with the growing kilometres downhill and the small dark grey spots in the resort valley gradually got larger. As we cut through the snow metre by metre, they became buildings, ticket turnstiles or bus stops. The distance between us and the valley covered by morning sunbeams got shorter with each new minute.

"What´s time?" Patricia tried to catch some air.

"8.48." Jacob answered her question.

"The coach must be here already."

"It´s at the stop." We piled our pairs of skis next to Jacob. Patricia quickly kissed him. We evaporated in less than an eyelid twinkle. The coach´s body shrouded us.

A microscope radiated rays at an insect sample braced between two tiny glass rectangles. He scrutinised it, compared it with a photo illustration in his book and scrutinised it again, checking whether he had understood correctly or not. All the students´ heads bent down over the microscopes were filled with knowledge. They memorised the subjects for an exam they were due to take in a couple of days´ time so they would be able to pass the first four sections that the exam would be divided into. They strived to examine the samples stuck under their microscopes.

Bang! An unexpected door slam distracted all the alumni from their work.

"Is Rudi already here?"

"It is nice to see you too, my dear colleague."

"Morning professor, I apologise. I need her. She is obligated to give me her project."

"I asked her for a favour. She left the lab just two minutes ago. I estimate she´ll return between 1 and 2 pm. Haven´t she given you her project yet?"

Keeping a smile on his face, his brain calculated all the possibilities that could explain Rudi´s behaviour. He had saved her a second time in an extremely short period. Flywick closed the lab door full of anger and furiously paced along one of the university´s many corridors.

As some of the passengers starting getting up from their seats on the Pacific Coach, the last stop in downtown Vancouver got closer than an instant before. The bus, after transporting the alumni to the university, reached the bus stop and waited for students, staff, the inhabitants of Vancouver and tourists to climb aboard.

"Such a great idea! Get up at 5 am! Switch our forehead spotlights on! And slide downhill! Hurray! Don´t you know who was the idea´s creator?" We laughed. I was sure our oversleeping would bring many problems, but I would manage to attend all my lectures on Monday´s schedule. Especially as I was obligated to deliver my project to our lecturer that day at the latest.

The audience patiently listened to the explanation of my project presentation; a lot of queries were asked to get more information from a detailed angle. I was grateful: their behaviour helped me to successfully conclude my work. Graphs, diagrams and photos had become the pillars of my project. They eased my swim through that lesson to its end.

"Nina, one minus point for delaying the project, but the topic was handled well." He told me his decision, squinting his eyes to adjust to the soft light coming from the projector. He scribbled points in the column next to my name.

"Thanks, Mr Flywick. Can I sit down now?" He nodded. I gathered all my project documents and headed to my seat.

"Rudi, can you lend me your work?" I stopped, turning to face him, my face was full of sudden surprise. I was not sure whom the question was addressed to.

"Possibly." Stretching my hand over to his desk,

I put the file right next to his notebook. Some classmates began giggling, whispering to each other. It might have seemed that my answer was rude, but that was not my intention. I wanted to disappear, evaporate or vanish as promptly as circumstances would allow me to.

"You can go, the lesson has finished," the lecturer said. I left my place next to the projector. The alumni groups covered the staircase, vividly chatted, joked with their heads together or screamed at each other, making fun. I grasped the rest of my things and joined them.

My guts created strange sounds in my stomach, announcing I had not had any lunch yet. Arriving at my residence, I threw my backpack into a corner of the room, took a rapid shower and hurried to catch the 12.35 bus to be at school at 1 pm. No time remained to allow me to satisfy my body´s demands. If I wanted to have a lunch I had to return to college. Breakfasts and dinners in our residence became a routine but lunch seemed like a great luxury, so students travelled a day to school to satisfy their hunger.

'Hurry, Rudi! Hurry!' Urging orders shouted at me from my head as I checked the time. The canteen would be closed in 18 minutes. Running, taking two stairs at a time, I headed along the passage to the canteen. I quickly shortened the distance separating me from my covetous lunch.

"A salmon salad and those three small French baguettes please, madam."

"Here you are, honey."

"Thanks, madam." I winked at her, silently laughing to myself. My hand shifted my tray to a drinks machine. Immense comfort flooded across my whole being; the idea of a meal cheered me up.

"Hi, Her Majesty," Mathew said. My lovely time had been spoilt in a few seconds.

"It´s nice to see you again." His supreme arrogance enclosed me.

"Princess, it´s hard to say this, but I need your help." Settling in a chair, I looked forward to the salmon but I did not want to listen to his stupid, selfish comments.

"It is sad, isn´t it?" I said with a grin, addressing the question it more to my late lunch than to him.

"Princess . . ." He rose up. His face wore a nervous expression as he paced to the canteen exit.

"I´m Rudi, firstly. And secondly, if it´s important, I´ll help you." My fairly loud response followed him. The area remained empty apart from two people, and the humming drinks machine and refrigerator were silent observers in the corner of the room.

"Thank you, madam. It was delicious."

"You´re welcome, honey."

"Have a nice day, madam."

All the students were swallowed by their classrooms. Every now and then, soft voices sneaked through the crevices between the doors into the hallway. I slowly strolled over to the forestry lab to ask the professor for his next orders. Three weeks remained until my departure home for the holidays. Nearing the lab, I could see a guy leaning against the wall. I passed him, approached the door, pulled it aside and slid into the professor´s kingdom.

Bang! I turned to face Matt. He raised his forehead; I expected an explanation. He cocked his head to the side.

"I´m Mathew, Matt Sander. Can we go back to the beginning?"

For a while we silently faced each other, then my hand shot out to him.

"Rudi, Nina Rudić, sometimes rude Rudi." He opened the door. I slid in. In the far corner of the lab, near a window, the professor was sat at a computer screen, fiercely tapping. His expression seemed scared.

"Hm-hm." Matt disturbed him to imply our company.

"Oh, Rudi, Matt." He shut down the windows on the screen, rose, went over to the racks crammed with files and dragged one of them from its shelf.

"Forms. Fill them in and I´ll send them off for confirmation." I began patiently reading, row by row.

"January the 4th is the departure date?"

"What´s the arrival date like?"

"I´ve passed one exam. There are three in front of me."

"I´ve not passed any." Our protests rotated, pummelling the professor.

"January the 26th is the arrival date."

"What? The winter term will have finished in two weeks, at the end of the first week in February!" Matt whipped his sentences into the air, not believing what the professor had said.

"One week for every exam, it could be enough."

"Enough? I have four."

"Matt, one is the proje . . ." He did not let me finish. With a loud bang of the door, he was gone.

"He´ll be back," the professor said. I did not comprehend. Looking at the professor, he went on.

"He has a hot nature. We casually argue every time we see each other. Something new comes up and we have a disagreement. But he is clever and slick: he´ll come back and take his place in the research." His smiling face persuaded me. I stuck my form inside my bag. I was about to leave when a phone rang.

"Yes, Professor Dragonsky, Faculty of Forestry." I supposed the caller had introduced themselves. The professor´s face suddenly went white. He swallowed hard. I should have left him on his own. With a wave to say goodbye, I closed the door and walked down the corridor.

The sky progressed from grey-blue to dark grey and the late autumn period sliced away the daylight more and more. Half past three in the afternoon was similar to late summer evening hours. The streets wore their twilight robes and glittering lanterns became their pearly accessories. A freezing breeze touched chilled noses, ears and lips, tinting them with shades of red. The soles of pedestrians´ shoes played a crunching melody. The instrument was the white snow on the pavement´s surface.

"The Irving K. Barber Learning Centre at the University of British Columbia." A direction sign solved my dilemma. I stood in front of an imposing piece of architecture: a beautiful residence building (I estimated from the 1920s) split into a central part with two wings. They had been built using extremely modern architectural techniques. Large glass sheets and metal junctions were the most important parts of them. A clock tower dominated over the small nice-looking park in front of it, which completed the whole picture. I was stunned again. The old times tangled with the present. I obeyed the counsel of the direction sign and walked around the majestic building. At the entrance, the same title was printed. A glass door gave me the approval to come in.

"Wow." I slid inside. Its walls were covered from top to bottom with pictures in massive frames. I supposed they depicted tremendously eminent people from Canadian history. Enormous glass windows let the lamp lights coming from the evening streets leak into the library, generating breath-taking optical effects. My eyes gazed at the ceiling; I rotated around my axis to not rip my eyes from the beauty.

"Can I help you?" I jumped. The query tore me from my thoughts.

"Oh. Just. Oh. Yes. I need the registration desk," I stuttered. I tried to put my words in comprehensible order. The woman ripped me from the world of great amazement. I was woken up in a reality.

"Follow me, please." The woman´s arm pointed to an information desk. She sat down, the familiar buzz of a working computer tickled my eardrums and data was typed in. A freshly printed form was put on the desk in front of me and, after a few seconds, I obtained a lecture on how to use the ASRS, the automated storage and retrieval system. The alumni and library staff liked to call it the library robot. Later, I learned that ASRSs were exploited in the most respected science libraries in Canada and in the rest of the world too.

"Madam, is Internet use included in the fee too?" The lady lifted her glasses from the nose and began explaining to me all the rules, responsibilities and abilities of the library. Simply said, she was a clerk to the core.

"Thanks, madam." I left the desk, smiling. It was the first time I felt as if I were at home. Sometimes people need to be taken more seriously than required.

Finally, I found all the texts from the recommended literature needed to pass my exams. Standing at a copying machine, I counted my coins to see if I had enough to complete duplicating the texts. Exhaustion crept in step by step with the growing minutes. Inputting my last orders into the copying machine´s panel, I toyed with the idea of a hot cup of coffee. Copies gathered and folded under my arm, the machine stopped as I headed into the cloakroom where I had left my jacket. A coffee aroma crossed my way. Stalking the transparent strips of the flying scent, I discovered the source. A coffee machine in all its beauty stood in the corner. No mugs, just Styrofoam cups.

Going carefully back to where I had come from, trying my hardest not to spill a drop, the dim lights emanating from computer screens along rows of library desks attracted me more and more. They persuaded me very easily to sit at one of them and log in. The cup full of steamy latte waited patiently for my next sip. Something inside me urged me to go online. My mailbox finished downloading my emails as quickly as the capacity of the university´s connection allowed it to. Skipping one row after another, I scrolled down the page. Four days had passed since I had last checked my emails and nobody had needed me. All my emails concealing advertising bullshit were ticked and removed. I reloaded my inbox to ensure nothing had been missed. One in bold capitals hit my sight. A spasm crossed my tummy.

"Nina, I´m sorry.´

Gregory wrote this on a piece of paper—he asked me to send an apology to you.

Minerva, Gregory´s granny."

I did not understand. He was no coward. I knew he would have been able to find the courage somewhere deep inside him to tell me he was sorry for himself.

"Dear Minerva.

What happened? I´ll try to connect every day around 11 pm. Please, ask Gregory to connect with me. I am not angry with him. In spite of the fact that I would love to help him, I can´t. I can´t solve it, he must do it on his own. But I am definitely not angry with him.

Cordially, Rudi."

I disconnected and slid my registration card with my connection data out from the computer´s body. Sipping the rest of my latte, I walked over to spend valuable moments with "Miss Important Librarian" to pay my fees.

The outside temperature must have fallen sharply below zero, as the snow crunching had become sharper. Subtle white flakes flittered in the air here and there. Frozen noses made breathing more difficult. Gloved hands asked to be shoved into pockets because the frost was quietly creeping inside them, underneath fingernails. Crossing the park, a great feeling of the residence´s warmth captured my brain. A couple of wild ducks swam on the free water in the park´s pond. I estimated a park warden or a member of the park´s staff had taken the thick ice shell off to make life easier for the pond´s inhabitants. I interrupted my walk and bent down to become a silent observer. I used to love doing that. In many autumn, winter and early spring evenings, my granddad used to discover a secret place among dangling willow twigs and make a shield protecting us from being seen. We used to sit there for many hours sucking in the intimate atmosphere of wild duck life. I landed in my childhood again, losing connection with the present. A warm wind whirling near my neck got more persistent. Slight jogs, they repeated again and again. I was back in the present, turned backward, I jumped. A pretty tall, dark silhouette stood in front of me. With a short snort, a horse´s muzzle tenderly touched my cheek.

"Hi." My heart´s thudding sounded so loud that it seemed as if it was echoing all around us.

"It isn´t clever to be alone here at this time of night," the rider replied.

"Are you a night rider? That´s strange too, isn´t?"

"I´m on guard duty today, it´s my job."

"A rider of the Royal Canadian Police?" A hesitant question pressed out from my lips.

"Yes, madam."

"I´d better go. Enjoy the rest of your shift." I was suddenly reminded that I was freezing, so my one desire was to get back to my residence, sip hot tea and savour a scrumptious cake from the canteen.

"I could take you home."

"Oh. How? Sit behind you?"

"Are you scared?"

"Oh, no . . . Just . . . your horse . . . will he mind?"

"Of course not. No worries," he giggled. Offering me his hand, I squirmed, not knowing how to get on the horse´s back without using a stirrup.

"Use the bench!" he said. I understood. I climbed on it and slid my hand into his. I sat on the horse´s back.

A blue cloud with a white "S" in the middle and a minuscule number one in the bottom-right corner of the button appeared in the toolbar. She checked the email addresses one by one, looking for one in particular. She had not noticed the Skype button had changed in appearance. She had heard about Skype but had never used it. Her generation was fully satisfied with the advantages provided by browsing the Internet or sending and receiving emails. Using and discovering new devices progressed terribly slowly.

"Yes." She clicked on the particular row. The six rows of text were eaten by her mind in a moment. Her fingers began cooperating with her brain, translating typed letters into sentences. Thoughts twisted in unsynchronised spirals in her mind; many ideas were born in that brief minute without thought for the right order that would explain Gregory´s behaviour. Eventually, she completed the email.

"Dear Nina or Rudi,

I can only guess why Gregory asked me to write to you rather than asking me to bring his laptop into the hospital to write to you himself. I honestly do not know. His head is full of mysteries. I would love to decipher them, but many times he lets nobody in. He became an adult when he could have been enjoying his childhood. The dystrophy became his nearest friend. It sounds awful, but I do not think he sees it that way. He is a highly sensible and intelligent boy and he understands everything. To live his life as enjoyably as possible is the one and most appropriate goal that he decided on. I am thankful that you are not angry with him. His words are sometimes more venomous than any poison produced by the most poisonous snake. But it is his defence, nothing more. Accept this please. Be his friend.

Sincerely, Minerva."

The room was soaked with the scent of chocolate cookies and a cinnamon fragrance coming from an oversized mug standing right next to Gregory´s laptop. An old rustic table lamp cast a cone of light on a corner table, which provided space for things like paper, envelopes, mugs crammed with pencils and pens, and bowls full of rubber bands and paperclips. She sipped her tea, took one bite from a cookie and double-clicked the SEND button. The mouse pointer swam along the lower toolbar, preparing to click the round button allowing the user to switch the computer off.

"That little button there, what can it mean?" She hesitated for a while, then she made her choice and clicked on it. A window consisting of two frames appeared. Its left part was a list of names with miniature photos or pictures. Gregory had probably added them as friends, she thought. The right frame was much bigger and contained two parts: a horizontal list of the same people that occupied the left frame and a pretty big text area beneath it.

"Oh, Rudi is there. Well, let´s see." After a double-click, a short query appeared above the text field.

"Hi, Gregory. What happened? Please write to me."

"What now? Maybe I use it like email." Speaking with herself, she typed an answer into the text area.

"What now? What now?" Looking for a SEND button, the mouse pointer accidently landed on a blue circle carrying a bubble with a miniature picture of a letter. *"SEND MESSAGE"* appeared. She clicked.

"It is me, Minerva."

"Perfect, I´m stuck here like a fool and princess has new company." He angrily rose, watching the movie scene from behind the residence´s foyer window. Although his scarf, cap, jacket and gloves had been put on in haste, his desire for a meeting had evaporated. He felt a piercing hurry that urged him to vacate the space. He hung his head down between his shoulders to protect him against the direct attack of the chilling frost, as well as against being noticed. The glass door was nearing its previous position; his boot hit it, changing its trajectory.

"Thank you. It was a nice ride. Enjoy the rest of your shift." Her chirping hovered through the air, approaching him, tearing his eardrums. Looking straight forward, he paced ahead, wanting to get away from that potential meeting place.

15

"I told you, everything is in progress. We will continue after December. I´m obligated to finish examining the alumni." The white tone in his face was slowly changing to red. His calm voice had risen two octaves higher in the space of a few minutes. It was his second call during a couple of days. An academic salary was not anything excellent, but that money allowed him to keep a relatively solid social status. He wondered where his mind had been when he had closed this lousy deal.

"What kind of references did he think? Why does he need to accept his company as a member of the FSC (Forest Stewardship Council)?! His rudeness doesn´t know any limits!" He extracted the phone flex from the plug in a great flood of anger. Throwing himself down on a padded sofa, his mobile began repeatedly ringing.

"Shit!" he snapped. He pressed the green response button. "Yes? Professor Dragonsky speaking!" He screamed so loudly that the person on the second side of the link remained silent for a while.

"Andrew? Is everything in order?"

"Oh, Trevor, I´m sorry."

"Can I speak? Will you stop shouting at me?" The voice had a teasing tone.

"Yes."

"The FSC received an application form a couple of days ago. The applicant is a company referring to you. Their lawyer mentioned in the attachment that you would confirm their reliability and business integrity. Do you know something about that?" He felt spasms squeezing his muscles. No exact words emerged to be said, although he had no idea how he could avoid directly responding.

"Trevor, is it possible to email or fax me that document? I´ll take a look at it," the professor said.

"No problem. How are things going, by the way?"

"It´s the end of the winter term, you know what it´s like. Got many exams to mark."

"I can imagine. But sometimes it´s pretty ridiculous. Alumni and their attempts to simplify their exams." Memories full of fun flashed in their minds.

"Do you remember . . ."

"Hi, Mum." A familiar mannish voice thundered. The man bent down to kiss her.

"I suppose you would like to go in, would you?" Irony snaked into in the air.

"Didn´t you invite me?" he asked. He had not expected her refusing attitude. She opened the door a little bit more. Following her, he thought back to several months ago when he had visited her the last time. She stopped at a kitchen sideboard, leaned against it and waited for his lies.

"Mum, I don´t know what Gregory told you, but . . ."

"What?" Minerva asked in such an icy manner that it caused him to squirm.

"Is there any reason to get totally drunk and let a bus knock you down?"

"Are you listening to yourself, dear Fillip?" Her query was so hostile, he lost all courage to do anything in his defence. "You didn´t want to tell me where he´s hospitalised. Could you be so polite . . ."

"You know where the local hospital is, don´t you? Or did you forget? Is it not enough noble for you?" Her voice remained calm but a great amount of arrogance flew through it. He nodded, approached her and tried to kiss her forehead. She dodged aside.

"I´m sorry, Mum." Turning, he left and his legs carried him along the hallway to the entrance. With a subtle click of the door lock, he vanished.

"No, you aren´t. You´ve never been truly sorry," she said under her breath. She strolled upstairs to finish her conversation, hoping that the chat with her son had not consumed too much time and Rudi would still be waiting for her. Minerva sat at the laptop. With the slight touch of her fingertips, the screen got brighter.

"My son visited me. We can continue." Sipping her cold tea, the nervousness increased in her tummy. No response.

"Minerva?"

Many happy sparkles shimmered in her pupils.

"Yes, Rudi. Rudi, are you Rudi or Nina?"

"My nickname is Rudi, my name is Nina. My full name is Nina Rudić."

"It's nice to write with you, Rudi."

"Thanks, Minerva. Please, can you tell me what happened?"

"Gregory went into one of the local pubs, I suppose for fun, got totally drunk and was knocked down by a bus on his way home."

"Is he O.K.?"

"Yes, he has been getting better over the last few days."

"Minerva, please stop me if my questions get too indecent. When I met Gregory, we became friends. He told me about his DMD. I looked for hours on the Internet, asking myself what his future will be like. I read something about physical therapy maybe helping. Muscle strength and muscle functions could remain operational for a longer time if the patient has regularly physical activity. There is no known cure, just drugs being developed. But, Gregory spoke about drugs, about his Dad's search for the best hospital, laboratory, scientist . . . How is it in reality? Did I grasp the interpretation of DMD wrongly?"

"Gregory told you the truth. And you comprehend everything correctly. Gregory's dad started searching from the first second when the doctors got the results from the laboratory tests and said loudly 'your son has Duchenne Muscular Dystrophy'. But I'm afraid he hasn't found a way to achieve his goals. He will not stop until he finds a drug to cure DMD or until Gregory is no longer alive. There is no way to stop him. Not one."

"Did Gregory say anything to you? About delicate affairs?"

"Do you mean if Gregory mentioned that his dad had sex with their landlady?"

"Yes, thanks. You said it exactly."

"Yes."

"He told me too."

"Can I ask you, what your response was?"

"Sincerely?"

"Yes, my dear," Minerva said, encouraging me.

"I'm not sure you want to hear it."

"Jump to it, Rudi!"

"He should forgive him."

Monika Pistovčák

"That was mature of you."

"Don´t disconnect, please Minerva."

"Rudi, be his friend, please."

"Did you hear it?"

"Hear what?"

"You don´t know how big a weight just fell from my heart. ;o)"

"What does ;o) mean?"

"A smile."

16

There remained one student in front of me before I would be asked to go into the office, where my examiner would throw my memorised knowledge out the window or my answers would be enough to convince him to let me proceed to the summer term. The score had been four to two: four winners and two losers. The student before me left the office.

"Nina Rudić!" I slid inside. I got lost in time: questions, responses, additional questions and examples fused together at the same foggy time.

"That's enough. I'm satisfied. I give you an A. You can go." The examiner's words dropped from his lips one by one, joining into sentences. The final result would allow me to finish my year at the university if I passed the rest of my exams.

Closing the office door, I noticed the professor standing in the corner of the far corridor. "Morning, professor!" I shouted. He stopped walking and waited patiently as I ran towards him.

"Hi Rudi!"

"I'm glad I've bumped into you. Would you be so polite and give this to Mathew?" He scrutinised the stack of papers that I suddenly thrust into his hands.

"Material for passing one of our exams successfully," I explained. His face lit up and he understood.

"Aren't you going to the practical exercise today? It starts in half an hour. Mathew will be there."

"I swapped it around, I've already done it."

"With Professor Creacher?"

"Yes. I did not know the finish time of the exam I just did, so I took the practical earlier than scheduled."

"O.K. Rudi, so see you at the next exam."

"Alright, see you on Thursday, professor."

"No, I don´t want to leave! Tell him, please!"

"Your father thinks . . ."

"Thinks what? That the treatment in this hospital is not the high level he demands? Is he a doctor?"

"He has legal responsibility for you. If he decides this, we will be obligated to accept it, Gregory." In an exceedingly polite tone, the doctor tried to calm him down.

"Mum, Granny, why don´t you do anything against it?"

"Stop, Gregory, you will have the opportunity to tell him personally," his grandmother´s gaze led to the room´s entrance.

"Hi. Mum, honey, could you leave us alone?" No shame, no politeness: power came out of his attitude. The bile boiled in Gregory.

"No, they stay here! Accept it or leave!" Every word was whipped with such mighty power, his face was hard like a rock. The doctor left the family to solve their issues.

The students in the university canteen were excitedly chirping about the Vancouver Christmas Market. Their chatting was so infectious that it remained hooked in my mind as I strolled along the university corridors and slid outside.

Beep-beep-beep. Patricia´s phone stubbornly sang the same response. I tried four more times, then I left her a short message.

"Hi kid, it´s Rudi. Join me, I´ll be at the Christmas market."

The university´s information desk trapped my view as I neared it. I approached the counter. "Good afternoon, sir. I have a little request. Could you tell me how to get to the Vancouver Christmas Market?"

"Hi, Rudi! How´s it going?"

"Wow! You remember my name?" He promptly gave me a wink. A big map of Vancouver was unfolded on the desk: his finger showed me all the routes, buses and bus stops needed to get to the Christmas market and enjoy magical moments.

"Thanks, sir. See you later." Putting all the information in my grey cells, I left the university´s gates behind me and followed the line drawn with pencil on a scrap of paper. I caught the number of a bus approaching me: it was the right one.

"Yes!" I climb aboard, bought a ticket and began counting the bus stops according to a plan hanging above the window. Eight days of memorising, studying, scrutinising and memorising again had cut me out from reality. Looking out through the windows, my eyes skipped from one Christmas decoration to another, each more pompous, brighter or more unique than the last. It was clear to anybody that the first week of Advent had arrived.

The sun´s last rays struggled in the dark grey sky, chains of lights along the streets were switched on one by one, shining stars achieved their full beauty and light bulbs wrapped around trees shimmered. "Ho ho ho" sounds tickled children´s ears, singing groups occupied each second corner of the streets producing Christmas carols and people forgot about the frost creeping into their gloves, chilling them under their nails. There was enthusiasm everywhere. My legs carried me, unconsciously dragged by the Christmas crowd. The mass swept me along with the rhythm of cramming people. I felt a ticklish bouncing inside the inner pocket of my jacket: my mobile vibrating distracted me from my spectator role.

"Hi, where are you, honey? What´s the nearest stand to you? O.K. Wait, I have a great meeting point." The acoustic scene in my ears coming from her phone disclosed immediately that she was at the market too.

"A stand with gingerbread hearts and an enormous Santa Claus towering above it. Look up, you must be able to see it!" Shouting into the phone´s microphone, I gave her all details to simplify her seeking.

"Yes, I´ll be waiting here!" Patiently pressing through the crowd allowed me to stand near the counter. Many variants of gingerbread hearts, angels, bells and lambs decorated in Christmas styles reminded me of the Christmas markets in Central Europe, at home.

"Can I ask you how much this is please?" I handed the vender an item that showed its beauty to the world, which had clearly been created by deft hands.

"Two dollars." She put it in a little plastic pouch and waited calmly. I took my purse out of my bag and handed her the money.

"Merry Christmas, madam. Thank you." I put my purse back into my bag. As I zipped it up, the teeth clutched my glove. The titillating tiny threads caused a sneezing feeling; somebody´s gloved hands covered my eyes.

"Patricia?" I asked. The giggling coming from behind me transformed into a warm hug.

"Hi honey, I´m so glad you called me. Where have you been hiding for more than one week?"

"I was cramming book pages into my small brain."

"Successfully?"

"Do you doubt me? My name is clever girl, it´s really nice to meet you Patricia." She poked me and we broke into laughter.

"Look!" I opened up my fist slowly, finger by finger. The tiny object was lying in my palm.

"Is it mine?" Patricia took it gently.

"An angel, almost the same as you´d find at the Christmas market in my country. I had to buy it."

"It´s a European Christmas market—the first German style market in Vancouver." Patricia hugged me immediately and very tightly. "Thanks, it´s sweet."

"Do you like it?"

"Of course, I do."

"Hi neighbour!" A group of five people was struggling in our direction. Their shouting disturbed us and we turned towards the noise, checking the faces surrounding us. Whether someone was there, who would have said them back ´hello´. Nobody.

"Oh! No!" The guy who lived in the same hallway as me was among the group. The manner-less boy wanted to be the focus of fun every time and everywhere, not matter what the consequences.

"Do you know him, Rudi?"

"I am afraid so, yes. Let´s disappear!"

"It´s too late, Rudi," Patricia replied.

"Hi neighbour, can we join you?" He screamed at us, standing half a metre from us and smelling like spoilt beer. His friends giggled stupidly.

"I´m sorry, we´re meeting someone, we have to go." My self-confident answer swiped through the air. I grabbed Patricia´s hand, dragging her behind me and struggling through the crowd.

"Hey neighbour!" He ran over to us, crossing our path.

"Let us go on." I sent him an ironic smile.

"No, no, beauties, today we´ll be your company."

"No, not today, step aside, dear neighbour." Sarcasm radiated from me in all directions.

"And if I don´t obey you?"

"Get out of our way!" Every word was pressed through clenched teeth. He theatrically laughed, leaning towards my face. A terrible stink flooded the narrow space around me. Grinning, his fingers squeezed my chin, pulling it up. My arm shot out, my palm grabbed his wrist and yanked it away.

"I´ve told you, leave us be!" Mighty anger circulated around me in numerous trails. I was shaking as I looked straight into his glazed eyes, caused by a great number of alcoholic drinks.

"I would love to kiss you, my little neighbour." His tongue tangled his words. It was hard to understand. His fist pushed my jaw.

"That´s enough! Don´t touch me with your stinky hands!" My arm shot out a second time to loosen my face. I grabbed Patricia´s arm and struggled among the people.

"You little bitch!" A painful grip of my forearm twisted my arm behind my back. I stomped on his foot so strongly with such piercing power that he repeatedly swore and his vulgarity grew. His grip was released slightly.

"Let her go! Immediately!"

"Why, my dear Ken?" His arrogant query was tangled with excessive self-confidence.

"I told you, let her go."

"These little bitches aren´t worth it," he hissed through clenched teeth.

"Say that again!" Mathew approached nearer. The nose almost touched the nose. There was no space for a pin. Looking round, seeking help from his mates, he recognised they had crept away so he vanished into the crowd.

"O.K. Ken, how I said those bitches aren´t worth it. Thanks." He gave up, offered his hand to Mathew. Matt refused his gesture.

"Are you O.K.?" Mathew asked.

"Yes."

"Rudi, you´re squeezing my wrist." Patricia protested.

"Oh, I´m sorry . . . oh . . . Mathew this is Patricia—she has the nicest heart in Vancouver." I switched my demeanour as the Christmas melodies hovering in the air reminded me of the reason I was there: I had come to suck in the Christmas spirit and enjoy the atmosphere. I tried to return us back to the comfort of Christmas time.

"What shall we do now?"

"There, can you see that stand? I guess you´ve never tasted it yet.

"What?"

"That stand with the Mozart Christmas punch. Let´s go, you must taste it." Vivid chatting helped to pass the time in the relatively quick queue; three handy vendors skilfully served people looking forward to tasting the delightful hot drink, which certainly cheered anyone who had any.

"It smells good."

"Wow, strong but good."

Time was quickly running away from us. Stands with sausages were exchanged with a stall selling a great variety of strudels. We stopped at a stall selling salt pancakes made in the European way. We got lost among the stalls, stands, people and fairy tale creatures running here and there. It created an unbelievable Christmas air.

"Guys, I must go, it´s late," Patricia said.

"I´ll accompany you."

"No Rudi, stay and have fun. It´s nice to meet you Matt." A small butterfly kiss shivered for a brief second on my cheek, two hands wrapped around my neck for a second and then she was gone.

"Let´s go! I glimpsed something beautiful." Matt swept me into the crowd, gripping my glove more than my hand.

"Wow," I commented. There towered before us a tremendous live Bethlehem scene: a cradle, a donkey, a cow, straw on the floor, Mary, Joseph, baby Christ, three kings and an angel on the stairs above all this. In front of the stage, a great string orchestra produced a breath-taking melody that radiated all around, which people enjoyed in silence or crooned along to. I did not know how long I remained standing there, amazed and wordless. He shifted himself behind me and crossed both arms around my waist, holding me gently and firmly at the same time. We unconsciously moved with the rhythm of the melody.

"Thanks, Rudi."

"For what?" Wrinkles decorated the small part of my forehead peeking out from my woolly cap.

"For the study material."

"Oh, you´re welcome." Turning back, I caught the horologe´s face beaming down from the tower. "It´s late Matt, I should go."

"I´ll accompany you."

"I´m a big girl, in case you haven´t noticed."

"Oh, I forgot. You´ll certainly meet your Royal Guard and he . . ."

"You are jealous, Matt Sander."

"Don´t be naive. Don´t make believe," he said. I got jammed in my mind. How did he know about my accidental encounter with the policeman?

"Are you stalking me?" I asked.

"No, Rudi, I´m not." He laughed and laughed.

"I don´t understand."

"I was waiting for you in the residence to say sorry, and I saw you . . ."

"Why did you leave then?"

"I didn´t want to disturb you."

"Disturb me?"

"Leave it Rudi, let´s go."

"What?" He dragged me, giving no further explanation or clues.

"Don´t ask questions non-stop, just walk with me," he said.

"O.K. you´re the boss."

Carols evaporated into the air. The market receded into the distance. We jumped onto a bus that approached us, just for one stop. In a rapid pace, we ran down a moving escalator; with no fragment of hesitation, he tugged me to the left. The ear-tearing noise of a coming train pushed billowing wind in front of the nose. The underground platform brimming with people transformed into a refrigerator. A chill frost clenched every waiting being in its shivery trap. Each of them desired to vanish inside a train to be cuddled by the warmth of the heating.

"Get off. Hurry!" Matt shouted at me. The music coming from a platform was too loud.

We ran on and on, abandoning the staircase below us. The crisp night air welcomed us as we reached the street. I had never been there during my stay in Vancouver. A far-reaching park sheltered a tall white building behind a veil of branches, twigs and tree trunks. An unrefined tiny path wound among black tree trunks with brushwood piles scattered across it. The frostbitten snow and tiny twigs lying on the earth crunched and creaked under our feet. I stumbled many times until we achieved Matt´s aim. My feet had changed to two icy units.

"It´s a decayed old church." My whispering distracted an invisible small animal from its dreams. I felt a subtle motion along my shoes.

"Come in," Matt said under his breath, so quietly that I would not have understood him if he had not pulled my jacket sleeve. Sliding into a private church world, I lost my breath. Walls so tall they almost touched the sky were covered with ancient fresco paintings. Moonbeams entered the space through slim vaulted windows built from many coloured small glass fragments. A pompous altar balcony stood in the far corner, maybe two metres above the floor, partly drenched in moonlight. The floor decorations had been created by dexterous fingers and artistic minds. Rainbow-coloured stone tiles were organised into many religious pictures, telling centuries-old stories.

A slight tap on my shoulder dragged me from my thoughts. We went up the staircase, moving patiently step by step, trying not to cause any subtle creaks. Matt constantly gestured with his forefinger pressed to his lips to keep quiet. The staircase, which stood next to the altar, twisted twice and I had not yet recognised what the mysterious result would be. The last step was missing. Matt stretched his hand out to secure my climb. I pushed down onto the penultimate wooden step in an attempt not to produce any more noise than necessary. It suddenly burst with a great din. All the pieces fell down, hitting building components on their way to the floor. I jumped. In one second, I pressed against the nearest brick wall. In the same instant, I protected my head with my arms against a pretty big bird that I had startled when I broke the step. I had not heard it until the bird's wing feathers almost touched my face.

"What . . ." A gruff word dropped from my lips. "Bubo Bubo."

"That's eloquent," Matt said to me.

We progressed along the wall to an unglazed window on the far wall.

"There," Matt whispered, pointing his finger at the ceiling. A sumptuous brass bell hung in the middle of a hexagon made from six massive square wooden logs. Each log was decorated with many small, undefined and angular miniature packs. They hung in groups. Their surfaces were covered with an icy coating and the moonlight's soft rays. It looked like a silver coliseum floating in the air.

"Go." Tapping on the frame of a ladder, he encouraged me to climb up. I followed his command.

"Wow." I looked around, rotating my head to all sides, not believing what I could see.

"They are sleeping bats." A smile stretched across his lips.

"Shouldn't they be in a cave? They'll get frozen."

"That's enough princess, I'm freezing," his whisper tangled with the creaking of ladder slats. Returning down the staircase, a thought occupied my mind. How could I reach the first unbroken step? I squatted, lay down on my belly and fumbled around to feel a steady step under my soles.

"Wait, are you crazy, I'll help you!" Matt said.

"Hush. The batmen have woken up." I began giggling unreasonably. I could not stop it.

"Rudi, stop it."

Finally, we reached the last step. Matt dragged me to the exit of the church.

"Ow, my arm. Matt, don´t grip me so hard."

"The batmen have woken up?" His voice was full of amusement and his eyebrows were raised.

"Hush and hush again. It hit me spontaneously. By the way, it was great but it was so scaaaaary."

"Did you like it?"

"Of course, I like it. I like mysterious places." He gave me a strange piercing look; I was wearing goose bumps. "Matt, what . . ." Pointing behind my back, he wore a frightened expression.

"I know there´s nothing there. Ha-ha," I said. His gaze continued. I turned. At the last moment, I crouched to the ground so rapidly that my legs slipped and I landed in the snow.

"Our new friend Bubo Bubo," Matt laughed.

"You said it was eloquent. What did you mean?" I asked.

"Bubo means a spook in my language. Mums use it to scare their children if they don´t want to go to bed."

"Matt, it´s 2 am. We must go to school tomorrow."

"Today, princess, today." His hand offered to help me up.

"Yes the main hospital, the church . . ." He paced up and down the hallway, giving various orders to a person on the end of the telephonic link.

"Sir." A doctor on duty tapped him on the shoulder.

"I´ll call later. Expect my call," he said, putting his phone back in his pocket. "Yes, doctor?"

"Gregory has psychological trauma. I would recommend you take him to a specialist. He really needs to be willing to do his daily exercises. He has DMD—I appreciate you have involved him in drug research treatment provided by the MDA, but muscle exertion is the most important aspect in alleviating his physical state."

"Doctor, my son is not a fool. I´m persuaded I´ve stuffed enough money into the Muscular Dystrophy Association to bear fruit in an exceptionally short period of time."

"You´ve misunderstood me, but his mental stability has a big influence on his physical state. Have a nice day, sir."

The doctor refused to go into a futile battle with a parent who probably thought he had eaten the whole world's wisdom. He understood Gregory's attitude towards his father.

"Neither money nor human effort can make a miracle happen," he percolated through his teeth. "Some people think they can achieve anything using an adequate sum of money. Unfortunately, diseases have a different opinion." His anger rose as he neared the end of the hospital corridor.

"Hi Gregory, it seems you´ll have a visitor shortly."

"Dad?"

"Yes."

"Visiting hours have already finished, haven´t they?"

"Yes. I´m afraid you´ll be disappointed. They finish at 6 pm, however, your father has his own visiting hours."

"And the manager of your hospital now has a pretty big budget?"

"That may be so. If you want, I can tell him that you are sleeping."

"It´s no good. He is patient. He´ll wait until I wake up. And . . ."

"And?"

"You cannot solve this, you´ll get into trouble. My dad is impolite to people who cross his path."

"I see. Have a good day, Gregory." He rose from the edge of Gregory's hospital bed just as the boy's father pushed the door open with such overwhelming power that it hit a glass sheet dividing the bed part of the room from a storage space.

"We´ve not seen each other for such a long time, sir." A sarcastic notice whipped through the hospital room; the doctor left them alone.

"Hi Gregory." Paying no heed to the doctor's comment, ignorance was his answer to the sarcasm.

"Dad." His eyes did not swerve to the side in the slightest: they pierced his father's pupils continuously.

"How is it going?"

"Come on! Give out your demands!" Every word cut the air separately.

"Alright, you saw me with the landlady," his father said. Gregory remained confused. He had expected his dad's orders related to his hospitalisation. Dad's confession without any sign of sorrow was like a starting flag, allowing him to shoot ahead.

"She has a name, doesn´t she? Or did you use her like a mat?"

"You are rude, Gregory."

"I know. Oh, I should not be rude to my dear dad. Do you deserve another way of treatment? I don´t know! I´m confused! Explain to me what is right according to you, my dear dad! I love both you and mum. Is that how it should be or am I wrong? Tell me Dad! Tell me!" His adolescent hormones tangled with his growing anger. His sense of fairness pushed forward to emerge and ask about everything that remained unspoken. An awkward silence and the worming of his dad became the long-expected response.

"Coward." Gregory´s little comment was spat hoarsely into the quietness.

"I´m terribly sorry. I messed up." No mercy touched his son´s ears. There was no encouraging squeeze of the hand or a slight tap on the back, nothing. His father decided to abandon the situation and leave. The door handle was pushed down, the door was opened and the generally arrogant and selfish man shrank into himself, attempting to be as invisible as it was possible to be at that moment.

"Dad?"

His heart jumped hopefully at the tone of his son´s voice.

"Could you come tomorrow? I´d be glad if you did."

Happiness circulated through his veins but his voice was pressed down by a hefty ball that had grown inside him during the last few horrible minutes.

"I don´t need a chaperone."

"Yes, you do," Matt replied.

"You´re not my nanny."

"Yes, I am."

"What do you think you´re doing?"

"I´m accompanying you to your residence."

"Stop! I am a big girl, Dad. I can go from the bus stop to my dormitory, Dad," I said unusually slowly, emphasising each word one by one and trying hard not to laugh.

"Monkey!" Matt exclaimed as he tugged my cap down over my eyes and laughed with me.

"So, Dad, can I go?"

"No! You´ve already had one accident today."

"What accident?" Wrinkles surrounded my nose. I did not comprehend what he meant by ´accident´. "Oh yes, you mean my boozy neighbour? He is certainly in the kingdom of drunk dreams."

"Or he is resting directly on your doormat."

"O.K. So, I´ll cross him as silently as a mouse crosses a cat´s tummy. Oh, I´ve got it, you´re trembling for me." A whopping great smirk occupied the corner of my mouth.

"Princess, you first," he said, holding open the door.

"Have you begun attending a school for gentlemen?"

"Ha-ha-ha!" he laughed. The warmth of the residence foyer cuddled us, offering as much the comfort as we were able to notice, given that it seemed our chit-chat was not going to end.

"See you in the lab," I said.

"Wait, wait, wait my little princess." He dragged me back using my hood.

"Matt, that´s enough, it´s getting late. Now, I´m going to climb that staircase and you´ll let me." Pointing my forefinger to the stairs, I walked up to the first step, trying to escape if Matt would allow me to.

"Hey princess, I´m not as stupid as I look." His grip pulled my scarf, shortening the distance between us.

"Are you totally sure?" We laughed uncontrollably. The scarf throttled me: I raised my palms, expressing I had given up.

"The lift has arrived," he commented.

"You´ll have to go in without me." He raised his eyebrows, not understanding.

"Claustrophobia," I explained.

"You faker."

"O.K. Let´s go." The lift door opened, a bell rang and we started going up. For the first two floors, I felt fine. The third got fuzzy and by the finishing tinkle of the lift, I felt like I was taking my last breath of air.

"I´m such a stupid cow." I gasped slightly, not able to develop a breathing balance as my lungs refused to pump air in and out.

"Rudi, Rudi, give me your keys." He left, unlocked my room and opened the door. He then picked me up, my legs horizontal and my head resting on his shoulder.

Bang. Matt´s back hit the door to widen the space. He lay me down on my bed and opened the window, which allowed fresh cold air to flow into the room. I could hear the sound of water coming from the bathroom.

"Here you are. Drink!" Matt instructed me.

"Thanks." The glass´s contents disappeared in a moment.

"Better?" he asked. I nodded. His expression was so scared. "It was a stupid idea."

Slowly taking off my jacket, boots and thick woolly sweater and putting them at the far end of the bed, I desired deep dreams.

"Thanks. I´m exhausted, see you in the lab." Returning to my horizontal position, I instantly fell asleep.

17

"It´s the Christmas season—people go out with their friends. Be patient. Write her an email." She caressed his hair and kissed his forehead. "I´m sure she is your true friend. I must go."

"Bye Granny." There was seven hours difference between their geographical longitudes. "I should put things in order," he said to himself. With a few clicks of the mouse pointer and after connecting to the Internet, his email inbox offered him many ways to spend his time.

"Gregory, get on with it. You caused it, so solve it. Don´t be a coward." His courage was stuck somewhere between his mind and his heart. Starting the first sentence was a never-ending struggle: he typed them, reread them and removed them, again and again. Finally, he successfully finished the email to his head teacher.

> *"Dear Mister Derbhall,*
>
> *I am afraid that I must postpone my examinations to a late date. The reason is simple: I was horribly stupid. I tried to solve my troubles by drinking a large amount of alcohol. I got drunk and caused a traffic accident.*
>
> *The shame is difficult to admit—it was the stupidest thing I have ever done. I´m in hospital and the doctors do not know when my treatment will finish. I would like to ask you for another chance to do my exams.*
>
> *Cordially,*
> *Your delinquent student Gregory."*

"Now all I can do is pray he´ll accept my apology." Teasing himself, he pressed the SEND button.

He scrutinised the rows of emails for a couple of seconds to be sure he had not missed any.

"She hasn´t written yet. Look again later, Gregory." He grabbed two school books from the top of a pile on a table near his hospital bed. Within a few minutes, he had dipped into the texts and was looking for analogies, connections and the basics of the subjects. He adored learning. It was his second most favourite thing to do: observing roofs during an evening drizzle won the battle between the two favourites.

"Mr Sander, your project disappointed my expectations. The topic is robust enough to be analysed in depth. You attended the last postgraduate term at the university. And your presentation? I wonder. A sixth form student would present this project at a higher level than you. I´m giving you a B and I´m being generous to you."

"Thanks, I appreciate it." He folded his pile of study materials into his bag and shot out from the classroom. A ´B´ was fine, but this project was worth more than that: he had worked hard for weeks.

"She was right—Flywick is an idiot feeling misjudged by other people," his murmuring dropped into the space, keeping his temper under control.

Bang. A door hit the nearest wall, a result of the unexpected power of Mathew´s hands.

"Shit." A muffled sound of steps echoing along the corridor vanished into the lab. "Nobody around. That´s strange, where is everyone?" The professor´s computer was working. A quiet buzz filled the lab.

"What´s that?" He squatted down to pick up a piece of paper from the floor.

Bang. With an immediate jerk, he bumped hard into a desk. His head felt incredibly painful and an uncountable number of pins radiated in sharp pain around his temples.

"Hell! Matt, what are you doing here?!" She snapped the paper from him before he could stop her. Her little fingers wrapped around his wrist. "We have to get out of here quickly."

"Why?"

Bang! The lab door flew into the wall again. The professor stood in the middle of the door frame, looking confused. He turned suddenly and left as though an idea had hit him.

"Now!" She shouted. We did not stop until we had reached the door, where we looked up and down the corridor. Rapidly running up and down stairs, corridors and floors, we eventually got to the bottom floor.

"Rudi, does the professor know you´ve been in the lab?" We had not stopped running until the everyday bustle of the university foyer did not whirl in our cochleas. We wheezed and gasped terribly.

"Yes. I gave him my last results from Belize and said hello to him."

"And your bag and that paper on the floor of his office?" He waved it in front of her face.

"Matt, we must get out of here," she balanced her breath.

"Anywhere. A private place," Matt added.

"My room?"

"A good try. But no." The university building vanished after we walked round the nearest corner and crossed the road. We looked for any place that could allow us a wee bit of privacy. "There is a bench." Matt pointed to a wooden bench hidden under maple branches near the George Cunningham Building, a biological science centre a few blocks away from the main university building.

"I was in the lab three times. The first time, I gave my materials to the professor, then I returned as I had forgotten my bag. His computer was on; I was curious, so I looked at the screen. The Professor had written a letter to a Liverpudlian company. The words ´red wood´ attracted me. So I clicked on the field of the sender and . . ." I laid all the printed papers between us. "Read them."

"This one is from my dad, a credibility confirmation."

"Yes, this first email from the owner of the company is full of threats, saying what will happen if the professor does not follow their agreements." She picked up the printed page and ran her fingertip along the typed rows. "And here is the professor´s reply to the company owner: he mentions that he evaluated his abilities the wrong way, so he must resign from their agreements."

"Where did you arrange to print it, are you crazy? The professor could have entered the lab and caught you printing."

"Yes, but he didn´t."

"It´s wrong." Matt studied each sheet of paper in turn. "Why did the professor do it? He is an honest man, my dad believes in him."

"Don´t call your dad."

"Why?"

"This should be said in person."

"Might I call you Minerva?"

"Of course, doctor."

"It would be best for Gregory´s mental state if he stayed with you for the first few days."

"He is living with me now. But I think the boy needs his parents, his mum at least."

"Is it a problem?"

"What? Oh, no. I can see no problem in him living with my daughter-in-law."

"O.K. Gregory is waiting at the reception desk—the ambulance will take you home."

"Thank you, doctor."

He observed as the most virtuous woman that he had ever met left the room. This woman was full of grace, life experiences and wisdom and could teach anybody about respect for life. The beauty hid in her was visible to those who wanted to see it.

"Have a nice day, Minerva." Smiling, he said it more to himself than to her.

Jing. The button light reported that one of the two hospital lifts had touched the ground floor. Minerva got out of the lift, approached the reception desk and waited until her daughter-in-law had finished signing hospital forms.

"Granny?" She turned. Her face displayed satisfaction and she radiated warmth.

"Yes?"

"Can I stay with you?"

"I would be happy if you did. You both can."

"I´m freezing. I should go." I piled and folded all the scattered pieces of paper into my bag. My fingers would have enjoyed the luxury of gloves.

"Wait Rudi, I´ll go with you."

"No."

"Leave it. I´ll go."

"I have a next exam on Thursday, I need to learn," Matt said.

"Me too."

"You´ve not done the . . ."

"I swapped it around."

"How will you learn without any study materials?"

"I was going to ask you . . ."

"You are a bad dream."

"Your bad dream."

"O.K. also will we go to my room or to your?" he asked. The comical gesture of Pinocchio that he made took the wind out of my sails. I smiled and made no comment.

"I desire to be guest in your kingdom, Princess."

"We´ll learn. O.K.?!"

"Princess, you are so bumptious." I ribbed him.

"Am I wrong, cowboy? Correct me please—didn´t you ask for my help?" My woolly cap was again pulled over my eyes.

"Hurry! Our bus is coming."

"I prefer walking."

"You´ll go by bus today, life is full of changes." I turned my sight to the sky and rolled my eyes. The constant swinging of the bus let me fall asleep, leaning my head against the window.

"Princess, wake up." Shy caresses dragged me from my dreams.

Twilight was falling on the ground, which slept under a snow blanket. Street lanterns whispered their nightly songs and the frost created a few new icicles from their bends. "Run," Matt said.

"Why?"

"I´m shivering." Our run was more similar to a roe deer walking immediately after its birth than a run defined by athletics terminology. We stumbled across frozen bulges and slipped on icy puddles.

"Yes," I muttered under my breath.

"Yes?"

"Don´t you smell it?" I disappeared into the canteen. The fragrance of baked cookies and fresh coffee was like a strong drug.

"Afternoon, madam," I said, addressing the serving assistant.

"What would you like today?"

"You know me, the same as last time?" I said. She giggled.

"I´ve told you, you need a boyfriend," she replied. Matt was pressing against me, pushing his chin into my shoulder.

"Oh madam, he´s a lost individual." She put my order in a paper bag in front of me. "Have a good day, madam," I said. She shouted something juicy at us, but it fused with the chatter in the canteen.

"A lost individual?" Finally, he spat it out. He strived to unlock the door of my kingdom, I laughed, his priggish tone ringing so loud that a deaf person would have heard it.

"I like it."

"What?"

"When you´re so theatrically priggish."

"You´re terribly rude."

"I know. Shall we start?"

The floor was covered by many papers. We memorised information, asked each other questions related to the subject, explained our answers and repeated the same sequence again and again. We went through our revision topic by topic. Drawing on paper when something was totally unclear, we crossed out the topics that we had absorbed with each inch of our grey cells.

Bump! I threw all the papers on the bed.

"Tomorrow?"

"Hm." He rose and gently pressed kiss onto my forehead.

"See you tomorrow. At 2 am?"

"Hm," he replied. The door opened and closed, leaving behind a gush of air.

"Minerva?"

A delicate sound disturbed him from reading. He typed a reply. *"No, Gregory."*

"Hi, are you angry with me?"

"No. It´s fine."

"How is your injury?"

"I´ve been at Granny´s for a few hours. Mum is going to come in two days´ time."

"And your dad? Don't disconnect! I was only teasing you. It was impolite to you. It's your problem, you must solve it. It's difficult enough as it is, you don't need my stupid advice."

"It's O.K., Rudi. I argued with him. Well, I shouted at him, he just spat out two sentences. Or was it three sentences? I don't know, I was angry."

"The result?"

"He left."

"Did you let him leave so simply?"

"I told him something like 'come back tomorrow'."

"Did he come?"

"No. The doctor sent me home one day early."

"Are you in Liverpool?"

"No, at Granny's. She lives in Lancaster, I'm not sure if I already told you. Mum is going to stay with me here—Granny invited her."

"Has he called you or your granny or your mum, or made any attempt to contact you?"

"No," Gregory replied.

"Perhaps he has not been to the hospital today. I suppose he'll certainly call or the door bell will ring in a short time. He loves you, Gregory, he's your dad."

"Sometimes I'm not convinced of that fact."

"That was an ugly thing to say."

"Life is ugly."

"I thought you loved life, in spite of all your handicaps?"

"I did."

"?"

"My muscles refuse more brain commands than before."

"What about your exercises?"

"The doctor gave me an exercise schedule. It starts on Tuesday, next week."

"Hey guy, you had a traffic accident. Do you remember? Even people without your diagnosis aren't able to move for weeks if they have a crash."

"Ha-ha."

"Was it sarcasm?"

"Do you think?"

"Gregory, hello! Peek your head out from your window for a while! What can you see there? It's Christmas time! Enjoy it! Life is too short to sit on any veranda!"

"That's mean!"

"It's true—for me, for you, for anybody."

"You are unfair."

"No, I like you. If I didn't like you, I'd write lies.

"Just one little lie. Please, Rudi."

"Maybe next time, if your mood is in a better condition. ;o)"

"That was impolite," Gregory typed.

"I know. And what about your school?"

"The head teacher allowed me to do some external studying."

"When are you going to take your first exam?"

"I'm waiting for his response to my email."

"Don't you have a time schedule?"

"It got more difficult after my boozing episode."

"But you are going to pass each exam, aren't you?"

"Are you my nanny?"

"Promise me!"

"Hey Rudi, you annoy me."

"Really? Promise me!"

"Why?"

"Do it! ;o)"

"Did granny give you some lessons?"

";o)"

"O.K."

Different sounds could be heard now and then: the rustling of paper, a spoon jingle stirring coffee, the subtle howl of a cold wind behind the window panes and the squeal of a writing pen. The time remaining to answer all the theoretical questions and complete all the results of the ten numerical calculations seemed too short. I fell into my own world, not noticing the room, the examiner, the spoon jingle or the howl of the wind leaking through invisible gaps between the window frames and their transoms. With a last check, my eyes slid across the questions, ensuring that my answers were correct.

"Your time is up, Rudi."

There was no time left to check the last two questions. A dreadful stillness filled every inch of the room. I dipped into the world outside, jumping from one tree branch to another and looking for birds sitting on them, or hopping along benches.

"What else is there to say? Excellent! Your grade is an A."

"Excuse me, professor, I´m sorry, I wasn´t listening."

"I said your grade is an A."

"Thanks." My experience in the lab began biting at me again. I had shaken it off during my exam, but the thoughts now emerged from my brain. I felt awkward. On one hand I liked the professor; on the other hand, I did not know how to forgive him. He had allowed the straw to break the camel´s back. Rooting around in my bag, I was not able to look at him directly. Finally, I found it.

"Merry Christmas, professor," his eyes fell on the gift, refusing to look away.

"An angel. It´s beautiful." His fingertips tickled my palm.

"Merry Christmas, Rudi." He hugged me warmly. I would have loved to scream or yell at him, but I did not do it. Loosening the hug, I wordlessly left.

"Rudi, have you passed?"

"Yes," I responded to my classmate absent-mindedly. Thoughts were flying inside my cranial cavity like horses rotating around a carousel. I tried to push an off button. There was none.

Ring-ring-ring. A comic well-known sound switched my thoughts off. The carousel stopped.

"Rudi, honey, get the bus at 11.30. But the 37 bus is the totally wrong choice. We´ll meet in the residence foyer." The voice died.

Beep-beep-beep. I redialled.

"That´s not a good idea, my flight departure is at 6.40 am tomorrow."

"No, I´m talking about today. Everything will be sorted. Honey, be in the foyer."

Driftwood was twisted by the waves as it hit the rocky shore. A strong, chill wind continuously scattered our hair across faces; a group of trees danced in rhythm, bowing their tops in the prevailing wind´s direction. A gang of guys, who were all about 20, stood on the giant blocks of rock, their views transfixed by the ocean water.

"There, there, look there!" Everybody jumped from one block to another rock, nearing the shore to see the magnificent ocean theatre. Great dorsal fins rose above the water´s surface in a stunning synchronised motion and large black parts followed after extensive white sections, again and again. Many giant black and white bridges emerged above the water and slid back under it again in one fluid motion. I kept jumping, I was not able to stop like a marionette controlled by strings in hands of an actor: their incredible performance attracted me more and more.

I could feel the water drops dispersed in the air landing on my cheeks, I heard the ocean waves angrily hammering the rock walls and I could see their skins. One wrong move and I would have become their dinner. The ocean´s surface suddenly rose up. A giant orca´s body was cast high into the sky. It fell slowly into the ocean depths in a circling motion and vanished under the water. The last few cold drops of water rolled down my face as the water´s surface was cracked. A flashing eye above an opened muzzle with a padded tongue unexpectedly appeared and disappeared in the same way.

"Phut." A spout of liquid was shot with enormous power into the sky. I jumped; my shoes slipped on the wet rock surface and my bottom bumped on the ground. The orca shoved its body under the water. It neared the rocks and slowly revealed its head bit by bit above the surface. Goose bumps covered my entire body.

"Wow." I was stunned, amazed and wordless. Our shared piercing looks had only consumed a fleeting moment, but it seemed like the whole day had galloped away. The orca swam off and I stayed there for several minutes.

I stood up. The driftwood played its rock song as it hit against the stones, waves leaked into the sand and the excited talk of the group freely hopped about in the air.

"You are crazy. I´ve never seen anything like it. I´ve never been so near to them." I nodded, unable to push a single word through my steady lips. I was cold. Every inch of my body was cold.

"Is everything all right?"

Bum-bum-bum-bum. My gesture imitated my heartbeat.

"Your clothes are completely wet. You need some dry clothes."

Patricia´s brother took off his jacket.

"Put this on, Rudi," he said. I obeyed him. My fingers were icy chips and my skin wore a slightly blue tint.

"It´s too late guys, it´s time to go." Somebody´s voice cut the air.

The engines of three vans woke up, sparkles jumped inside their ignitions and the rocky bay was left alone. Six headlights stung the dark. Darkness settled on the shores of Lighthouse Park; the local lighthouse sent rays of light into the ocean.

A white cone, created by a table lamp near a newspaper being read by our night security guard, was the one shining point in the residence foyer.

"Thanks, sir. How was your duty today?"

"Fine, I´ve already read the whole newspaper." He locked the entrance door of residence, carefully checking each one of the four locks placed on them.

"Enjoy the rest of your night. By the way, we might not see each other again this year, so Merry Christmas and a Happy New Year."

"You too, mademoiselle," he replied politely. Leaving his wishes trailing on the ground floor, I ran up the staircase to the first floor, the second, the third and finally I reached the fourth floor. The picture of my warm bed got more and more attractive. The excitement circling around my veins had helped me to forget I was freezing. I shoved my hand inside my pocket to find my keys: I chose the wrong one. A small object wrapped in paper touched my fingertips. I dipped my second hand into my other pocket and pulled the keys out. Trying to find the keyhole immersed in the dark stretching along the corridor, I detected the wrapped subject in my other hand. The genial warmth invited me in. I snapped on the light switch, sat on a wooden shoe cupboard and unwrapped the item as quickly as my frozen fingers would allow me to.

"An orca, how beautiful. Thank you, Patricia. Merry Christmas honey." I bowed down to loosen my shoelaces. A creak distracted me.

"Hell! You are such an idiot!" I screamed at him, my heart devilishly jumping in my chest. "You´ll kill me one day!"

"I´m sorry. I didn´t mean to frighten you." Matt muttered under his breath.

"Close the door." I placed my outer clothes on the radiator. I desperately needed to occupy my mind with any activity to calm myself down. "I need a hot shower, so spit it out."

"I´ll wait."

I vanished behind the bathroom door. Hot water drops tingled everywhere: they hurt my skin and processed deeper, near to my bones.

"I got an A." Zipping up my jogging jacket, I sat down on the floor. I liked the tickling sensation caused by the carpet´s many small woolly threads.

"Fine, I congratulate you. Is that the reason why you were waiting for me for hours, stalking me in the dark?"

"No."

"What then?" A silent gap rose in our conversation. "Fine. I´ve got three hours to pack, call a taxi and sleep. I´m really happy you came, but I need a short sleep."

"Where are you going?" His voice wore a tone full of wonder.

"Home?"

"You´ve not mentioned it to me."

"You´ve not explained to me what I did wrong. Have I humiliated you in some way? I can´t understand it."

"Why?"

"Why? I didn´t think you were that stupid. Your fan club full of nice faces enjoyed your jokes on my account greatly. Unfortunately, I accidently went by. I heard every word. Wait, I remember. No, rather no, I might vomit, and there is no time for cleaning. Could you close the door from the corridor side?"

"No."

"O.K." I resigned. Untidy things were piled in the bottom part of my luggage and tidy things and cosmetic cases were put on top of them. I packed in the materials for my last exam, books and my laptop. Finally, I placed my personal documents in my smart backpack. After half an hour, I buried myself under the quilt like a mole in its home.

"3.10." I had woken up before the alarm had begun beeping. He was sleeping opposite me. The upper part of his body was spread on the desk. The rest was in a sitting position on the chair. Moving mouse-like, I grabbed all my items and evaporated from the room.

"Merry Christmas," I whispered. Running down the stairs, I left four floors behind me. I waved to the security guard as he locked the door and my baggage was swallowed by the car boot. I slid into the taxi.

"Hi Rudi, to the airport?"

"Yes, sir. It´s nice to see you again."

The taxi parking lot at Vienna airport was snowless; all the pavements were naked, the entrance and exit roads were without any snowflakes or icy strips and salt grains were visibly scattered across them. In spite of the fact that Mrs Winter held the mace strongly in her hands, there were no snow-stains on the roads of the airport. Taxi left its taxi lot, its aim was my home city. Routes were edged by fields under heavy layers of snow, icicles decorated tree branches, herds of roe deer grouped around feeding places, rabbits and pheasants looked for food here and there, and villages decorated by the white and grey surroundings were scattered along these roads. In the distance, a brightly coloured castle towered on a hill keeping an eye on its city, a bridge with a UFO-tower-restaurant invited newcomers and residents alike. Old Mr Danube equably flowed along his watercourse, dividing the ancient part of the town from the new. A lovely-looking park dedicated to eminent writers slept. A shopping centre with a business tower at its edge patiently guarded this cluster of trees night after night. I had missed this scene so much. I was home.

After a few minutes in the taxi, Svatopluk´s Fort waved at me from its hill, towering above the confluence of the two most famous rivers of this part of the world, where history had been created at the hands of clever emperors.

"Thank you, sir." He handed me my luggage from the boot, wished me a nice day, slammed the taxi door and drove off.

The phone tune disturbed my mum from her unfinished activity.

"Hi, Mum."

"Rudi?"

"Is it possible to take the key out of the lock?"

"Excuse me?"

"The bell isn´t working."

"Which bell, Rudi?"

"Your doorbell, Mum. I would love to come in."

134

18

The everyday bustle of the high school corridors flooded through every metre of their lengths. Two examination-filled weeks made sense of a never-ending story. Chit-chat, jokes, laughter or some repines echoed every now and again around the school´s walls. Christmas time did not make any of the test questions easier and did not affect the minds of any teacher in examining the answers. A marvellous-smelling fir or spruce stood in the corner of every classroom, decorated with many rainbow-coloured glassy balls, bells, angels or stars in a variety of sizes, reminding the students the whole time that amazingly generous gifts awaited them.

"Morning, madam. Mr Derbhall confirmed that I can join my class and take your test today."

A lock in the door frame separated the class space from the potential corridor rustle and provided a safe silence for students attempting to answer test questions as well as their knowledge enabled them to.

"O.K. people, put your pens down and put your test papers at the edge of your desks. Katy, would you be so polite and gather the tests, then bring them to my table? Thanks."

A fairly loud murmur, chatting and vocal answer comparisons danced among the desks and streamed out into the corridors through the door. The now-recognised results became the basis for pleasure and for depression too.

Two wheels crossed the door line, spinning around their axes and slipping on the tiles. He knocked on the door and it opened.

"Oh, Gregory, come in."

"Thanks, madam."

"Did you enjoy your equator holiday?"

"It was fine, madam."

"Just fine?" A mischievous grin hopped around her lips and coquettish sparkles burned in her eyes. Her behaviour switched on indescribable flames inside him.

"Madam, I would like ask you for a date for a vocal exam."

"Next week, on Tuesday?" Looking at him directly, her attraction increased.

"Tuesday is fine."

"Fine, is that your favourite word? Here are some URLs that will help in your studies. Check them out, they are really very interesting texts." Her fingers accidentally swept the sheet over the table's edge. It glided fluidly down, landing on Gregory's lap. In an attempt to capture the paper, their hands met; he gently grabbed her wrist, checking whether she would deny his grip or she would pull her arm away, but nothing happened. His lips brushed her skin inch by inch, rolling her sleeve up. Her reaction took his breath away: there was no hesitation, no tendency to finish a few tactful manoeuvres. Just a straight attack. Her fingers vigorously dragged the zip of his jeans down, freed the way and wrapped themselves around his member, moving up and down in a skilled motion. Her other hand forced Gregory's palm to knead her mons veneris. The wet emulsion leaking through the fabric of her underwear startled him. Clothes were scattered on the floor in a fragment of time. She shamelessly straddled his lap, looking directly into his eyes as her palms squeezed his shoulders. His fingers played continuously with her private parts and her nipples were tenderly cuddled by his fingertips. Her tights slid down. She slowly neared to his lap. His member slid into that kingdom of secret delight, their lips fused into one, their tongues became tangled and the motions of her pelvis caused many shots to pulse around his pelvis, again and again. He wanted to scream to tint their sexual act and lead it to perfection, but he could not afford to do it. The office walls were too thin to keep a delightful howl behind them. Nobody would accept their behaviour.

A tram rattle leaked through the windows into the inside: the repeated sound of metal tracks caused me to fall asleep every now and then. Almost all the seats were empty. The majority of the passengers had got off the public vehicle a few stops earlier, in the old town. Only alumni remained. The upcoming city district consisted of several university buildings and residences scattered across local valleys and hills closed in a grey and white forest amphitheatre. The mid-tram door stretched open to both sides. The empty space offered the resting people a possibility to inhale the fresh chilled air and hit the icy pavement and create a few awkward dance figures, unintentionally. The old habit of the public pavement services in my home town was, that this company had never noticed, than the frost changed pavements of the city to one big ice-stadium. Any pair of skating shoes would have been a better choice than the commonly used boots. A concrete staircase towered in front of me, leading from the stop to a bridge and levitating above the road, trails and pavements connecting residences and dormitories to a university yard. It reflected the lamp light rays falling on its frozen surface. After a moment I had made my decision: I slid across a zebra crossing, climbed a short slope and reached the first quarter of my alma mater's area.

"Morning, sir. How's your duty been?" I asked. The familiar clerk in the information cabin continued solving his crossword puzzle.

"Morning. Well, thank you." Smiling, he kept on with his former job. I was almost at the canteen's entrance when he suddenly shouted at me.

"Oh, I almost forgot. The chemistry lab practice today has been cancelled—Professor Davidova is ill." Standing in the middle of the corridor, he shouted the pertinent information. He was waiting for my answer, I supposed.

"It is alright, sir. I´m going to the Department of Soil Science." He satisfyingly nodded and entered his glass cabin to continue his work.

"Strange." I checked the actual time.

"6.55, where are they all?" I sat down on the steps that headed directly to the Department of Zoology. Time was flowing and I got bored.

"I´ll check my emails." Unzipping my laptop bag, many thoughts tickled my grey brain cells and many memories bounced around my cranial walls, tangling together and causing confusion. And then they unexpectedly loosened and everything became clear.

Ping-ping.

"Who is online?" I wondered out loud. I clicked on the Skype button.

"Hi Rudi, you´re on holiday, aren´t you? Why aren´t you sleeping yet?"

"Me? It is 6.15 in Britain, isn´t it?"

"Yes, I´m revising my project. It needs to be finished today and given to my history teacher."

"So what´s new?"

"I made love with my teacher."

"?"

"I made love with my teacher."

"Wow!"

"Wow?"

"What was it like?" I asked, shocked.

"Are you joking? You are from a different unknown dimension."

"Wow. Which seduction trick did you use?

"None. She seduced me."

Monika Pistovčák

"Wow! Where?"

"In her office."

"Wow! ;o) Have you fallen in love with her?"

"She is a teacher."

"And?"

"I love making love with her. If you tried it, you would like to do it again. You know it."

";o)"

"You have experienced it, haven't you? ;o)"

"Hm."

"Rudi, have you experienced it?"

"NO!"

"No? How old are you?"

"O.K. What are you doing for Christmas?"

"Rudi, you are, let's say, 23 years old. Am I right?"

"Almost twenty. And, no, I haven't made love. Is that a crime?"

"No, but I can't understand the reason."

"Probably just that men don't like me."

"You? Is that a joke?"

"No, it's reality. What is the topic of your project?"

"Don't change the subject, Rudi!"

"Gregory, I don't want to continue with this conversation."

"O.K."

A long time later my senses perceived a moving in the corridor; alumni trickled into a classroom in front of the steps where I sat waiting for my dear friend of the Department of Soil Science.

138

"I don´t believe what my eyes can see," someone said. I knew that voice.

"Gregory, I´ve got to go, I´ll cross my fingers for you. Bye."

Several quick actions closed the whole operating system, the screen got dark and the laptop slid into my backpack. I wondered, looking for the source, why I thoroughly wanted to be erased or evaporated at that moment. Why?

"Where have you been for such a long time, fuck!"

"It´s nice to see you too." I grinned. Perhaps I had found the reason: Daniel´s manner.

"It´s nice to see you again, my chocolate." Lifting me up and embracing me in a bear hug, he scrutinised me like a microscope lens, not giving me a chance to be offended.

"A new nickname for me?" I asked with a theatrically hoarse voice.

"Your skin is brown, baby."

"Of course, turn left twice, round the next corner to the right and five metres from Honolulu there it is, Vancouver."

"How I´ve missed your sarcasm."

"Could you put me down?" The left part of his face made an unidentifiable grimace. Nearing some corridor windows, the space between the window and us got smaller. Feeling the cold radiating through the glass from outside, my feet touched the floor.

"Hey Daniel, is the practice cancelled today?" The approaching voice was so familiar. The Skype chat must have swallowed my whole mind. I had not noticed when he had arrived or if he had been there earlier to prepare things for the lesson. The head tried to peek out above Daniel´s shoulders without any success. I squatted to escape his trap.

"Morning, professor."

"Professor, I´m joining your lecture. That´s O.K., isn´t it?" The professor´s unexpected appearance saved me. Without waiting for a response, I landed on a chair inside the projection room of the Department of Soil Science.

"I am already going. Checkmate, professor." Daniel looked down at him from his height, passing by him through the door frame.

"I´ve missed this, the tomcat and the mouse," professor grinned, entering the space as the lecture started.

"Be calm, Madam Minerva. Everything is under control. He´s stabilised. His heart is pumping properly." Minerva´s glance had pierced the doctor´s face for more than a quarter of an hour. Storing data in her brain cells, she strived to identify the cause.

"His specialist gave us all the details of Gregory´s DMD. He mentioned it, but . . ." The words got stuck in the middle of her larynx, refusing to proceed upwards.

"You knew that congestive heart failure is one of the many possible symptoms accompanying DMD," he spoke the words singularly and carefully to not frighten her. Her eyes kept piercing his side, sucking in each line of the doctor´s explanation.

He continued. "I´m sure Gregory has regularly attended all his medicals, so I´m persuaded that you are familiar with all the possibilities related to the progress of DMD. Right-sided heart failure can appear as one of the many possibilities of heart failure."

"Right-sided heart failure?" Her pupils jumped from one corner of her eyes to another, searching for the correct answer on the doc´s lips.

"A condition that causes failure mainly affecting the heart´s right side."

"That means . . ." She had a confused expression. There was an awkward silence and an uncomfortable wait for an explanation; the corridor felt busier than a brief instant before and a peculiar apprehension leaked into every cubic millimetre.

"There are two causes for heart failure: chronic conditions that influence the heart´s state in the long term, or heart failure that arrives suddenly without any warning. In the majority of cases, this kind of failure causes greater damage to one half of the heart than to the other."

"Is that Gregory´s case?"

"Yes, it is."

"What are you going to do, doc?"

"First, I am going to monitor his heart for several days. Following that, I´ll start an appropriate treatment."

"Is it possible that it will happen in the future?

"Yes, many times."

"Can I see him?"

"Yes, I think he would like that." He squeezed her delicate shoulder and gave her an encouraging smile. He left. She stood there, on her own. She looked through the glass wall into the room, took a deep breath and mustered all her remaining courage. The uncountable variety of tubes, which helped his body to control his respiratory system, looked terrible. He seemed so fragile. She squeezed the door handle, which gave an unnoticeable click. His eyelids fluttered and he slowly stretched a painful and weak smile across his face. He drew breath trying to press words through his lips. None were heard, just the sound of mouth muscles in motion. With a goose bump-inducing dragging noise, she pulled a chair up to his bed and sat on it. She caressed his forehead, touched his wet hair and let her calmness flow via her palm into his skin. Deep silence, serenity and warmth said everything that could never have been said with words.

"Where is Mum?" A hoarse, trembling voice filled the space with childish dread.

"At the desk, she´s just signing all the necessary paperwork. She´ll come, don´t worry honey."

"Почиму это невозможно зделать? Это уже две недели, когда мой запрос выл отправен."
(Why is it so difficult? It took two weeks when I sent my request.)

He constantly paced around his office. The panorama behind the window attracted always his attention. He let his eyes drift down roofs powdered with tiny snow blankets, but then his impatient nature distracted him and forced him to pace at a more rapid speed from the window to a small coffee table in the middle of the opposite wall, again and again.

"Никакое подтверждение у них ненаходится до сегодняшнего дня. Это очень интересноя информация. Способо дорогая Анна, я позвоним Вас когда это дело будет наделёное полномочиями."
(They haven´t obtained confirmation yet; this is frightfully compelling information. Thank you, dear Anna, I´ll call you when they have confirmation.)

Their phone call finished, he set at a computer, connected to the Internet and a hellish typing hovered in the room. Each cubic inch of the air was crammed with growing aggression as rows were added to the text.

"Дерьмо!"
(Shit!)

The majority of the written text was unfortunately wiped off the email by a sudden touch of the bottom of his palm on an optic and extremely sensitive mouse. A ringing phone dragged him out from his wrath, which absorbed his person completely. He jumped.

"Yes, I´m listening." His snapping answer cut through the air. As the call progressed, his face got more and more stiff and lifeless.

"Сердце, в катораю больницу он был транспортирован?"
(Honey, what is the hospital that accepted him like?)

"Кде ты была, когда ты допустила что они переезли его в ту саму грязную больницу?"
(Where have you been, you let him be transported to the same dirty hospital?)

"Что!? Кде я был? Что? Это какой то вопрос?"
(Excuse me!? Where have I been!? What´s sort of question is that!?)

"Я буду визжать, всё время, когда мне это будет нравиться."
(I will shout whenever I consider it is appropriate.)

Beep-beep-beep. He looked at the receiver in surprise: he did not believe that she had been brave enough to finish the call first. His fierce re-dialling was disrupted by the buzzing of a mobile phone vibrating on the coffee table and twisting around on its axis, without any let-up and impatiently. He left the receiver at the computer. With two long steps, he grabbed it.

"Yes?"

"Филип, тебе надо приехать безотлагательно. Вещи в Спаныш Лоокоут двинуться не правильныйным курсом. Пошли детально твое данные для твоего прилёта."
(Fillip, it is necessary to arrive immediately. The issues in Spanish Lookout are progressing in the wrong course. Send me your arrival information.)The urgent voice flew into his ear from the mobile.

The caller did not give him an opportunity to protest or negotiate. The order was clear: get there as quickly as flights during the Christmas period would allow him to.

19

"Any questions, people?" I scrutinised their faces one by one during the lecture on forest populations on the equator, their production of biomass, their sustainability and the potential and real dangers to them. Finally, I made a direct comparison with forest populations in central Europe, including all the aspects of our, later my, research. I hoped that the presentation was interesting enough that the audience would not think that their time had been wasted.

"Any questions?" I repeated

"Yes, I have one."

"O.K. Ask away."

"Why did you choose the equator?"

"The most visible differences among species conception, maybe." I knew that voice. He had no interest in the project. His intention was hidden, known by him and me only.

"Any other questions, anyone?" Encouraging them, I switched projector off, piled files, stuck them in my backpack together with the laptop.

"What about boys, Rudi?" He drilled an imaginary screw in a hole to detect any piece of information that could be useful to him. People giggled and turned towards him.

"Not bad. No problem to choose," I laughed. I had not expected such a frontal attack. It seemed I would be forced to play word ping-pong with him. Our audience encouraged us. Note taking, laughter and a pretty loud buzzing sound floated in the classroom.

"Would you like to do your verbal graduate exam earlier?" The professor caught me off guard, requiring an answer immediately. I doubted whether his decision to save me was done at the right moment. Nobody had known that I had joined the last two school years together to apply for the scholarship at UBC. This project had only been offered to graduate alumni in this year. I had wanted to win it or bunk off: I was not sure what the genuine reason was. An awkwardly long silence stretched in all directions around the classroom. Nothing hit me, nothing clever was said.

"A call of nature urges me. Thank you, everybody, see you next time." Such a stupid comment had not dropped from my mouth since I had been in nursery. I evaporated from the space, wanting to fuse with the linoleum spreading along the corridors. The bathroom door slammed behind me but I did not snap on the light switch. Hidden in the dark of the women´s bathroom, I calmed myself, trying to fix the emotions messing with my feelings. I had thought, I had forgotten, I had forgiven.

"Something was grasped wrongly," a male voice said. I jumped a little bit, not expecting him. I closed the door of my stall to consolidate myself.

"O.K. What´s the problem? Tell me." Face to face, Daniel´s eyes pointed at my eyes. My chin cocked to the side.

"No problem, honey," I replied. "So leave me be if you are able to be so magnanimous."

"What about that guy in the photos of your project?" he asked. I smirked. A pleasant, delicate tickle suddenly appeared in my tummy.

"Wow, the young chap is jealous. I don´t believe it. Don´t worry, I´ll be silent like a grave." I shoved my hands in my pockets and whistled, leaving him with his sarcasm. Swinging my hips from side to side, I enjoyed provoking him.

"Rudi, stop! I was an idiot!"

"Is that a sorry?"

"Hm."

"Is it?"

"Yes."

"Fine. When shall we see each other next?"

"A small, dirty pub?"

"At 1.20? Did you lose your last grey cell?"

"At 6 in M.A.S.H," he replied. I liked that student pub. All the university´s alumni from every surrounding institution went there to have fun, to let it all hang out.

"O.K. See you at 6."

"Where are you?"

"On the shopping centre bridge, just two minutes away. I´m looking straight ahead."

"O.K. I´m at Saint Oliver."

"I´ll be there."

I had always wondered why Laura´s thumbs weren´t bigger, as every time I met her she was chatting with a friend via her BlueBerry mobile phone. I was the happy owner of a simple Nokia mobile, which did not supply the free chat feature that BlueBerry phones did. So I was saved: I did not have to answer her queries a hundred times a day. Snaking over to her, my palms covered her eyes. She stopped writing, turned around and hugged me very tightly.

"Honey, honey, wait, I can´t breathe!" Almost three weeks had passed since I had returned home from Canada. Laura´s school responsibilities and her synchronised swimming training occupied all her free time. It was nearly impossible to meet up with her. Our battlefield was closed when we recognised that our physical ability was at the same level and there could be no winner. Mum surely wrote it in her memoirs as one of the most pivotal events in her daughters´ lives: she had not believed that our rivalry would end. A pair of Siamese twins was born in front of her sight. It would have been fine if we had not been wearing gadabout shoes. Muddling along, we went through an unbelievably crazy episode and got into big trouble many times. We simply enjoyed the presence of each other, carelessly. This had not changed.

"Let´s go, I want to show you something," she said. I hated it when her voice got mysterious. Her fist clenched my wrist. We passed a flock of people worming through a vast shopping centre. They had woken up and recognised that the Christmas period had pressed a door handle down and the door had been left ajar. They were everywhere, swarming around each shop, occupying seats in open cafés and pushing fruit cakes down their throat pipes, or elbowing at shop counters to win first place in a queue and snap up the last piece of anything that could be transformed into the perfect Christmas gift.

"I hate this Christmas shopping madness. Laura, stop!"

"Shout up, darling!" she replied. I stomped on one of the ends of her extremely long scarf. A loop wrapped around her neck and choked her a little bit. Her warning face appeared a few inches in front of mine, nose to nose. We giggled.

"It is worth undergoing this torture. You will be a nice girl and you will pretend you love it, honey." She emphasised every word, the corners of her lips dancing up and down. "You´ll pay for that, honey." She held my gaze with strong, direct contact; neither her eyes nor mine moved at all. "Let´s go." She grabbed my wrist again. A wooden village hidden in the belly of the central shopping corridor showed us its beauty. Old handicrafts came to life. They painted all the stalls with a kind of nostalgia and kindness that did not support an absurd and unreasonable Christmas rush.

"Look!" Laura shouted. A transparent glass globe was covered with an uncountable number of engraved ornaments and holes in different shapes. It was placed on a wooden desk among other nice objects, but none were as amazing as the globe.

"What is it?" I wondered how to use it. The practical part of my character would have liked to know how, but admiration for the aesthetic aspect overwhelmed me. "A lampshade. Is it for mum?" I asked. With a nod, no words and one triumphant wink, she satisfyingly smirked.

"Wow, unbelievable," I commented.

"Who is the winner? Say it loudly and emphasise each letter. Laura is the winner," she said. With my head cocked, I laughed. My whole body laughed, from my insides to my lips. My hands had to hold my belly, it hurt me so much.

"Laura is the winner!" I screamed above the heads of the crowd. They noticed nothing and hurried on.

Uproarious laughter, the tapping of pint glasses, clashing, creaking and many other different noises hovered under the ceiling of the M.A.S.H pub. The air was rich with cigarette smoke or some other kind of smoking fragrances mixed with the fresh air molecules coming in from the entrance. Colourful glass baubles, tears with snowflakes, stars and chains made from coniferous twigs decorated the banister and walls, or a sticky bar full of beer or coca stains. The alumni were enjoying their last pre-holiday drink with their classmates and girl or boyfriends, perhaps with their favourite professors or lecturers as well. I again sucked in that familiar atmosphere. It was my last Christmas at the university. It sounded strange. I had decided to leave these things that I liked for one year.

"Good evening, people." I finally found a table, my classmates and friends sat at it.

"You owe me five euro, Daniel." Hummingbird, a quiet classmate with an eloquent nickname, stretched his flat palm directly under Daniel´s chin, shaking his fingers up and down to urge him to pay.

"Did you bet? I don´t believe that half of your win is mine." My arm shot out to Hummingbird.

"Why?"

"How many euros would you obtain if I didn´t keep my word?"

"Also . . ." My palm remained in the same position. Two euros landed on my palm.

"Fifty cents, I miss them," Professor Somak giggled. I joined in. Fifty cents were picked up from the table we were sat around and placed unwillingly in front of me.

"Thanks, darling, now everything´s O.K. Seven beers please!" Shouting at a waitress, I attempted to attract her attention: success came after the first try. Seven pin glasses full of cheering liquid met the flat table surface.

"Seven euros, please." The waitress was waiting for her money.

"Seven fifty." A ten euro note, flatted between my fingers, slid into the waitress´ hand.

"Thanks."

"You are welcome." A pourboire-bell rang a few times.

"Where is your darling Daniel?" A question full of irony addressed to Daniel flew above the table.

"Here is my darling." His look pointed at me.

"I didn´t think Rudi, I´m spiking about your Camilla." The remaining members joined Christopher in teasing Dan. Dan dragged me aside from the professor and Iva, my head tutor.

"Can we finish our chat, darling?" I produced an affected voice. The whole table broke into sniggers.

"Have you already experienced her theatre performances?" Christopher´s teasing went on.

"What?" I was not able to understand the topic of their conversation.

"It was the perfect Cam imitation." Iva silently cleared the shot message addressed to Daniel.

"It was a joke." The repetition of my tone caused uncontrollable comments to be flung in all directions. I had never seen a boy address as many jokes to his girlfriend as Daniel did. Tears were rolling down my face as I laughed. My jaw muscles hurt me, and my belly as well. I could not stop it nor did I want to. I simply enjoyed that moment. Dan´s arm rested on my shoulder. We exchanged looks from time to time, teasing each other to entertain the rest of the group. With the growing number of rounds of beers and my colas, my eyes constantly checked the wall clock. It read 7.55.

"What are you doing?"

"I´m leaving."

"No."

"Yes, darling, I am."

"I´m going home tomorrow," Dan protested stubbornly, like a spoilt child.

"Oh, I almost forgot." Lifting the small items wrapped in paper sheets, decorated with tiny twinkling ribbons, I put them under the noses of their new owners.

"Rudi, I told you, I´m going home tomorrow."

"I heard you, darling, but I promised. I´m expected at the Christmas market in the old town at 8.30."

"So, see you in May?"

"It seems that way, yes." No hint of a taunt.

"That was an ugly thing to say."

"Yes, it was. Merry Christmas, people." I hugged everyone sincerely and tightly. I really liked them.

"Don´t run again, Rudi. Is that possible?" The professor´s whispering tickled my eardrum. Surprise and incomprehension covered my face. "He adores you," his whisper continued.

"He adores himself, and his girlfriend too, I hope."

"Are you blind, Rudi?"

"I used to be blind and naive, but no more. It hurt."

"Running isn´t a solution."

"I don´t run. I must go. Merry Christmas." I kissed him on his cheek warmly and pressed a small thing in his palm. I felt for a short while like his granddaughter again.

The cold air took me aback. My squinting lids allowed me to more clearly see a number on the top of a shield screen. A tram was nearing me. My feet started running towards a stop approximately a hundred metres away. An awkward snap halted me, making me jump.

"The next one will come."

"Why did you do that? Do you think it´s funny?" I loosened his grip, slipping my forearm away. I ran again, more quickly, more angrily. The tram was my aim.

"No, wait!" A grip caught my shoulder, a weak hint of an unspoken prayer obscured under a temporary veil of his arrogance. He spat the words, but his eyes were soft.

"Leave me alone, please!"

"No! I´ll accompany you if you listen to me, just for a second."

"Why? Have I asked for your company?"

"Stop, please." The ´please´ I had never experienced before; ´please´ had never dropped from his lips. "For you." His opening fist divulged a miniature round thing. Our shadows made the space between us seem much darker than it really was. No ideas, no guesses came to me. I stood there, frozen, not able to give any reaction, wishing my ears would have listened to the rattling sound of tram rails and wanting to be swallowed by its doors, trapped inside.

"A walnut?" My teeth helped me to remove a glove, revealing my fingertips to the pretty strong frost. They traced along the nut´s shell.

"Open it," his eyebrows disappeared behind his woolly cap in expectation.

"A ring?" As if I had been stung by a bee, I shoved the walnut box into a pocket of his jacket, turned around and headed to the closest zebra crossing. Big sky blue neon letters cast their light rays one the pavement. The sign contained many small twinkling light bulbs and read *"THE INSTITUTE OF HYDROMETEOROLOGY"*. The banner, which was placed on the twelfth floor of the building, winked at passers-by. His arms wrapped me, preventing me from continuing my rapid walk.

"I was an idiot, I know." I was lost in the middle of a bear cuddle. "Don´t run, Rudi." A desperate urge to shrug off this illusion fought against the feelings trying to win their own battle inside me.

"Am I good?" His question attracted me. Looking at him through blades of grass and the stalks of flowers, I sought to discern what he meant by his strange question.

"No. Why should you be?" His fingertips played with a tiny ring.

"Wow." Putting my arms at right angles, I propped myself into an upright position and looked at the beautiful little circle braced between my two fingertips. I was afraid of touching such a fragile thing. Stalks tangled in one natural wire, forming an almost true circle. They connected into one piece under a subtle daisy head surrounded by forget-me-not miniature blooms, creating the most breath-taking jewel I had ever seen.

"Am I handy?"

"Nature is handy."

"Say it. Daniel is handy." He raised his eyebrows, cocked his head and a giggling dropped into the air. His head popped up above the flood of flowers and grass around us and he rolled towards me. Face to face, he demanded my clear answer.

"Say it. Daniel is handy."

"No. Why?" I laughed.

"Because I am."

"Daniel is selfish and bumptious." Chuckling, I pulled myself out of his body snare.

"You lie."

"Look there. Can you see that thistle?"

"That tall one with the enormous purple bloom on its tip?"

"Yes, exactly."

"What?"

"That's you, a tall, bumptious and arrogant young man covered with many prickles that allow nobody to touch him."

"You are a rude little ladybird in the middle of that thistle," he retorted. My raised eyebrows were brimmed with some low wrinkles. A slight touch to my chin directed the head to catch the topic. A small red beetle swung on the thistle, basking its dotted wings and soaking up warm sunbeams. My body shivered all over, causing many fluttering butterflies to tickle the insides of my tummy. My sight slid down to my hand. The flower ring decorated my middle finger. The twinkles in his pupils produced unusual goose bumps on my skin. His forefinger brushed my lips and our noses touched for a fragment of a second.

"Marry me, Rudi," he said. I recoiled away.

"Is that a joke?"

"No, marry me."

"It's a bet, isn't it?"

"It's no bet. Marry me."

"Do you love me?" After a silent gap I stood up and brushed all the stalks, leaves and other parts of plants off my clothes. On a path below the meadow's hill, a group of guys were returning to our camp. As the minutes passed, I scooted closer and joined them.

"Where's Dan?"

"There!" Hummingbird pointed to his direction.

"Hey, Rudi, has he told you the news?"

"News? No, I have no idea."

"He has been engaged for four days."

"Oh, that's good."

"Do you know Camilla?" I put the earphones of an MP3 player into my ears, which protected me against the world around me. The French music arrested all my senses. No bad joke, no teasing or snickering got a free ticket to accompany me during my own movie created by the different stories coming to me via my earphones.

I loosened the bear cuddle. Blue neon rays coloured our faces. A bus was nearing its stop several metres away from us.

"Merry Christmas, Dan."

"Wait."

"I would love to, but Cam trusts you. Don´t be a jerk again. Merry Christmas." The bus opened one of its three doors. I got on and pressed the door knob to close them.

"I´m so sorry!" His words trailed behind the shut wings of the doors.

"It´s too late, Dan. Being a coxcomb is pretty hard work." I was glad this chapter of my life was over. I locked it away deep within my heart, hoping to never draw a key out to unlock it and allow my stirring feelings to act instead of my brain. But I had expected something different. I was waiting for a flood of pleasure or freedom. None came. I felt like a loser.

20

"Looking good, girls." Many wrinkles caused by pillows marred our faces. Our pale skin absorbed all the freckles that could have perhaps created a healthier look. Our hair was bundled with brown rubber bands into uncertain forms: the final masterpieces were remarkably similar to bird nests. The one difference was the hair colours: red honey blonde against raven black.

"Mum is joking. Have you noticed?"

"Look in a mirror, darling."

"No, I´m not going to spoil my morning. Meeting ghosts is postponed to a later date," Laura said, she made a grimace.

"I estimate, it was a pretty good Christmas party, tomorrow, wasn´t it."

"A little bit more drinks than usual, Mum."

"Our Christmas tree is still naked."

"No, really? Where?" It was hard work to keep our poker faces and to not break into laughter.

"It stops the dog´s kennel from toppling over." Mum accepted mine and Laura´s game.

"Mum, we haven´t have breakfast yet. Later, mum, later."

"Breakfast at eleven?"

We settled in front of our TV set to absorb as many fairy tales as the TV offered; it was hard work deciding because of the number of channels. Christmas traditions forbade us from eating meat during Christmas Day. Vanilla crescent cookies were available among a number of other sweet Christmas goodies, as well as salt pastries and other dishes related to Christmas. Our traditions included lentil soup for keeping money in the house during the coming year, honey spread on an extremely tiny and fragile circle pastry for a pleasant life and fried fish with boiled potatoes as a reward for anybody who fasted the whole day. When we were children, we used to steal pieces of food when we thought the coast was clear. Our childhood naivety had caused a smile to play on Mum´s lips. The theft of forbidden food was the second best thing on Christmas Day. The first best came immediately after finishing Christmas dinner. When a small glass bell tinkled on the Christmas tree, of course at the hand of some adult family member, we had to go into the living room to discover all the secret gifts placed under the tree. That was the first best thing. I had liked this time as a child and I still adored it.

"Where is Dad, Granny?"

"No idea, but I´m sure he´ll appear at any moment." She was playing with his hair, observing the changes on his face after reading each of his many Christmas greetings emails. Happiness and warmth could be seen in his expression; he became cheerful and satisfied. Any stress was evident neither on his face nor within, she supposed. The strange sounds of working machines buzzed and beeped in repeating periods. Christmas decorations created a faded illusion of home: there was no cinnamon or gingerbread smell and no carols hovering in the air. In spite of this, it was enough. They enjoyed the presence of the decorations and soaked each moment up. They shared their wishes, composed responses to his emails and laughed at crazy pictures. After one tiny click and a minute of loading, their idyll was disturbed by a familiar voice.

"Hi, Gregory. I want to wish you Merry Christmas. Some issues arose a few days ago and it was necessary for me to solve them. I´m sure you´ll get better. We´ll see you soon. I love you." Gregory clicked on the small cross in the corner and Dad´s face disappeared. The application was shut down.

The twinkling stars in Gregory´s pupils died and he submerged deeper and deeper. Any explanation was refused: an uncontrollable anger rose in him from second to second.

"Granny, I would like to sleep." The words dropped through his clenched teeth. She stood up, left her chair and hesitantly vacated the room. She understood but she was disappointed as well. His reaction was exaggerated. His father had never been there for anybody. Living with Gregory´s father was always according to his exact rules. She had thought Gregory had got used to living with his dad´s egocentric decisions. She recognised she had been wrong. Approaching a coffee machine, all her thoughts focused her son.

´Why is he like that? I never brought him up that way. Where did I go wrong?´ Questions whirled around her brain, creating a never-ending circle. A button was unconsciously pressed, a Styrofoam cup was filled and a lovely scent tickled her nose cells. Sitting on one of several padded chairs connected in a line, she sipped the coffee, relaxing in the calmness of the hospital corridor. She was exhausted. Her head lolled against the wall. Her approaching sleep was interrupted by a sudden rush. Orders cut through the air and doctors and nurses ran along the corridor. She straightened up.

"Oh, no!" She jumped up immediately as the last nurse disappeared behind the door. She watched the rescue scene as if it were a bad dream. Every member of the team became part of a precise machine inside an expensive Swiss watch. No instructions flew in that hush: looks were enough to determine whether each of them should act or move back to make room for someone else to fight for Gregory´s life.

"Установи этой факт! Я не ехал здесь что бы ты мне сказал что нашу торговлю не возможно произвести! Жди!"
(Check it! I have not come here to listen, it´s impossible to deal with it! Wait!)

He specified a particular address to the taxi driver and leaned against the seat to continue his phone call.

"Оговори условия для нашей встречи!"
(Sort out all the meeting conditions!)

He listened for a short while. His face reddened and his lips trembled.

"Как же это нет необходимное! Зделай как я скзал! Позвони когда ты будеш знать определённый срок!"
(Don´t tell me what is necessary! Do what I say! Call me after arranging an exact date!)

The municipal airport parking lot yawned with emptiness, so the taxi easily chose a place. A minute passed and then the passenger´s baggage was swung in a walking rhythm, gripped by the taxi driver´s hand. Several small runways supplied a couple of private six to twelve-seat airplanes with narrow stands. The captain and first pilot, both the same person, checked his airplane accompanied by a co-pilot, probably comparing values.

"San Pedro?"

"Mr Fillip?"

"Put my baggage on that step. That´s for you." A few coins jingled into the driver´s palm. With a polite nod of his head, he left. The captain pointed his arm at the plane´s entrance and remained in the same place until his passenger had climbed aboard. The oval door was closed, all buttons and levers were put into their correct positions, the engines purred and propellers the rotated around their axes. The latitude grew and the city spreading under them shrank, abandoned behind a coastal line. A turquoise liquid painted the horizon in all directions around them; a few subtle islands built by corals were scattered here and there. Thoughts buried him under their surfaces, forcing his consciousness to give up and recede into his brain. The hot weather produced a great amount of air bubbles, which caused the plane to relaxingly seesaw. He fell asleep.

A brassy panel placed half a metre up a massive wall next to the entrance gate read the words:

"Russian Federation—Honorary Consul
Princess Margaret Drive."

Life behind the thick walls of the consulate was treated in the same slow manner as life in the rest of the Caribbean country. Months had passed before he had accepted the lifestyles of the local people. No rushing, no rocket careers and conversations and disagreements were mainly handled in a very calm manner. His loud strong orders cut through the air like Othello´s yelling in Shakespeare´s play. Everyone´s attention pointed at the man furiously clenching a portable phone.

"It´s my order, don´t ask questions!" With the last sentence, he cast his mobile on the desk, grabbed his car keys and vacated the office.

"Darria Fillipovna, did he tell you when he is going to come back? There are some unfinished issues." A clerk, observing the whole scene, asked the assistant for the information.

"No. Maybe I can help you?"

"There are two appointments this afternoon."

"I have contact numbers, I´ll re-arrange them."

"I appreciate it."

Life in the consulate returned to as it was before. A hot sweltering lunch time sneaked in offices, and people went out to lunch. The short unpleasant episode became a little sweet cherry on the tip of a gateau, which ordinary life problems would swallow in a few bites.

More than an hour remained until our Christmas Eve dinner would be served. Bird feeders hung from silver fir twigs in the centre of our garden and the fence around the doghouse was decorated with many pine cones bundled together with brass jingle bells, red ribbons and pine needles, scattering green and red flakes everywhere. I had just got back from the local cemetery, where candle lights festooned the graves of our departed nearest. The lights trembled in a silent dance hand in hand with the wind, mutely blazing.

A water splashing sound could be heard: Laura was having a bath, enjoying every bubble of the floral foam. Mum ignored all her kitchen work and read her favourite book in a rocking chair in front of the fire place, listening to the relaxing cracking of burning logs. The shadows of flames hopped across her cheeks, playing with the tone of her pupils now and then. I liked observing her sitting there as I leaned my back against the wall in our hallway, which connected all the rooms on the ground floor. Standing up straight, I thought about all the possibilities, open to me. Reading emails or chatting on Skype became the winners.

> *"Merry Christmas and a Happy New Year*
> *Best wishes, Charlie, Trevor and Matt."*

The email had been sent by Trevor. Too short, too impersonal; it was hard to translate the hidden meaning of the words. None may have been there.

"It is nice that Trevor did not forget me, or maybe it was Charlie that emailed me?" I liked the little boy, with his never-ending chirping and his busybody questions that he asked anybody anywhere.

> *"I wish the same and many fulfilled secret dreams.*
> *Rudi.*
> *P.S.: One kiss for Charlie. ;o)"*

"Here is one from Patricia. Look at it, Rudi." After a short click, a gigantic picture was displayed on the screen. All the members of her family smiled at me in their native clothes and reindeer horns towered above the heads. A small hand appeared when I crossed the picture with the mouse pointer, so I clicked on it.

"Jingle bells, jingle bells . . ." The well-known song poured into the room. I hummed the melody, smiling.

"Oh, Minerva has written to me." I looked forward to the next click, even though I had never met her.

> *"Dear Nina,*
>
> *I would first love to wish you a Merry Christmas and a Happy New Year.*
>
> *Nina, I was summing my request for two days. I have constantly checked Gregory's state—nothing has changed, unfortunately.*
>
> *He has had a second heart failure during a very short period.*
>
> *I am frightened and scared and my faith grows weaker. Nina, if you agree, I will pay for your ticket to visit him. I know you are a student, take it like my Christmas gift, or rather my gift to Gregory.*
>
> *I think your presence would help Gregory get along with his disease much better. I hope so.*
>
> *Minerva."*

A hefty lump paced up and down in my throat. Reading it once again, no right words came to my mind: no response was good enough to cheer her up, to draw her thoughts out and throw them in the bin. Almost a quarter of an hour passed before I began typing.

> *"Dear Madam Minerva,*
>
> *It sounds a little bit strange to wish you Merry Christmas and a Happy New Year. Be patient. Everything will get better. I'll write to you soon.*
>
> *Rudi."*

Bang! The door handle thudded into the wall behind it. I jumped, not expecting Laura's invasion.

"The bathroom is free, darling."

"I thought you had evaporated into beads of vapour."

Click. The tongue in the bathroom door latch swam into its hole. A weak water whisper crept up to us.

"Too late."

"Some wishes, sirs?"

"No!" All three men flew at him. The waiter bowed respectfully, accepting the powerful client´s decision and left. Nobody was interested in the magnificent panorama on offer: there was an increasing furiousness at the table. Waiter´s hands braced a freshly washed glass in the shadow of his cane-roofed bar. He shined it to perfection and raised it to let the sun stream orange and purple beams through it. Clinks of glass mixed together with the whistling of Caribbean songs and occasional tapping on the bar. He loved the early noon and his job in Victoria´s resort.

"You have been cheating me for a long time." One of two men shouted.

"You are completely wrong."

"If I admit I´m wrong, you can surely explain that vast newly found habitat of red wood to me."

"Red wood? I thought our business was related to crude oil. Or not?" His poker face and calmness threw the opposing side off their balance.

"Our business is finished."

"I don´t think so."

"Why? You are just an investor, an outsider."

"Your signature is placed at the bottom of our agreement."

"And?"

"Correct me if I´m wrong, but do Mennonite rules assent with your activities?"

"Is that a form of extortion?"

"Don´t use such a strong definition!"

"So you´d never condescend to threaten anybody, would you?"

"I can´t see a reason not to."

"Stalin was a bastard, but the whole world knew it! The worth of a streetwalker is higher than he had or you have."

"Hitler was a mass killer and I´m so polite not to blame you like his offspring."

"Hitler was the son of a Jewish Austrian woman. My family has Prussian roots—there´s a tremendous difference, my dear ex-business partner.

"Not so fast, sit down. An agreement is an agreement." This time, cold sharp prickles of arrogance and dominance emerged from his voice.

"Such ridiculous behaviour. Report me to the Office for Business Competition, if you want. Now, I´m going to get up and you´ll let me go."

"No problem, my friends will visit you in a short while." An arrogant leer covered each section of his pale face.

"No problem, we will cope with it." Old-fashioned pride forced him to tower over his rival.

"So, have a nice day, my fellow."

"You too." His steps died into the distance.

"A drink, sir?"

"Yes."

"The same?"

"Of course, my taste buds love it."

"Who is missing?"

"Granddad."

"Mum?"

"I have no idea, he´s gone to the vineyard."

Ding-dong-ding-dong.

"Grandpa!" Both grabbing him, we hung on his neck and laughed.

"Has grandma already begun screeching?"

"No, everything fine, it´s Christmas Eve," he winked.

A thin piece of tiny crunchy Christmas biscuit spread with honey started the Christmas Eve dinner. The spacious oval table was occupied by people close to our hearts: family members, friends and even their friends that had not found anybody to spending the evening with.

"I met Joseph." Granddad announced.

"Did he recognise you?"

"Yes, all pubs were closed. He was celebrating."

"Celebrating?"

"His first non-drunk day this year. He was sober." Many of us giggled at his simple joke.

"Did you write your letter?" Granddad continued his ride of teasing people.

"Me?" The question surprised my Auntie.

"Let him have fun." Mum tapped the back of her hand.

"Yes, Santa wrote back to me . . . He is going to come." She jumped on his wave.

"What did he write?"

"Supplies of Christmas gifts were used up. I should stop bugging him." She replied.

Martin nudged me, letting me know it was time to disappear. He became one of Santa´s helpers every year, which involved shaking a small jingle bell in the middle of the Christmas tree and announcing to the audience that the time to unwrap gifts had arrived.

"It´s for you Rudi." My raised brow asked instead me.

"Daniel called me." Martin immediately answered my unspoken question.

"Martin, are you his nanny? I regret taking you to that volleyball match."

"You would do the same for me."

"What?" I could not believe what I heard.

"Did you send him to hell?"

"It´s not your concern! Mind your own business!" I whispered, but the tone warned him.

"Don´t you want to open it?"

"Why, I know what it is." My cousin´s expression halted my protests.

"Just open it!"

"No." I stuck the gift in my trouser pocket.

"You're the most stubborn mule I've ever met," he ribbed me.

Jing-jing-jing-jing. The bell was trembling, its tip squeezed between his thumb and forefinger. I disappeared. That time was his.

Teasing, laughter, warm thanks and rustling paper were accompanied by sounds of a fairy tale broadcasted by one of the many TV channels. The hours were galloping rapidly; the midnight knock banged on the kitchen wall clock. We left the room.

"Good night, girls."

"Good night, Mum."

"Good night, darling."

I felt like a coward—I did not want to hurt her. The door of my room was closed. The minutes passed extremely quickly. Browsing and looking for the easiest combinations of flights and coaches or trains to Lancaster, I strived to find a solution to get to the city. The dim light tinted my face. Shadows ran across the web pages as they changed. There was a sharp firm click; I ignored it, thinking Laura had come for an evening chat. Flights offers were downloading one by one on the screen, saved in the top bar for comparison later.

"Did you wrap your tongue like a Christmas gift this evening?" The preceding silence was not like Laura. A pair of arms cuddled me tenderly and perfume tickled my nostrils.

"Mum?"

"What's going on, honey?" No anger or annoyance came from her, just calmness and understanding. She knew me. There was nothing that mum's receptors could not reveal. The mouse pointer landed on the email icon and our eyes followed the pointer's motions. Mum's former work with international companies had forced her to learn different languages: one of them was English. I offered no explanation as she silently read the email.

"When?"

"Aren't you sad?"

"It's fine. I'm proud of you," she replied. I turned and buried my nose in her soft sweet-scented jumper, my arms cuddling her waist tightly.

"I don't know when exactly. Either tomorrow evening or early the next day." She dragged a blue pouf near to my desk, pulled a pen from a rainbow-coloured round container and ripped a piece of paper from a block: she was prepared to write.

"Dictate to me." Times of possible flights and coach links were written down and combined. The result was decided.

21

"Consolidate, Rudi!" My thoughts screamed at me. I knew it. I was obligated to do it. I was scared. It would not have helped if he had woken and seen my expression full of sorrow, regret and dread. I was grateful for that glass wall, which became witness to my hesitation. It gave me an opportunity to leave, stay or enter the room. I had seen this kind of picture in the movies, but the reality was much worse. I squeezed the handle for a while.

Bump-bump, bump-bump. My heart shouted. I felt it in my throat pipe. A lump jumped with each bump. I coped with it and approached the bed. My hand stretched to drag a chair next to the side of his bed. Slowly, quietly and pulling it nearer, a muffled sound gently cut the beeping of the respiration devices. I sat on it, listening to the periodical beeps and looking at his silhouette.

"Merry Christmas, Gregory." Holding his hand, I tried to restore myself. I could hear his quiet breathing as I observed the subtle motion of his rib cage and felt his heartbeat bumping in his wrist artery. No change; he slept on. I dipped into that tranquillity, absorbing his presence and the calmness of the room. I appreciated the shades of twinkling stars among the tree decorations. Hours passed.

"I'll come tomorrow, your granny is waiting for me in the corridor." I returned his hand to its former position, kissed him on the forehead and caressed his hair.

"I like you, Gregory."

Satisfaction: that was an accurate description of his emotional state. Threats became his work tools many times. They performed effectively and brought fruits almost immediately.

"Your drink, sir."

"I'll pay."

"Fillip!" The voice diverted his attention from the waiter.

"Trevor! It´s nice to see you."

"Happy Holidays. Oh, bring your son and wife, we would like it if you would dine with us. It would be nice."

"Oh, sit down, please."

"I can´t, Charlie is waiting for me at the information desk. Have a nice day. See you in the evening." He backed away as he said his last words, smiling and waving goodbye.

"Oh . . . Trevor, I´m not sure . . ."

"See you later. At 6." He butted in and left.

"It is pretty ludicrous how a small amount of money can create friends that occupy extremely significant public posts," he grinned to himself. He raised his hand to request a new drink.

"Help yourself, Rudi. They are still warm. I got them out the oven about half an hour ago."

"They smell nice." A mug full of morning coffee stood in front of me. I could feel the warmth radiating from it.

"You look different," Minerva commented.

"Oh, my hair colour. If I had lived in the medieval period, people would have sentenced me to death by burning."

"Rudi!" Minerva´s expression seemed confused. "I didn´t mean your hair, but your outlook on life."

"I know. Many people challenge themselves to understand me. They take it on like a scientific task."

"A scientific task?"

"It´s a joke," I replied. She cracked a smile.

"Why did you choose him as a friend?"

"He chose me. We met at the airport shop in Vancouver, accidentally. Then our destiny played a valiant card game and we met again."

"He´ll die soon."

"Everybody dies. Gregory knows an approximate date, at least. That is the one difference. It´s his advantage," I smiled.

"Why?"

"I love living."

"Why did you choose him?"

"Have you seen a rain puddle full of tadpoles?"

"Yes, I was a child too."

"We are those tadpoles."

"Tadpoles?"

"Yes. Some will change into tree frogs and some into toads. Which are winners and which are losers?"

"I don´t know what you mean."

"Did you used to like those tadpoles?" I asked.

"Oh, yes. They were nice and fragile."

"Do you like toads?"

"Not really."

"Why? It was not their choice to change into toads. It was nature´s decision."

"Oh."

"It wasn´t Gregory´s choice, nobody wants to win a theatre ticket to see the play called DMD, or become one of its actors."

"You are different," Minerva mused.

"Can I take one more cake?" I asked. She gave me one with a sincere smile. I sipped my coffee. The wind´s song blew behind the window and a quiet tune produced by the radio created a warm air.

"Señora Isabella, I´m not going to argue with you." A kind of resignation sounded in Trevor´s voice.

"Did he say yes, exactly?"

"No."

"Did you tell him 6?"

"Yes."

"O.K. Eat, children. Your dad can wait for that mysterious Sir Fillip, if he wants." Charlie giggled.

"Dad?"

"Yes. I rebooked my flight."

"Why?"

"The young man fell in love and she refused him." Another bout of giggling bounced around the room.

"Charlie!" They shouted at him together.

"Two exams remain. I need to learn. Some materials . . ." Mathew stopped in the middle of the sentence.

"Charlie, shouldn´t you turn your attention to your dinner?" Isabell weakly slapped him.

"There is the whole of January for exams."

"Not for me." Trevor´s questioning brow awaited an answer.

"We´re going to return to Belize at the beginning of January to finish the research." Mathew continued.

"Stop it, Charlie!" Charlie´s grimace immediately transformed into a perfect poker face.

"That was delicious, Señora Bell, thank you." With a polite brush of her cheek, he left.

"Charlie, come to me." He jumped from the chair and settled next to his dad.

"Who is that brave rude girl who refused our king?"

"You answered yourself."

"What?"

"Repeat your sentence, Dad. Who is that rude . . ." He stopped.

"Rudi?" He eagerly nodded, his pupils shone and little mischievous sparkles twinkled in the middle of them.

"Thank you, my fellow." They high-fived and Charlie slipped from the chair to snake into the kitchen and steal a piece of Bell´s masterful cake.

"Minerva, I would love . . ."

"No, Rudi, it is your time to enjoy spending time with each other."

"I´m afraid."

"Me too. You are brave, I´m sure." Her fingers encouragingly squeezed my shoulder. My palm slowly travelled along the glass wall; my hand gripped the handle.

"Hi, honey," I said. His almost sightless eyes intermittently looked at me. He cracked a smile.

"Yesterday . . ."

"Yes, I was. You slept."

"No, I absorbed your warmth."

"Oh . . ."

"I´ve brought you a present." I strived to hide the awful visible shaking of my hands, shoving them in my bag and rooting among the items inside. "Merry Christmas." The rustling paper caused a tension in my belly: innumerable fluttering butterfly wings tickled me once again. I was annoyed with myself. His fingers fought with my perfect packing.

"The fox. You bought it." His eyes pierced its silhouette as it stood on his flat palm.

"You impressed me, and not just me," I said.

"Rudi, what . . ."

"I´m envious."

"What of?"

"Your sexual experience."

"It was just once, no more."

"You´ve a great secret." I conspiratorially winked.

"Rudi!"

"It was a joke."

"But the most horrible I have ever heard."

"Never mind, you are laughing. The end justifies the means. Nice accessories, but a little bit old-fashioned." My finger pointed at the strange-looking knotted plastic tubes decorating the beeping devices.

"Have you got a serious interest in them?"

"No, they don´t go with my outfit."

"Here." I handed him a paper sheet from the bedside table. "Write."

"What?"

"It´s our bet."

"Our bet?"

"The loser has to climb to the peak of a Mayan pyramid and scream I AM THE LOSER."

"That´s unfair, I´m in a wheelchair."

"So, you must win."

"What is the challenge?"

"The last day of your hospitalisation."

"Why? It´s not important."

"Yes, it is."

"The purpose of our bet?"

"I would like to book our flight to Belize, finally. I can´t do it yet."

"Why?" Hoarse mirth struggled through his slightly opened lips.

"Because you´re lying in this bed."

"And?"

"You´ve not seen the butterfly cave yet, I promised I´d show you."

"That was pretty crazy chit-chat."

"Write it down."

"Why?"

"No reason, just write." I shot him a rude smile.

"You are rude."

"Write it down."

"A pen?" he laughed. His chest let the infectious sound stream into the rooms. Two fools, two buffoons delighted with each other. I pulled a pen out from my bag and passed it to him. His fingers touched it; a delicate shaking pulsed around his fingertips and travelled along his fingers to his palms.

Beeeeeeeep. An ear-tearing sound blasted around the room. Everything changed. Gregory´s mouth tried to gulp air. I desperately searched for an emergency button. I found it and pressed. Seconds passed, the door was shot open and doctors and nurses flooded the room. I mindlessly backed away.

"A new heart failure! Adrenaline, please! How . . ." All the sounds fused into one.

"Rudi . . ." Palms squeezed my shoulders. "What happened?" Two ladies eagerly awaited my response.

"We were laughing . . . he was happy . . . it seemed . . . I don´t understand." The words jumped in my throat as I stuttered.

Beep-beep-beep. Minerva´s expression lost traction.

"Madams?"

"Yes, doc?"

"Gregory is stabilised for a while. I hope."

"Oh, gosh."

Snowflakes mutely fluttered downwards, changing the road into wide white strips. Cars slowed their speeds, some people opened their umbrellas and others bowed their necks to protect their faces against the cold touches of winter flakes, their soles slipping aside. There were others who slid consciously along the white snow-covered pavements. A taxi stopped at a kerb, its nearly shining letters announcing the taxi company to anybody passing by. They crossed the property of Liverpool John Lennon Airport.

"Don´t you want to stay?"

"No, madam, it´s time for me to go."

"Anne—Marie, please Rudi, or just Anne."

"Anne." I was confused. I had only known her for a very short time, but I was thankful for each second I had spent beside her. A noble fighter, she loved her son, loved her life and loved all the people she met.

´Very awkward circumstances must have been encountered when Gregory´s father decided to cheat on her,´ I thought. I was glad she could not read my thoughts. It was rude to root into such a delicate matter.

"Have a nice flight."

"Thanks." I griped the handle of luggage and we exchanged a friendly hug. I confusedly waved back at her as I entered the building. A great glass-panelled door hit a wall, separating the traffic sounds coming from the street outside. I disappeared into the vast hall of John Lennon airport.

22

Small plastic wheels rattled as they crossed the snow-cleared tiles of The Gallery Plaza. Some little abandoned spots of snow swerved the light toy vehicle left and right. The boy's tiny booted feet kept going straight on for a short time. His bottom jumped a bit as he crossed another snow bulge and his car began to swing from side to side again. His father, with one of his hands shoved in his coat pocket to protect it against the chilling frost and his nose stuck in a wrinkled scarf, pulled a red rope, dragging the car along. A small hand covered in a mitten was raised: he waved at me, smiling. The vehicle then met other snow spots, which attracted his whole attention. I laughed and waved back at him.

The silhouettes of two creatures in the heart of an oval brim towered above the snow-blanketed floor of a fountain. Paging through my brain, I remembered the sculptured faces of the two creatures from the gallery photos. Turning to face the main entrance of the Vancouver Art Gallery, I pressed the trigger on my camera. The composition of the square surrounding the gallery was incredible. Different centuries, architectural styles and building materials combined into a symphony. Even though an enormous board reading "*RENOIR´S LIFE*" informed people of what lay inside, they could not fail to be amazed by the deeply hidden feeling of this beautiful composition.

The grey winter sky got lower among the buildings and white filmy fluff flew through the air, settling down next to other white fellows on tree branches, grass or next to kerbs in narrow ditches. I noticed a direction sign stating "*CHRIST CHURCH CATEDRAL, Burrard Street*"; I followed it knowing that there would be many opportunities to use public transport because the crossroad of Melville Street and Burrard Street was spotted with different kinds of stops. I was leaving West Georgia Street and crossing a zebra crossing when an old Anglican brick building squatting under a multi-floored construction attracted my attention. Ascending the steps leading to the cathedral's gate, a gospel song streamed through the air. I went in, sat down on one of several wooden benches and let myself become a part of the truly ubiquitous holy atmosphere.

Buzz, buzz. Fortunately, I had put my mobile on silent mode before I had entered the cathedral. In spite of that, I reddened. Nobody could have heard it, but I felt like I had committed a crime.

A short text message arrived in my phone´s inbox. "Happy New Year, darling. Love Mum and Laura."

"Oh." I checked the time, rolling up my sleeve: my watch showed 1.15 pm. My thoughts had been swinging with the melody in the cathedral, dragging me out from reality. I had almost forgotten that the New Year had started just a quarter of an hour ago.

"Happy New Year, enjoy it. I love you. ;o)." Some countries around the world had already begun the following year, and some were still waiting for this annually awaited point. The globe constantly twists around its own axis and we are small marionettes observing this thrilling theatrical performance.

The gospel song stopped; the calm voice of a priest flew into the space. I stood up and left my seat at the edge of the bench. A tiny creak stopped the silence, but fortunately nobody noticed it. Darkness had set down on the streets outside. Lamps sent their cones to the ground and the miniature flying fluff had adjusted to become bigger snowflakes during the time I had spent in the cathedral, as the pavements now wore a pretty thick layer of fresh snow. A small orange vehicle rolled snow from the roads towards kerbs, creating low white puffy barriers. If a car stood in the way, the vehicle avoided it and continued its job.

Buzz, buzz. The mobile phone screen lit up. After sliding along the pavement and then descending down a subway staircase, I undid my glove. My fingertips touched the screen, which revealed an expected text.

"Hi. Happy New Year. Martin." Responding, a number of vibrations tickled my palm. I read and answered each one. Sometimes I had to loudly laugh. Their texts were more jokes than New Year´s wishes. A strong chill wind announced to all the passengers waiting on the subway platform that their train would arrive in a couple of seconds.

It seemed that the last guest had been served at Whistler Blackcomb Rentals. Minutes passed and the bustle of the last day of the year died. A sharp tick, coming from the opposite wall, disturbed them. They both threw glances at the clock: 4.30 pm. Two hands clapped on an Atomic pair of skis together. They flattened the bottom part of the skis with hot wax and sharpened the metal edges. This pair could have been put in the rack among other treated pairs of skis.

"Could you put them on a free shelf?" He leaned over to her, planting a small gentle kiss on her nape. She clutched the skis with her free hand and carried them to a rack. A new version of a song by Alexander Rybak sounded in her pocket once again.

"Yes?" As she looked for the right information in her mind related to the caller, she smiled. "Oh, I remember. Of course, I know. Rudi´s classmate—we met at the Christmas market." Chirping, she held the mobile between her cheek and shoulder as she continued trying to put skis on the shelves.

"Wait a second, I´ll search my contact list." She clicked through her phone´s menu to send Rudi´s contact card to the new caller´s number, then she chose the SEND option and pressed YES. Rudi´s number was sent.

"Are you there?"

"I´ve sent it."

"Thank you."

"No problem. Bye."

"Don´t look at me like that. He wanted Rudi´s number."

"Are you sure Rudi will appreciate your helpfulness?"

"What?"

"Sometimes people have reasons for not offering their numbers to anybody."

"He´s her classmate." An incomprehensible expression appeared on her face.

"O.K. It´s time to go. We need to get off—the guys are waiting for us. Everybody has gone to Horstman Hut." His fingers played with keys, snapped off lights switches and the rental shop dipped into darkness.

"Your hangovers are famous around Vancouver, at least." The rest of the adolescent group laughed so loudly that it was impossible not to be attracted by their conversation. Some passengers of a train smiled while others were shocked, mainly seniors.

"Why is that Lighthouse Park logo on that car rental advert?" I wondered, sitting at the seat opposite to the window. I skipped through the digital list of stops hung above the window. The last was approximately ten kilometres from Lighthouse Park. I looked at the green figures in the bottom corner of the digital panel: 4.49. I decided to postpone my return to the residence.

"Every day of every year, our cars are waiting just for you!" My fingertips slid across my mobile phone´s screen and dialled the telephone number printed on the advertisement.

"Lighthouse Car Rental, can I help you?" Surprise clutched my throat for a short period.

"Oh, yes. I would like to rent a 4 x 4 car. Is that possible?"

"Of course, what´s the rental date?"

"Today, is that still possible?"

"Oh, we close at 6 today, it´s New Year´s Eve. But I can . . ."

"No, it´s all right. I´ll manage it, I´ll be there till six. I appreciate your help."

"O.K. So, 31st December, 6 pm. What´s your name?"

"Nina Rudić."

"Can you spell your name, please?"

"R-U-D-I-C with an accent over the C and my first name is N-I-N-A."

"O.K. Thank you. I´ll look forward to seeing you."

The train became empty. I got off, seeking the narrow exit. A long sheer escalator transported a handful of people up to the world above the surface. Remembering the maps on the advertisement, I strived to identify the points printed on it. The same advertisement slogan shone on the roof of a bungalow behind a small fenced car park in front of the subway exit. I needed to cross the nearby playground. An intensively kissing couple occupied the end part of a plastic slide, cuddled against each other very tightly. Their kissing was so loud almost everybody was forced to turn in their direction. A chap in his forties almost ran me over attempting to catch a bus. A group of young people sat on and surrounded a bench, hidden in the shade of an extremely widespread and tall spruce, having fun. They teased each other, laughed at rib-tickling jokes and gave the place a particular warm atmosphere.

Ding-dong. Thumbing the bell button, I listened to a joke being spoken so theatrically that its elocution flooded the space around the group.

Buzz. The low door loosened its adhesion to a magnet positioned on the opposite steel bar.

"Good afternoon, madam." A woman shot her arm out to me. "Daisy Grimould, rental assistant."

After asking questions and reading the rental terms, I confirmed I had comprehended fully. I checked the car visually and finally shut the driver´s door behind me. I left the rental car park, joined the road and let the wheels roll on the tarmac. I gave a GPS several orders to find my destination more easily. The device woke up. An attractively tinted male voice chosen from the GPS menu began accompanying me. I smirked.

"Not bad. Hi Ken, how are you?"

A dense coniferous forest swallowed the last rays of the town´s lights. I switched to distance headlights to magnify the beaming cone on the road. The road bent left; as the minutes passed, it started sloping downwards. Transparent yellow beams rotated in regular periods around the lighthouse, crossing giant rocks, a flat beach and driftwood scattered along the sand. The quiet rattle of the car ceased. With a click, the SUV was locked. I raised my hood, protecting my head against an unusually strong and chill wind. A rip-roaring ocean song spread all around me. The beach was constructed of many tangled strips of sand and snow created by the wind´s powerful hands. I was amazed. My limbs were led by unseen tiny ropes, like a puppet without a brain.

Ring-ring, ring-ring, ring-ring, ring-ring, ring-ring.

Beep-beep-beep.

"I don´t believe this. Is she deaf? Maybe she is sleeping?" He rolled his sleeve up. The longer watch hand pointed to a green phosphorous twelve and the shorter to six. He counted the time difference.

"At two? On New Year´s Eve!" He shoved the phone in his jacket, finished lacing his boots, put on his cap and gloves and locked the dormitory room.

"Hi, I´ve just decided, I´m going to join you." A snappy jingle was followed by the opening of the lift doors.

The streets started waking up. Squads of people, couples and singletons trickled in all directions. Bus stops were spotted by potential passengers. Chit-chat, talking, shouting and laughter hovered in the air. Buses came and left in the same minute, the numbers and destinations written on the information boards placed above their windscreens changing with each new bus. The streets were full of a New Year´s Eve rush.

Approaching the giant rocks and struggling with strong blasts of wind, I noticed two small circles piercing the darkness. I halted for a brief while then kept moving on, not giving up my former intent. Climbing across those slippery rocks, I fought to maintain my balance every time my rubber soles slipped on the wet surface. I had almost reached the edge of the block when two shining spots emerged in front of me. With a gasp, I backed off a little bit. A sudden beam from the lighthouse tower revealed the whole silhouette. The light rays made its bared fangs macabre. Its growl did not reach my eardrums due to the thuds of the extremely powerful ocean waves, but it was obvious that it was snarling at me. I backed away, one careful step after another. I did not estimate the distance growing between us. My foot unexpectedly slipped and got stuck in a narrow crevice among the rocks.

"Shit." In spite of the burning frost, my leg and my entire skin felt like they were on fire. The two glowing spheres neared me with bared teeth growling so loudly that my ears caught that strange sound. I fought, pressing my arms against the rock surface and wanting to loosen my leg from the crevice. My leg hurt but my attempt was successful. I rolled on my tummy and stood up. I ran, stumbling and limping, to the end of the rocks to reach the flat beach. I looked back to check the situation behind me. It followed me, keeping the same distance, neither shorter nor longer. I was stunned. An enormous wave stood for a second behind the last rock, then suddenly fell down in an ear-deafening roar and gushed around the rocks. The animal, which was more similar to a fox than to a dog, ran to the side, reached the beach and fused with the darkness.

´Man, have I lost my mind? What have I thought? All orcas have already gone off.´ I asked myself. I was frozen to the bone and my wet trousers adhered to my thighs. I had forgotten one glove on the rocks, so my fingers were icy sticks. Feeling inside my jacket pocket, I gripped the keys and unlocked the car.

"Where are you going again?" Bob shouted at him over the glass pints, the music produced by a live rock band and the noises of revellers.

"I need to make a call."

In comparison with the air in the pub, the street rush seemed to be a synonym to silence.

Ring-ring, ring-ring, ring-ring, ring-ring, ring-ring, ring-ring.

Beep-beep-beep. The same response. He shoved the mobile back in his pocket.

"Hey guy! Can I cheer you up?" A lovely-looking girl´s arm wrapped around his waist.

"It depends on the price," he winked.

"It´s worth it."

The next blasting song invited them into the entrance of the pub. Everyone at the tall table downed their next pint. The fun accelerated and the dance floor got fuller; half an hour passed, then an hour. She pressed against him, their hips swinging to the tones of a love song. There was no gap between their pelvises. She looked at him and their eagerness increased. Both nodded. The door of the ladies´ toilets was slammed open and one of three stalls was locked. His lips brushed her neck, his fingers fought with his zip, her hand got off to a frontal attack and set just the head of his member free.

"No." He pushed her away.

"What? Have you gone mad?"

"I´ve just realised, I´m gay."

"What the hell?!" She smoothed her clothes in a hurry.

Bang! The toilet cabin vibrated for a while.

"I´m gay." Zipping up his jeans, he leaned his back against the wall, chuckling at his sudden epiphany.

23

A strangely sinister silence hovered above the small farm. It was feeding time and each one of the animals clamoured for its daily breakfast. A cheerful chirping cut through the air from time to time, but nothing else.

"They can´t still be sleeping," he said.

Approaching the low shelter of his favourite pony, he sang a merry childish song. Something dark with tiny yellow stripes across its body and eye-catching yellow antennas rested and swung on a cane blade, copying the subtle seesawing of the plant. He pinned his gaze to the slim subject. He had never seen one before, just in a photo in a book. Touching it gently with his fingertip, the grasshopper suddenly jumped up high, spread its wings (showing their strawberry-coloured inner parts) and landed on a neighbouring blade. He stalked him, sparkles twinkling in his pupils. His childhood eagerness utterly consumed him. The red-winged grasshopper kept hopping from one blade to another, then the cane field became privy to a short strong squall, the grasshopper fused with shaking stems and leaves and he could not find it any more. He went back to the path and headed to the pony stall to visit his friend. His small fingers rooted inside his pocket: some sugar pieces rested in the bottom. He adored the gentle touches of a horse´s muzzle tickling his palm. A great surprised halted him; he stood in consternation.

"Dad, Dad, Dad, Dad!" he screamed at the top of his voice. "Dad, Dad . . ." Great capital letters were sprayed in red on the side of a water container.

"DON´T DRINK THE HIGH-PERFORMANCE POISON!" A lowly positioned voice thundered behind him.

"Are they dead?" His question was hard to hear; the words percolated through his teeth and dropped into silence. He did not hear an answer. He looked over his shoulder, looking for his dad. There was an empty farmyard and their house stood nearby. He turned back, not believing what had happened. There was a jerking motion in the left corner of the fence. He ran, squatted next to the brown mare and cuddled her, caressing her forehead patterned with a white big star.

"Go home, son," his dad's voice thundered. His hand squeezed a long gun hidden behind his body.

"No!"

"She is suffering. Let me help her, go home!" The boy's small lower lip trembled and tears glittered in his eyes. His eyes pierced the ground as his legs shuffled across the yard.

Boom! The shot sound totally absorbed the creaking of hinges. His small fingers played with the sugar pieces in his pocket and tears rolled down his face. Wiping the tears with the back of his hand, he pressed down the door handle and looked for his father. There he was. He had climbed into a tractor, which pulled a trailer. The enormous wheels spun along massive gate pillars of the horse-yard and its wings swung slightly as the earth began shaking under the weight of the machine. The tractor stopped and his father jumped out. The man crouched down to the mare, bound all four of her legs together and returned to the trailer to loosen its side and pull out a capstan. He wanted to have the mare on board and finish the mad spectacle as soon as possible. The trailer's side fell down. Large letters were sprayed on the side: *"HAPPY NEW YEAR!"*

"Are you still in Belize?!" he shouted so loudly that anybody within a radius of twenty metres could have heard every word. His mobile microphone sent a creaking back to his ear. He stood, his stunned face went pale and his lips shivered in fury.

"You are a bastard!" He pressed the miniature red phone on his mobile and finished his call.

My numb fingers fumbled around the front seat next to me. I was trying to grab my ringing mobile. The heating finally blew a little bit warmer than the outside temperature and many sharp needles tinkled through my fingers as they melted. They finally met the phone and grasped it in haste to avoid missing the call.

"Oh shit!" My mobile slid down to the floor, rang there for a pretty long while then clamped up. The screen went dark. The darkness outside changed to dark grey as the first rays of the town's lights illuminated the road, beside lines emerged and made my drive easier. I turned into the nearest parking lot, switched off the engine and left the key in the ignition. My body bowed across the next seat as my hand strived to find the phone.

"Shit." I had to leave the warmth of the car and deal with the frost outside in order to reach the phone from the passenger's side. "Look at that! Who was that caller?" My trembling fingers touched the screen. Sitting on the passenger seat, I slammed the door to protect against the coldness snaking inside.

"Matt, three times?" With a light tap on the screen, I re-dialled his number.

Ring-ring, ring-ring, ring-ring, ring-ring, ring-ring.

Beep-beep-beep.

"Never mind. I´ll try it later." Leg by leg I carefully clambered into the driver´s seat. I settled in it and turned the key to the right. The engine purred his low-toned song, lights pierced the air, wheels went backwards and the SUV slowly left the car park, joining the traffic on the road.

"Your bottom is shining." Bob approached the bar.

"What?" he shoved his hand into the rear pocket of his jeans, touching his phone.

"Why did you tell her you are gay?" Bob asked. He listened to Bob, wondering why he had not noticed any ringing.

"Sorry, what did you say?"

"You told her you are gay."

"Oh, yes." He kept trying to solve the ringing problem.

"Why?"

"She wanted to have sex."

"And?"

"Bob, she is like an oven—my ´fella´ would have changed into a baked sausage." A grin of contentment radiated from his face.

"What?"

"Nothing. Get the next round of drinks in! I´ll be back in few minutes."

"Matt!"

"The same as I had before, he knows." His gesture was directed at the barman. The crowd closed around him and Mathew vanished.

The extraordinary pompous hall of Victoria House Hotel´s foyer seemed more luxurious than any time before. The New Year´s Eve celebration oscillated around the space, not leaving even the smallest inch of the room untouched. Excitement for the coming night transformed everybody into happy and cheerful creatures.

"My dear fellow, there is no reason to shout at me." Holding his mobile half a metre from his ear, he spoke calmly, hardly able to hide his amusement.

"Bastard is such a strong word." The red button put an end to their conversation. His deal was done. Steps echoed around the foyer, dying on the stone tiles that joined into a path among the sand. Ocean waves splashed in several drops, hitting the poles of hotel jetties or soaking the sand. The night was full of joy, which changed now and then into genuine thrill. There were just a few hours until the year´s end. He dragged his phone out again and dialled a number.

"It´s me. No, don´t . . ."

Beep-beep-beep. The number was re-dialled.

"I would like to know how he is doing. Better? Is he O.K.? No! Don´t hang up!"

Ring-ring, ring-ring, ring-ring, ring-ring, ring-ring.

Beep-beep-beep.

Hot drops hit my hair, face and shoulders. Rolling down, they sent thousands of tiny sharp prickles across my body. I was melting, enjoying each small water droplet. I dried my hair somewhat with a towel and a soft bathrobe sucked up the last splashes scattering around my body. Sipping hot tea, I waited until my computer had connected to the Internet. A hairdryer buzzed loudly, blowing hot air. My earphones delivered French songs from the musical "The Hunchback of Notre Dame" to my brain cells. Goose bumps rose on my skin when the solo part was sung by Quasimodo. The clouds in the column of Skype-friendly souls were empty. I wondered, as the 31st December rolled to its end, why anybody would not want to steal a last little bit fun.

"Never mind."

> *"Happy New Year folks.*
> *I love you all.*
> *Rudi."*

I added the email addresses of all the friends who I had not sent greetings to via text message. Typing the last email was terrible: I was afraid of the response.

> *"Dear Minerva, Anne and Gregory,*
>
> *It is terribly hard to write what is hidden in my heart. I really believe this New Year will certainly be HAPPY.*
>
> *I send you a lot of hugs.*
>
> *P.S.: Write me, please. ;o)"*

A bus drove alongside the pavement in front of the pub. A red traffic light halted it. Listening to a phone ringing, he became a spectator of a strange performance in the bus. Some guys in the bus had celebrated a little bit early: they swung bottles of champagne from side to side high above their heads. The red light changed to yellow and then the green light shone on the board. The bus set off. A standing chap lost his balance and a small volume of liquid splashed on the coat of the passenger sat next to him.

A SUV headed into a parking lot, copying the bus´ line several metres behind the traffic lights, then the car went into the left-hand lane. A machine offered a parking card, the barrier was raised and the entrance to the car park opened up. A pretty large number of cars was scattered there.

A green pedestrian figure glowed. Pedestrians crossed the zebra crossing, their feet met the opposite kerb and each one of them continued on their way. I left the group of people and took my direction. I was in a hurry. An hour remained until the end of the day. The canteen announcement had clearly stated that 5 pm was the last call for serving. Its employees were going to relish the evening too. (So, I had jumped in the SUV and drove to the city centre.) I passed by quite a tall boy who was making a call and nervously pacing. Maybe his girlfriend had not answered him, or his mum. A smile cracked on my lips. I imagined my mum, nervous and impatient, waiting for my season´s wishes. Sliding downstairs to the basement, where everybody was, I joined the crowd revelling in the pub. Looking around and searching the bar, my eyes noticed the whished object—the bar a second later. I stumbled, pushing bodies away from me. Finally, I stood at the long brick bar.

"Hi!" I shouted at the top of my voice, striving to increase my volume several octaves higher than the surrounding creatures produced.

"Hi beauty, what would you like," the barman replied. I wondered how he could smile and scream at the same time: years of practice, perhaps.

"One bottle of wine, please."

"How about these?" His arms pointed to a row full of green elegant bottles delivered from the French region of Champagne.

"Oh, no thanks, that´s too luxurious for my purse."

"These?" The vignettes on some bottles of Californian wine attracted my sight.

"O.K., that sounds good."

I paid, grasped the bottle and my cap, and shoved my purse into my inner pocket. Zipping it, I turned to leave the jammed space.

Bump! The glass of my bottle hit a man´s elbow. His hand wrapped around the contact point.

"I´m sorry," I said. He revealed his entire set of teeth, pushing into me. I smelt a terrible alcoholic odour.

"A kiss darling and everything will have been forgotten."

"I don´t think so." I favoured him with a grimace, ducked and made a path through the revellers.

"Wow, silence." The boy, who was calling few minutes ago, had not called yet. He had probably gone back into the pub to celebrate. My legs carried me to the parking lot. I looked like a right alcoholic: the slim elegant claret neck of the bottle peeked out from the brim of my jacket.

With the bubbling of water then a click, the kettle was taken from its electrical base and the boiling liquid was poured into a flask, where a tea sack hung in expectation. The fruity aroma tangled with the fragrance of cinnamon cuddled every air molecule. The cookies that had been bought at a petrol station had been placed on the cut-up cardboard bottom of a box.

"The bottle is in my pocket, the flask is thin enough to be stuck in my other one and my hands will remain free. Ça vas." Spinning a lemon half in my palm, I checked how I would deliver all the items to the ground floor safely.

Putting soles patiently on steps and attempting not to fall down, I thought how it would have been a great pity to lose the delicious articles on the way to their final destination.

"Can I join you?" the man behind the glass turned down the sound blasting from the TV set. He faced me.

"Rudi, what are you doing here? What did I tell you?"

"You are alone during New Year´s Eve?" My smile broke his serious facial expression. He seemed amused.

"And the next excuse is?"

"Wait. Hm. Something about a breath-taking firework in the downtown area? We can observe it together. The sky will be full of many twinkling colourful stars." I wandered into the cabin and placed the card tray, the bottle and the flask on a wooden table, close to a lovely little artificial Christmas tree. I propped my legs on the table´s edge.

"Will you kick me out?" I asked.

"No."

"O.K. good. Have you got some cups?" Screwing the flask´s lid off, I observed his confused searching.

"I have some." Two blue transparent plastic cups were squeezed in his palms.

"Wow, that fragrance," he commented. The tea drops fused into one long stream and filled both cups. We sipped the drink and tasted the cookies. All our senses felt the same delight.

"Guardy, let´s go! Put on your coat and let´s go!"

"Rudi!" Several minutes of hesitation passed, then he joined me. It was both ridiculous and nice to see a man in his late sixties join me in building a snowman. Our gloves pushed a small amount of snowflakes together to create a white ball. The white ball was rolled around and grew and grew. The first section was done, then the second and then the smallest as the snow man´s head was put on top of the second. My scarf decorated its neck and a thing twig became its nose. I was pressing in stones to represent eyes when an enormous rattling sound attracted our attention. We turned our sights to the sky.

"Wow. You didn´t lie," he said. An ocean of multi-coloured sparkling fountains emerged from the dark. The dying rattle of one firework accompanied a new one. My companion disappeared for a moment, but I did not notice.

"Happy New Year, Rudi." He handed me one of the blue cups. Delicate wine bubbles swam from the bottom to the surface. We tapped our cups together.

"Happy New Year, Guardy," I winked. He gave me a kiss on the cheek.

24

"I´m missing one passenger." A steward skipped from one name to another, ticking them off one by one.

"Hello, I´m Nina Rudić."

"Oh, where have you been? All right, I have everyone." The steward ticked off my name and checked my boarding pass. I took off the bag belt that crossed my middle. It unfortunately hit someone´s shoulder as I loosened it and let it freely fall with the rest of the bag.

"Sorry, I´m really sorry," I apologised to the woman.

"Never mind." A strange accent whirled in her tone. Continuing to struggle along the narrow craft´s aisle, I thought about the familiarity of the accent. There was an empty seat at the window: its number corresponded with the number printed on my boarding card. My bag landed in one of the two boxes above the three seats and I took my seat. The stewards´ arms flew in different directions, showing all the necessary emergency procedures. A loudspeaker welcomed all the passengers and gave the exact details relating to our flight. The craft floor vibrated more and more, a short strange pressure expected by everybody came and the plane took off.

"It´s nice to hear that you are feeling better." The doc was writing some notes in his papers.

"I must take away your old friend."

"My friend?"

"Yes." The doctor´s palm drummed on the respiration device.

"Oh, my guardian angel. I´ll miss its beeping."

"You have more than one guardian angel. I would be a happy man if such a beautiful creature guarded me." Gregory cocked his head.

"The one with light red-honey hair, usually tied up in the same ponytail every day."

"Enormously big green eyes?" Gregory asked. The doctor smiled, and made a gesture using the pen braced between his fingers.

"Yes, two great blinkers."

"Rudi."

"For three days, your mum and grandma brought her clean clothes every day. She left you occasionally, to get a drink or use the bathroom. Sometimes she would go for a small walk along the corridor, but she always kept an eye on you through the glass." A noisy gulp disturbed the quietness that reigned in the room.

"This was found on the floor—a cleaning lady passed it to me," the doctor said.

"Thank you, it´s a present from Rudi." He squeezed the small cinnamon figure.

"I think it´s quite similar to her."

"Hm."

"Does she know . . . everything?"

"Everything?"

"About your diagnosis . . ."

"Yes. Sometimes I have the feeling that she is more educated in this area than any doc." The doctor raised his eyebrows. "There is no excuse that I can use with her if I´m too lazy to exercise or my mood is low . . . simply, I get annoyed with her sometimes . . . ´promise me Gregory´ . . . she teases me until I do it."

"Do you hate her?"

"Are you crazy? I get fed up with her from time to time, but . . ."

"But?"

"I don´t understand her favourite phrase." The wrinkles on the doctor´s forehead deepened more than they had one minute ago. He waited for an explanation. "´Life is too short to sit on any patio´," Gregory quoted.

"I thought you were clever?"

"I´ve got DMD. It´s the main focus of my life. And a long interesting life is spreading in front of her, isn´t it?"

"No. An approximate prediction of the final day for you has been made, but nobody knows the exact date of their last day. She is right. Life really is too short to sit on any patio." The doctor tapped him on the shoulder, stood up and left him in his own world.

On the 6th January, the day of the Three Kings, my thoughts wandered into my country, where all the Christmas trees would have been taken down and the period of carnivals began. In comparison to the sweltering heat, any frost would have been redemption from this hot and wet hell. Sweat beads rolling down my temples, our ascent got more and more difficult because of the dense foliage, stems and plants. Several kilometres remained before we would reach La Cuevas Research Station, hidden somewhere in the heart of the forest. Samples were picked up from new areas, all the required comments were written down and our backpacks were stuffed full of items related to the different research fields.

"Rudi?"

"Yes, professor?"

"Has something bad happened? Have I done something wrong?"

"Have you?" Not turning, not stopping, I just addressed the question to him and walked onwards, struggling through the thick vegetation.

"Rudi." The sudden brace of his hand halted me.

"Professor, let it go, what hasn´t been responded, it doesn´t hurt anybody." I brushed off his grip and went ahead.

The following kilometres passed quickly. There was a momentous vacuum in my brain. I had to stop thinking about it so I would not get angrier with him. The other members of our five-man group had no idea about the real reason for our research. I did not fancy mixing the circumstances and knowledge that I had discovered with our co-living in the camp. Not noticing the world surrounding me, I caught a familiar buzz produced by the engine of a device generating electricity for the entire research station, now and then. Not consciously, I abandoned them to be welcomed by the staff and the other guys from the station. My legs walked forwards, crossing the meadow and heading into a building that was used as a shelter for a laboratory. I pulled at the handle but the locked door unexpectedly stopped my progress.

"Shit," I whispered. Sliding down the wall, the cold pleasant touch of its surface against my back let me enjoy a short rest. My head leaned against the wooden surface, my eyelids got heavy and a nauseous feeling grew inside me.

"I´ll do the blood analysis—his fever is too high to just treat it with drugs. I would like to be sure." I did not know that voice. It intermittently came from a vast distance away. Thousands of native drums thundered in my head, causing a sense of exploding. I fell asleep again.

"Tell him personally. I´m not a courier."

"Why?! You´re living with my mother!"

"Have you forgotten the way?"

"Have you forgotten whose money you are spending?!"

"Ha-ha, ha-ha . . ." She started laughing uncontrollably. The cessation of their call might have been the better way to settle this extremely ridiculous question. After her sarcastically humorous act, she felt better because his rude behaviour had not touched her inside. This extremely funny business became his favourite coat, his habit. He was not able to recognise the starting point, the real cause of his everyday dishonour of other people. She laughed and laughed, put the mobile phone on the edge of the sink and returned to finish the cake mixture. Her thumb pushed a button, small metal shovels twisted at a rapid speed to make the mixture smooth and the kitchen robot blasted its ear-tearing song into the air.

"What the hell is this? Anne!" No answer, just the annoying roar of a machine.

"Anne—Marie." She jumped a little bit as an unexpected touch on her back made her shiver.

"Oh, Minerva."

"Your phone isn´t switched off." Showing her the shining screen, she smiled. Amusement and understanding were written among the wrinkles created by her raised brow.

"Will it be rude if I switch it off?"

"I don´t think so." Minerva´s thumb decided.

Beep-beep-beep . . .

He looked less surprised than the last time, but it could not be said he held no fury. The first stone, which met his trajectory, flew up in the air when his shoe tip met with it. His mood was greyer than the sky above, which prepared for rain.

"Sir, your massage is finished. Shall I write your next appointment down?"

"What? No." He grabbed a towel, wrapped it tightly around his waist and put on his flip-flops. He vanished into a cabin made from cane stems to put the rest of his clothes on. A crumpled note was stuck in the glass.

"Sir?"

"Yes?!"

"Your phone." The masseuse handed him the device. He violently snapped it from her without any thanks.

The walls were getting nearer and nearer. It looked like they wanted to crush my bed. I jumped, ran, squeezed the handle in a hurry and opened the door with such force that it slammed into the wall. I gasped for breath, my arms leaning against my thighs and my middle section bent over. The night delivered the mysterious sounds of animal or insect voices above the Las Cuevas clearing to the veranda. Standing there, I tried to listen to anything that could distract my brain and drag the phobic visions outside of my head. My legs shuffled along the wooden floor to find a place to relax. They were trembling; in spite of that fact, I balanced bit by bit. A canvas bed, with both ends hanging on sturdy metal hooks, was swinging slightly from side to side. I headed to it, desperately wanting to rest in any place without walls. I climbed onto it, slid in and let the breeze caress me. I might have dreamt. There was a quiet knocking, then silence again. I was not sure, but I could have sworn I heard feet shuffling, then silence once more. It was certainly a dream. I pressed all my senses away from my head and attempted to fall asleep.

"Rudi, are you sleeping?" A light tap tickled my arm. As Matt appeared over my bed, I realised it was no dream.

"No." Both my legs hung from the rim of the bed; I sat up by seesawing using one leg to touch the ground.

"Did you need the air?"

"Yes, the room is too narrow, the walls wanted to crush my bed."

"Did your phobia visit you?" His chin gestured to get her approval to sit down.

"No, go sleep in your own bed, your fan club would be disappointed to see you sitting with a mad fool," I jibed. He settled next to me in spite of my comment.

"I was an idiot. You listened to what you shouldn´t have heard, I´m sorry."

"Have you just apologised? I don´t believe it. Listen! Did you hear that?"

"What?" He did not comprehend.

"Your crown fell down." Looking at him, I felt a compelling urge to laugh.

"I called you during the whole of New Year´s Eve."

"I know. Me too."

"I know, twice. I saw."

"The doctor said he would send my blood to the hospital. Did he?"

"I think so."

"Why? I was too exhausted to hear."

"Your fever was extremely high and your body was covered with many purple spots."

"Did I take some pills?"

"Of course, they needed to push the fever down."

"Which?

"Aspirin."

"The secret has been solved. I´m allergic to aspirin. It was my body´s reaction."

"It looked awful."

"Matt, I would like to sleep, I´m tired. Sorry I must send you away."

"Of course, princess." He jumped down. I stretched along the length of the canvas.

"Hi Gregory!" Surprise and thankfulness entered his voice when he noticed who was calling.

"Yes, I know him." A great number of his own taunts forced him to listen to. There was no request that he would not fulfil his son.

"I´ll call him and ask him." After a short gap, his hesitation changed to doubt.

"I would like to visit you." His breathing stopped for a while; he was prepared for a refusal.

"O.K., I´ll be there on Wednesday at 5, not a minute later. I promise I´ll be polite to anybody who crosses my path," his attempt at a joke went down badly: nobody laughed, not even him. He was thankful Gregory did not refuse his request.

Taxis were readily available at the building of the Honorary Consul. He did not call his assistant to order her to book his flight: he decided to do it himself. The thrill of Gregory answering his call pulsed through his veins.

"To San Pedro Airport." The distance between the consul´s residence to the airport consumed less than twenty minutes. It was not worth dialling the Belizean information service to obtain the phone number; the taxi would reach the airport quicker than his search would finish.

"Good morning, children." Trevor´s words woke me up. Sitting up, I switched each of my senses from a resting to a working state. "Are your beds occupied?"

"Morning, Dad." The greeting came from the floor. Matt´s back leant against the banister and his legs rested onto the wooden slabs, crossing each other.

"You lost your purple stains, Rudi."

"Yes, the aspirin has evaporated."

"Oh, no secret virus, just a negative bodily reaction to drugs."

"Hm." I shrugged my shoulders and smiled.

"Breakfast is done."

Trevor explained the plan for the next few days during our short walk to the mess hall. An enormous amount of picking up samples, working in the lab, putting the results into the computers and changing them into graphs and diagrams was described to us. I was glad. I needed to focus my mind to not think about the professor´s illegal deal and Gregory´s physical state. I knew if I had confessed and told Trevor everything, I would have ridded my troubles of. My inner fight between doing what was right and protecting my favourite professor would have been solved. A chair rattle distracted me from my thoughts. Everybody was sat at the table so I joined them.

"Where are you, Rudi?"

"I´m eating."

"I can see that. Where is your teasing? It´s strange. Did you forget it?"

"Is it a hangover? A terribly good New Year´s Eve?"

"Yes, Joseph, a two-week-long hangover. Put me in the Guinness World Records, would you?" A poker face blinded the surface of my face. I stood up. "Thank you for the breakfast, it was delicious." I slightly kissed the chubby cheeks of our landlady, who was cleaning the sink to prepare for dinner. Nobody needed any lunch. Anybody could ask a member of staff to prepare a packed lunch if they wanted one, which would supply the necessary energy for a long day full of physical work. Everybody from Las Cuevas Research Station left their temporary dormitories an unusually short time after breakfast. It was not worth starting their scientific work unless they arrived at the research areas when the watch hand reached 11. Twilight was at 6 and darkness came to the forest approximately one hour before it.

"I´ll be in the device storage area packing the necessaries. Trevor, have a nice day."

"Can I disturb you for a moment? It´s me, Fillip."

"Oh, it´s nice to hear from you again. What can I do for you?"

"I just need your confirmation that I can give your phone number to my son."

"Of course, I can´t see a reason why not. Do you know why he wants to call me?"

"I would like to, but I have no idea."

"O.K., tell him I´ll be looking forward to his call."

"I appreciate it. Goodbye."

"Have a nice day, Fillip."

No info panel announced the arrivals or departures at San Pedro Airport, just an aluminium board where cardboard rectangles, with big black letters creating destination names, were stuck in many horizontal rails, obeying orders blasting from the airport transmitter. People advanced to the plane: its number was identical to the flight heading to Philip S. W. Goldson International Airport.

"Hi honey, I spoke with Trevor. He is looking forward to your call. I´ll send it via text message." He managed to deal with all the things that bit at his mind. He wondered how he had not sensed any taunts for years. His ability to push all human weaknesses, such as empathy, mercy and sympathy, to his farthest brain lobe had enabled him to climb his career ladder at a cosmic speed. A truly tiny jolt of satisfaction shivered in his stomach.

The engine purr twisted around our Land Rover. I dragged the last packs of equipment and pushed them up onto the boot floor. I slammed the boot door with all my power, climbed into the driver´s seat and drove the car to collect all the members of our team.

The horn honked. The brake halted the car. I crept from my seat to the benches in the back positioned to the sides of the car. The door opened, the Land Rover´s crew settled in their usual places and we set off. I reposed, my head bouncing against the padded side each time the car wheels met a new rail built from hardened mud or hit an unexpectedly large stone. This west mountain road seemed rougher than any I had experienced before. Metal tools and equipment knocked against each other; the bottom of the bumper chafed against the ground from time to time when the wheels moved into the deepest part of a rail. The car unexpectedly stopped. We were thrown in the driver´s direction and some packs rolled down.

"What happened, professor?" Joseph asked, climbing back on the bench.

"Yesterday´s storm knocked that tree down, it´s blocking the road."

"Have we got a chainsaw?"

"No, just three axes."

"That is a joke, isn´t it?

"No."

"Where are they?" Every male member of the crew turned to me.

"Under the benches." My fingers fumbled for a moment, then they hit things similar to small latches. I squatted down to look at how to loosen them. They worked in the same way as locks on suitcase bags: I had to pull down and the upper part would be shot into the air. There was just one on my side. I took my axe and jumped down, looking at where would be easiest to begin cutting. Minutes passed; I was thankful for the last storm. All my boiled emotions were disguised as a great effort to free the road. I chopped using my whole strength. Wooden chips flew around me. My muscles stretched with each cut and sweat beads rolled down my skin.

"Leave it! Rudi! Leave it!" the professor shouted.

"Why?!" I was furious, confused and disillusioned. The axe slipped from my palm and landed on the ground. The professor bent down, took it and started chopping. I stood there, observing him mutely.

"Shit!" Turning on my heel, I disappeared among the dense foliage of a nearby forest. Within several steps the amount of plant growth got smaller, then got rarer and in the end the floor was almost empty. The canopy trapped every sun beam, which were absorbed by leaves and transferred into oxygen. I was walking unconsciously, deep in thought, when the edge of a nearby extremely dense section of forest stopped me. I was sure there must have been another route or stream that went across the forest and the sun could have sent an arbitrary number of rays that no canopy could restrain. I found a less thick area of growth and pressed through it. A lake with turquoise water spread in a round ditch. Bushes and trees surrounded it, bending their crowns downwards. They tickled the water´s surface with tiny leaves or twigs. Circles were made and dispersed across the water´s surface each time a leaf or twig touched the water. I settled on the ground in a ball, my arms bracing my legs and my chin pushing down onto the top of my knees. I slightly swung forwards and backwards, crooning and trying to calm my temper. I did not notice any movement beside me, any subtle shuffling. My eyes pierced the lake. My thoughts bit at my mind.

"Spill it." The words sounded dumb, like they had come from a different space. I did not jump but strived to find the direction of the voice. Then the volume got louder and I caught the source.

"What happened, Rudi?" Mathew asked.

"Nothing." I withdrew into a ball and began swinging again without finishing my response.

"Spit it out, Rudi. Please."

My words scrambled up, one by one. "I knew he´d die, but I did not expect it to come so early." The first sentence was the most difficult. The next flowed from me easily. "I knew the entire diagnosis. I studied the DMD´s progress for many nights. But there was a small hope: a website wrote that some patients can live until their forties. I had hope. He is dying, I know it. I couldn´t even recognise where the respiratory tubes began and where his body ended." I spat it all out as he had asked, with one sentence immediately following another. I could not have stopped if I wanted to. His arms cuddled me, holding me tightly, and his lips pressed against my temple. I felt as if all my guts had been torn from me. Just a giant hole was left.

"What is DMD?" he asked.

"Duchenne muscular dystrophy," I replied. Mathew swallowed.

"Are you taking about that boy who went diving with us?"

"Yes. He´s Gregory."

"Do you like him?" I loosened the cuddle and looked at him in incomprehension.

"I like you, too. And he´s never asked me such a strange question."

"Do you only *like* me?"

"No, I´ve actually realised I hate you." He dragged me back and brushed my forehead. We laughed. I enjoyed his company. I felt much freer than I had a few minutes before.

25

"I´ll ask him. I can´t tell you why without his confirmation, but I can see no reason why he refused your proposal." A silent pause ate the next few minutes. He listened to him.

"I have it. I´ll spell it out so you can check it and write it down correctly." Another gap consumed a short time period.

"O.K. That´s a solution, too," he said, waiting again for a reply.

"I wrote it down correctly." The pencil in his hand skipped from one letter to another until he arrived at the last letter of the email address.

"Thank you, you, too." His fingers shoved the piece of paper into his shirt pocket. The pencil occupied its former place again, stuck in the plastic circle of a sunshield protecting the driver against sunbeams. The engine woke up and the car kept driving. He had checked the west side of Chiquibul National Park today; the south peak remained, but it was too late to go in that direction. He decided to go back to Las Cuevas Research Station. Kilometres were abandoned behind him. Suddenly, the top part of a Land Rover trapped his attention.

"A day called by name AN IDIOT?" A polite smile accompanied Trevor´s question.

"Yes."

"Don´t you have a chainsaw?"

"No."

"Are you crazy?" He disappeared behind his SUV, returning with a big chainsaw in his hand and smiling. The tree was finally cut into many pieces. Each one of them became part of the timber road trim.

"Can we leave? Is everybody on board?"

"Yes," Matt responded. He sounded so convincing that nobody noticed we had climbed aboard just a second ago. The Rover reversed for two kilometres to reach the last junction. With a manoeuvre involving many partial reverses and awkward shifts forward, the car set off to the research station.

A black Jaguar turned into a private little park on Church Lane in Lancaster. Its driver's soles touched the ground outside and his door was slammed shut. Another door was opened. The walls of the house had witnessed his boasting and pride numerous times. The house seemed half a metre lower than usual, as if he had shrunk. The handle was pushed down by the palm of a genteel old lady. No invitation, no comment: there was just that open door telling him to go inside or leave. He bowed down to her in an attempt to kiss her cheek. She automatically avoided him in the same way as last time. His legs carried him along the hallway to his old childhood room. He hesitantly knocked on the door but nobody answered. There was the sound of water splashing, a mute period and then a quiet handle click.

"Hi, Dad." The greeting came from the bathroom. He could not read Gregory's emotion from his expression or from his voice.

"It's nice to see you."

"Let's skip the formalities."

"You called and said you wanted to speak with me. Am I right?"

"Yes."

"And? . . . Has anything changed?"

"Nope." Wheeling his chair to the children's bedroom, he did not look at his father as he passed him.

"I'll put my jacket and cap on, and we can leave."

"Leave? For where?"

"To have lunch."

"Lunch? O.K."

The driver helped Gregory to climb off his wheelchair onto the rear seat and checked Gregory's comfort.

"Excuse me," Gregory said. The driver halted on his way to the car boot and went back to wheeling the turned-up chair in front of him.

"Yes, Gregory?"

"Do you know St John's C of E Church, on West Derby Road near the crossroad with Green Lane?"

Monika Pistovčák

"It's in Liverpool, isn't it?"

"Yes."

"And?"

"I would like to ask you to take me to a particular address."

"Anywhere," he winked.

"11 Green Lane, Liverpool. Is that possible?"

"Liverpool Men's Centre is there."

"Yes."

"Mum and Anne." Fillip bade his adieu and left the house. Confusion and uncertainty accompanied his departure. He did not want to face their direct refusal again. His self-confidence and cowardice prevented him from trying again. Instead, he headed over to the luxurious car.

"Where are we going to eat?" Gregory asked. The car wheels stirred and the vehicle joined the road. An hour passed and a response had still not been given.

"Alex."

"Yes, sir?" The driver paid his attention to Mr Fillip.

"Do you know our destination?"

"Of course." The rear mirror reflected his secret satisfaction. They reached the end of motorway junction 58 and passed three entrances into Liverpool before the blinker announced their intent to turn. The board above the road spoke of a variety of direction possibilities. The driver chose the exit to junction 57. Letting several vehicles go before him, he moved into the next lane and they progressed on their journey.

"Liverpool Men's Centre," Fillip read aloud. The voice full of wonder swam in the cab. He faced Gregory, waiting for a response or explanation.

"Our first lunch, Dad," Gregory said. Alex left his seat to get the wheelchair from the boot.

"No, thanks Alex. You are too polite to me. I think it's a dad's job to help his child. Am I wrong?" No protest and no arrogant order was given to assert his boss position. His father's shoes met the ground, the door was slammed, the boot was unlocked and the unfolded wheelchair stood poised and waiting for Gregory. Gregory slid in it with his dad's assistance and the wheels set off towards the main entrance.

The noisy clatter of dishes invited them into the room as soon as they left a long narrow corridor. Two glass door wings allowed them to walk into a giant hall. Several table rows were occupied by men of different ages, looks and mental or physical states. The one thing, which was related to every man in the hall, called the bad social situation. They were homeless.

"Why are we here? Is this my punishment?"

"No, I love to help." Gregory wheeled over to a person who neared them. They shook hands and exchanged information. Gregory moved his chair over to an unusually long table carrying one dozen giant bowls full of hot soup. Ladles binged every time they hit the porcelain surface of a plate. The queue on the opposite side of the table stretched across the hall: it seemed there was no end to it. The frost reigning outside on the streets, parks and even the suburbs too, forced them to look for any kind of sanctuary.

The job consumed him totally. Men approached his part of the table, put their empty plates on the board and thanked him for their dishes honestly. It was not easy for him to bow down to get plates from the low shelves. His muscles did not obey him each time his brain sent information to them. It was worth fighting with them. It helped him and the men in the same way.

"Sir," someone said. Fillip jumped.

"Can I ask you for a job?" A man wearing an expensive faded coat offered him his hand.

"Call me—this is my address card." Shame might have been one of the many reasons why his manner became polite and full of respect.

"I appreciate it, thanks." The man nodded goodbye and disappeared among the people in the hall.

Darkness fell on the streets. Lamp globes dispersed light rays into the space, big fat snowflakes full of water drops built up on the ground and the frost changed them into a slippery hard shell.

"Sit down. Calm down." She had been pacing for almost an hour, looking through the window to check the black street. No lights pierced the dark hue of the January evening. No limousine stopped at the pavement between the house and the small private park, no door slam deleted the silence of the late hour: just big heavy white flakes landing on the windowsill.

"Anne—Marie, don´t call him." The palm of a gracious old lady wrapped around the mobile phone.

"Anne—Marie, he behaves like an idiot the majority of time, but he´s his father. Nothing will have happened. Believe me." She faced her, calmly pronouncing parts of the sentence to emphasise them and erase doubts from her mind. Shadows of trees ran across the kitchen as the lights illuminated the park.

"They´ve arrived," she smiled. She observed her daughter-in-law, squeezing her shoulder. She left her stood at the window and walked over to the unlocked door. She was impressed: she had never had the opportunity to see an image similar to this. Her son gave no orders. Everything was done on his own.

"Hi, Granny." His infectious enthusiasm woke her up. He turned the wheel on his chair; it slipped. His thumb pressed a button, the chair moved by electrical engine and then slipped again. His hands braced the chair handles and forced it to move forwards.

"Good evening, Mum."

"Good evening. Bad road?"

"Yes, icy roads."

"Can you come tomorrow, too?" The question caught him out. Gregory waited for dad´s reply.

"Dad?"

"Oh, yes, of course, why not. I´d be glad."

A shining cone ending with an oval made an uncountable amount of light rays. All the measurements were written in my notebook, and the single samples were zipped in plastic sacks and labelled with a detailed description, the species, the area number and the date. Items of many piles disappeared, the rows on the papers were covered with semi-results, which were written in pencil as I had known they would be erased and swapped for the final results. I withdrew into the work. The click of the digital wall clock, with its figures stating the exact time, threw me back into reality. My eyes burned me like they were on fire. I placed the remaining samples in the bottom of a cardboard box, added labels and filled them in with all the necessary data so they would not be filed in the wrong place. Putting things in order, all my body parts yelled at me in exhaustion. A key locked up the lab. My legs conveyed me to my temporary home.

Bird chirrups and insect fiddles tickled my sensitive ear cell membranes. Beams glanced when they hit dewdrops swinging on blades, leaves and spider webs. The dawn painted the sky a whole scale of hues, weaving the clearing into a breath-taking gown. The intensity of the morning scent overwhelmed me. It streamed through my nostrils and whirled down my pharynx to be transported to each inch of my body. Heading to the dining hall, I imagined boiling water in the blue kettle beside a mug with grains of instant coffee and milk poured into the coffee at the end.

A sound similar to an engine purr distracted me from my lovely thoughts. It was unusual at that early morning hour, but our work the day before had neither started nor finished, so the professor might have decided to leave at dawn to do some of the incomplete work before we joined him later. I paid attention to the purr as I continued in my previous direction. My growing desire for a mug full of fragrant coffee surged me forward. The purr suddenly changed to a strange rattle akin to the motor roar produced by a car crossing a road five decades ago. My curiosity forced me to check the sound´s source. Creeping along the pillars holding the construction of the wooden main building, I saw him. A man in a round black hat and a dark shirt or jacket leaned against a Chevrolet van from the sixties, arguing with the professor. The roar absorbed their entire conversation. I squatted down and awkwardly approached the other side of the van using a duck-like walk. The rear bumper served me as a handle to keep my balance while I crouched.

"Don´t be stupid, together we could manage it and put this bad business in order."

"His tentacles are longer than we can imagine."

"Yes, and that is the reason why we must co-operate."

"Can you tell me the right way?"

"The government is the only way."

"Are you so naive?"

"The legal way is the solution. His people won´t recoil at anything. I already experienced this recently and I´m worried they won´t finish yet."

"I was blind when I agreed to his deal. I would have never supposed such horrible conclusions."

"It´s too late to regret it. You´ll tell him everything was done according to his conditions. That´ll give us two or three days, at least."

"Then?"

"We´ll confess to somebody trustworthy and with useful connections to the government."

"Call him today." They departed. I saw their legs disappear over the van´s edge. It was necessary for me to evaporate immediately. A big tree with a wide trunk became my sanctuary. I pressed my arms to its body, held my knees together and tried to mingle with its bark. Allowing him time to leave the place, I observed as the van crossed the station´s clearing towards the forest edge. I had never met the mysterious man, I was sure of that, but I knew the conversation was related to the professor´s business with the red wood in an ambiguous way.

"My coffee." Peeking my head out from the trunk´s shelter, I recognised the coast was clear. My run to the dining hall building seemed never-ending, in spite of the fact that it took less than a minute.

A small green figure lit up to allow the pedestrians to cross. He neared a taxi rank at the local bus station. Behind the last taxi, a luxury Jaguar stood waiting. Alex came over to him and took his school bag, accompanied him to the rear door and helped him slide onto the seat.

"Where is he?" Gregory´s voice was full of curiosity.

"At the kiosk. He needed some newspapers."

"Hm." He had just fastened his seatbelt when the fresh chill air flew into the cab.

"Hi son."

"Hi."

"Do you think there would be a possibility in the near future to pick you up directly in front of your school?"

"None." He looked at him for a short moment.

"O.K. Where would you like to go today?" Changing the topic of their talk, he veiled the sudden disappointment in his voice.

"To the swimming pool."

"Where?"

"Sandpiper Leisure Club, Lancaster University Sport Centre, on Green Lane." Fillip addressed his question to his driver.

"Do you know it, Alex?" He nodded wordlessly. The car abandoned the place and joined the traffic.

"Could you pass me my bag?" He reached over to the free seat and handed it to him.

"Thanks." It became the last word for a long mute period. The figures on a digital display positioned next to the dashboard changed their shapes and values as time run. The turquoise small cloud with a chubby white "S" was the first icon that his mouse pointer clicked on. Disappointment circulated through his body.

"Rudi hasn´t sent me any e-mails. There is no signal perhaps." Granny´s old remark popped out for a minute, hit his mind. His email inbox showed several new rows in bold. He skipped through them until the last results of his winter exams caught his interest.

"Mathematics A, History A . . ."

He did not need to continue reading: all the subjects had the same grade. The next email was his rehabilitation schedule for the following two weeks. He quickly flicked through all its content. It was not bad, easy to cope with. Running from the first to the last unopened row a few times, he saw none had been sent from the expected email address.

> *"Hi*
>
> *I know you must have been scared. Several heart failures could scare anybody. I´m O.K., the breathing accessories were returned to the hospital storage, I began attending school again, going to physio . . .*
>
> *Please answer as promptly as possible. I get bored. ;o)"*

"Sir, we´ve arrived." Alex disturbed him from his emailing. The unconscious light touch of the heel of his palm on the sensitive PC rectangle turned off his inbox.

A delightful nostril-tickling coffee aroma hovered around the kitchen´s corner and into the dinner hall. My thoughts wandered to around a quarter of an hour ago; numbers and figures flashed through my mind. I tried to collect them in order to drag them out the hole in my imagination. Sipping my coffee, a pencil stuck in the rails of a notepad on the refrigerator door caught my attention. I approached, pulled the pencil out, tore a small piece of paper from the block and drew a rectangle, placing all the items from my brain onto the small paper square.

"BELIZE C.A." The name of the state created the first row, the left edge had "O" and "W" one under another, and the central position was occupied by "C" and the number 15073. I folded the paper in half and put it into my rear trouser pocket. The pencil was again pressed into its little rail. A silhouette emerged from the door frame.

"Do you have any idea what time is?" Matt approached me.

"Good morning, nice to see you," I winked at him. I raised my mug in his direction and sipped my elixir.

"Is the water hot enough to make more coffee?" Answerless, the next mug was put on the sink board. Grains of instant coffee fell onto the bottom. The sound of boiling water was ceased with a click as the kettle light switched off. The water was poured into the mug. The nostril-provoking fragrance conjured warmth in the early morning hours.

"Have you already slept?"

"Why?"

"I saw you disappear into the lab and the light was still switched on at 1.30 am."

"Did you spy on me?"

"No, I was reading. Don´t make stuff up," he replied. I was not fed up with his grinning. It seemed that sometimes he did it unconsciously. I picked out the folded paper from my pocket and put it under his nose.

"What?" he asked. As my fingers flattened the paper, he read it.

"It´s a licence plate number, isn´t it?"

"Yes, can you help me?"

"How?"

"Is the Belizean register of licence numbers accessible to anybody?"

"No, it´s in the hands of the police."

"Do you know somebody with access to the database?"

"No, but I hope that Dad does. Whose number is it?"

"If I knew that then I wouldn't be asking you, would I?"

"Why is it so important to know it?"

"I think it's related to the professor and his business with the red wood," I replied. He froze.

"Where did you obtain the number?"

"As I was returning from the lab about an hour ago." His brows were raised in incomprehension. "They made some verbal agreement against an enemy. They didn't name him, but from the context, you could understand it was connected with the professor's business. They both won't continue. It sounded as if they wished they had never been a part of it. They dislike it but have no idea how to get out of it."

His expression remained frozen. "Describe that man to me." I did so, point by point from top to toe. There was no aspect of him that I did not mention. "It's similar to a Mennonite member," he commented. "The letters O and W are the initials of Orange Walk District. They live there in Spanish Lookout."

"Is it a big city?"

"A little bit bigger than a big village."

"You are bad—small country, small cities."

"Rudi, have you fallen in love with Belize?"

"It's a much better choice than with you, isn't it?"

"And, yes I am bad. But I'm just an amateur in comparison with you. My heart is bleeding."

"Press your hand on it and your bleeding will stop." The last sip flew down my larynx. He stood up, the paper braced between his fingers, and wrapped the palm of his other hand around my wrist. "Have you finished?" I asked. He twisted his mug on its axis for a while. Its landing in the sink was done more quickly and with stronger power than necessary.

A chlorine odour slapped anyone as soon as their foot touched the first tile of the swimming pool area. Turquoise water rippled in many subtle waves produced by the motions of several swimmers in three trails separated from the rest of the pool with red plastic tubes. The remaining half of the pool was left for public use. Nobody's attention focused on the wheels crossing the blue tiles to reach the pool's edge.

"To the edge?" his father asked.

"Hm."

"I don´t know how. No experience."

"Put your arms under my armpits and around my chest, hold your hands tightly together and shift me towards the edge," Gregory instructed him. His father slowly lifted his body down. Gregory´s knees shook and doubts entered his mind: he was not sure if his muscles worked in the same way as several months ago, before the heart failures.

"Dad, don´t worry. The water will help me." Fillip undid his hands. The liquid surrounded Gregory´s middle. A marvellous feeling circulated through his body and his arms let the water caress his skin. He swam. His arm muscles moved his body forwards, leaving the rest of him floating a few inches under the surface. One metre, then two, ten, twenty, thirty, fifty . . . finally, he hit the opposite side of the pool. Satisfaction, cheer and exhaustion mixed inside him, emerging and immersing in unexpected circles.

"That´s enough, I´m afraid," Fillip commented.

"Why?"

"I don´t know, just a strange feeling."

"Fifty metres? I used to swim more."

"But, that was . . ." He fell into silence.

"It was before the heart failures?" Gregory asked. His dad nodded, pressing down a huge lump in his throat. He was nervous: showing feelings in public was new to him, he had never experienced it.

"Relax, Dad. Put your arms behind that bar and let the water play with you," he smirked. Tiny waves splashed against the tiled walls. Whistles cut through the air, then a swimming coach instructed his swimmers to start. Loud clicks as the wall clock ticked away were periodically repeated. They relaxed, hanging on the chrome bar with their armpits.

"Why did you choose Bernicia?"

"What?" The sudden question caught him unprepared. His breath was taken away. His grey cells worked to invent the perfect response that would not sound like a prevarication.

"What has she got that Mum doesn´t?" Gregory pierced his father´s thoughts with the new query.

"Nothing."

"Why did you do it? I can´t see the purpose."

"Too much testosterone?"

"Mum is a beautiful, clever and nice person, where is the real point?"

"Too nice, too polite and too fragile."

"No, you are wrong, Mum is strong."

"Strong?"

"Yes. She is." Stretching his body on the water´s surface, he left his father at the wall. He swam to the side beside the entrance.

"Excuse me, please." Gregory shouted at the lifeguard passing by. "Can I ask for your help?" His chin gestured to his wheelchair.

"Of course." The guy easily helped him to settle in his chair with a few professional movements.

"Thanks."

26

All their daily responsibilities done, every one of the scientists returned to the station before twilight. No lost members were announced and no illegal logging groups or signs of their work had been discovered. He was exhausted, but no further problems affected his mind that would prevent him from enjoying his son´s company. Walking along the corridor, he approached the staircase to the rest of the station. The lights streaming from the windows of the dining hall lit up the clearing beside them; a head or a silhouette flitted there for a short period. Dull sounds from the steps neared him. He saw two shadows of heads emerging from the staircase.

"Dad?"

"Mathew?"

"Good afternoon, Mr Trevor."

"Oh Rudi, have you had a nice day?" There was a mute gap.

"Do you have a minute?"

"Yes, what´s happened?"

"We need your help."

"Now?"

"Is that possible?"

"Of course."

"Can we go into your office, Mr Trevor?"

"O.K., follow me." Trailing him wordlessly, we walked into his room. His hand snapped on the light switch and he offered us chairs.

"Thank you, Mr Trevor, I´ll stand." Mathew dragged the paper out from his pocket and flattened it on the desk.

"A licence number from the Orange Walk District. And?"

Trevor asked.

"I would like to know its owner."

"Why?"

"Hm." Hesitation hovered above us. I did not want to accuse the professor before I had evidence that he had seriously crummy intent when he agreed with that absurd business. I was fighting against my emotions. One part of me wanted to say that because they were friends, Trevor should understand and help to solve the problem. The second part of my personality screamed at me to shut up and keep the secret until I had gathered more evidence. I clutched the handle to leave, to finish the fight inside me.

"Rudi?" I halted in the middle of the door frame. "Is it related to the thing that you mentioned that night?"

I swallowed and looked at the ground, hoping I could find the right response there. "Yes." My sharp hoarse agreement drifted into the air.

"Please, come back." A chair was dragged to the side. Looks were exchanged. I slowly sat down, crossed my legs under me and wrapped my palms around the edges of the chair.

"Rudi. Look at me."

"I think I´d rather go."

"I know you like the professor, I do too, but it´s necessary to put everything in order. All right?"

"Hm."

> *"It is nice to hear from you again. I´m not sure if the station is the right place for handicapped people, but I´ll try my best to change it.*
>
> *I can easily answer your second question: yes, she is here and she is going to stay here until the end of March at least. So, if you are confident and decide to do it, write me.*
>
> *Sincerely, Trevor"*

A smile spread across his face. Life suddenly wore a pinker shade and the upcoming hour of rehabilitation seemed more attractive than it had a minute ago.

"Please come in." A polite voice invited him to enter the kingdom full of ancient torture devices.

"At last?"

"Finally," she replied. He gave her a polite wink.

"You are too young to flirt with me."

"Age is just a shell that people hide in," he retorted. She raised her eyebrows. A tiny smile flew across her lips.

"Too young to be a philosopher." She kept writing her comments. His sight became glued to the paper sheet.

"Too young to become an observer."

"An observer?" she asked. She shifted her body, interested in his last remark.

"How many hard lives have you observed between these walls?" She froze for a while, then smiled.

"You may wonder that, but it has taught me to smile at common problems. Can we start?" His wheels moved towards her. Exercise equipment was scattered in all directions in the room. His arms were put along two parallel bars. He pulled himself up using all his arms' muscles and the power streaming from them. Beads began rolling down his temples and his hair got wet.

An awkward silence hovered under the office ceiling. Eyes pierced the floor, refusing to look at anybody in the room.

"Did Joseph tell anybody?"

"I don't think so. He didn't attach any importance to it."

"Today, were you there on your own? There was nobody who could have seen you?"

"No! What a strange question." I raised my head to try to perceive the purpose of the query from his facial expression, or another clue that could convince me and help my attempt to answer questions regarding the obscurities occurring around me.

"Rudi, don't worry. I don't intend to hurt Andrew, he's one of my best friends. I just need to make circumstances clear so I can help him." My lower lip was partly concealed under my upper as I continually dipped my teeth into it. "Rudi?"

"I don´t know what threats and means that Russian man used, but they were scared of something. And believe me, Russians don´t usually act in the way of white-gloved gentlemen." Both their heads cocked and their foreheads wrinkled. "It´s simple. I come from a country in the former block of communism. Don´t get involved with anything related to them, don´t start any business with them."

"Apparently, Andrew did." Trevor´s remark was strained through his teeth.

"Yes. And the man from the morning too."

"It´s time to go, or there won´t be any dinner left for us." With a short look at his watch, he urged us to leave.

A long phone ring ignored the mute air in the waiting room. His hand slipped into his inner coat pocket. Checking the shining display, satisfaction appeared on his face.

"Yes?" he asked into his mobile phone.

"I´m glad I can listen to this kind of news. I know you are one very clever man, no doubt about it."

"I´ll send an e-mail with all the details." Pacing and smiling, he looked like he had won first prize in the lottery, or got a free flight to the moon.

"The old art of threatening." He spoke under his breath, grinning and not noticing his surroundings. The pupils of a teenage girl sitting on the sofa in one of the waiting room´s corners got larger and wider. She had no idea about the reason for his cheer, but she could not see any intelligent connection between cheer and the word ´threat´.

"Paula, it´s your time, honey." The rehab nurse asked the girl to come in. She took her crutches that leant against the sofa beside her and folded them under her armpits. Swinging forwards, she vanished behind the door of the doctor´s office.

"Gregory´s having a shower, be patient. It´ll just take a few minutes," the nurse informed him. Thrill, happiness and the feeling of winning circulated around his veins. The insignificant speech of the nurse did not have the power to pierce his bubble of glory and reach his ear drums.

"Is Gregory still exercising?" She smiled wordlessly, leaving him in his own world. She backed away and closed the door, silently. A short irritation boiled in his tummy but his previous feelings pushed it down. He approached a coffee machine, read the labels covered with the names of different types and made his choice, in the end. He pressed the round metal button with the label "Italian latte". Several sips dropped through his larynx; he started coughing, his eyes reddened and tears seeped around the edges of his eyelids. The glass door was opened. He unconsciously jumped. The rest of the latte landed on his luxurious coat and some drops hit his trousers.

"Shit!"

"Dad?" Handing his dad a soft hankie, Gregory laughed. His father, who kept his stony poker face during any circumstances, was brushing his clothes furiously and expressing a gesture of desperation. It seemed like a colossal disaster had happened to him. Gregory kept smirking and wheeled towards the exit.

Mathew halted the Land Rover at the edge of Spanish Lookout. He flattened a map on the dashboard, browsing around the sheet. I re-read the address of the owner of the licence plate number, which Trevor´s unnamed friend had pulled out from the police database and wrote on a piece of paper from a notebook. Trevor had never broken any rules. I could imagine the size of his self-denial when he had asked for that ´small´ favour from the guy.

"Here." Holding the shred of paper above the map, my forefinger pointed to the coloured line.

"Fine."

"Matt, it´s just two blocks, we could walk." Matt reversed the Rover along a tiny path, leaving a couple of centimetres on my side so I could get off. I skipped down and left the place. Mathew locked the car and followed me. Multi-coloured bungalows without fences lined both sides of the main road. Children played in the yards in front of them, animals ran along the road and grandparents sat on benches smiling, absorbing the sunbeams.

"Here." Mathew turned into a street, obeying the direction sign on the opposite side of the street. Minutes passed; we found it strange. We had abandoned more than two hundred metres behind our backs and we had not met any house, building or construction that indicated a human being lived there.

"We should go back," I said.

"It´s here." Matt´s fingertip poked part of the line drawn on the map.

"I know, but nothing is here. We can return and drive the car there." An enormous dislike was written his face.

"Here." The keys loosely dangled between his fingers. Then they were lost for a second in his fist and were offered to me a second later.

"I´m so glad that real gentlemen are not extinct." Flattening my palm at his eye level, the keys dropped into my hand. He settled on the ground, ironically waved at me and crossed his legs. The sun had risen to the top of the horizon, creating an angle of ninety degrees. Hot sharp beams stabbed my skin. I started rushing to be sheltered in the Rover´s cab. A group of three guys chatted at the corner of the crossroad. Their voice intonations whirled the air around. Excitement, discord and an intermittent higher tone bounced between them. I passed them by when a flash in the back of my mind halted my legs for an instant.

´I know him,´ my brain screamed at me. Less than two blocks remained. My shoulder hurt me more and more. Consciousness kicked me forwards and I was curious to observe the men from the comfort of the Rover.

"Тебе ненадо бояться."
(There is no reason to worry.)

"Я не планирую . . ."
(I´m not going to . . .)

The caller on the phone was shouting at the top of his voice, so some sequences of their talk were fairly audible.

"I assure you there is nobody who could notice any connection."

There was a short break while he listened to a screaming man. He did not bother to communicate in Russian any more. The caller´s behaviour became nonsensical. Nobody had ventured to talk to him that way before.

"Calm down! I know! You won´t lose your position at the embassy!" A wordless gap spread its tentacles across the car´s cab. An engine croon flooded the space. The former stressful air flew outside through miniature pores in the glass panes.

"All right. The next appointment will be arranged after my arrival." He looked at the boy sitting approximately half a metre away from him. His sight was glued to a screen and his lips stretched towards his ears now and then. No interest in the phone call, the chap enjoyed his own world.

"Gregory?"

"Yes, Dad?" Not quitting his typing, his sight still attracted by the computer screen, he answered because it was polite.

"Can you give me a couple of seconds?" He raised his eyebrows.

"O.K. Are you irritated with my writing?" His dad pretended he had not heard his question.

"I´m going to leave for two or three weeks."

"And? You´ve never told me before. Don´t taunt me."

"I would like you to accompany me."

"Fine." His fingers started criss-crossing on the keyboard again.

"Gre-go-ry." He emphasised every sound.

"Speak. I´m listening." His father made no motion towards him. Many dumb clicks and the purr of an engine could be heard.

"Jump in." My arm held the Rover door open.

"Finally."

"You are rude!" I did not believe what had hit my eardrums.

"What are you doing, princess?"

"I´m reversing."

"I can see that," he replied. I stamped on the brake. He flew forward: only a devilishly little amount of free space remained between his forehead and the windscreen.

"I´m fed up with you. Comprende, amigo?!" Seriousness reigned in our battlefield for a while. Mathew got confused. "Have you got sunstroke?" I giggled.

"You are terrible," he commented. My foot pushed the pedal down again and the car neared the crossroad.

"There, that man with the dark grey hat with a round brim."

"And?"

"He´s the owner of that licence number. He was talking with the professor."

"Drive forward. We can wait for him on his yard." The Rover moved at the right moment when the men had finished their conversation. Each one went his own way. Our wheels cut shreds off the hard uneven road and hit many bumps and rails of tyres in dried mud. If the wheel springs could have sweated, they would have.

"A car is driving behind us. Stamp on the accelerator!"

"No, I´ll damage the car."

"Turn in there," Matt instructed me.

"Those are bushes!"

"It´s just a pretty tall weed on the former lane, bushes line its sides."

"O.K., you´re the boss." The massive iron bumper forced its way into the weed. Tiny young bush twigs hidden among the long stems were smashed.

"What now?"

"We'll wait until he drives by," Matt said. My heebie-jeebies got stronger, mangling my guts, I missed the fresh air. Mathew kept observing the scene in the rear mirror. I skipped out into the mass of untrampled stalks. The thick soles of my track shoes pushed plants aside as I tried to reach the edge of the road, but their sharp blades caused many little cuts on the bare skin of my thighs. It might not have been the right decision to wear shorts.

"Shit," I swore as a thorn pierced the limb's surface and a teeny nick went red. The rattle of an engine distracted my attention. I squatted down, thrill climbed along my nervous system and my heart rate dramatically increased, its thuds almost making me deaf. The car continued bouncing from one hard bump to a temporary ditch then to a rail, and repeated it once again. I got back into the Rover.

"Hell! You frightened me."

"I'll knock next time," I smirked at him. The keys were turned in the ignition and the engine purr flooded the cab. The wheels hit the roads. No car was in the distance. Kilometres passed and our vertebras clapped among themselves as the surface's raggedness compelled the Rover to jump instead of glide along the terrain. The next metres were cut from the road when a farm emerged from bushes. The wide-fenced yards were without animals; there were no sounds coming from the stalls and a powerful tractor had a semi-trailer joined onto it.

"Shit." My curse dropped into the air. The man in the hat with a round brim was squeezing a shotgun in his hands as he neared the Rover. The door handle clicked and the door of Rover got opened. The gun end pushed the door back and the lock clicked. He gestured for me to roll the window down. I did.

"Have you followed me?" My head shook from side to side. "Who sent you?"

"The professor."

"Does he have a name?"

"Dragonsky, Andrew."

"Reason?"

"Let me get out and you will know."

"If I don't?"

"You'll be a mad jerk."

"I wouldn't be so rude if I were in your skin, honey," he said sarcastically. I did not respond but pressed open the door.

"What? Will you shoot me? Go away!" My fingers were rooting in my pocket angrily, pulled a piece of paper out and energetically shoved it into his breast pocket. "If you want, you can shoot me now." Turning on my heel, I climbed back into my seat and the Rover headed in the town´s direction. I could see in the rear mirror how he stayed there for a while. He was stunned perhaps, standing there motionless.

"Have you gone crazy?" Matt queried.

"Are you alive? So, don´t shout at me." Gripping the steering wheel, emotions mangled my insides. I had enormously good luck.

27

The periodical rhythm of his pacing got irritating. The situation was serious enough without pouring hot iron in the water.

"He might have decided not to come. It´s too big a risk. It´s not worth him hanging his career on a rusty nail."

"No panic, he´ll appear in a moment."

"Good afternoon, Trevor." He stopped his never-ending pacing and his face lightened.

"My research fellow Andrew. Andrew, this is Mr Bastian."

Oral testimonies, evidence and printed papers carrying emails massages sent from the same address, from the same company, written by the same person, arrived in the professor´s inbox. The one that contained the application to become a participant of the Forest Stewardship Council was delivered directly to Trevor´s email inbox. Trevor had already read each one of Andrew´s emails several times before he forced his old friend to reveal the truth. He had broken Mathew´s and Rudi´s obstinacy: when things gathered a terrible quick pace and took a decidedly dangerous direction, they gave up. Pages full of orders and different kinds of threats were put on his desk.

"O.K. people, here is the scenario." Minutes passed; the voice of the one man hovered near the office ceiling. One piece of information fused into the next, slowly creating sense and a plan. No orders, no questions, no demands. He explained just the modus operandi, nothing else. There remained one possibility: "TAKE IT OR GO!" The monologue stopped and his last words echoed for a period in their brains.

"Did you open the right window?"

"Yes, princess!" He barked under his breath. Irritation peeked out from each gesture.

"I can´t hear anything."

"Be quiet and you will do." The conference hall part of the building towered above us. No information escaped from the open window, unfortunately.

The boy´s head repeatedly knocked against the window pane as he slept. The eleven hours of travel had beaten him. He let him rest, gluing his sight on the scene running beside the road. Valleys with forest vegetation changed into roads lined by savannahs with occasional bushes. The Maya Mountains peeked at them from their majestic heights in the distance. The screeching of vultures, which caused goose bumps on his skin, trailed off. The shrill cries of monkeys and parrots crossed the way from time to time, sounding similar to a strange language. The sound intensity got stronger as the Land Cruiser went deeper into the rainforest. He hated these uncomfortable parts of the job; if his son had not persuaded him to become part of the secret expedition, he would have instructed his guys to lead this affair to its end. The dark grey threads of twilight started dropping down and filling every free space. The driver switched the headlights on, stabbing the rays through the descending darkness. They danced according to the car´s bounces, increasing the feeling that the dark was in progress. He leaned his neck against the padded part of the seat, closed his eyes and allowed his brain to think. His eyelids got extremely heavy. He fell asleep for a period. Black dreams varied in short flashes. He slept.

"No problem, amigo. I´ll reverse a little bit." The driver´s shouting woke him up. The Land Cruiser was carefully backing into the wider part of a road. Twigs overlapping the edge covered with a rich green mass met the car door and a couple of long scratches were created by the prickles or other malicious parts growing on them. The car halted, the window was rolled down and the driver peeked out for a while, waiting until the opposite vehicle passed him.

"How far is it to Las Cuevas Research Reservation?" the driver asked the man in the other car.

"A few minutes, fifteen max. Thanks, amigo."

"You are welcome." The SUV set off slowly to pass the Cruiser without the smallest touch. The passengers in the rear seats gave each other quick glances. They returned to their previous activities, uninterested in each other. He leaned his head against the padded seat. The man in the strange car focused his attention on some documents in front of him, trying to catch every tiniest ray of the car´s roof light.

"Hi fellows . . . oh . . . and madam. Sorry, I didn´t notice you." Mathew reddened. Her strong lecturing glance forced him to bow his head. He dragged a chair away, slipped down onto it and joined the rest of the professor´s team. The fragrance of fresh coffee deleted his shame, a stainless steel fork stabbed food items one by one and his plate got piled up.

"Have you listened to the radio news?"

"Why?" Mathew did not understand the question.

"I only ask. They didn´t mention that a famine will break out?" She winked at him and put a jar of coffee on the table. Smiling, she went back to the sideboard. Everybody in the room giggled.

"Madam, can I ask you for a paper napkin?" Matt asked. She raised her eyebrows, did a half step towards the microwave and picked up one from the rails standing on it. "Thanks." Two bread slices were glued together with a napkin wrapped around them. All eyes kept observing what he was doing, wondering, but no word was spoken.

"Is that big mug with butterflies on clean?" No remarks or ribbing. She finally understood the reason of his strange behaviour, handed him the mug and looked straight into his eyes.

"Can you pour the coffee into the mug?" A strange feeling of shame jabbed him. He lowered his eyes, grinning and marvelling at the same time. He was sure she could read him like a book.

"No, I´ll help myself, thanks." Leaving the dining hall, he adored vanishing.

"Tell her I said hello." All eyes popped; some spluttering sips caused coughing.

"Rudi and Mr Important?"

"Hey fellow, gossiping is strongly forbidden!" Landlady´s finger pointed to Joseph for a second, then chit-chat, jokes and the vivid morning air filled the hall.

"Morning. Wow, what a scent. You are a sorcerer, madam." I kissed her on her chubby cheek, opened the cupboard and halted.

"Somebody hasn´t put back that butterfly mug." Everybody giggled and laughed and the woman leaned her bottom against the sideboard.

"Honey, your breakfast is on the way to your room."

"What?"

"Didn´t you meet him?"

"No."

"Did you climb along the banister again?"

"No problem. I´ll take another." I rapidly said.

"How old are you, honey? Climbing is for children. Or for him, if his natural urges force him to try to slip into your bed." The last bite of food stopped on its way down my throat.

"Who?" She shifted her forehead, many wrinkles spreading across it.

"Mathew."

"What? . . . Oh . . . No, no . . ." She faced the wall. Pretending she was cleaning the sideboard, she laughed under her nose.

"Did you meet Mr Sebastian yesterday?" Joseph helped me.

"No, unfortunately." Sips of coffee soaked my lips and the liquid caressed my tongue. I hoped that he would expand his simple query into a longer chat and the people at the table would forget the previous topic. I was lost in my feelings and thoughts. I put my empty plate in the sink and vanished.

Thrill, shame and excitement circulated through veins; they chilled me in one moment and burnt me just a second later. My feet walked on unconsciously, knowing their daily routine perfectly.

"Rudi! Rudi?" A shy tapping on my thigh disturbed me when I absentmindedly approached the banister of the conference hall.

"Wow," I whispered, unable to demonstrate such enormous surprise in words. I hugged him, squeezing him and not willing to loosen the hug.

"Rudi, please . . . You throttle me."

"Oh. Sorry. How . . . What . . ." Happiness flooded each part of me as I babbled incomplete sentences.

"How long has it been since you checked your email inbox?"

"Three weeks. It may be more."

"I wrote to you. Why didn´t you reply?"

"Oh . . . maybe I´m a coward? I was afraid you were . . ." a giant lump trapped the last word.

"You thought I was dying?"

"Yes." I forced a smile.

"We made our bet, didn´t we?"

"Oh . . . Yes, yes I forgot."

"I´ve become the winner."

"No, no, the date of expiration finished approximately a month ago." I laughed finally. The knot in my neck evaporated secretly. The joy came back.

"Yes, I am. My education tells me to be a correct gentleman. Also, I offer you a good deal: our bet for the butterfly trip."

"Will you give me time to consider?"

"Yes, one, two, three. Oops, it´s gone."

"All right, the deal has been done."

28

The entrance to the office of the Airport Police had been left open. A poker-faced man, whose company consisted of two men in black, stepped inside. The man at the desk stood up, approached the man and offered him his hand. The poker face melted.

"It is nice to see you, David. Nice office."

"Yes." He held a sheet of paper. An official stamp decorated its bottom-right corner. Several lines related to a particular name; the owner of the name would be given an unpopular official stamp in his passport.

"No arrest, just a stamp?"

"Yes, politics is a chess game of the slow kind, unfortunately."

"Some coffee, tea or chocolate?"

"Ha-ha. No thanks, I appreciate your offer, but I´m afraid that my diabetes wouldn´t agree with it." He rose up and shot his hand out to say adieu.

Approaching the window, he looked out at the car park of Philip S. W. Goldson International Airport. A spacious comfy limousine was waiting for his old friend, accompanied by men in black. Diplomatic etiquette demanded some definite rules, but Sebastian liked to add some of his own.

"Diplomatic duty can stand in front of my threshold, waiting for me until I come back. One step more and everyone is obligated to obey my wife´s rules."

The limousine vanished around the next corner. His guts grumbled and a loud clock click announced him that lunch time was coming. He snapped the document from the desk and put it between the sheets of a copying device. The number seven shone on the small screen, buzzing whirled in the space and copies landed on the tray below.

"There is just one kilometre in front of us." Sweat beads were rolling down our temples and necks and into the ditches lining our spines. Our clothes got wet and our physical power decreased. We tried to catch our breath. The engines of the chainsaws got hot. The path, which was constructed of cut twigs, branches, giant leaves, lianas and roots, lead back to the beginning of our journey, disappearing behind the horizon.

"Show me the map." I handed it to Emanuel, our guide. Mathew looked at me full of anger.

"Calm down, Mathew! She is right. It´s a thousand metres, maximum." He bowed down to Gregory and his finger skipped from the map to the GPS and back again, giving him orders. It made him a valuable member of the small expedition. In spite of the terrain transformations we had made to the wheelchair (making the tyres wider, the engine mechanism more powerful and adding massive springs to the wheel system), Gregory´s transportation got exhausting. I took a plastic bottle of water from my backpack. Refreshing drops were slowly poured on the nape of each member sat on the ground or leaning with their arms against their thighs and their heads almost at knee level, sucking air into their lungs and new energy into their burning muscles. Joseph straightened up and reached out his hand for the bottle. A few long swigs pushed his Adam´s apple down every time he swallowed.

"Thanks, Rudi."

"You´re welcome." I was grateful for his politeness. The chainsaw engine indicated it was functional again. Pulling its handle, a thread jumped out, bringing the device back to life. Twenty, forty-five, fifty metres of vegetation were cut down. A subtle tapping on my back stopped me. Looking at Emanuel, I moved aside to let him continue my work. Gregory´s chair neared me. It halted from time to time when the pile of green waste got too tall. With Mathew´s hands, Joseph helped Gregory to cope with it.

"I´ll help him. Relax for a while. Please." Joseph was unwilling at first but he knew there was a pretty rugged terrain in front of us.

"Rudi?"

"Yes."

"Your estimations were wrong. We´re here. Just a few steps to the Chiquibul cave system." Gregory pointed his finger at a point on the map. According to the map scale, we were at the edge of the rainforest.

"Have you made a mistake?"

"No. The map scale is . . ."

"Shit!" Swear words died in the distance, they distracted me. Our attention turned to that shout.

"Wait!" I ran.

"Stop! Stop, Rudi!" His warning came at the last moment. A steep short slope separated me from the floor half a metre under me. I would have certainly landed beside him had I fallen down the slope.

"Are you O.K.?" I asked. He nodded wordlessly. I swivelled to go back to the guys.

"What . . ."

"Nothing, he fell down. That´s all."

"Oh."

"No problem, we´ll all slide from time to time. A little bit of mud never killed anybody." Mathew and Joseph put his arms around their shoulders; their hands created a comfortable seat for him. The wheelchair slipped on the terrain. I ran over and halted it, shifting it under his bottom. The sound of a steam locomotive pierced the air as they strived to suck enough oxygen molecules into their bronchial sacs.

"Wow!" The volume of excitement in Gregory´s voice flooded the scene, which he faced with wide-opened eyes. Thousands of shimmering hues fluttered above the shining water´s surface, around cave mouths and among hanging plants. Nobody moved, breathed or spoke. We were an audience and our breaths were lost looking at such vast beauty.

"Would you like to go inside?" Emanuel asked.

"In the cave system?" Gregory replied.

"Yes."

The sparkles in Gregory´s eyes answered immediately. Emanuel pulled out a rubber thing from his backpack, unrolled it and fixed a plastic pipe from a foot pump to it. The air began streaming inside. Its shape grew, changed and modelled into a boat. Joseph continued pumping while Emanuel gathered all our things, putting them into the boat one by one.

"Rudi?" The boat´s floor floated on the water.

"Thanks but I´d rather not."

"Rudi?" Gregory protested.

"Mathew will keep an eye on you."

"Gregory, I will help you, don´t be afraid." Matt tried to calm Gregory. It was obvious, he was frightened.

"I´m sorry. I can´t."

"I don´t understand." I got confused. The look in Gregory´s eyes persuaded me and I approached the boat. My first sole touched the rubber.

"No, she remains on the shore!" Mathew´s voice stopped me. Everybody´s gaze skipped from me to Mathew, expecting an answer.

"I´m claustrophobic. I won´t cope with it," I said, reddening.

"No?" Emanuel asked.

"No," I replied.

"All right. Gentlemen, you can start boarding. Rudi will be our lighthouse." Emanuel winked at me. Chose, Gregory, Joseph and finally Mathew clambered into the boat. I settled on the ground on a tuft of grass, loosened the laces on my track shoes and let the liquid of the pond caress my feet.

"Rudi?" Mathew jumped back on the shore and squatted down, facing me. "You do believe me, don´t you?"

"Hm."

"I´ll become his legs. O.K., princess?"

"Hm. I´m a weakling," I replied. The warmth of his palm heated my cheek for a second.

"No you aren´t." He stood up, theatrically stamped on the boat´s floor and pretended to fall into the water, saving himself at the last second, of course.

"These documents are falsifications. All members of the departments related to this delicate job were provided with all the necessary details and facts. It is expected that Andrew´s performance will take place with success."

"An officially authorised logging in the Chiquibul National Reservation, they will get suspicious! They are not idiots."

"No, they will not. They are too covetous and self-confident and that is our biggest advantage: they are convinced that success is their privileged right anywhere and anytime. It doesn´t matter what way it happens."

"What happens next?"

"It is important to leave the reservation. There is a conviction that we can advance further in the area of Belize City. Put the right smelling carrion on the ground and the vultures will swoop in."

"He is playing the role of the responsible father redeeming his debts to his ill son."

"Really? Ridiculous. Invite him to be your guest."

"But, he is a guest of the station. He has all the necessary confirmation. He has the right to stay here."

"You've not comprehended me." The real purpose of Sebastian's demand rang in Trevor's brain.

"No, you're mad. Charlie is at home. No."

"Send him on a holiday. Your mum will be happy. Call her. Today. I'll arrange everything. Have a nice day, Trevor."

29

"Grannyyyy!" With a long jump, he hung like a little monkey with his legs wrapped around her waist. She cuddled him.

"Ha-há-ha." Wet touches tickled him on his neck, cheeks and ears.

"Stop it! Ha-ha. Stop it." Charlie screamed and giggled all in one. A coati cub climbed along his shoulder, licking each inch of his naked skin.

"Thank you mister . . . hm." She addressed her thankfulness to a man standing at the front of her yard, observing them.

"Come inside, I invite you. I baked a delicious fruit and cream cake. Your tongue will thank you." There was no space to deny her conviviality.

"Have you forgotten your smile?" She rubbed man´s arm in a friendly way, he melted a little bit and he tried to spread an uncommonly tiny smile spread his lips.

"Don´t kiss any animals, young man! I´ve already told you many times!" Charlie immediately jumped.

"Granny, how long can I stay with you?" He had been caught so he found a clever way to change the topic to avoid his granny´s lecturing look. She giggled under her breath, offered the guest wooden chairs and vanished into her house.

Two new coatis joined the first; they spent their time playing with something similar to a mango pit, rolling it across the yard, stealing it from each other and chasing after each other to grab it. His granny´s presence was revealed with a nostril-tickling fragrance. She moved like a ghost. Nobody noticed when she appeared on the veranda.

"Help yourself. I´ll serve Charlie," she said. The first bite melted his poker-faced expression. Marks of his professional deformation disappeared.

222

"Madam, I´ve never eaten anything better," he commented.

"Thanks, I´m sure you can learn it." His forehead got wrinkled. He did not understand her remark.

"A simple smile."

Pillows basked in the lunch time sun, sucking in its scented rays and absorbing as much of the warmth as their surface enabled them to. Belle´s arms hugged one of them to carry it to a bed, then the second, third and fourth. She trotted into the kitchen to check the meal she was cooking, threw a brief look in the refrigerator to see if her cold dessert had gotten stiff enough and then returned to putting all the rooms in order. A strange loud slam distracted her from her activities. Two pretty large taxis stood at the edge of the sand field. Pressing her stomach against the banister, she squinted her eyes to try to recognise the people, who looked as though they were mooning about the cars purposelessly.

"I don´t know how, you must tell me."

"It´s O.K., but . . ." He stopped in the middle of his sentence.

"But?"

"I need somebody to help me with my legs." I looked at Mathew. He nodded and slid into the car to ease Gregory´s swing from the car seat into the wheelchair. His hands clutched the hardy side handles and his arms trembled in his effort to reach the wheelchair. My knees pushed the chair against the car´s side to prevent it moving, my arms shot under Gregory´s armpits and I dragged him towards me.

"Thanks my good fairy." No reaction, just a faint smile. I bowed to the ground to collect all the luggage and changed into a pack mule, with my backpack on my back and Gregory´s two bags hanging across my middle. My right hand was occupied with a paper bag containing sweets for Isabella bought at the airport in Belize City.

"Rudi?"

"Has something happened?"

"Oh, no, no, I don´t think so."

"Are you sure?"

"Yes."

"You´re sad."

"Oh, no . . . no . . . just exhausted."

"O.K." His hands surged the wheels forward.

"Give it here, honey," Trevor said as he freed me from one bag.

"Can you smell that delicious scent, people?"

"Mathew." It was expected that our arrival would be decorated with many hugs, Belle did not leave anybody out.

"I´m Belle, young man." She energetically offered Gregory her hand.

"It´s nice to meet you, madam. I´ve heard just glorious things about you."

"I´m glad you are flattering me." She gave him a flirtatious wink. Gregory´s chair reversed to the edge of a temporary ramp made from a wide long wooden board, which had been built to ease Gregory´s ascent onto the patio. Everybody vanished behind the villa walls.

"Take your old room, Rudi," Belle shouted from nearby.

"Thanks," the quiet word dropped from my lips. I passed the kitchen, my feet touched the last step of the staircase and I gripped the door handle. My backpack was thrown into a corner, my shoes were abandoned near the door and my clothes created a snake along the floor.

The splashing of spring water flicked all my thoughts away. I enjoyed the silence in my brain for a while. I had not expected the remarkably rapid progress of his illness. I was not able to absorb it, to accept it or to give up without a fight. I felt like life had cheated me. I slipped down to the floor, crouched in a ball in the shadow of the shower and let sorrow and despair stream into the room.

"В пять часов, да у памятника, да в Парке Возпоминаня."
(At 5 pm, yes beside the memorial monument, yes in the memorial park.)

"Ты идиот? Где ты?"
(Are you an idiot? Where are you?)

"Это кде?"
(Where is that?)

"Пятнадсть минут, ни минуту долже."
(Fifteen minutes, not a minute more.)

His mood boiled and irritation, furiousness and tremendous anger surged in him at the prospect of their new meeting point. After crossing the lawn of the memorial park, he met the crossroad where Park Street joined Marine Parade Boulevard. There was a jetty nearby, a few cabin cruisers anchored in the water and a booth at the end of the slabs covering the jetty.

"Why did they name it Fort George Jetty when there is no fort?" he murmured under his breath.

"Да я тебя слушаю, но я тебя не вижу. Где ошибка?"
(Yes, I´m listening to you, but I can´t see you. Is something wrong?)

He energetically walked on. The jetty neared him. His foot touched the first slab and he continued on, observing his surroundings. Nobody was there. His eyes squinted; he shielded them against the sun´s sharp rays with the flat of his palm. Under the roof, in its shade, his eyes caught a movement. He kept walking. A man left the shade of the shelter and approached him. A dossier was handed to him. He thumbed through the pages then satisfyingly slammed the sheets together.

"Здраствуй Филип, кажется, да мой молодец был убедительный."
(Hello Fillip, it seems my chap persuaded them.)

"Доверши это, конешно."
(Finish it, finally.)

Then Fillip showed him his back, walked along the jetty in a hurry and headed in the direction of the memorial park. A scratched limousine stopped next to the pavement. The man in the booth´s shade did not pay any attention to the two men getting out of it. His eyes dipped into the dossier and a feeling of great contentment soothed his ego. The sudden creak of a loosened slab disturbed him.

"Can I have a look at that?" A stranger gestured for the dossier to be put in his hand.

"Can I know your reason?" he queried him arrogantly. The gloom of the shade forced him to take several steps to reach the light.

"I´m from Belize Police Department."

His brain understood the meaning of the short sentence. "And your evidence against me?" His arrogance was not going to trail off.

"In your hand."

"Don´t be silly. Nobody has ever been arrested for confirmation documents."

"No, but for falsifications, many people have been."

He looked at the officer in utter amazement. His arrogance died immediately.

"Yes Madam Belle, that cave system was marvellously decorated with many stalagmites and stalactites, dripstone veils and cave ponds. Then Emanuel took us down an unknown aisle and there was such a big crevice that some sunbeams were streaming down through it. It looked like they tickled the water . . ." Gregory gushed. Mathew rolled his eyes and sighed. Gregory´s chirping was like a maestro´s fingers playing the piano, but Mathew´s nerves were the keys. He was going to eat, but Gregory´s often repeated story broke his decision.

Tap-tap. Tap-tap. There was an answerless knocking on the nearby door; he gripped the handle and slid into the room. Steam was snaking into the space from the gap under the bathroom door.

"Rudi?" Water splashes drummed on the floor. "Rudi?" He snapped on the chrome handle of the shower, switched the water off and wrapped my body in a towel.

"Let´s go, princess." He turned to give me place to stand up and hide in the towel. I disappeared into the bedroom. I put some clothes on and rubbed my hair to dry it somewhat.

"Enjoy it. There is no time for sadness. Time is the only thing that he hasn´t got. You can´t change his destiny. Keep the memories: you created beautiful adventures for him. Be proud of yourself." He gently pulled my chin up, then hugged me and provided me with a nest where my sobs were not heard and my tears were not seen. He hugged me so tightly, it seemed like nothing bad could happen.

"You must eat. Belle bakes the most delicious cakes in the world."

Ring-ring-ring-ring. A policeman was writing down a list of the possessions of the last man that had arrived at the department. He picked up the ringing phone from his desk to study the caller´s number and added a new line to his list after several others. The same caller rang seven times.

"Such a patient chap." He cocked his head. The newcomers were still in the same positions: legs straddled, elbows on their thighs, their middles bowed downwards and their views piercing the same point as they had a couple of minutes ago.

"The guys told me there is a big fish in the cell." The sergeant dragged him out from his observations.

"Wait, here it is." His fingers paced from side to side under the right part of the row.

"Wow, Embassy of the Russian Federation, that is a fairly big fish." The sergeant whistled.

"Calm down, he has diplomatic immunity."

"Just the next guy who thinks he can do anything and won´t be punished." His ringing laughter trailed along the corridor until he vanished around the corner of it.

"The cake was extremely delicious, Belle." I glued a kiss on her cheek.

"Did you like the cave trip?"

"Oh . . . how . . . Belle . . . how I . . ." I was ashamed. The prospect of saying it publicly for the second time in a day caused me to stutter.

"Belle, is a band playing at Rosalie today?" Mathew saved me.

"Kids, it´s such a great experience. Every time I go there, I fall in love." She took one of the free chairs, hugged her arm around it and floated it a few inches above the floor. She sang, danced and whirled around its axis. The unexpected theatre entertained us; we smiled, our feet stomped on the ground and our palms drummed on the table.

"With whom?"

"With the music." She shot her melodic answer at us.

"What time?"

"At 8, I think. It´s 7.53 now," she sang.

"Gregory?"

"No, go with Mathew."

"Trevor, help me, please," I pleaded.

"Gregory, this girl has asked you out for the evening."

"Will you go with us too?" I gestured to Trevor to say yes.

"Of course, did you doubt me?"

"I´ve something for you, honey." Belle braced both my wrists and dragged me away from the kitchen.

"Guys, you can leave, I´ll accompany Rudi to Rosalie. Enjoy the local girls," she shouted at the top of the voice, dancing and crooning a song.

"Sit down, honey." There was no way they could disobey her order. I settled in an old beauteous rocking chair in her room, my fingers gliding along the carved and curved handles. Slightly swinging, I waited to hear what her artistic soul had to say. She rooted among a large quantity of dresses in all hues, shapes and types of fabric.

"I´ve found it," she announced, singing the fact in the tune of a familiar opera sequence. She placed her winning dress directly to my face.

"Wow." I sat up and shifted to the edge of the chair. It looked like it had been created by thousands of small handy spiders, working for uncountable number of hours to complete their artistic creation. It was a silky cocktail dress tailored from a blue-tinted cloth with many fragile blooms.

"Put it on," she instructed. I felt like the word NO was strongly forbidden, so I obeyed.

"Trevor?"

"Yes?"

"Do you know when Dad is going to return?"

"Tomorrow, in the morning."

"Where did he go?"

"Gregory, listen to the music and ask a girl for a dance." He screamed to be heard—the music was too loud.

"Hi Mathew, have you had a long holiday?"

"Tristan, how is it going?!"

"Things would be better if you had brought Rudi."

"She isn´t for you."

"Hi boys." One of local girls approached him and dragged him onto the dance floor. There were skilful motions, music and the harmony of bodies. Gregory did not know which way to look.

"Hi Gregory."

"Tristan, I´m glad I met you."

"Me too, fella."

"Oh." A girl pulled Tristan´s arm in the middle of Rosalie´s club. Gregory swayed with the rhythm of a blasting song. A tap disturbed him; a subtle kiss on his temple forced him to find out who was the sender.

"Can I ask you to dance?" I tangled my fingers with his and his wheels followed my steps. We danced. I immersed my pupils in his to be able to drink in the smallest sip of his spirit, of his soul. I decided to listen to Mathew´s advice. Bell join her friends at the opposite side of the Rosalie´s dancefloor.

´Enjoy it. There is no time for sadness,´ the thoughts vibrated in my head. I liked him and his never-ending battle, in spite of the fact that he knew his fight had been lost before it had started. I respected him for his bravery.

"We have an audience," Gregory commented. His voice was full of amusement.

"Is that bad?"

"No."

"So, dance." Song by song, dance by dance, drink by drink, the hours passed extraordinarily quickly, like a horse´s gallop.

"I would like to go home, Rudi."

"No problem. I´ll go with you."

"No." Trevor´s voice could be heard piercing through the music. "I´ll take him."

"Oh."

"No problem, honey. The night is still young." I watched them leave Rosalie´s club, the darkness swallowing their silhouettes. Something clutched my guts and squeezed my heart. I needed a drink. I struggled among the dancing bodies, happiness, laughter and agreeable mood that whirled around the floor.

"A cup of strawberry juice with white rum, please." A nicely decorated glass landed next to me. I sipped the pleasant drink, admiring the dancers twisting in sambas or rumbas. Legs flew high in the air and hips sashayed with the rhythm of the music.

"The same again, please." I downed the glass. It tasted better than the first. "The same again, please."

"Surely the girl would love to dance?"

"What? No, I would love to drink. The same again, please." The barman laughed.

"Mathew, that girl has courage," bartender´s laughed echoed in my ears.

"Leave it, Rudi." His arms embraced me. I was dragged onto the dance floor.

"You´ve committed a crime," I informed Matt.

"Really?"

"Yes, you kidnapped me."

"And the punishment?"

"Let me drink."

"Later." He loosened his grip so I could move as he led me. I felt each touch and every muscle that met my body. Goose bumps rose on my skin; his lips brushed my nape and my shoulders. We fused among the dancing mass. Sweat beads rolled down our bodies and feelings seesawed through me.

"Do you hate me?" Matt teased me.

"Yes. I need a drink."

"I know something better."

"Go, Rudi!" He gave me no chance to decide. The music of Rosalie´s dance floor trailed off as we moved away. Darkness, silence and the song of the waves accompanied our running. We crossed a palm field, avoiding coconuts that had fallen on the sand.

"Here." A lagoon hidden in the shelter of palm trees spread among the sand dunes. Low bushes were spotted with little light yellow blossoms, their intensive fragrances trapping me. My fingertips skipped from one petal to another; I was afraid of touching them in case they vanished. Mathew tore one.

"Why did you do that? It will wilt," I raised one brow. He stuck it behind my ears and bowed down to brush my neck, shoulders and arms. Then he stood up, brushing every part of my skin.

"Do you hate me?" he asked.

"Yes," I laughed, counting the sparkles in his pupils. His arms lifted me behind my knees and he carried me to the shore. Sand grains tickled my skin and waves poured over my ankles.

"Do you hate me still?"

"Yes."

His lips brushed my skin again. I could feel his warm breath. Heat circulated around my body. I was shaking as I ran my fingers through his hair. He ascended upwards to my chin. His lips pressed kisses on my skin. We kissed, fiercely and hotly. My palm glided downwards, copying his body curves. My fingers found the zip of his jeans.

"No, stop," Matt said.

"Did I do something wrong?"

"No, I don´t want to."

"What don´t you want to do . . ."

"Make love."

"I´m not drunk! Oh, I´m sorry." I shot up. I ran. I was so ashamed; I would have loved to vanish, to evaporate. The breeze caressed me and the splashing of waves became my comfort as I continued running, not wanting to stop before I could see Sander´s villa. A light shimmered on the empty patio. Trevor´s rocking chair rested in the corner, expecting a newcomer who would settle on its seat and begin rocking. I switched the light off and curled into a ball between the chair´s handles. The wooden floor of the patio creaked as its curved rails swung. The first step squeaked and he gasped, coming over to the chair.

"I don't want to make love to you because we drank. I would love to do it because we love each other." Squatting down, he faced me.

"I appreciate it." I kissed his forehead and left. "There's nothing new under the sun," I said to myself.

Climbing the stairs, I was angry with myself. I was thankful for my room, which was first in the row of rooms and situated a maximum of two steps away from the banister. The dark in it was a balsam for my sole. Crossing the space, I took off my sandals and left my dress on the striped rug. The quilt tickled my jaw. I strived to fall asleep, to forget that horrible part of the night. I had the uncomfortable feeling that somebody had opened the door, but I adored boarding the first ship of a dream so I did not pay any attention to it.

"Hush . . . I didn't mean to startle you. Hush." Cuddling me, he whispered and pressed his lips against my hair. "Look at me please." his palms pulled my face up. "We won't make love tonight. But it doesn't mean I hate you."

"You're such a big fool." I was confused and amused all at once.

"May I stay?"

"In my bed?"

"Yes," he said. I laughed. We cuddled each other. I was not able to comprehend the disorder in his head.

"I like you more than I want to," he whispered into my hair. He lifted my chin up again and pressed his lips to mine.

"What do you really want, Mr Mathew? To love me or to make love to me?"

"Both," he replied. I pushed the lump growing in my throat down and settled deeper into his hug, balled in his nest.

"Me too." My heart thudded so loudly that I was not sure he could hear it.

30

The seagulls had been calling excitedly for a pretty long while; the clapping of pelicans´ beaks met their yelling for several seconds. The ear-tearing sounds hovered above the ocean. Fishermen anchored small faded trawlers near the jetty, solid ropes were knotted around piers and engines stopped working. Their dexterous hands sorted fish, cut them, pulled out their guts and cast them over the boats´ edges into the water. Gulls circled above the boats, waiting for new pieces of fish waste, then turned their beaks and fiercely flew down to snap up the discarded shreds. A chair in the middle of the shore caught my gaze. I snaked down from the balcony, tiptoeing.

Silence reigned in the morning house as everybody slept. No fragrance came from the kitchen and there was no rattling of pots: just silence. The slabs on the patio squeaked slightly under my weight, sand grains tickled me as they streamed through the gaps between my toes and wind a little bit stronger than usual played with my hair, commanding me to stick hair strands behind my ears repeatedly. I caught sight of Gregory´s head floating on the sea´s surface: he was swimming. I settled beside his wheelchair and sank into the moment, observing his slow arm motions consuming a fairly large bite of his energy. He enjoyed it and allowed the water to cuddle his body, caress his muscles and titillate his chin. I admired and respected his bravery in facing life, fighting and smiling at the same time. I liked him.

"Hi Rudi." He rolled on the bottom of the sand. I joined him. Waves splashed across our legs and wrists and hit our waists from time to time. My clothes got soaked. We sat together, observing the horizon, fishermen and seagulls. His head pressed against my shoulder, his hairs tickling it.

"Has my dad arrived? Have you seen a car behind the house?" he asked.

"No. I´m sorry."

"Never mind."

"I can give you a lift to the airport, if you want," I offered. He nodded. We listened to the beautiful sounds of the surroundings, absorbing each other.

"Он есть как плохое сновидение."
(He is like a bed dream.)

He gave up his effort to contact him. His plane would take off at 1.35 pm. All his remaining affairs would be finished from his office. Duplicates of the confirmation document authenticated by a noted public figure had been delivered by UPC to Liverpool. His advocate should be signing the currier´s documents in the next few minutes. The mahogany area was his gold mine. Thirty per cent of the profits from the operation would flow into the account of the Muscular Dystrophy Association and the DMD Research Centrum to advance their work and finally launch the DMD drug into the medical market. The last seventy per cent would make his account more valuable, increasing his fortune. His pocket began shining. A familiar song blasted into the air.

"Yes, I´m sorry Gregory, I had to work." He stopped to listen, his fingers drumming on the dashboard. "Ask Trevor to take you to the airport, we´ll meet there." The voice in the mobile phone died and the car set off from the hotel car park. The agreeable odour of her perfume touched his nostrils as the car´s air conditioning fans blew in the right direction. He smirked. His member got stiff as his memory played back flashes from the last hot night they had shared. If time had not urged him on, he would have reversed the car, tore her clothes off and dipped his penis between her delicious chocolate thighs and permitted his lips to lick her young steady tits. An aggressively long horn honk brought him back to reality.

"Have you lost your mind?" a driver shouted at him. The light on the traffic lights was red.

"Dad is here. Thank you, Rudi. Mathew, I would like to say goodbye to her."

"No problem, fella." Mathew left us on our own.

"Can you kiss me?" Gregory asked. I laughed.

"Of course." My lips pressed against his then I squatted down, facing him.

"I´ll visit you, if I can."

"No."

"No?"

"I´m sorry, but I must say NO. Life is too short to sit on any patio. I don´t want to become your patio, Rudi. You gave me your heart, your legs and my dreams. That´s enough. I won´t allow you to sit on the patio." His palms pushed his wheels. He reversed, turned the chair on its wheels and left red-white cones leading to the check-in area of the local international airport behind him.

"Rudi?" Matt said. My teeth bit my lower lip.

"He is right."

"But it hurt."

"Fight, Rudi!" His arm clutched my shoulder.

"Persona non grata? Do you know who I am?"

"Yes. If I didn´t, that man would arrest you and lock you up with your friend." A customs officer pointed to a room that was used as a temporary cell for people who were accompanied by a police officer to their destination.

Gregory´s wheels rotated forwards and backwards, waiting for dad. "Is something wrong?" he asked.

"No and yes all at once." An airport officer bent down to him, whispering. "Your father obtained a new stamp in his passport."

"Me too."

"Yes, but he has two new stamps." Gregory´s forehead wrinkled in incomprehension. "He´s a persona non grata."

"That means I´ll fly alone."

"No, with your father this time. However, in the future, you can visit Belize but your dad won´t be permitted to do so.

"And now?"

"Have a nice flight. Good luck."

Gregory saw his dad at the counter. He noticed his gestures were full of anger. His palms shifted his wheels onwards. He lost interest in observing the disgraceful performance.

31

Six little mottled ducks swam in a queue following their parents. The grass fields around the pond in the university park wore the brightest green I had ever seen. Small heads of dandelions knocked against my arms, as the breeze blew stronger and longer than a while ago. Daylight hours stretched and people sucked in the fresh air and listened to birds chirping, walking along the paths in the park. I had almost two hours: the rendezvous time was set at 8.

Buzz-buzz. Buzz-buzz. The vibrating of my mobile compelled me to shove my fingers in my pocket. I looked at the display.

"Yes!" I screamed. The noises of a crowd of people blasted out from the phone. My head swerved to protect my eardrum against the enormous noise.

"Where are you?" I could hear every question pretty well without putting the phone back to my ear.

"I´m at the pond."

"Have you forgotten?" I repeated Patricia´s question.

"No, the meeting was to see Devil Dawn at 8. Am I wrong?"

"No, at 6 in the City Square Shopping Centre." Patria corrected me.

"Oh! You´ll kill me. That gift. I´m sorry, Pat. Give me fifteen minutes. I´ll be there." The chequered Scottish rug was rolled and folded. I jumped up and ran to the closest bus stop. Scanning row by row, I looked for the most simple bus link to City Square.

"Yes, Broadway—City Hall Station is quite close to it." I spent the remaining seven minutes putting the things in my bag in order.

"The 39, fine. I´ll be on time."

"Fifteen minutes." Patricia checked the time.

"Pat. Pat, wait." I could read great reproof in her facial expression. She broke into laughter.

"I hate you," she joked. I joined her ringing tone.

"Let´s go. I found such a beautiful creature."

"Is it for a boy?"

"Don´t grumble, mademoiselle," Patricia patiently answered. The glass lift tower got nearer. I took a breath: I was determined to persuade her in any way to use the staircase.

"The shop is on the first floor, we´ll up run the stairs," I said.

"Fine, yes, it´s fine." Patricia looked at me in amusement.

"Are you O.K?

"Yes, I´m fine." Ascending the stairs, we completely dived in our vivid chit-chat. Pat was excited: her and Jacob were going to spend their first summer vacation together. They had decided on France.

"No, I spent two months in Côte d´Azur but I´ve never been to Paris," I commented.

"You must have learnt something about it at school."

"Yes, but you can find out everything on the Internet. But I´ll give you some pretty good advice."

"Yeees?"

"Go alone."

"Why?"

"French men really know how to satisfy a girl." I gave her a conspiratorial smirk.

"Rudi!" She laughed.

"Good afternoon, madam. Please could you show those wings to my copine?"

"Wings?" I wondered.

"Hush."

"Mademoiselles," the woman said as she presented us with silky rainbow wings shimmering in a miniature box. I was lost in my thoughts for a while: it really was a beauteous butterfly.

"It´s similar to one from Belize, isn´t it?" she asked. I nodded wordlessly. I wanted to touch it, but I was afraid of breaking it.

"It´s marvellous. Have you got some birthday cards?" I asked the shop assistant.

"Yes. There is a post office opposite."

"Thank you, madam. Have a nice day."

> *"Have the most beautiful birthday.*
> *I love you, Gregory. From Rudi."*

I slid the card into its envelope; the wings in the small box would accompany the envelope for a few days during their journey to the United Kingdom.

> *Gregory Wronskij*
> *9 Church Lane*
> *Lancaster, Lancashire LA4 5*
> *The United Kingdom*

I finished filling in the address on the dispatch ticket and gave it to the clerk at the counter.

"$12.25 please," he requested. I handed him the money.

"When will it arrive at the address?"

"I estimate it could take one week."

"Thank you, sir."

"I´m sorry people, I must go. I would like to sleep a little bit. My plane is leaving at 11 am," I shouted at the top of my voice. The rock band in the pub (called ´Devil Dawn´) shot their new song into the space. It was a terribly well-done song, but the room was too noisy for chatting.

"Are you going to come back?"

"It depends on the faculty´s confirmation."

"Your name was written on the dean´s webpage."

"I know, but they must send it officially by post. I´ll be sure to check when I get home. I´ll write you, Pat."

"Lecturer Rudi, could you help me? I´ve not comprehended this question correctly." I bowed down to hug him.

"My ears desire to hear it." I replied in the same teasing way as Matt. His lips brushed my neck.

"I´ll go with you."

"That´s not a query, Mr Sander, it´s a declaration." I went around our table to say goodbye. Mathew left the place during my rounds and my attempt to find him was not successful. I backed away from the table and waved at them.

There was darkness in the streets and the scent of spring. The last buses transported revellers, guests of pubs and alumni back to their homes. My destination was clear: the park. I loved its ambiance. Each season it attracted me and took my breath away when I crossed it.

"To go to me or to go to you?" A sudden tight clamp halted my walk.

"Is that the question." I finished a verse.

"Is it?" Our daily verbal chess had started. It had brought about many comical situations in the past. From time to time, we were trapped in our own nets. But, we tried best to snake from every situation and win. Passers-by turned their heads towards us, giggling and smiling at us as they continued their journeys.

"Wait," I asked him.

"I´ve won. You´ve lost the thread."

"No, wait, hush." He raised his brow.

"Here it is." My fingers rooted around in my bag to fish out the right object. "Open your hand." He shot me a suspicious look. "Have a look, don´t be so silly."

"O.K., princess, you´re the boss today. It´s your night." A shred torn from a newspaper landed on his palm.

"Are you crazy, is John Rockefeller your dad? Flights into Europe several times a year, luxurious gifts . . . What else?"

"Nothing, why?" His reaction was exaggerated. I did not know the financial value of the miniature mahogany creature.

"It´s too expensive."

"No, the owner of that shop gave me it!"

"It´s from the dolphin shop, isn´t it?"

"I helped him to persuade his dearest pet Nana to begin to eat. And . . . it was my reward."

"When?"

"You´re too curious. Don´t you like it? You looked at it for a long time. It hit your sight every time you walked by. What´s wrong?"

He bowed down and kissed me. "Sorry, I love it."

"O.K. I forgive you." I grimaced and laughed.

"You´re such a monkey, princess. You´ve not answered me."

"Yes, I have. It was my reward."

"No, your scholarship budget isn´t enough to cover your study, your lifestyle, your flights . . ."

"Hey! Aren´t you a little bit too curious?"

"No!"

"O.K. Two years of hard work."

"Hard work?"

"Yes, four hours as a croupier in the Crown Plaza Casino and four hours as a garbage woman, three times a week for two years."

"Are you joking?"

"No! From 8 until midnight I was a croupier and from 4.30 to 8.30 I was a garbage woman."

"What did people say?"

"Nothing. Only my mum and Laura knew about it."

"Good evening, sir." Mathew remained stunned and held the door open without pause.

"Are you going in?" Matt did not notice that question addressed to him.

"Good evening, sir." Guardy replied.

Lost in his thoughts, Mathew approached the lift and pressed its button.

"We´ll meet on the floor." He accepted the offer of the lift and walked in. The bell announced his coming. I struggled with the door lock. It refused to cooperate. His limbs braced my legs, his arms crept under mine and his hands pushed forwards.

Monika Pistovčák

"You´re welcome princess."

"I would be lost without you."

"Yes, you would be." He neared me, leaning both arms against the wall so my escape exit was closed off. He bent down. I felt the warmth of his breath and the gentle touches of his lips brushing my neck, jaw, ear and finishing on my temple. There was a short gap as our eyes absorbed one another´s smiles.

"I´ll kill you if you stop," I said with a coquettish smile. He bent down, brushing every small part of my skin. His lips must have been tickled by the goose bumps that grew immediately as they felt his breath.

"I don´t think I want it to end." His whisper increased my lust. My fingers snaked to his jeans and I awkwardly unzipped them. My hands hesitantly went back to the familiar parts of his body.

"Don´t be a coward, Rudi." My brain shouted at me. One of his hands crept under my jacket, helping it slide down the wall. Two glued bodies shifted ridiculously around the room, knocking down things crossing our direction. Pieces of clothes created a trail on the floor. I landed on my bed. He gently slid next to me.

"Can you help me?" I asked. My teeth braced the corner of a small packet, trying to tear the top away.

"Why not?" It was such a big flub. I had never done it before, but did my best to disguise it. His fingers lead me to achieve my goal, then knitted among mine and dragged me to him. His touches and brushes covered my body. Our limbs got tangled, our lips were glued together and his fingers walked downwards to cause more wetness between my thighs. The air was full of love, lust and desire. He skilfully rolled onto me. My body was screaming. I was shivering through my whole body. He gently glided inside. His initial slow motion increased, changing into a hot dance. The gentleness, the beauty of his manner and his expression when he looked at me sent flames through my veins. I shook, praying he would never stop. He did, not willing to unglue his eyes from mine.

"Wow."

"Yes, wow. Was it your first time?"

"Oh . . . how did you . . . oh . . ."

"Nina, it was breath-taking."

"Yes." I was glad for the gloom in my room, as I reddened from shame.

"How did you know . . ."

"That you were a virgin?"

"The condom . . ."

"Yes, and your fear to continue to meet my little Mathew." I closed my eyelids and giggled. I got totally red.

"Don´t be silly. Nina, open your eyes," he whispered into my ear.

"Never." His fingers attacked my sides and I broke into laughter. He titillated me until I glanced at him.

"Will you come back?" he asked. I was confused. His expression scared me. I had been familiar with it during our rivalry time. Then a wide smile stretched across his cheeks. "Will you come back?"

"Do you mean to tell me you´ve fallen in love?" A parcel of silence separated his next answer from his last.

"I hate you Nina Rudić."

"I hate you too."

The steward in front of the first row took care of all the necessities and settled in her seat. The passengers fastened their seatbelts and the plane took off. Minutes passed; the plane hit the right altitude. The plane´s loudspeaker informed people of all the facts relating to the flight, trolleys were pushed along the narrow aisle and stewards offered drinks, meals and sweets, smiling at passengers as they strived to make their flight more comfortable. I pulled my laptop out from my cabin baggage placed in the box above me and switched it on.

"Coffee?"

"Yes, thank you." I waited for my coffee until my computer came to life. The connection to the Internet was extremely quick: after one or two clicks, my emails came rolling down. Just two new ones, strange.

"Never mind," I said to myself.

> *"Confirmation.*
>
> *I would like to announce that your application for doctoral study at the University of British Columbia has been accepted and you are allowed to finish your education at our university. The official confirmation will be sent to your official address.*
>
> *Sincerely,*
> *Dean of the Faculty of Forestry."*

Thrill, happiness and pleasure mixed inside me. I looked over my neighbour to the round window to calm such a powerful stream of emotion.

Ring. The heel of my palm touched the rectangle on the bottom of the PC and my second email was opened.

'Nina,

Thank you for the patio that you conjured for me.

I love you, Gregory.

Date of birth—19th January 1999
Date of death—7th May this year

With love, Minerva."

I slowly shut the laptop and folded it into the stowage space on the back of the seat in front of me. I let my eyelids drop, not wanting to show the world the tears streaming from the corners of my eyes. I collected all the wonderful memories from my brain one by one and played them again and again. I was afraid of forgetting his face, his voice, him. Hours flew by and exhaustion fought me. I dropped off.

32

The second guy came out from the exam room. He looked like a steamroller had gone over him. All his energy had been left behind the door. I had a sudden whim to check his throat to see if two bloody holes were there.

"Rudić." I stood up. I was sure I was going to pass.

´Fight, Rudi,´ my mind spurred me on.

"Good morning, madam, professors."

"Your topic is ´comparison of processes influencing different forestry associations´?"

"Yes. Can I begin?"

"Of course, the projector is yours."

"As the title says, there will a comparison. My choice was much easier as I had the opportunity to study at the University of British Columbia, as it was near the geographical area for easy comparison. And when Professor Dragonsky, Dean of the Faculty of Forestry, asked me if I would join his team in Central America, in Belize, I was glad because the third area was born. So, as you can see on the wall, the three pillars of my work are three geographical areas: two forest areas situated in the North Temperate Zone, each with slightly different climate conditions. The first forest has a cold climate and the second is situated in a medium climatic zone. The last forest is situated directly on the equator . . ."

Knowledge flew fluently in the space; graphs, diagrams and photos appeared on the wall one by one and lines of text were scrolled upwards or downwards depending on the questions asked by one of the four examiners. The months I had spent in the terrains gave me a great advantage. I had touched every one of the facts projected on the wall until they were transformed into the rows of my work. As the presentation came to its end, I got happier. My voice and body were in the room still, but my thoughts walked through all the places that I spoke about.

"That's enough, you can go."

"Thanks." Every face in the corridor had expectation in their eyes as they waited for my opinion. Unfortunately, I had none. I settled on a chair near some glass shelves where a number of soil samples were placed. Reading the names, I was lost in the past.

'Where is Daniel? I wrote to him about the date of my examination. He didn't answer me or turn up! And why did the professor avoid my query?' The questions flew around my head.

"Rudi?" The professor's tapping on my shoulder cut through my thoughts.

"Yes?"

"The results will now be read." I wordlessly followed him.

"Professor?" He faced me. "Where is Daniel?"

"Later, darling."

Our hands shook as the results were read; everyone passed.

"For you." My glance pierced the sky.

"No, no, it's yours Rudi. It's an official document stating you are a Master of Forestry and Soil Science." I smiled on that misunderstanding. Those words were not said to professor.

"Oh, thanks."

People trickled out of the exam room, chatting and cheering. I bent my head into my bag and rooted around in it. I hit my forehead on the frame of the glass showcase. I straightened up unconsciously to find out what the object was that had thwarted my progress. I froze. Daniel's photo look down at me from it. I immediately headed to the professor's office and gripped the handle, pushing it down fiercely. It was locked. Turning on my heel, I decided to go to the secretariat of the Forestry and Soil Department. Without knocking, I flew inside. He was sitting in an old chair and sipped his coffee.

"Why?! Tell me why!" Professor faced me, his bottom lip trembled.

"Daniel's wife asked me to do it."

"Daniel's wife?"

"Yes, he got married to Camilla."

"Not to write to me? We were best friends! Why?!" My pupils gazed directly at his heart. An enormous seesawing was enacted in my tummy.

"Why? I thought you were my friend. Why?" Professor looked at me wordlessly. I left. My words vanished inside me; I needed to disappear.

33

The sunny day was aiming to complete its journey. The pictures of many towns, villages, mountain ranges and fields were exchanged for images of the capital. Tall street lamps along the motorway invited me and my body relaxed with the familiar atmosphere. The feeling I could have said hello made me calm. But those eyes: I needed to pay attention to them. It was strange to face that animal and ask him for a favour. I smirked.

"Oh." I grasped the mobile phone buzzing on the dashboard. "Mum?"

"Of course. Yes, I´m going to come to my goodbye party."

"How long? I don´t know. I´ve crossed the edge of the town. Fifteen minutes, twenty?"

"No Mum, I´m not going to change my mind. It´s a good opportunity. I worked hard, I deserve it."

"No Mum, I won´t leave you forever, just for three years."

"Yes, the plane is flying straight to its final destination."

"Ha-ha, ha-ha, ha-ha." I broke into laughter. It was evident from the start of our conversation where Mum´s investigation carousel was leading. Her shame outgrew her curiousness, so snaking to her aim seemed less degrading.

"Yes, it´s possible."

"Yes, I can tell you. No, it won´t kill me."

"Now? All right, there is somebody who is worth it."

"Ha-ha, ha-ha."

"Of course. Mum, I need to go. I´m nearing the motorway exit and I´m breaking two rules, at least."

"Which two rules? First, I´m on the phone while driving a vehicle, and second . . ." I hesitated for a while.

"I´ll invent the second when I get home."

"Rudi accepted Dragonsky´s offer."

"Did you speak with the professor?"

"No." His forehead was raised.

"I emailed her. I like her emails. They charge your battery."

"Are you writing to my girl? Dad it´s a little bit rude!"

"Yes, we´ve dragged Matt´s secret out from him, Charlie." They exchanged high-fives. Charlie beamed like the sun.

"I´ve told Dad."

"You´ve misunderstood me . . . She is my best friend."

"You´re such a big fool, bro." Charlie started giggling again. Trevor pressed him to his thigh. They laughed.

"Flight number . . ." The transmitter blasted details about Mathew´s flight into the air. He bowed down to pick his luggage up.

My foot intermittently pushed down on the brake. The car stopped. Some cars drove along the road that flowed from the exit. I joined the first lane, then the second, and followed them. The sounds and fragrances of late evening flew through a gap in the slightly opened window of the car. A great amount of traffic signs lined the toad. The town hall was determined to obey the pressure from investors and a new housing estate was growing on former wheat fields. A small cone of light penetrated the dark in the car; my phone was ringing.

"Yes, Mum, five or seven minutes, maximum." I switched my phone off and put it back on the dashboard. Four shimmering points pierced the night extremely close to the road´s edge. My eyes checked the rear mirror quickly: no car lights appeared behind me. I stamped on the brake and slapped my hand on the triangle danger button. Four orange lights regularly flickered in the black. Two animals ran across the tarmac surface carrying rabbits in their muzzles. It looked like two parents coming back to their young after a successful hunt. The white ends of their bushy cinnamon tails waved me and vanished among the fences of the nearby gardens.